VERTICAL

A NOVEL by

REX PICKETT

Loose Gravel Press, Ltd. is a wholly independent publishing house owned by Rex Pickett and Timothy T. Moore.

www.loosegravelpress.com.

Title page art by Kraftwerk Design, Inc., San Luis Obispo

Library of Congress Cataloging-in-Publication Data

Pickett, Rex.
    Vertical by Rex Pickett
        p. cm.
    ISBN 978-0-615-39218-9
    1.Automobile travel-Fiction. 2. Man-woman relationships-Fiction.
    3.Male friendship-Fiction. 4. Divorced men-Fiction 5. California–Fiction.
    1. Title

    PS3566.1316 S55 2010
    813 ..6-dc22   2003027209

Also by Rex Pickett:
Sideways

20 19 18 17 16 15 14

Acknowledgments

First and foremost, I'd like to extend my appreciation and respect to the energetic and risk-taking Tim Moore for making this self-imprint a reality. There wouldn't be a book without his hard work, business acumen, and bottomless belief in the project.

I'd also like to heartily thank attorney Krista Carlson and veterinarian Dr. Shiri Hoshen for their indefatigable, and scrupulous, work on the manuscript. I want to doubly thank Krista for her legal counsel and Shiri for her detailed input on all matters relating to veterinary medicine. Not to mention their unwavering support and close, valued friendship.

Also, on the manuscript, I want to commend Jess Taylor for his sparkling line edit. And Todd Doty for his final proofing.

The entire team at Kraftwerk Design, who created the book cover, the Web site, and were involved in all the advertising artwork.

For advice on wine and the Willamette Valley I want to single out writer Katherine Cole and Fred Gunton. For her medical expertise on stroke and heart failure, Dr. Jen Vakharia. And on all legal matters regarding the LLC, our tireless attorney Scott Creasman.

My support group of friends and representatives: David Saunders and Steve Fisher at Agency for the Performing Arts; my generous brother Hack; Barbara Schock, as ever; Wade Lawson; and my caring, always-there-for-me, manager Peter Meyer.

And, I can't forget, Pamela Smith, for her sage advice in too many matters to enumerate. Without her friendship, creative input – everything from reading of the manuscript to overseeing all the art work – I would be rudderless.

Anything that involves Miles and Jack, I would be utterly remiss if I didn't thank Alexander Payne – and everyone responsible for the making of *Sideways* – who made them come to life on the big screen.

For my Mother
(1921 - 2000)

I got up on my feet and it took character.
It took will power. It took a lot out of me.
And there wasn't as much to spare as there
once had been.

– Raymond Chandler, *The Long Goodbye*

VERTICAL

chapter 1

The surf crashed thunderously against the cliffs outside my spacious seaside hotel room in Shell Beach. Golden sunlight filtered in through the white curtains. Stretched out on a bed big enough for three, I absently watched a golf tournament. I was at a wine festival, incongruously, to promote a book. Though it had been published, not that anyone could have noticed, a year earlier, the movie adapted from it had recently come out. So I was back on the promotional trail. Critics—and real people—had gone wild for the film. The story was a week in the life of me and my friend Jack, on a carousing two-man bachelor party rampage through some world-class yet little-known wine and golf country. My mom had appeared in a cameo role in both versions, and garnered a serious fan base of her own.

Thanks to the movie, my fortunes had changed. Jack, sadly, was, as I had long ago predicted, divorced and having trouble finding work. My poor mother had suffered a massive stroke that left her wheelchair-bound and sequestered in an assisted-living facility.

But I had my own problems to focus on: What was I going to say as the keynote speaker at the kickoff dinner? I had nothing prepared. Should I regale them with stories of the destitute existence that led me to *Shameless*? That would have them all in stitches. Should I deliver a rote speech about how my book had felicitously impacted the wine world, and how delighted I was to see them all beneficiaries of its success and... hey, where are my royalties? Nah, too self-serving.

Maybe just go extemporaneous. Wing it.

The surf went on pounding the cliffs, sending spray high enough that I could actually see it beyond my balcony every time a wave crashed. I poured a half glass of a David Family wine '09 Pinot that the owner had been so generous as to send me to sample. *Shameless* had celebrated my love for that unique grape variety and made Pinot producers and distributors want to celebrate me. Maybe a little too much. I glanced over at the dresser where stood dozens of bottles, wines I couldn't afford until just a few months before. I'd thought about re-gifting them, chortled I should peddle them on eBay for a little reserve cash in case this gust of fame ended and I was back to my former penniless life. But the gust didn't seem inclined to abate any time soon. I had a new publishing agent who was arm-twisting me into a deal *if* I could come up with as little as a concept. "Just a couple pages! That's all!" I couldn't, but that didn't stop her pestering. I had new movie/TV agents sending me out on meetings to pitch projects and hawk myself for assignments.

Life was good. Too good? No. But I still felt, acutely, the absence of a woman to share my life. Good fortune's not as much fun as a solo act. I needed that special someone I could vent my frustrations to, negotiate life's vicissitudes with and all the rest. Oh, there were women aplenty, but I had not found my soulmate, and I wondered–still licking the wounds of my divorce–whether I ever would.

Maybe that was what I should talk about, it occurred to me, as I sipped the David Pinot and exulted in its glories. No, too personal, too self-indulgent, and though I was accustomed to wearing my heart on my sleeve–hell, my book's story couldn't have been more personal!–the subject of my solitude would be a buzzkill. The crowd, estimate nearly five hundred, would want humor. I could do humor. The protagonist of my book, whom I was here to play, got a lot of laughs out of the life of a failed writer, a broken middle-aged man who couldn't figure out where the front door was.

Done. Now I just had to come up with an opening line.

There was a determined knock at my door.

"Come in," I called from my sprawl.

Marcie, my somewhat zaftig publicist–yep, I had one of those, too!–blustered in. All hips and limbs and curves and loose body parts, especially her disorganized mouth. A walking stereotype. She pulled up a chair. "How're you doing, Miles?"

I muted the TV. "Trying to think of what to say."

"Just be yourself."

"If I'm myself, there's no telling what might come out of my mouth. I'm not used to giving speeches. Except to the walls."

"They just want *you*, Miles. They just want to hear your rags-to-riches story."

"They want Martin." I looked at her, but she was suddenly captivated by the stupendous view. "I should have a basic speech prepared or something, but I'd come off like a politician. Besides, I'm lousy at reading from prepared text. Even when I do readings from them I sound like some academic bore."

She patted me on the knee. "You'll be fine. You changed the world of wine, Miles."

"The movie did," I chopped her off.

"Okay, but it was your book. You created the world."

"God created the world. I just wrote a book."

She laughed her throaty laugh. "And that's why they're here to hear you. You're playing for an audience that loves you already."

"I just got lucky. Nobody wanted that book, except one hot writer/director, and he changed my life. I don't deserve all this."

Marcie was looking at me impatiently. Had I done this rap before?

I held up the glass of Pinot. "Try it. It's the David."

She accepted the glass and ventured a sip. "Mmm," was all she said.

"Yes. Very Burgundian. Tremendous finesse. I've never drunk wines like this. That bottle goes for nearly ninety bucks. And there's lots more." I pointed to the dresser.

"Enjoy it, Miles. But not too much. Remember the Santa Barbara County Harvest Festival." She wagged a reproving finger at me.

I coughed a laugh. "I'll do my best," I said. "But, no promises. There's going to be barrels of wine at this dinner. You know that. And let's not forget: you got me into this."

"Miles, you're a celebrity. Specifically, a celebrity in the wine community. I'm just trying to help you promote your book and make you beaucoup bucks. I thought that's why you hired me?"

"It is. And I appreciate all you're doing. But I'm wondering if it's too much. Wine and I don't always mix."

"You'll be fine," she said, in an effort to reassure me. There was an edge in her voice along with the reassurance.

The sky out over the Pacific was growing orangey, semaphoring that the time for my kickoff speech was fast approaching. I was getting more nervous. What if I just clammed up? I worried. I fretted. My mind was turning in vertiginous circles. Part of me wanted to bail, get in my Prius (yes, just off the lot) and ride into the sunset, hit a wine bar, and have an anonymous evening alone with a raft of Pinots.

"How do you like your room?"

"It's nicer than my place in Santa Monica, that's for sure."

"Got everything you need?"

"Exquisite wines, ocean view, plasma TV. What more could a literary figure ask for?"

"You want to get a massage? You seem tense." She flipped open her cell. "I'll arrange it right now."

I held up my hand. "No, that's okay, but thanks. I might get an erection and do an Al Gore."

"We don't need that," she laughed. "I don't want to bother you right now, but I need to run some important things by you tomorrow, okay?"

"Okay," I said wearily, fearing a spate of speaking engagements and more wine festivals.

My iPhone–yes, it's pretty much the whole package–rang. I glanced at the number flashing on the screen. My mother. Or, rather, one of the numbers for Las Villas de Carlsbad. Ever since her "incarceration" at the assisted-living facility she called me three times a day, sometimes five. "It's my mom," I said to Marcie. "I should take it."

"I'll come get you in an hour," she said. She stood and exited.

I tapped Accept. "Hi, Mom."

"Miles! Where are you?"

"I'm up in Shell Beach."

"Up where?" she screeched.

"Shell Beach. Central Coast. Near Hearst Castle. I'm supposed to give a talk here in an hour or so. It's a big wine festival."

"Oh, no," she said.

"Oh, yes," I said. "They've got enough wine up here to keep everyone on Capitol Hill inebriated for a week."

"You'll get drunk and be thrown in the pokey," she said.

"No, I won't. I don't have to drive anywhere, Mom."

"When're you coming to visit?"

"I don't know. My publicist and publisher have a lot of events planned for me to promote my book. They all want to make money. I'll get down soon. I'm supposed to give a talk at a faculty event or something at UCSD, so maybe then."

"I'm so miserable here. The food is shitty. The help is shitty. They treat me like an invalid."

"You are an invalid, Mom."

"I am not!"

"I'm sorry. I didn't mean it that way. But you did have a pretty massive stroke and you need care, and until someone convinces Medicare to cover assisted living, Las Villas is the best I can do."

"Why can't I go live with my sister, in Wisconsin? She'll take me."

This was a regular part of her litany. There was no way they would let a woman with full left-side paralysis board a plane on her own, and I hate to fly. No, I'm terrified by the mere prospect.

"Mom, I've explained to you a hundred times. There's no way to get you there. Unless you want me to pack you up and put you on a boxcar."

"Stop joking me. You can find a way. You're always showing how smart you are."

Unless I shifted gears, she'd go on indefinitely and indefatigably. "How're you doing otherwise? Has Hank been up to visit?"

"No," she retorted nastily. "Your brother hates coming here and seeing all these old, dying people. That's what he told me."

"So Melina hasn't been coming up with Snapper?" I knew my cantankerous mother had long-ago alienated the old girlfriend of mine who'd adopted her horrendous Yorkie.

"No. I haven't seen Snapper in months."

"I'll talk to Melina," I promised.

"Please come and visit," she beseeched... no, wailed!

"I'll try, Mom," I said, with exasperation now in my voice. "But I'm real busy these days. This is my time. It comes but once in a career."

Why should she give a damn about my windfall fame? "Oh, please. Try. I'm dying in here!"

I couldn't take it anymore. "I've got to go, Mom. I've got a speech to give to five hundred people and I have no idea what I'm going to say. Okay? Goodbye. Sleep well."

As soon as I hung up the phone rang again. Same number. I hit Decline and muted the incessant ringing. She left an evidently lengthy voicemail I had just as little interest in hearing. I rose and ambled out onto the balcony. Now I could finally see the waves I'd been hearing. Sailboats bent sideways raced across the coastline, leaving white wounds in the water behind them, the rich and adventurous, living the good life. Fuck them, I thought. Gulls wheeled overhead, cawing hungrily. The air was redolent of the sea: brine, kelp, dead shellfish. The David Pinot was really opening up. It had started out kind of barnyardy with notes of hay and wet tea, but now it was fragrant with raspberries and black cherries, a truly splendiferous wine. The more I drank the better I started to feel about the upcoming dinner. In fact, I was getting fired up. *I can do this* I intoned over and over. I can do this.

I topped off the glass and went back to the golf tournament, but it was just as boring as before. The wine, though, was energizing me, propping me up, fortifying me for my talk. Hell, I could say anything and I'd be fine. I undressed, crossed to the ridiculously capacious bathroom and indulged in a long, hot shower. When I came out I felt better. Much better. An opening line had even flared in my head during the shower. From there, I reasoned, I would be off and running.

I donned a pair of black corduroys, a long-sleeve white button-up shirt–sans tie–which I purposely didn't tuck in. Hey, I was a real writer now, I could dress the part. I could show up with my hair looking like a tumbleweed, my eyes bloodshot, my left shoe on my right foot, walking an oblique trajectory without clear destination. Hell, that's probably who they were expecting!

At seven Marcie came to retrieve me.

"How're you feeling?" she asked.

"Great!" I said, probably a little too exuberantly.

She glanced at the empty bottle on the nightstand, but held her tongue. I was her client; it was her job to get me through this. After all, I was being paid five thousand for the speech, and her ten percent commission probably covered most of her BMW payment.

We left the hotel room and ambled along a meandering cement pathway toward the venue. The sky was starting to purple. The ocean had grown calm and glassy and the swells had abated from their earlier fury. The sailboats were gone, back safe in their harbors, their owners no doubt dining on lobster at seaside restaurants. The gulls, fed now, had quieted. There was a peace in it all. A peace everywhere except my soul, in my gut, in my re-escalating nervousness about what I was going to say, how I was going to get through this.

"You'll be fine, Miles," Marcie kept saying.

"I'm sure I will," I tried to reassure her, not believing my words for a second, the Pinot in my belly no longer buoying my sudden surge of confidence.

"Just like the last one. They'll get easier." She placed a hand on my back and prodded me forward. "Remember. They're here tonight not just for the festival, but for you. They just want to see and hear the guy who wrote *Shameless*. It doesn't have to be long. Twenty minutes. I'm sure they'll be over the moon."

"I hope they will. Disappointment disappoints me."

She laughed.

The auditorium was packed and noisy as hell when we entered. At the back of the large room, fifteen sommeliers–many employed by famous restaurants in L.A.–were uncorking Pinots and sniffing them for cork taint, sometimes emptying whole bottles of expensive Burgundies they deemed off. Some sixty white-clothed tables, each ringed by eight of those fake-gilt fake-bamboo chairs, crowded the room. Numerous wineglasses sparkled on the tables, indicating that many wines waited to be sampled. All the tables boasted the same centerpiece: a large aluminum spit bucket. Winemakers and wine aficionados were hobnobbing.

It was good no one recognized me by face. I wasn't, after all, a movie star. I was just a writer and they're generally known, if at all, by name. Especially if they were first-time novelists as I was.

Marcie took an elbow and led a reluctant me to the director of the festival, a middle-aged, pleasant-faced woman standing near the raised stage. Marcie introduced me.

On Marcie's introduction, Jean hugged me profusely. "Miles! It's so great to meet you finally. Congratulations on your book and your movie. I'm so excited you're with us."

"Thank you so much for your hospitality," I said humbly, adding in a mumble, "Beautiful hotel room."

"It's our pleasure. You're the guest of honor. In fact I bumped Stephen Tanzer from your accommodations."

It was little consolation, in my state of rising anxiety, to learn I'd usurped one of the great critics of the Burgundian world. Tanzer's lectures at this festival had been sold out from early on.

"Really? Wow. That wasn't necessary, Jean. I would have been fine in a first-floor room with a view of the parking lot. He'll probably trash my book now on his site."

She laughed. "We wanted to make it special for you."

"So, what's the game plan here?" I asked, businesslike.

"Well, I'm going to get up and give a short introduction to the festival, then I'm going to introduce you. You'll come up and do your thing."

"Okay," I said. I raked a hand through my hair, half out of nervousness, and half combing it into some vague notion of presentability. "Sounds like no big deal. How long should my speech be? I have nothing prepared."

"Just keep an eye on me. At some point I'll give you this"–she raised a flattened hand and, smiling, made a gesture as if slitting her own throat–"and you can wrap it up, go back to your table and enjoy! Menu's marvelous. And there's plenty of wine!"

"I noticed. Wow."

"We're going to be going through hundreds of bottles tonight."

"Looks like it." My panic had seemed to be ebbing, but no–it wasn't high tide yet.

"All Pinot. No Merlot," she laughed.

Marcie joined Jean in the standard guffaw, and I gave my now rehearsed smirk.

"Let's get seated," my publicist suggested, "shall we?"

"Again. Great to meet you, Miles," Jean said. "And really curious to hear what you've got for us."

Me too! I wanted to say.

Marcie, with her profession's sixth sense that the client was a little wobbly, re-gripped my elbow and steered me to our assigned table–front and center. Winemakers and wine writers I didn't recognize made up the rest of our group. They introduced themselves all around, smiles on their already ruddy faces.

The white-coated sommeliers–most of them surprisingly young and some of the females equally fetching–threaded their way to tables, pouring wines into the four or five glasses set before each place now occupied by an attendee. Temptation was calling its siren song. I started sipping, just to get over the dry mouth that had set in. The speech I was to give was still uppermost in my mind and I wanted to keep my wits about me. Wine kept arriving. All Pinot Noir, of course, my favorite grape, in an absolute, ridiculous embarrassment of riches.

At one point a winemaker I thought was from an outfit in Monterey showed up at the table with a magnum of one of his single-vineyard Pinots, inscribed to me in silver ink, and presented it as a gift. "Maybe you'll put it in your next novel," he suggested, winking almost lewdly.

"Thank you," I said, hefting the huge bottle with a glance at the label, which I didn't recognize, and placed it on the floor next to me. Other winemakers made their way over to our table, also bearing bottles. By my position in the room they were all now apprised of who I was, nondescript physiognomy and deer-in-headlights look notwithstanding. The sips of Pinot that kept arriving were definitely improving my resolve, even my comfort level. Fawning attention, as any aspiring tyrant can tell you, is useful: it bolsters confidence. Hell, I remember thinking at one point, I can say whatever I want.

As the appetizer plates started appearing, Jean took the podium, adjusted the mic, and spoke to the five hundred Pinot mavens. "Hi, everyone. Welcome to the World of Pinot Noir here at beautiful Shell Beach." Applause greeted her opening line. The sommeliers kept appearing with more and more wine, pouring tasting dollops. Spit buckets filled up so quickly that they had to be replaced almost every half hour. "Tonight we have a special surprise guest." She paused for effect.

I turned to Marcie with alarm. "You didn't tell me I was a *surprise* guest."

"That's how they wanted it," she said. "Just go with it."

I reached for one of the four glasses in front of me and drained it.

Jean soldiered on. "As you all know, a man, an extraordinary writer"–I murmured under my breath that I wasn't an *extraordinary* writer–"created a wonderful tale called *Shameless*. His book was made into a movie I'm sure all of you have seen." More applause interrupted her introduction. "Most of us more than once. That book and movie glorified the grape we all love. Pinot Noir." The applause was now interspersed with whistling. "Well, that author is here with us tonight. So, without further ado, I want to introduce... Miles Raymond!" Jean looked down at me and applauded, that reliable real-estate broker smile brightening her countenance.

The five hundred Pinot-philes broke into wild applause. Many of them stood. I fortified myself with another blast of wine. Marcie grasped my elbow and helped me get to my feet. It was a short walk to the stage and the podium, and that was a good thing.

As I approached the dais and made my way to the lectern where the microphone was, Jean stepped aside from the microphone, still clapping. The audience continued with her, urging me on. Despite my discomfort with my sudden ostensible fame, my determination was strengthening.

I adjusted the mic to my level. I held up both hands as if I were saying, *I'm guilty, I'm the guy.* The guests resumed their seats, but the applause went on. "Please," I said. I paused, looked around a bit sheepishly, then roared: "I've never seen so much goddamn wine in my life!" Hilarity greeted that opening. I had brought a glass to the lectern and took another invigorating quaff. "I don't know what this is in my glass, but man this shit is da bomb!" I sipped a little more. "Before I wrote *Shameless* I was so poor all I could afford was five-dollar Merlot. And, man, that stuff was crap!" More laughter encouraged me. "When I wrote my book I never thought in a million years that it would have such an effect on the most noble of grape varieties. And kill that damn Merlot industry, which right-fully earned its ignominy." More whistling and applause. I was on a roll. I held up my glass. "Would one of you kind sommeliers refresh me here with one of your finest Burgundies? I'm Pinot parched!"

As the audience laughed and cheered, a young, beautiful female sommelier strode to the stage bearing a bottle with some arcane French label I couldn't even read and generously poured me half full. I took a healthy sip, sudsed it around in my mouth and swallowed. "This is ambrosial," I hollered to the crowd. "My God, I wish I could take all this wine and back-date it to seven years ago. Backdate the stock options like all those dot-com guys almost got away with doing." That got another laugh. "When it rains it pours, I guess." I took another quaff, and noticed Marcie looking a little anxious. But the wine and the crowd's approbation were driving me on. I was theirs now. "I don't know how you people can spit this wine out. It's so good. Maybe that's why my marriage failed." I paused, sipped, shrugged, and added dryly, "She wouldn't swallow."

The crowd roared. I may have been halfway to the crapper, but the one-liners were firing on all eight. I don't know where it came from. All my usual neurotic inhibition had left me.

I rambled on. "Never in a million years, in my penurious days, when I sat down to write *Shameless* did I think it would have such an effect on an industry. Never in my wildest dreams did I think someone would make a movie out of a book no publisher wanted to publish. I am so grateful that all of you, and the millions of others, have responded so favorably. Hell, I was just hoping to make a few grand, pay my rent, hire a hooker maybe, and be able to write another novel." More hilarity. "I was so low when I wrote *Shameless* that if I could have afforded a gun I would have killed myself." Gut-spilling, jackknifing laughter. "Seriously. Tall buildings had a mysterious pull on me. Freeway overpasses beckoned. Fistfuls of Xanax." For some reason at that moment I took out the vial of Xanax I always carried with me and shook it. There was more laughter. "But it's funny how success can soothe one's anxiety." They couldn't stop laughing. "And wine! Great wine! The kind of wine we're all imbibing tonight." Many of the attendees raised their glasses in a mass salute. "Man, I'm in a two-room suite on the ocean–sorry, Mr. Tanzer–with some of the finest Pinots in my room, courtesy of you munificent and talented winemakers. I don't deserve this. I was just a guy with a laptop and no girlfriend, a feckless fool with an aversion to a real job and nothing better to do than type to pass the time. And now"–I swept my hand with my glass, sloshing some onto my white shirt–"You all and a fine movie have made me a writer. I get to write now, and even tell people that's what I do. It's positively surreal." I took another sip. "I could go on and on about the inspiration for the book, how I fell in love with Pinot–and a waitress who no longer chooses to be in my life–how I weathered my mother's stroke, was down on my luck, how I was so broke when someone blew off my car door on Wilshire Boulevard as I opened it a little too quickly I didn't have the money to get it fixed and how it became the Motel 6 *du jour* for the homeless, how I defenestrated out the back of my apartment when my landlord pounded on the front door. But, those days are past."

I sensed I was growing maudlin, so I stopped. "So. Some of you might have questions for me."

Arms shot up. At this point, in my recall, comes one of those blackout ellipses that only hardcore alcoholics fully understand. I remember at one point someone's asking me about the notorious scene in the movie in which Martin, the protagonist, is so frustrated with his life that he drinks from a spit bucket at a high-end wine tasting. The questioner wanted to know if that had really happened. I think I explained that it was wildly exaggerated in the movie. And, yes, I remember that some besotted oenophile brought a spit bucket overflowing with Pinot to the stage. I was so intoxicated, with the Pinot and the adulation, that when he approached me all sense of reason went out the window. Time to deliver the coup de grace and reenact the scene as it happened in the movie. At first I pretended just to sip. I heard chants and exhortations from around the room. They grew louder, urging me to imbibe. Finally, in a move I can't explain, I lifted the bucket high over my head and poured the entire contents over my uplifted, grateful face.

The audience went wild!

Marcie looked at me like she had wandered into a locker room after the Super Bowl and was thinking sports publicity was not for her. Jean was practically sawing through her own neck. I must have ignored them because I babbled on some more.

I have little or no recall of the dinner. Or any of the wines consumed. I half-remember when the event concluded that the sommeliers gathered in a private room and drank until the wee hours of the morning, welcoming me into their cabal. They debated obscure wines and tried to outdo one another in their oenological knowledge. I must have tasted some sublime grape, but my palate was so shot it was wasted on me. Recalling my performance, several of them laughed until tears watered their eyes. Then, there were these two young, beautiful female sommeliers, one pressed to each side of me. That I vividly remember. Vaguely remember shambling back with them to my cliff-top room, groping them, stopping to kiss them, reaching an unrepentant hand into their clothing.

Depending on whose perspective you were relying on, the kickoff event was either a rousing success or a total disaster. I had either made a total fool of myself or regaled the audience with one of the great opening speeches they had been lucky enough to hear. I can't say, since it was all a blur.

chapter 2

I woke heavy-lidded, my head a molten ingot of lead as the room–what room?–kaleidoscopically rearranged itself into a solid. I sniffed the air. It was a malodorous mélange of perspiration, pussy, and plundered bottles of Pinot. As I blinked my surroundings into focus I vaguely recognized the brunette sommelier-in-training from the night before. What a pretty young girl like her was doing lying next to me I had trouble imagining. I was afraid if I closed my eyes I would be plunged into a dream in which I was homeless, a soiled rucksack slung over my shoulder, my extended thumb buffeted by rumbling 18-wheelers.

I felt a stirring to my port side. What's this!? A strawberry blonde had risen from the tangle of pillows and sheets. She looked like some model materializing mermaidlike from an infinity pool in a slick perfume commercial peddling happiness and youthful, hard-body romance.

"Mornin', Miles," she cooed.

She started to kiss me. Then she snaked hand down into my nether regions and attempted to restore me to life. I didn't know if this 45-year-old wreck of a body could take it anymore. I had bitten off half of a Viagra to counteract the effects of over-imbibition, and it now had me turbo-charged as if someone had dropped a Rolls Royce engine into a VW chassis. While the blonde lightly snored and the brunette stroked me I came to the felicitous realization that these were the spoils of the life of a now celebrated author.

But all the receptors in my brain just cried out for a glass of Pinot. It was tantalizingly just out of reach and I didn't want to spoil the brunette's concupiscent fantasy. "Enough concupiscence!" I almost shouted, my penchant for polysyllabics having had them in stitches the previous night. *Where was my publicist?* I suddenly wondered. As the blonde came awake, the brunette had, without warning, disappeared under the sheets to make *my* fantasy come true. I turned and kissed the blonde with the bed-tangled hair. Her lips were big and moist and, best of all, desiring, wanting, in unapologetic terms.

I closed my eyes to the unbidden ravishing and let the both of them have their way with me. Two women in my bed—had I expressed this fantasy to them the previous besotted evening when I had charmed them back to the room with promises of autographed books and a glimpse into the personal life of one Miles Raymond, erstwhile failed Hollywood scribe turned successful novelist? *Shameless* was, for better or worse, a humiliatingly frank book that laid bare my soul. I thought it would be my ruination, my Hail Mary shot that would end up fluttering into the proverbial void, but instead it miraculously turned my life around. Unwittingly, I made wine appreciation cool. Everyone wanted in on the act. OK, I wasn't handling it well. Who could blame me? Here I lay, two women devouring me, when a year before I couldn't get a date to save my life. And still, in my jaded state of degeneracy, needing desperately to sandpaper the edges of a sledgehammer-pounding hangover, all I really wanted was a glass of Pinot. Pinot for pussy, I almost pleaded to the two wanton wine whores.

The girls thrashed me finally to a perspiration-soaked, if awkwardly, limbs-entangled, conclusion. Pfizer made sure the crown jewels stayed in fine form for the final assault on the ramparts of young womanhood, but I almost fainted getting to the Promised Land. There was some requisite and obligatory hugging and nuzzling before they minced off to the shower, complete with hard-muscled naked asses the likes of which I hadn't witnessed in a while, prone as I had once been to any body type in my desperation for any kind of female affection. I struggled off the bed and climbed into a plush terrycloth robe, knotted it at the waist, and poured a healthy glass of Pinot from the many uncorked bottles still littering the dresser. Feeling blissfully dissolute in the postcoital respite, I fired up a half-smoked Cohiba I found in an ashtray on the dresser. I didn't smoke, especially cigars, but some ruddy-faced winemaker–who now loomed like a demonic elf in my fractured memory–had pressed it on me the night before, along with a bottle of his winery's finest, and it seemed to complete the image of my shameless and unapologetic plummet into depravity. *Success, mess*, I muttered to myself.

The picture window beckoned and I donned my new Revo sunglasses and stepped out onto the balcony into a blazingly bright morning, the sky as blue as my ex-wife's eyes. The waves crashed against the cliff below, their explosions deafening. The ocean was an unobstructed amplitude of dark blue. Pleasure boats, disgorged from a nearby marina, listed against the strengthening wind and pimpled the sea. I felt sore–and at the same time, sated–everywhere. It had been a long time coming. The previous decade could have been written off with the pathetic trope of a snail crawling on hot asphalt en route to Bakersfield. This fame shit is great, I thought, as I lifted the Riedel sommelier's glass to my lips, coaxing in some of the delicious wine. *But why am I feeling so wretched? so miserable?*

The girls re-emerged and flanked me. In the past, they would have disappeared after a shower (had they bothered with one), leaving no note, only the scent of their drunken abandon and the redolence of their ambivalence for having slept with someone they shouldn't have–marital guilt? The ignominy of awakening to the realization of having just bedded down with a loser? This view was decidedly different, one I could get used to, if only my circumspect self wouldn't keep shrieking in my ear that it was all ephemeral, an evanescent dream. *Live it while you can, Miles*, I intoned to myself. *Live it while you can.*

"Wow, that was amazing," I said, shaking my head.

"You were amazing, Miles," the brunette–whose name I was blanking on–said in a sultry voice. She was a tall, leggy woman, combing back a wet mane of hair, and I drank her in, raked her nakedness with lusting eyes.

"I was?" I said, having little recall of the evening, remembering only being pitched and tossed about in a frenzy of sex and more sex.

"How does it feel to be famous, Miles?"

I shrugged. "I'm not famous. I just got lucky."

She pinched my cheek. "You can dispense with the false modesty, Miles. You *are* famous."

"I am? I don't *feel* any different. But I realize that people perceive me differently, if that's what you're fishing for."

The blonde poured wine into a similar piece of Riedel stemware and handed it across to the brunette. The bulbous, pretentious glasses were a gift from the man himself for my having autographed a poster for the movie–*Without Riedel I Wouldn't Drink Wine!* I had grandiloquently scrawled; he loved it. Did the '07 Bonaccorsi Pinot taste better in these glasses as some suggested? I couldn't tell. All I knew was that it was a hell of a lot better than the $5 plonk that until recently had been all my budget could swing. It was big, voluptuous, fruit-forward, a true expression of the Pinot variety. The truth is, I didn't know shit about wine. Experientially. I made it all up, relying heavily on Jancis Robinson's brilliant encyclopedia on the subject, *The Oxford Companion to Wine.*

"You look a little down, Miles," said the blonde. (What was her name? Damn it! Sherry? Sarah? Started with an *S.*) I turned and gazed into her too-young, freckled face and smiled wryly. How could she read me so well, I wondered? I guess the twin emotions of elation and depression were warring inside me and my tired and spent expression bore both equally.

I held up my glass. "No, I'm happy," I said. "Two beautiful girls, a hit movie, the honeymoon suite with the ocean view. All the Pinot I can drink. What more could a guy like me ask for?"

"Do you have a girlfriend back in LA?" she probed.

"No," I said.

"How come?"

"I'm picky about wines, and I guess that spills over into my feelings for women. When my life was shit I would have married a parking enforcement officer I was so desperately lonely. Now, I feel like everyone wants something from me, including women. I'm having trouble differentiating fact from fiction." I held up my glass in a toast to the sea, to the world, and all that awaited me therein, and said, "Maybe I just got so used to the fact that I would never find the right woman–and that the right woman would never have anything to do with someone as fucked up as me–I had given up."

"Maybe you just want to serially date for a while?" the blonde chimed in.

"I don't think so," I said. "It doesn't appeal to me." I held up my glass and stared into it, ruminating. "I'm really looking for love."

They raised their eyes circumspectly, smirks on their faces. Wasn't the Miles Raymond *they* had imagined. Because they had thought they were meeting Martin West, *Shameless*'s protagonist-narrator, not me.

"Seriously," I said. Then I cheered up. "But since you two both have boyfriends back in LA"–actually, one was engaged if memory served!–"you're out of the running. Plus, I'm not sure it'd be good for my liver to be falling in love with sommeliers."

They laughed.

"You were funny at the dinner last night, Miles," the brunette remarked.

"Was I? My recall's a little fuzzy."

"You wouldn't think from reading your book that you would be the type who could do speaking engagements," she said.

"Yeah, well, I just, I don't know, drank myself through it, I guess."

The blonde ruffled my tousled hair and said, "When you lifted that spit bucket and poured it over your face and shouted out 'No more fucking Merlot!' that crowd went berserk."

"What?" I said, suddenly alarmed.

"Don't you remember?"

At the memory, both broke into irrepressible, eye-watering laughter. My chin sagged to my chest in mortification. As after a lot of drunken blackout nights, my own recall could be snapped quickly into focus by someone's painting a vivid picture of an incident that alcohol had mercifully occluded. Now, it all came back to me in a stinging, humiliating rush. Holy Christ! I remembered now how the crowd had grown positively primitive and tribal about it, pounding the tables with their fists and imploring: DRINK! DRINK!

I turned to the brunette. "Did I really do that?" I asked, feigning ignorance.

"Oh, yes," she said.

"I don't believe it."

She turned and went back inside the room and a few seconds later returned with a white dress shirt, extended the sleeves and modeled it. The entire front was Rorschach-ed with red wine, a rag-like testament to my public opprobrium and refutation of my selective memory.

I glanced at it with increasing embarrassment. I brought the wineglass to my mouth, deciding I needed a little more memory obliteration. "I'll never live this one down," I said. "Fuck, that's going to be on YouTube tomorrow," I muttered.

"It's already up," said the blonde. "But the quality's poor. Cellcam, I think."

"Oh, what a consolation!" I said, genuinely aggrieved. I tried to sort through the potential repercussions of this now viral dissemination of disgrace, but it was too much to deal with, so I just took another healthy sip of the sublime Bonaccorsi to chase it away. Still feeling guilty that I didn't remember their names, I glanced at each of them, then settled on the blonde. "Forgive me, but I... can't recall your names."

"Sera, with an *e*," said the blonde. "Like the evening, in Italian."

I turned to face the brunette.

"Jessica."

"Sera and Jessica. How the hell did I end up with you two impossibly beautiful women?"

"We thought you were cute," Sera answered.

"It's the World of Pinot Noir, Miles. We all let our hair down. You know, like that pagan German beer festival where everyone takes off their wedding rings."

I nodded, suddenly feeling a little weary. The wine festivals, the book signings, they were starting to take a toll on me.

Sensing perhaps I was a little down, I don't know, out of nowhere Jessica snaked a hand through the crease of my hotel robe and throttled me. Damn Sildenafil! Build it for a 70-year-old who shouldn't be having sex and then cleverly and disingenuously market it to 40-somethings. There should be a limit to how much we can cajole out of our bodies, I thought, as my cock magically sprang back to life.

"Oh, no," I protested.

"Oh, yes," she said. "You look depressed. We don't want you to be depressed."

"You're going to give me a heart attack. I've got a mother in a wheelchair in an assisted-living facility who depends on me."

She ignored my expostulation. Succeeding in arousing me, Jessica set her Riedel on the stucco partition, knelt down and started to fellate me again, twisting her head this way and that as if to impress me. Sera, apparently not wanting to be left out, and not interested in philosophizing on the infinitude of the sea and sky, turned to kiss me. Out of the corner of my eye I noticed a young couple with their two kids walking on the cliffside cement path. Thank God the partition shielded their innocent eyes from the pornography below my waist. For a brief moment I thought wistfully about the prospect of kids, flashing back to a memory of Victoria, early in our marriage, agreeing to an abortion after an accidental impregnation that sent me spiraling into a high level of anxiety. Nah, I thought, as my cock stiffened in Jessica's confident mouth. If I'd had kids I'd never have written *Shameless*. And I wouldn't be getting blown at the World of Pinot Noir in the honeymoon suite with the ocean view at ten in the morning....

We potato-sacked it back into the bedroom and, hangovers be damned, resumed the orgy, each of them taking turns now, no one giving a prudent pause to consider prophylactics or personal sex history confessions, boyfriends, fiancés or whatnot. I think we all believed that all the wine would kill any transmittable viruses and concomitantly disembarrass us to any guilt we might suffer when we returned to our quotidian lives. I let them cavort on my enervated body as if I were fresh kill and they were a rogue pack of coyotes. It felt good to be adored so unconditionally, made love to until there was nothing left in my imagination or testicular chambers. There were moments when I thought it was a vortex pulling me down somewhere chthonic where I would have trouble resurrecting myself, but I let myself surrender to it.

The wine industry girls were really lovely, if a bit over-enthusiastic, but I was glad when they had finally evaporated, leaving business cards, kisses, specious promises, sashaying behinds, half-empty wine samples, the wreckage of an all-night bacchanal, and me, on the bed, TV remote in hand, benumbed by a golf tournament, feeling utterly relaxed, a fat pasha, my upper lip reeking faintly of, well, *Woman*!

I lay contentedly on the bed, sommelier's glass resting on my expanding waistline–I made a mental note to get back into the gym, even though it didn't seem to matter one whit to these wine worshippers–and reflected on how everything had changed so dramatically in my life in just the last six months. Emceeing wine festivals, hosting faculty dinners, women looking at me with a whole new aspect and degree of attraction. Okay, admittedly I had been sipping wine since waking–and I would have to work on that as well, I mused ruefully–but I wasn't sweating rent, wasn't scheming stealing from my poor mother, was no longer in a state of paresis over how I was going to get through the next damn month without succumbing to the St. Vitus's Dance. All the years of suffering–living on the edge, the divorce from Victoria that capsized me into despair, my mother's debilitating stroke, my career in tatters—all of that had been magically wiped clean with one book, and a glorious movie. Sure, the press had first cluster-fucked the director and the stars, but finally they realized this wasn't the Immaculate Conception and that indeed there was a novel behind the whole éclat. And suddenly, I was the go-to guy for Pinot Noir. It was a riot. It was all just too incredible. And a lot to deal with all at once.

I was basking in it, though. I had nowhere to be. I could afford to let my phone ring off the hook, even when I knew it was someone important calling, many of them clamoring for a piece of my soul. The more I blew them off the more they wanted me. What a novelty! The women found me sexy. Yeah, sexy! The salacious things they drunkenly whispered in my ear. Married, affianced, committed relationships. They didn't give a shit. The married ones were the most uninhibited. Christ, don't you men fuck your wives anymore?! I almost shouted out loud as I mused on this phenomenon. God, these women. I didn't understand them. What was it about some middle-aged guy who had written a moderately successful book? Had my looks suddenly, supernaturally, transmogrified into those of a movie idol? Did sleeping with me and receiving my bodily fluids constitute some irreligious category of christening into the numinous realm of creativity where, it seemed, everyone dreamed of residing, but which few could actually attain? Was I a genius and didn't even know it? Hell, film people, agents, others, were using the "G" word with regularity now. *Best not to get too big a head* I spoke out loud to myself—a tic I had developed from spending too much time alone—as I continued sipping my wine and reflecting on my newfound good fortune.

My new iPhone jangled on the nightstand. I glanced at it. It was Jack. Did I want to hear *his* boozy voice? In the seven years since we made that serendipitous and novel-inspiring trip up to the Santa Ynez Valley, he had fallen on hard times. Shortly after his opulent wedding his wanton philandering had picked up where it had left off. Assistants on the TV shows he directed, location groupies, scuzzy barflies, any willing woman he could get his meaty paws on and seduce with his outsized charm—it was as if he was on a self-destructive tear *to* destroy his marriage. Because once you cheat on your spouse and get away with it a couple times there's no more moral superego. The libido runs riot. The fresh pussy feels intoxicating, transformative. You can't get enough of it.

Then, invariably, the wife gets wise. She kicks you out of the house, lawyers up after couples therapy dismally fails. Throw in a kid–a cute little boy named Byron–and the inexorable, nasty, venomous divorce from Babs, the custody battle protracted and expensive–and your life becomes a living hell, the stress nerve-shattering, drink-inducing. And Jack was drinking more now than ever. His benders were being bruited about by an already too-gossipy industry. Like a lot of people who drink too much, he didn't care about the fallout; they're so immured in their misery that they lose all touch with reality and soon it's too late and they find themselves unemployed, sans wife, visitation rights stripped away from them by an unsympathetic judge, bank-gutting child support payments, alimony, and all the other detritus of a wrecked life. That's where Jack had landed with a thud and being around him had ceased to be fun. His usual bonhomie had turned lugubrious and sullen. Still, I felt an obligation, what with all my success, to be his ameliorant, if that's what he needed. Hell, his lovable roué of a character had made me thousands. I owed him. And he was not shy about reminding me that our financial situations had flip-flopped.

"Jack," I said. "What's happening?"

"Where are you, Miles?"

"Up here in..."–I glanced at a brochure on the nightstand; I didn't even know the name of the hotel I was staying in!–"Shell Beach. Shell Beach Lodge. The World of Pinot Noir. Two women just left."

"Bullshit," he roared.

"I'm not pulling your leg, Jackson. It's fucking nuts up here."

"I told you you were going to get laid off of this."

"Man, they were off the charts, dude. These women in the wine world. You'd think they'd be dehydrated from all the alcohol and come with purses overflowing with Astroglide, but, no, they're lubricious. And you'd think they'd pass out, but, no, their tolerance levels are Falstaffian, they want to fuck all night! It's wild, dude, it's wild!" It was a stunning reversal of fortune, our discrete lives, and I enjoyed needling him about it.

Jack listened without saying anything. I thought I could hear him dragging on a cigarette, disgruntlement or envy rasping his silence. "That's great, man," he finally allowed. "When're you going to take me on one of these extravaganzas of yours? Let me be your factotum," he bellowed, somewhat pathetically. "I need the money. And you need the protection."

I chortled. "From what?"

"All the women, short horn."

"You just want me to deflect the rejects into your coop."

"That too," he said. There was a pause. Jack dragged on a cigarette and I sipped my wine.

"Look, Jack, I got your message a couple days ago. I know you asked me for five grand and I haven't forgotten."

"Well, I wasn't going to bring that up," he said proudly.

"No, it's okay, it's cool. I've been there. I know how hard it is to ask for handouts."

"I mean, I *was* the inspiration for the Jake character in *Shameless* after all."

"That you were. And I'm tired of your using that as a fulcrum to lighten my wallet."

He grew silent. "You owe me, short horn. You had a good run with Maya, didn't you?"

"Yeah," I said, my euphoria dipping a tad. I reflected for a moment on the relationship, now petered out, with the Hitching Post waitress–the commute, a new love interest in her life that derailed me for a while, and then my descent into unbridled hedonism a few months ago when the movie hit.

"Whatever happened with that?" Jack prodded. "We never really talked about it."

"I don't know," I said. "The movie. The attention. I don't know. I don't think she was happy with that hot tub scene where I licked a '90 Richebourg off Renay's–meaning her–pussy."

"Yeah, but it didn't make the movie. And it made her the hottest fuck-ing waitress in the Santa Ynez Valley."

"True. True," I conceded. "But, you know, I'm not sure I'm ready to settle down, big guy. There are weak moments when I think I am, then another side tells me I've still got some wild oats to sow here. Relationships are a tough gig. Tell me? How can I possibly be faithful at this magical juncture in my life? And at least I have the smarts to recognize that, and if I find myself inclined to get into a committed relationship, the likelihood that I'm going to hurt some wonderful woman like Victoria is too omnipresent. And I don't like hurting people. It's very taxing."

"I hear you, brother, I hear you." I heard a gurgle of liquid. Jack was warming up, the glow was slowly returning to his morose mood. I had an image of him sliding slowly into a hot tub, the ills of his life melting away with every inch of immersion. I didn't dare bring up Byron, Babs, the directing gigs that weren't there as they had been, the one-bedroom walk-up in Silver Lake where he was now unhappily ensconced with futon and TV and six-packs of cheap suds and little else.

"Look, I'll loan you the five. No, fuck it. In fact, I'll give you ten."

"What?" he said.

"I just sold the German rights for twenty. Wasn't expecting it. Euros dropping out of the sky. But, I want something in exchange."

"I'm listening," he said, tugging on the cigarette.

"Okay, I told you that I've been invited to be the master of ceremonies at the International Pinot Noir Celebration in McMinnville, Oregon, right?"

"I think you mentioned it, but you didn't want to go or something."

"Well, I wasn't. These festivals are killing me. I want to get back to my writing. But I've decided to accept this one."

"What?! You weren't going to tell me?"

"Jack! I was planning to take the Coast Starlight all the way up to Portland. I was going to make a relaxing week out of it. Read a good book. Tap out some ideas that have been rattling around in my brainpan."

"Jesus, man, we talked one night about going up there together. Where's the loyalty, Miles?"

"I confess I was just a little too afraid it was going to be another bacchanal with the two of us."

"Bullshit. You met a chick who wanted to go. Miles Raymond. Celebrity author. I get it, dude, I get it."

"Well, okay. But the chick and I had a falling out."

"Uh-huh," Jack said, incredulous.

"No, seriously. She told me she was looking to get married, I told her I wasn't, so I didn't want to string her along. Especially because she wasn't really right for me."

"What was the problem this time?"

"She waxes."

"Ah."

"You know I like some fur down there."

"I know, brother, I know."

"So, anyway, I was going to cancel, but then a flare went off in my head. Why not drive? Schedule a couple book signings along the way, take in the scenery, get out of the hurly-burly of LA…"

"Road trip!" Jack interrupted excitedly. "I am all in, brother. I am all in."

"But there's more to the plan."

"Okay, I'm listening."

I sipped my wine. "So, my mother's very unhappy in Las Villas de Muerte"—our moniker for her assisted-living facility–"down there in Carlsbad."

"Yeah, that visit last month was sad, man. Sad. God, I hope we don't end up like that."

"Okay, well, I have to hear about it every day. I did the best I could after her congestive heart failure almost killed her, but even I have to admit that's no life for anyone. Anyway, she wants to move back to Wisconsin to live with her sister. Her sister needs the money, and my mother could use a little more of the home-cooking touch, if you know what I mean." I took a sip of wine to fortify myself. "Plus, the whole thing is draining me cash-flow wise. Not that I mind, but…. So, I was thinking, I don't like to fly, my mother can't fly in her condition, if we rented one of those handi-capped vans, drove to the Willamette, gave my mother one last big send-off, then drove her to Wisconsin and dropped her off at her sister's... Anyway, that's the plan."

"Dude." I could see Jack's eyes bugging out. "Your mom's a…"

"Hold on," I chopped him off. "I know it sounds wack, but bear with me. My mom's got a favorite nurse–a little Filipina named Joy. I've sort of floated the possibility of her accompanying my mother on such a trip. And she's totally willing. Especially for the cash I was offering."

Jack slurped whatever alcoholic beverage he was drinking. "I'm still listening."

"Five days to the Willamette Valley. Three for the festival. Two-day blitzkrieg to Wisconsin, drop my mom off at her sister's with Joy who'll oversee the transition, I get hammered, pop some Vicodin, and you get me on that flight back to LA. We have a great time, I give my mother this gift of being with her sister and liberating her from that depressing assisted-living facility. Plus, I get her out of my hair, get her expenses down to a more manageable number before she bankrupts me–the woman will not go down. What do you say? I know it sounds like I'm a little twisted right now–and I'm getting there–but I think it could be fun."

"I don't know, man. Your mom's in pretty bad shape, dude."

"I know, but I know how to handle her. Hand her a glass of wine and she's putty. Remember, I was the one who had to take care of her and get her into Las Villas after my little brother ripped her off. Plus, she's going to have 24/7 with the highly trained Filipina caretaker. But I can't do all the driving. I cannot do this without you!" No response. "Jack? You want to be my co-pilot? Make some coin? That's my offer."

"I'm trying to wrap my head around this," he said. "Why don't you just FedEx her or something? Ground rate. Should be cheaper."

I laughed at the image. "Ten grand. Hard cold. Post-tax. The finest restaurants. Five-star hotels. And, of course, all expenses paid. We'll have a blast."

"You're fucking nuts," he laughed.

"Not exactly breaking news. No, honestly, Jack, this is for my mom. She's really miserable in that place. And I've got the means now to make her potentially happy. It'll be good for my soul."

Jack was easing into the possibility, lubricating the path with cheap wine, or rotgut vodka. I knew ultimately the money would sway him. "The Filipina can totally handle your mom?"

"Yeah, I've seen her transfer Mom from her wheelchair into a car. Chick's strong, man. She does this for a living for Christ's sake!"

"Ten grand?" Jack asked, as if to be sure.

"Yeah! Jesus! How many times do I have to say it? Forget the salvation of my soul for a second. It's going to save me money in the long run because it's going to be cheaper for my mom to be with her sister. I just got to fucking get her there."

There was a pause. I don't know if it was the booze speaking or if he just wanted to escape his abject life, but he spoke with unbridled exuberance, "All right, dude, let's do it. Let's get Phyllis to Wisconsin."

There was a familiar loud rap at the door. "Hey, Jackson, there's someone knocking. I think it's my publicist. Can I call you back?"

"Your *publicist*," he said sarcastically. "You crack me up, Homes. All right, call me back." He hung up.

Whoever it was knocked again, this time more sharply. "Who is it?" I called out.

"Marcie! Are you decent?"

Before I could respond, she barged in. It struck me for some reason that she was most likely lesbian, but the thought of some pretty young thing going down on her made my jittery stomach retch.

She pulled up a chair next to the bed and slouched her corpulence into it.

"Jesus, Marcie," I said, quickly pulling my complimentary robe over my exposed groin. I muted the volume on the TV. The sound of the crashing waves filtered in through billowy curtains covering the sliding glass door. Marcie was wearing some sort of sweater-like poncho over a blouse and a skirt that mercifully ended below the knees. But even then one still got an eyeful of the vast network of varicose veins that road-mapped her calves. "What's up?"

She sniffed the air like a narcotics dog and said, "What's that smell?"

"Sex. And a lot of it," I retorted, just to needle her.

"Oh." She glanced circumspectly at the monstrous glass of wine in my hand and said, "Aren't you starting a little early?"

"I'm on vacation," I said, holding up my glass in a toast to her sneering presence.

She shook her head wordlessly. Out of a satchel she produced a MacBook and pried it open. "Do you want to see yourself last night on YouTube?"

Depression surged in and ruined my mood. "No, Marcie, I don't."

She shook her head again in overt disapprobation. "I can't decide if it's good or bad publicity."

"I heard it was pretty damn funny."

"You *were* funny, Miles. But, did you have to outdo yourself with the spit bucket? I sincerely hope that's a one-off."

"You heard that crowd, Marcie. They were going to riot if I didn't re-enact that stupid scene for them! You said just be yourself, so I was. Fucking wish I hadn't written it."

"Well, I'm going to write it off as being caught up in the moment," she said, closing her laptop, adding admonishingly, "and hope it doesn't happen again."

"So, what have you got for me?"

"I've got a wine festival in Santa Clarita…."

"Screw that," I chopped her off. "Santa Clarita Wine Festival. That sounds like an oxymoron. What do they want me to do? Sit in a booth all day and sign books. Screw that, Marcie. It's a bastion of John Birchers out there." It was exhilarating to be in the position to turn offers down.

"It's five thousand."

"I don't need five grand that bad. Forget it. What else?"

"This high-end cruise line wants you to be their enrichment lecturer."

"What high-end cruise line?"

"Silverseas Cruises. Ever heard of it?"

"No."

She passed me a brochure. I leafed through it. Looked pretty high-end. "Only 300 passengers. One-to-one crew-to-passenger ratio. Thirty wines free, which might intrigue you." I kept paging through it. It looked mostly like rich retirees sailing off into the sunset.

I raised my voice to a histrionic level: "Silverseas Cruise! Free morphine drip! Burial at sea! 24-hour Medevac to nearest ER! The last cruise you'll ever take for more reasons than one!"

She laughed, pausing to inject a little sense of humor in her usually splenetic temperament. "This one might do you a world of good, Miles." She adjusted her reading glasses and read from her handwritten notes: "Let's see, it starts out of San Pedro and goes all the way down the coast of Mexico, stopping for golf along the way–Cabo, Mazatlán, Acapulco, Costa Rica–then it passes through the Panama Canal, sails all the way to Ft. Lauderdale where they'll fly you business class back to LA."

"Business class!" I shouted, divalike. "Fuck that! I'm Miles Raymond. Author of *Shameless*."

She pointed a finger at the glass of wine resting on my stomach. "You've got to slow down, Miles. I'm sure I can negotiate it up to first if that's a deal-breaker for you. Fourteen days. All you have to do is screen the movie, tell a few choice anecdotes, conduct a wine tasting…."

"Drink from the spit bucket."

"No, not drink from the spit bucket, but hobnob friendly with some very wealthy people."

"*Friendily*," I scoffed. "That's not a word, Marcie. The correct word is *friend-li-ly*."

"Whatever."

"Where'd you go to college?"

"Vassar."

"Vassar? That's a great school, or so I heard." I paused and took a sip of wine. "Do you know a good lawyer?"

"Yeah, why?"

"Because I think you have an ironclad case to sue for a refund on your tuition. Then you could afford the cruise. Or at least the weekend in Santa Clarita you're hankering for."

"Ha. Ha."

"Marcie, facetiousness aside, you know I have trouble boarding jetliners. Remember I told you I once had to be deplaned in Rapid City, South Dakota, off that 50-seater Canadian Air. That panic attack cost me $2,500 because I had to drive home. Forget it. I told you, anything involving flying is not in the cards for me."

"Miles," she said in an exasperated tone, "you're going to have to get over your aerophobia if you want to take advantage of these opportunities I'm bringing you. This is a lot of money you're turning down. This is your fifteen minutes of fame."

"What do you want me to do? I've tried Biofeedback. Total waste of money. Mountebanks! I spent a grand on a series of DVDs from some airline captain and that didn't do shit. I've tried meditation, medication, even mediation. I just get claustrophobic on a plane. Have you ever had a panic attack where you thought a giant octopus was planted on your chest and wouldn't relinquish its grip?" I didn't want to launch into the story of the time I had to be hospitalized because I hypochondriacally believed I was in the throes of a heart attack because the story was too involved and I had told it too many times and it was starting to sound apocryphal.

"Heck," she said, the publicist in her anxious to find a solution to everything, "I'll meet you in Florida and fly back with you and hold your hand. I'll go on the damn cruise with you if you want. It's thirty thousand a person, Miles! They're putting you up in one of their better suites, offering a ten thousand honorarium, view of the ocean…."

The thought of spending two weeks with Marcie on a Mexico/Central America cruise made my eyes bulge a little. Sure, two weeks playing golf and basking in the sun on a luxury boat did sound tempting. But then I worried that it would just turn into another one of those boozy affairs that go on indefinitely. "I don't know, Marcie, I'll think about it."

"As the enrichment lecturer you might meet that wealthy woman you've been looking for."

I scoffed. "Love's not in the offing for me, Marcie. Once these women get past the allure of the whole *Shameless* phenomenon, they discover this insecure guy who can't fly, is afflicted with frequent panic attacks, drinks too much, and is an inveterate commitment-phobe. I'm just too messed up."

"A woman would do you a world of good," she advised.

I took a sip of my wine and grew reflective. "Yeah, you're probably right. But Victoria just set the bar too high," I finished wistfully.

"You've got to move on, Miles."

"I know, I know. Let's drop it."

"Okay, so anyway," she said, turning to other matters. "We've got the tasting at The Wine House next Wednesday, a second faculty dinner at your alma mater UCSD, then the Willamette Valley event the following week…"

I cut her off. "There's been a change of plan."

She looked up from her notes with consternation. "What? You can't cancel, Miles. They've already done all this publicity around your coming and everything!"

"Celebrities cancel all the time, Marcie," I said, with deliberate indifference just to rile her and get her jowls shaking.

She stiffened. "Jesus, Miles, you're going to give me a damn heart attack!"

"I'm going, Marcie, okay? Relax. Okay?"

"So, what's the change of plans?" she asked warily.

I told her the change of plans.

Her eyeballs bulged out like sprung headlights after a head-on collision. "Let me get this straight. You're trading in a nice Amtrak trip, sleeper car, everything I arranged for you, to what? Rent some handicapped van? Pile in Jack"—she said it affectedly in a nasty way with a

shake of the head–"your stroke-addled mother, who's in a wheelchair,
and... a... Filipina caretaker?"

"And my mother's precious Yorkie, if I can get him back."

Marcie laughed so long and loud, when she was done her face looked like Baked Alaska with two maraschino cherries for eyes. "Are you out of your fucking mind?"

"Marcie? I didn't know you used the F-word."

"Unlike you, I save it for when it's really meaningful."

"Why does everyone keep asking me if I'm out of my mind?" I raised my nearly-empty sommelier's glass. "Could you bring me that bottle?" I said.

Marcie ignored my request. Instead, she reached for the hotel phone and dialed room service. "I'd like to get some eggs, bacon and toast and coffee up here ASAP," she said brusquely to whomever was on the other end of the line.

"I'm not hungry," I said to Marcie.

"You need to get something in your stomach, Miles," the mother in her admonished, jabbing a finger in the air at me. "And you need to *fucking* rethink this cockamamie trip of yours."

"I need to get out, Marcie. And I want to do this for my poor mother."

At the mention of my mother she cut short her remonstrations about my "cockamamie" trip. "So, you'll still do the event I set up at Justin Winery?"

"Absolutely. It's on the itinerary." I tipped my head back and chugged the rest of the wine in the glass as she, a teetotaler, looked on, aghast.

Marcie, still shaking her head, rose cumbrously from her chair and left. I got out my iPhone and logged onto the Net. Went to YouTube, typed in my name. And there it was: my boozy emcee speech, complete with my pouring a spit bucket over my head and the audience erupting into laughter. It was as if I were looking at a ghost of myself. Total mortification descended on me; more wine assuaged me.

chapter 3

It was night when I angled off the freeway at Sunset Boulevard and headed toward my house, feeling weary after the three-day debauch at the World of Pinot Noir. I still lived in the same rent-controlled house on 12th Street in Santa Monica. Didn't seem there was any reason to move. I'm not big on cars or real estate. And even with a little money in the bank and the knowledge that property ownership was smart–tax write-offs and all that responsible financial stuff that artists never pay attention to–I wasn't known for doing the prudent thing when it came to managing my finances.

Mail had piled up in my too-small mailbox. A quick perusal revealed a plethora of wine-related brochures and a pair of manila envelopes from my publishing agent. I tore open those first, smelling money. As I suspected, both contained checks. One was payment on a foreign sale of my book and the other contained yet another royalty check from my American publisher. Five years ago I would have fainted on the spot. Or, at the very least, knelt on the floor and invoked the Almighty, even if I had lost faith in Him over the past years. Now, it was a deluge. Money *and* women. Feast or famine. Beast or gamine–stupid little ditties were springing up in my head I was so giddy with my new good fortune.

My cell rang just as I came in the door and tossed my mail aside. "Hi, Mom," I said in a cheery voice, as I made my way into the kitchen and uncorked another amazing artisanal bottle of Pinot–that one of the girls had left on the credenza in Shell Beach–while balancing the cell between ear and shoulder.

"Hi, Miles," she said. "I'm in bed."

"That's good," I said. "How're you feeling today?"

"Oh," she said in her occasional singsongy voice, "okay, I guess."

I poured a glass of wine, reversed back into the living room and stretched out on my new Eames replica couch, a plush tuck-and-roll leather version that replaced the ghastly 20-year-old IKEA one where the polyester batting flared out of like disdainful tongues. "Did you get your glass of wine tonight?"

"Oh, yes," she said. "Joy was good to me."

"Well, that's good, because I know you didn't like that other girl, what was her name?"

"Dolores. She's no good," my mother said.

"Hey, Mom, have you spoken to your sister lately?"

"Oh, yes, I speak to her every night."

"Well, you know we've talked about the possibility of moving you out to Sheboygan."

"Uh-huh."

"Well, what if I told you I think I can make it a reality?"

"Oh, don't joke me, Miles."

"I'm not joking you, Mom. I know you're not happy at Las Villas. I know you blame me for putting you there. Even though you're the one who had the stroke, not me."

"I know. I'm such a burden." She fell into uncontrollable blubbering. Ever since the massive stroke she had the tendency to break into tears at the most trifling of things.

"Don't cry, Mom. I can't handle that, okay?"

"Okay," she said, sniffling.

"So, here's the deal: I'm invited to be the master of ceremonies at this big wine festival in Oregon. You know I don't like to fly, so I'm driving."

"Oh, no," she said. "You'll get killed!" She also, at any mention of travel or change in the lives of her sons and caretakers, waxed maniacally paranoid that we were fated to die and leave her all alone, abandoned to a tyrannical system of truculent nurses who didn't give a "god damn" about her welfare.

"Stop being dramatic, Mom. Jesus."

"Don't take the Lord's name in vain." She had also rediscovered religion after her stroke.

"If there were a god you wouldn't be in Las Villas, would you?" I teased her. She fell silent. "Anyway, Mom, I talked to Jack yesterday and he said he'd come and help with the driving. But we need Joy. Remember last time I was down and we all had lunch and talked about this?"

"I thought you were fooling me," she said.

"Maybe I was then. But I'm not now. Do you want to get out of Las Villas and be with your sister or not?"

"Joy'll come," she chirped. "She hates it here as much as I do."

"Okay, Mom, I'm sorry it's such a hellhole. Stop guilt-tripping me. I know I'm a bad son. Even if you are setting me back three grand a month because you refused to go down like a good soldier."

"Oh, stop joking me," she said, laughing at my sometimes twisted sense of humor, which she had grown accustomed to, and which, startlingly, she enjoyed.

"So, Mom," I said, "you're not lying"–she also had a conniving side now–"you *have* been talking to your sister?"

"Yes, every night," she replied.

"And she's still willing to take care of you if we can get you back to Wisconsin?" I asked rhetorically, knowing the answer.

"Oh, yes," she said.

"Does she know what's involved? The toileting? Preparing all your meals? The frequent doctor visits? Your waking in the middle of the night and calling out? Not to mention your cantankerous new personality."

"I am not cantankerous," she bristled.

"It's a lot of responsibility."

"I think Alice can handle it," she replied.

I wasn't completely convinced. "Well, we'll definitely hire someone to help her out if you're too much for her. But I want to make sure she knows what she's getting into here."

"I think she does," my mother replied meekly.

"Does she drink?"

"Oh, no. Never."

"And she knows you're a wine lush?"

"Oh, stop that. You should talk," she snapped.

I laughed. "Yeah, well, it's making me a good living."

"Oh, I want to go on this trip so badly," she pleaded.

I got back to business. "And you know for sure that Joy's still willing to make the trip?"

"Oh, yes," she replied, back in her lilting voice. "It's all she talks about. Getting out of this shithole."

"Okay, Mom, let's get off the subject." I paused and took a sip of my wine. What was I getting myself into? I wondered. Maybe Marcie was right; I should rethink my priorities. "All right, I'm coming down to speak at my alma mater. We'll have a nice lunch and talk about it, okay?"

"Oh, please, don't disappoint me."

I sighed to myself. The three-day Shell Beach wine-and-sex wickedness had worn me out. Marcie's shunting me from one wine-related event to another was not only diverting my focus from my writing, I was so over-booked I didn't know if I was coming or going anymore. Maybe I needed this ten days away. Maybe it was the most foolish thing in the world.

"You really want to go back to Wisconsin? It's cold there in the winter." I found myself trying to talk her out of it.

"I need to get out," she shouted. "I don't feel human anymore!"

"I understand. All right, Mom, I'm tired, I need to return a few calls, okay?"

"You're not going out drinking, are you?" she admonished.

"No!" I replied peevishly.

"And you're coming down?"

"Yes!"

"And we're really going to Wisconsin?"

"Yes. If all the pieces fall into place, Mom, yes."

Her voice went slack. "Oh, that's such good news."

After quashing a few more of her neurotic apprehensions, we hung up. I lay in the dark sipping the wine. I felt sorry for my mother all alone in that small room at Las Villas de Muerte, sleeping next to a puddle of urine and feces. However, without the ability to toilet herself, she would have been in a nursing home–and the ones I had visited were like necropolises where the near-dead were still breathing. Taking her back to Wisconsin, however foolhardy an idea it was, seemed like the least I could do for her. Her poignant words, "I don't feel human anymore," reverberated in my head and distressed me to no end.

Three years earlier my mother had suffered a massive stroke. The fall-out: all the cells in the right side of her brain became necrotic, to use the neurologist's term, and she had been rendered totally left-side paralyzed. After two weeks of touch-and-go in the ICU she was moved into a rehab unit where highly trained physical and occupational therapists were helping her relearn how to eat, how to speak, how to perform the simplest of functions a healthy person takes for granted. The doctors, worried there was the likelihood of another "event," offered me and my two brothers the option of putting her on what's called a "no code": if she were to suffer another stroke they would only give her morphine and let her go. There had to be unanimity among the family members and my younger brother, Doug, didn't want to go along with my older brother, Hank, and me. As fate would cruelly have it, halfway into her stay, still dependent on a feeding tube, she suffered a heart attack in the presence of a PT. Because she was on a code blue, she was cardioverted, flatlined for thirty seconds, then the cardiologist employed all-out heroic measures to resuscitate her. After another stint in the ICU she resumed her grueling physical and occupational therapy regimen. All in all, she spent three months convalescing in the hospital before they felt she was fit to be released into the world.

When she was well enough that we could resume custody of her, she had relearned how to eat and how to talk–though her speech was still badly aphasic and her needs were copious. Hank and I wanted to put her in a nursing home, but Doug, out of seeming altruism, wanted to bring her back to her seaside condo in Carlsbad, offering to oversee her care. Out of pity for our mother, Hank and I agreed. Doug, unemployed and weathering an emotionally, and financially, draining divorce, went into action. He installed 24-hour care, then hired himself to oversee that care. Because of my mother's semi-paralytic state, she could not walk; she could not, initially, go to the bathroom without assistance; common reason said she should have been in a convalescent home. But Doug was adamant. He had visited my mother every day of her three-month stay in the hospital and the two of them had forged a kind of co-dependent bond. She wanted to come home; he needed the work.

For a while things seemed reasonably under control, but the money pulled from her savings to fund this in-home 24/7 care was astronomical, and after a year and a half all she had left was the equity in her condo and her Social Security. It had become clear that Doug, who was destitute and rudderless at the time of her stroke, had used her as a cottage industry to provide a stable income for himself. He lived it up on her dime. They dined out often, they bought a new car, and, in no time, the money was frittered away on the 24-hour care and other extravagances she couldn't afford. She had no concept of money and she let Doug run riot with her savings. When they had bottomed out, Hank, a five-o'clock alcoholic and unable to deal with the situation, implored me to come down and take over. Reluctantly, I did.

I moved down to Carlsbad where I found my mother virtually warehoused in her condo. The 24-hour care had been slashed to part-time. A girl came in the morning to get her up, bathe her, fix her breakfast, then leave. For the next three hours my mother sat parked behind her desk in her wheelchair, babbling incessantly to Snapper, her darling Yorkie terrier, and staring benumbed at a TV, waiting for Doug to come and make her lunch. After he left she sat all alone for another five hours before the second shift arrived to fix her dinner, administer her eye-popping cocktail of medications and then put her down for the night. It was a sorry, pathetic situation I had inherited.

My goal was to get her into an assisted-living facility as soon as possible and return to LA. Because she had learned, through using a series of handgrips strategically mounted on the wall, to toilet herself, she might be saved the horrors of full convalescence and go into the more benign world of assisted-living. But, it wasn't easy. Some were too expensive, others turned her down, and some my picky mother didn't approve of. The appointments were depressing. At the time my life was in shambles. *Shameless* had been turned down by every publisher and every film company to which my indefatigable agent submitted it. My money, along with my patience, was running out.

Living with my mother, I was sleeping downstairs on a couch, and she was upstairs listening to her radio. Several times a night she would call out and I would rush up to see what the problem was. Sometimes she had toppled to the floor in trying to transfer herself to her small portable toilet. Sometimes she just wanted to tell me a dream she had had. The stoic, unfeeling mother who had raised me now wore her heart on her sleeve. Nothing was too unimportant to express.

One night, three months into my stay and still striking out at the assisted-living facilities where we were making the rounds, I woke around

4:00 a.m. when I heard someone faintly calling out. The husky voice just said over and over again, "Help me. Help me." I threw my covers off and climbed the stairs, still in my underwear. I found my mother propped up on her pillows, her breathing stertorous. "I can't breathe, I can't breathe," she kept intoning over and over. I asked her if she wanted me to call 911, but she just shook her head. She was struggling, suffering, but I thought I would wait until it passed. I held her hand and stroked her forehead, but the labored breathing grew worse. Suddenly, her breathing ceased, her head slumped forward, and she slipped into unconsciousness. It was as if someone had lowered a dimmer on a light and her world had transited the Rubicon of life and was forever plunged into darkness. I sat transfixed, straddling the worst decision in the world. Did I let her go? It seemed like the humane thing to do. My God, stroke, heart attack, and now whatever this was. I was frantic. Or did I call for the paramedics? A huge part of me wanted to let things be. A peace, the likes of which I had never experienced, had descended over her. Her face was almost haloed. It was the weirdest sensation I have ever experienced. She had died. I was convinced of it. And, in death, she had finally found the serenity that all her infirmities had warred against. But another part of me didn't want to have this decision weighing on my conscience the rest of my life. As she lay there, her chin slumped on her chest, I broke down and dialed 911.

Five firefighter paramedics arrived and, again using all-out heroic measures, barbarously brought her back to life. Once in the ER she was stabilized. It turned out she had suffered congestive heart failure. She spent another two months in the hospital undergoing occupational and physical therapy in an effort to, once again, bring her back to some semblance of normalcy. During that time, I put her condo on the market, found an assisted-living facility that would take her, gave her precious Yorkie terrier Snapper to Melina, an attorney I was dating, and made the transition upon her release.

Mom was not happy. She didn't understand why she couldn't go back "home." On a daily basis, she berated me in her puerile manner over the phone. Eventually, her caviling abated, but she still hated Las Villas de Muerte, and she longed to escape. When she finally realized that she was never going to go back home, her new scheme was to be with her sister, Alice. Once she had hatched it, it grew into an obsession, as if her mind needed a hopeful fantasy to help her get through the dreary days at Las

Villas. In part, my final agreement to take her was simply so she wouldn't talk about it anymore. She was driving me insane. That, and the fact that my fortunes had dramatically changed in the year she wasted away at Las Villas. She had suffered so much, nearly died three times, that my sentimental side–yes, I have one–truly believed she had the right to live out her life with some kind of dignity.

I picked up my cell and auto-dialed the nurse I'd liked. She answered on the fifth ring.

"Is this Joy?"

"Yes," she said, somewhat warily.

"This is Mrs. Raymond's son, Miles."

"Hi," was all that came back in her high-pitched voice.

"Look, the reason I called–and this might sound a little weird–is that I'm thinking of taking my mother back to Wisconsin. We'd have to drive. Remember we talked about this?"

"Yes."

"Are you still interested?" She would be. She was making barely above minimum wage attending to the needs of depressed, moribund elderly, drooling, urinating in their pants, kvetching at the world, which they were soon to exit. Every week someone died.

"Yes. I'm interested."

"You think you can handle her all by yourself for ten days, Joy? I mean, I'll pitch in, but…."

"I can handle it," she said confidently.

"All right. Okay. I'll pay you $500 a day to accompany us and take care of her."

"Really?" she said, perking up. "$500 a day?"

"A day. However, we're not going to be going directly to Wisconsin. I have to attend this big wine festival in Oregon. From there we'll head to Wisconsin. You'll probably be gone about two weeks, maybe longer if I need you to stay on to help with the transition. Can you take a leave of absence?"

"$500 a day?" she said, apparently disbelieving what she had heard.

"Yes. And all expenses paid. No Motel 6's. No Mickey D.'s." That at least got a giggle. "You'll travel in relative luxury, Joy. I'm a generous guy. These days."

"When would we go?"

"End of the month."

"Okay, I'll ask Yvonne." My mother usually referred to Yvonne, her nemesis and Las Villas' nurse, as Nurse Ratched.

"She'll probably be happy to get rid of my mother." Joy chuckled at that. "But don't tell Yvonne the reason for the two weeks off. All right?"

"Okay."

"And don't talk about this with my mother until the plans have been set. I don't want her spouting off about it. There're probably a lot of formalities before they'll release her into my care. I'm just going to kidnap her and walk away, okay?"

"Okay, Mr. Raymond."

"Miles. Please."

chapter **4**

We launched the "cockamamie" Oregon/Wisconsin wine/invalid journey from my house the last week in July. Since hatching the plan I had been extremely busy. I conducted two sold-out signings/tastings at the Wine House, one of which ended with Jack and me being spirited away high up into the Hollywood Hills by two sirens of the thespian world, both of whom wanted me, but one of whom had to settle for Jack, now drafting off me, pleading his case by telling riotously funny stories about himself, as the inspiration for Jake in *Shameless*. The evening was mostly a blur, ending with traded phone numbers, drunken endearment, a floor littered with empty bottles of wine from the owner's cellar (turned out the woman I did was one of ten mistresses of an eccentric and peripatetic tycoon!).

I also made the trip down to my alma mater, UCSD in La Jolla, for a faculty wine (of course!) dinner/book signing that had been sold out weeks in advance. I drank my way through the event, delivered what I was told was another funny, extemporaneous speech, recounting how in my college days I couldn't get laid while all the foul-smelling Marxist/socialist professors had their way with the female undergraduates. They offered me a visiting professorship in creative writing, but I told them it wasn't time to put the cowbells on just yet.

While down there I also visited my mother. I took her and Joy out to lunch. I wanted to make sure they could work as a team, and Joy proved she had no trouble transfering my mother from her wheelchair to the car and back again. Joy may have been slight of stature, but she was surprisingly strong, and she had transfer technique down to an art. Reassured, I asked Joy, a few days before the departure, to gather up, as unobtrusively as possible, my mother's personal effects and hold onto them. I also inquired about her meds. Joy, excited about the trip now, had quit her job, but she had a close friend who said she would get them for me the day of departure. I gave Joy some cash to take my mother shopping and buy her some new clothes for the journey.

My mother's main concern was reclaiming her dog. I told her I would try to do my best, but that Melina had grown attached to Snapper and probably assumed he was her pet now. My mother didn't understand. Snapper, in her fragile and deluded mind, was merely on loan until the day she could get better and move back to her condo.

On the Hollywood side of things, my new flotilla of agents was all over me. The TV guy kept telling me "funny is money, funny is money." The film guy implored me to write a comedy in the spirit of *Shameless*, after ascertaining that I didn't have anything in my filing cabinets that he could peddle immediately. My publishing agent, to whom I felt a certain fealty, kept pushing me to come up with a one-sheet, anything that could score a book contract. And Marcie had big plans for me once I was able to conquer my fear of flying, a project she had made her express mission.

On the appointed day, Jack showed in ebullient spirits. He was easily twenty-five pounds heavier than in our *Shameless* days and he sported a wild, untrimmed rust-colored beard that made him look like some kind of satanic Santa Claus. In his customary slovenly manner, he was wearing a white button-up shirt, the sleeves rolled back to his meaty elbows. His girth obviated fastening the lower buttons so he just left them open, his hairy belly exposed. Describing him as "gone to seed" would be an understatement. But he was still Jack: he still had that infectious laugh; he still lived for the moment; and when he was in the right mood, he was still the life of any party.

"Give me a hug," he said as I opened my front door and greeted him on the porch. Without waiting, he wrapped his arms around me and pulled me toward him tightly. "This is going to be great trip," he said into my ear, the twin odors of tobacco and wine enveloping him in a miasmal stench.

I patted his stomach. "I don't know if you make the weight limit."

"Fuck you, short horn. You're not exactly Charles Atlas these days," he said.

I laughed. "Hey, help me with these," I said, turning back into my house.

Jack came inside and saw boxes and boxes stacked up all around. "These your books?"

"No. They're wine. Artisanal, hard-to-find Pinots from the Willamette Valley. Ever since I committed to being master of ceremonies at this International Pinot Noir Celebration they started sending me wine. Wine and more wine, hoping, of course, I'll write a sequel to *Shameless* and that Martin and Jake will make the pilgrimage to the Willamette and bestow a little recognition to their quaff." I turned to Jack and winked. "Okay, so I admit I told them a little white lie and said there was going to be a sequel and it was coming to their region. They fucking went nuts."

"Holy shit!" Jack exclaimed.

"I figured why waste money on wine when I've got all this awesome stuff."

"Fucking A."

"Did you know the Willamette Valley is planted 65% in Pinot Noir?"

"No."

"Hell, they're more passionate about my favorite grape variety than any other region in the world. I guess I'm kind of a rock star up there. Anyway, I put together a couple of mixed cases, and I've got a cooler over there with some awesome whites."

"All right," a financially strapped Jack said excitedly. "You've got to unload some of this grape on me."

"You can have all you want, big guy. *When* we get back."

We loaded the cases, Jack's battered portmanteau—the bamboo one emblazoned with the colorful ports-of-call stickers—locked up and motored off in the Toyota Sienna I had rented for the trip. It was a specially outfitted handicap vehicle with a movable ramp for easy transfering of my mother in and out. Joy would be pleased to see it.

Jack told me, as we started out of Santa Monica in the direction of the I-10, that he had spent the weekend with his three-year-old son and that had rendered him both maudlin and elated, a strange admixture in a man of his size. On an even sunnier note, he admitted, relations had normalized between him and his ex-wife Babs. The more he had come to terms with the fact they were now officially divorced and she was seeing another man, whom Babs had confessed to Jack she might marry, the easier it was becoming for him to adopt the new role of mostly absentee father.

"There *is* life after divorce," I said, after he had recounted the salient events in his life since I had last seen him. "We can love again with scars."

"That's beautiful," Jack said, semisarcastically, as I merged onto the 405 and headed south toward San Diego.

"That's why they pay me the big bucks."

"Now," Jack reminded me. "You always had the ten-dollar words, dude."

"True," I said. "I'm just milking this little window. I'm sure soon I'll be back on the skids, dodging slumlords and eating Baja Fresh."

Jack laughed. He snaked an arm around to the back and flipped open one of the mixed cases. He indiscriminately slid out the first bottle and said, "Do you have a corkscrew, Homes?"

"Jack. We've got a lot of driving to do today. Let's hold off."

"We're on vacation, man," he protested.

"I don't want to start this trip off with a DUI."

Sullenly, Jack returned the bottle to the case with the expression of a kid scolded to put the candy back on the counter, folded his arms across his chest and battled the temptation.

"We'll get a couple of glasses when we get to Carlsbad, okay, big guy?"

"Aye, aye, captain," he growled.

The first half of the drive from LA to San Diego is one of the most abominable drives on the planet. The five-lane freeway cuts sinuously through a hideous landscape of filthy white-stucco apartment complexes, car dealerships, franchise enterprises, windowless factories and other soul-destroying eyesores for which Southern California is notorious. It reaches its nadir in Long Beach where sprawling oil refineries, belching flames and God knows what else into the atmosphere, lend the impression of an industrial Hell feeding energy to a city starved for oil. Past Long Beach, the drive starts marginally to improve as Orange County gives way to multi-national corporate office complexes where lives are destroyed in a more insidious, less blatant, fashion. Not until you reach San Clemente does the ocean finally show its blue limitless face. The relief is tremendous.

It's as if you had staggered out of a war zone and happened upon a clearing
where the fight was no longer being waged. For the next 17 miles there is
nothing but ocean and parched brown hills, all of it owned by the military.
If the Pentagon ever went bankrupt and decided to sell, pricey gated con-
dominium and housing complexes, interspersed by emerald golf courses,
would quickly surge in to fill the void known as Camp Pendleton. LA to
San Diego would become one long, butt-ugly contiguous city, the grand
alimentary canal of all of Southern California.

Jack wasn't impressed with my analysis. "Yeah, yeah, yeah, I hear that
every time we come down here. Come on, let's pop a bottle. A little bubbly never hurt."

"Just hold your horses, Jackson," I said.

This was our first road trip since the now semi-famous sojourn in Santa
Ynez and my writing the novel it inspired, and we both felt buoyant about
getting out, wine notwithstanding, and leaving our cares in the wake of
the retreating freeway miles. Still, worry corrugated Jack's brow, and I
could palpably feel why he needed a glass or two to obliterate the wreckage
he had made of his life.

Halfway down the untrammeled 17-mile stretch of freeway, sensing
Jack was growing antsy, I said, "All right, Jackson, there's an uncorked
bottle in the Willamette case. Pour us a couple sippy cups."

Jack turned to me and beamed. "All right. Now, you're talking." Jack
pivoted around and rooted in the cooler until he found the bottle I was
referring to. He uncorked an '08 St. Innocent Freedom Hill Pinot Blanc
and filled two plastic cups and handed one to me. He held his up and
toasted me. I toasted him back. Wine in hand, alcohol in the belly, he
grew more garrulous.

"God, this is nice," he exclaimed.

"Great weight. Almost glycerin-like. Just a beautiful balance of fruit
and acid."

"Fucking awesome," he said.

"Willamette's the next Burgundy," I hyperbolized.

"So, what's on the horizon, writing-wise, Homes?"

"I don't know," I said. "I don't know if I want to go back to screenplays. The pay's good, and I've got this gust of wind behind me and all,
but they never get made. It's kind of dispiriting."

"Well, it's good that you have the luxury of choices," he said, a tinge of ruefulness in his voice.

"I guess, yeah," I said. "I don't know, Jackson. *Shameless* took a lot out of me emotionally and creatively. That's why I'm happy to be getting out, getting away from it all. I hope to come back transformed, fresh with ideas. Road trips can be revivifying."

"Amen, brother. Amen." He toasted me and I touched him back. "I'm so glad to be out of LA, man. I cannot tell you."

The shoreline stretch came to an abrupt end in Oceanside, the first of many seaside hamlets that dot the coast all the way to San Diego proper. By the time we reached Carlsbad we had polished off the bottle and were suffused with that emollient feeling a little wine–for Jack and me, that is–delivers.

When I sped past Las Villas de Muerte, visible from the I-5, Jack turned to me and said, "Isn't that where your mom lives?"

"We have to make another stop first," I muttered.

"What's that? Let's get this party on the road."

"I was dating this attorney when I was taking care of my mom," I tried to explain. "When she had her congestive heart failure and went into Las Villas I stupidly gave Melina–the attorney–my mother's precious Snapper, the dog we're taking on the trip."

"Yeah, so?"

"Well, I kind of blew her off when fame went to my head and she stopped making visits with Snapper and my mother blames me for it. So, we have to get him back."

"Okay, so how're we going to do that?"

I left the freeway at the Leucadia Boulevard off-ramp and steered the Rampvan in the direction of the ocean. Jack stared fixedly at me, looking puzzled, waiting to hear the plan. A mile down the hill, just before the Coast Highway, I turned left at Hermes Ave., a neighborhood street that dead-ended in a cul-de-sac. A couple of houses before Melina's I pulled the Rampvan over and braked to a halt.

"Okay, here's the deal," I began, looking into the perplexed countenance of Jack. "Melina knows we're coming. In fact, she's really looking forward to our company. In her world, after all, we're demigods. Anyway, we're going to go in, with a nice bottle, act friendly. She took the day off for this visit, in fact. We're going to get her looped. I'm going to get frisky with her. I've already been buttering her up with phone calls and e-mails. Hell, when I was dating her she offered me ten grand for my sperm because she was desperate to have kids."

"Why would she want your seed?"

"I don't know. Good point. Anyway, at the appropriate moment, you're going to offer to take Snapper for a walk so he can relieve himself. She's not stupid. She'll get the message. She knows I came down here to give her a thumping. While you're walking Snapper to the van, I'm going to take her by the hand into the back bedroom, grit my teeth, and give her the fuck of her life." Jack's eyes bugged out at me. "After sex she always showers. Always. It's a Brazilian custom or something."

"Maybe just with you. Scrub the crabs off."

I ignored his jab. "While she's showering I'm going to get dressed and boogie, meet you in the van with Snapper."

Jack continued to look at me unblinkingly, his mouth now frozen agape. "Let me get this straight. This woman you used to go out with, we're going to go in there, you're going to romance her, fuck her brains out, I'm going to kidnap her dog, and you're going to ditch her?"

I held up both hands, palms open. "On paper I realize it sounds a little cruel. But it's not her damn dog. It's my mother's dog. Of eight years. Melina has only had him a couple years. My mother *will not* go on this trip without her dog. We're going to hear about it for ten fucking days if we don't get that little critter. *Comprende?*"

"How do you know you're going to be able to get her into the sack if you blew her off?"

"I told you," I said in a rising tone, "we've been corresponding. I lied and said I might be moving down here to write my next book. It took a few flirtatious e-mails, employing all my literary skills–scant as they may be according to the critics–and a long phone call that almost ended up in phone sex to butter her up, but she extended the olive branch I knew was coming. The chick just turned 40. She hasn't been with anyone in almost two years. She loves sex. She rarely turns it down, even when she's menstruating. Plus, now with the success of the movie, she's re-enamored of me, if you know what I mean."

"Jesus, Miles!" Jack shook his head in befuddlement. "This is wack, man. Totally fucking wack. This wasn't in the job description."

"Well, we've done some wacky things. We did some surreal shit on that Santa Ynez trip. Some of it so wacky it couldn't even make it into an R-rated movie. Shit we don't need to recount," I argued.

"No, we do not," Jack said, flashing back to some wild moments immortalized in *Shameless*, with a sardonic grimace. But, he still had his doubts. "How's this chick going to feel, man, when she comes out of the shower?"

"What do you fucking care? It was her kind that caused you to lose your joint-custody battle," I argued.

Jack pinched his lips thoughtfully, as if rehearsing the plan in his imagination. "Yeah, you're right. I'm not fond of attorneys."

"Now, could we just do this? I'm not looking forward to it either. This is the ultimate mercy fuck. I'm doing it for my mother. And for our sanity on the road. Because she's going to blubber about that little Yorkie the whole fucking way. Trust me. Ever since her stroke, she's a different person. No Snapper would be the leading edge of a tsunami of crying jags."

"The attorney's not going to give up the dog to your poor mom?" Jack asked.

"I didn't ask her. If I came clean to her about taking my mom to Wisconsin and wanting the dog and she said no, she would be totally suspicious of our visit. So, no mention of this voyage, okay?"

Jack erupted into laughter. "What a way to start this trip!"

"Are you ready to rock and roll?"

Jack shrugged. "I'll do my best." He brandished a finger at me. "But don't blame me if it goes awry."

"Just follow the cues, okay? Don't blow it. In an hour we'll be on the road and tonight we'll be eating steaks and drinking Highliner at the Hitching Post."

"I'm down with that. All right, dude. Let's get it over with."

I slipped the Rampvan into Drive and crept forward. I executed a cumbrous U-turn and parked so that we could make one of those police squad car exits. I switched off the motor and handed Jack the keys. "Lock and load, dude," I said.

Jack took the keys from me, closed his fist around them and shook it in mock support of the plan.

Melina greeted us at the door in a black, low-cut dress that showcased her new surgically enhanced breasts. She was a short, full-figured,

bespectacled woman with shoulder-length rodent-brown hair. I was
gladdened by her appearance because it was blatant what the nasty little
zaftig attorney had uppermost in her mind. She was cordial to Jack
when I introduced the two, but I sensed she felt a little uncomfortable
with his presence, as if I had deliberately brought a third to thwart her
amorous advances.

Jack, sensing her mild disappointment upon seeing him, switched on
the charm in all his ebullient, erstwhile-actor phoniness. After I had enveloped her in a more-than-friendly hug, he wrapped his arms around her
and lifted her up off the ground—no mean feat! Jack! your lumbar disk! I
almost shouted—and said, "It's so nice to meet you, Melina. Miles said
you were beautiful, but, my God, look at you!"

Melina giggled. She possessed one of those tittering laughs that started
innocently, then rose and rose like a hot air balloon, spiraling upward in
volume until you were never sure when it was going to sputter to an end.
It had been a contributing factor in my decision to dump her. That and
the annoying HPV I had contracted from her, which had me in a urolo-
gist's office getting the damn wart freeze-dried off my member—yet another rationalizing motivation to kidnap Snapper.

Jack uncorked a bottle of another splendiferous Willamette offering,
an '08 Witness Tree Vintage Select Pinot. Melina didn't have much of a
palate, so anything at all better than Two-Buck Upchuck usually thrilled
her to the core. The wine was silky, with beautiful texture, redolent of
blackberries and black cherries. It was so good I almost wanted to hide in
the closet with the bottle and just conduct a private tête-à-tête with it.
But, unfortunately, I had other, even more sordid, things on my mind.

In a festive mood, Melina put one of Enya's vomitous New Age albums
in her CD player as Jack and I, more alt-indie and retro—Hendrix, The
Doors, Nick Drake—inclined, exchanged wide-eyed glances. As the music
wafted putridly over us I sighed and, with Melina's spreading ass staring
at us, mouthed to Jack, *How the hell am I going to fuck to Enya?!*

Jack threw a fist to his mouth to stifle a laugh with an eye-watering cough.

I took a seat on her couch and Jack sprawled expansively in a matching
wing chair as Melina went to fetch glasses and a cheese-and-cracker-and-
charcuterie plate she had thoughtfully prepared for our visit. Seeing me
alone on the couch, she parked herself next to me, close enough that I

could feel the warmth of her thigh through the nearly diaphanous fabric of her dress. She looked at me with an expectant smile. "Hi, Miles."

"Hi, Melina. It's so good to see you. Really." For good measure, I brushed a reassuring back of the hand to her cheek.

I poured wine all around. We sipped it as Jack and I regaled her with some risqué anecdotes of the *Shameless* trip and how the movie differed from the book. Melina wanted to know what the Academy Awards were like, which celebrities I had met, who I had slept with that night–ha, ha, ha. Not wanting to gloom the mood with the real story of how I had been relegated to the upper balcony by the insensitive studio heads who develop rapid-onset amnesia when it comes to the inconvenient fact there was a book behind their film, I prevaricated recklessly, employing all my fictive skills, about the celebrities who hugged and kissed me and bought me drinks, how I had stumbled from one after-party to another meeting the likes of Nicholson and Blanchett and other enchanting, ethereal Hollywood personalities. She seemed enthralled by my outrageous fabrications.

"And I remember when you were down here taking care of your mom and were totally broke," she said, smiling at me. "What's the secret, Miles?"

"How low can you go and still turn on your laptop? That's what I tell writers today. Success doesn't come without pain." I snapped my fingers, and produced another whopper. "Oh, I'm pretty sure I'm going to accept the visiting professorship that UCSD offered. Fall quarter."

"That's nice. You can see your mom and, um…." She blushed to a stop.

"…and take you out to dinner at the finest restaurants. Now that I can afford it," I finished, rubbing my shoulder against hers, the tacit implication of a regular sex partner not lost on her.

In no time, the first bottle was killed–Jack's hangover, my anxiety–and I dispatched Jack to the van to fetch a second. As soon as he closed the door, I turned to sex-starved smiling Melina and said, my speech a little hobbled by the powerful Witness Tree Pinot, "You look beautiful, Melina."

"Thank you."

"Have you lost weight? Doing Pilates? You look like you've been working out."

"Maybe a little," she said. "I've been taking long walks on the beach. And I cut out all carbs." Realizing the paradox, she held up her glass of wine. "But today, I'm celebrating."

"Well, you look great." I lowered my voice to a more sincere register. "I missed you," I shamelessly lied. "That's why I had to take the chance and write you that e-mail."

"You must have a lot of women now that you're a success?"

I waved her off. "Totally meaningless. All this Hollywood glamour does-n't mean shit to me. It's so shallow. I mean, you were there when I was nothing, down on my luck, and that means more to me than all these wine chippies flinging themselves at me. You're a woman lacking in pretense, a woman of substance... intelligence..." I chopped myself off because I feared speciousness was growing detectable in my slurry voice. "That's what I'm really looking for," I finished. "A real, down-to-earth woman. Like you."

Her eyes batted with the emotion of the moment and I seized the op-portunity to plant my lips on hers. It was a fervent kiss, mouths slammed together as if we were an adulterous couple meeting in a motel room for an hour. Without hesitation, she placed her hand on my groin and coiled her fingers around my cock. The half Viagra I had taken an hour before–non-performance was *not* an option!–primed me for her advances and my cock sprang to life, bulging in my jeans.

The door burst open with a blast of unwanted sunlight and Jack re-emerged. Melina, however, kept kissing me, the exhibitionist in her rising to the occasion. "Excuse me, lovebirds," Jack said.

Melina unlocked her mouth from mine so that I could reply, "It's okay, Jack. Uncork that second bottle. I realize it's a little early in the afternoon, but, hey, I'm an artist, Melina has her own practice, and tonight I'm going to take us all out to The Wine Brasserie."

"Really?" Melina said.

"Absolutely. We're going to celebrate!" I turned to Jack. "Wine Brasserie's one of the finest restaurants in all of San Diego."

"Awesome." As Jack disappeared around the corner to find the corkscrew, Melina attacked me again. Her hand was back on my tumesc-ing cock and I matched her gesture with my hand sneaking up her dress and slithering catlike under the band of her panties to beach itself on a verdant island of a pussy. For a moment I felt a twinge of nostalgia because I did miss that barbarian bush of hers.

Jack returned with the open bottle of an '07 Witness Tree Claim #51–another blockbuster, a heartstopper–and refilled all our glasses.

Melina and I were now half-entangled in each other, but a pang of concern struck me when I realized that I hadn't seen or heard the familiar yipping of Snapper.

"Hey, where's Snapper?" I said insouciantly, not wanting to arouse suspicion. "Where is that little devil dog?"

"He's out back in his new doggie house I bought him," Melina said, incipient inebriation beginning to slur *her* speech. "I had it custom-made by this cabinet-maker friend of mine. Cost me $2,500."

"Wow," I said. "You must really love that dog."

"Do you want to see it and say hi to Snapper?" she suggested, starting to rise from the couch.

With my hand still on her thigh I gently pushed her back down and said, "No, it's okay, Melina. He's your little bundle of joy now. My mother is so addled she doesn't even remember him anymore. Besides–" I paused, kissing her lightly on the mouth to reassure her I hadn't forgotten the moment that our flirtatious e-pistolary exchange had promised her. "I came here to see you, not Snapper."

She fixed her gaze on me with flashing, lovesick eyes, smoothed down her dress and said, "I've got to go to the little girl's room. Excuse me."

I took my hand off her thigh so she could straighten herself up from the couch. When her footfalls had receded down the hall and she was safely out of earshot, I turned to Jack with an expression of urgency. "Offer to take Snapper out for a walk. Give a little wink-wink to let her know that it's going to be a *long* walk. Say you want to leave the two of us alone so that we can have a *private* moment. And be insistent."

"Okay," Jack said, screwing up his courage with another quaff of Witness Tree's finest.

Melina returned. We shifted desultorily to the topic of her law practice, but Jack was bored and cut her off, "Where's your bathroom?"

"Around the corner," Melina said.

Jack got up and lumbered toward the bathroom.

I turned to Melina and said, "This is such a lovely afternoon." We kissed again. I didn't stop–and neither did she–when Jack returned. The way she was clutching my cock I really imagined that she wanted to do it on the couch with Jack watching. She was that kind of a naughty girl. She'd once fellated me on a beach in broad daylight.

"Hey, you know what," Jack started, "maybe I should, oh, I don't know, take little Snapper for a walk." He actually performed the wink-wink, which almost had me in stitches. "Maybe go down to the beach, leave the two of you alone to catch up. I need some fresh air; it's getting a little... steamy in here."

Melina laughed her tittering laugh. She loved all the verbal foreplay.

"That's nice of you, Jack, to offer to take Snapper for his afternoon constitutional," I said with both deliberate sarcasm and double entendre for Melina's salacious benefit.

Melina, her pussy slicker than a sea urchin, took the bait and rose. "Come on," she said.

As she spearheaded a path toward the kitchen and out to the back yard, Jack and I exchanged bug-eyed looks.

A few minutes later she returned with Snapper on a leash, barking and yelping.

"Don't let him off the leash," Melina admonished.

"Don't worry, Melina, I'm in no condition to chase a dog."

She passed the loop of the leash to Jack and I exhaled a sigh of relief. Jack lashed the leash around his wrist and set off out the front door. I smiled to myself—Part I had been beautifully executed.

As soon as the door closed, Melina and I fell on each other in a torrid deliquescence of bodies. Within minutes I was unzipping the back of her dress and she was fumbling with the buckle on my belt. Half-clothed, we stumbled tangle-footed into the bedroom where we quickly dispensed with the rest of our attire. She was vocally impressed with my pharmaceutically enhanced erection, worshipping its totemic magnificence with her ardent mouth. While I worried what I would do in the event she skipped her customary post-coital shower, she pulled open a drawer and produced a vibrator. She liked to be on top and work the vibrator on her clitoris for the first half, her torso vertical, her eyes drifting ceilingward like a clairvoyant in the throes of some providential vision. It was a pruriently hilarious image that once, after we had smoked some pot, sent me cascading into uncontrollable laughter, halting her mid-thrust and causing her to dismount, so I learned to keep my eyes closed as she went through her swooning ritual. The second half had her cooing underneath me, coaxing me toward a last-minute-withdrawal climax on her perspiry thigh. But I was having trouble coming. Anxiety was closing off my imagination to the erotic images I needed to recreate in order to finish. With eyes closed, I went through practically every woman I had ever been with–and it was a pretty eclectic gallery!–as if desperately shuffling through a deck of cards searching for a rare joker. I debated faking it, but the blue magic had me so erect I didn't think she would buy it. Finally, I alighted on a woman I had made love to on a beach in Mexico. I concentrated hard and could suddenly make out the full moon that eyeballed us, hear the roaring surf pounding the sand, and smell that pungent pussy stuffed into my face. Mixing dirty talk with romantic love talk, I drove her to new heights of expressiveness.

"Fuck me, Miles. Fuck me hard. Don't ever stop fucking me." It did the trick. Just before I came I pulled out. She grabbed my cock and finished me with her piston-pumping hand.

When it was finally over I felt like the last vestige of humanity had been sucked from my very being. I felt like a whore. But my agenda remained unchanged. I kept intoning to myself: *My mother will not get in the Rampvan to go to Wisconsin if I don't get her stupid dog.*

"That was the most intense sex I've had in a long time," I whispered in her ear as we lay on our backs, our hearts still racing from the exertion. "God, I missed you, Melina. I forgot what a fantastic lover you are."

"I wish you had come inside me. I really want to have a child."

"Let's talk about it when I move down," I said, as sincerely as I could muster.

She tilted her head onto my shoulder. "You mean it?"

"Yeah." I touched her cheek affectionately with the back of my hand. "Do you want to take a shower?"

"Take one with me," she suggested, to my consternation.

"No, I just want to lie here and bask in the afterglow of this wondrous moment." I kissed her. "Actually, I want to leave your scent on me all day."

"Okay," she said, kissing me on the mouth as she coiled her Rubenesque body away and clambered off the bed like a baby sea elephant off a moss-covered rock. A minute later I heard the shower running. She broke into one of Enya's treacly uplifting songs, which further inspired me to get out of there. I leapt from the bed and hurriedly climbed into my pants. I grabbed my shirt and shoes, not wanting to squander precious seconds.

The front door, through which I attempted to make my escape, was locked. I remembered that Melina always locked it from the inside with a key. And you had to have the key to unlock it. My eyes frantically ransacked the room. The key was nowhere in sight. Suddenly, my blood froze. I cocked my ear to the hallway which led to the back bedroom and heard a faint voice call out, "Miles, come shower with me." Fuck!

I strode briskly through the kitchen and fled out the rear sliding-glass door. But now I was trapped in her fenced-in back yard. My eyes shot a glance at Snapper's new doggie house. It was a magnificent, alpine-style domain with Snapper's name painted in blue on a shingle hanging over the entrance. I ran past it and scaled a head-high wooden fence, clawing to get over it, piercing my hands with splinters and scuffing my knees. A little walkway where the neighbor's trashcans were parked led out to the street and I made a dash for it, pulling on my shirt and trying unsuccessfully to button it mid-sprint, and knocking over one of the metal cans in the process.

"Hey, hey!" a man's voice shouted.

I hit the Rampvan half-naked. Jack shot me a look of alarm and turned the engine over so frantically he produced an ear-shattering screech from the starter motor. Snapper barked like a maniac in the back, knowing in his sentient canine way that something was amiss.

"Hit it," I said, "hit it!"

Jack shifted into drive and floorboarded it. The Rampvan lurched forward like a startled leviathan and Snapper lost his balance like an astronaut in outer space and tumbled backward, whimpering, flummoxed.

"We're not dognappers, Snapper. We're taking you to your rightful owner."

He cocked his little box-shaped head to one side as if he understood me.

I directed Jack to the freeway onramp and we sped north to Las Villas, dog in hand, splinters in hand, semen still sticky and warm on my thigh, mission accomplished.

Once on the freeway river and safely away from Melina's, Jack started laughing uproariously as I buttoned my shirt, laced up my Patagonias and combed my hair with splayed fingers. I regaled Jack with the sordid sequence of events, beginning from the point he took Snapper for a walk, and he couldn't stop laughing.

"How was the lay?" he asked, bearing a gleefully obscene expression, always interested in the rehashing of sexual details.

"Nerve-racking. All I could think about was you waiting outside with Snapper. Couldn't concentrate. I was afraid I couldn't come. Remember that gorgeous Mexican babe I screwed on the beach in Cabo?"

"Yeah."

"I used her. Worked like a charm."

"Excellent," Jack said. "Say, whatever happened to Isabel what's-her-name? She was pretty hot."

"She was using me to get a green card. So, I bailed."

"Oh," Jack reflected, "it's always something. Babies, green cards, dinners. I want to meet a chick who just wants to fuck, you know what I mean?"

A sudden wave of nausea swept over me. "I'm looking for true love," I said. "Stop living this crazy fucking life of mine."

"Oh, bullshit! Don't lie to me. Ever since the movie came out you've been getting laid like Clinton."

"I'm sick of it."

"Bullshit!" Jack threw me a look. "What'd you write the book for? Art?" He cackled maniacally. "You wrote it so you could get laid. Don't lie to me."

I turned slowly and looked at him. "You're projecting, dude."

"Don't psychoanalyze me, short horn." He paused and sipped on some wine from a plastic cup. "How many women have you had, Miles?"

"I don't know. I don't care."

"No, come on. How many?"

"I don't give a shit. I was married for ten years and faithful for seven of them."

"I've had over a hundred and fifty."

"Outstanding, Jackson. Is that what you're going to remember on your deathbed when the Great One snatches you away and drops you off in some celestial sports bar with scantily-clad San Diego State cheerleaders?"

Jack, sensing that I was still a little bent out of shape by the unpardonable dognapping antic, said, "Hey, Homes, it was not my idea to have you go in and fuck that chick and steal her dog."

"Yeah, I know," I said, still a little nauseated. "I really didn't want to do that to her, but I had no choice."

"What'd you do? Tell her you wanted to get married and have children?"

"Might as well have," I said, shaking my head in disgust.

"Hey," Jack consoled. "You got your mom's dog. That's awesome. And you can put it in your next book."

"Yeah," I said, brightening a little. "My next book."

We bent off the freeway at Carlsbad Village Drive and headed in the direction of Las Villas de Carlsbad. As orchestrated, we hooked up with Joy, who was parked on the street in a beat-up Ford Escort. We pulled up behind her and I climbed out of the Rampvan to greet her. When she rolled down the window the piquant smell of marijuana wafted from inside her car. She hastily extinguished the joint in an ashtray, hid it in a small tin that mints come in and smiled at me. She was no more than 5'2" and her short-cropped black hair ended at her slender shoulders.

"Hi, Joy," I said.

Out of the driver's-side window, Jack telescoped his head and said, "Hi, Joy."

"This is my friend, Jack," I said. "He's going to be helping me with the driving.

"Nice to meet you," Joy said demurely.

"You got my mother's things?"

"Yeah. They're in the trunk."

"Meds and everything?"

"Yeah."

"Good job, Joy." I squatted to her level and said, my voice still harried from the canine abduction escapade, "I'm going to go in and get her. Jack will help you load your and my mother's things. Okay?"

"Okay."

Las Villas de Carlsbad is a three-story assisted-living complex situated next to the roaring Interstate-5. Every time I visited my mother I popped some Xanax for fortification against a panic attack, the place was that depressing.

I left Jack and Joy together on the street and crossed Las Villas's expansive lawn and entered the main lobby. My cell rang urgently in my pocket. I glanced hurriedly at the incoming number. No surprise, it was Melina. Shit! I put the phone on mute and quickened my stride.

I wended my way up to the third floor on a glacially slow elevator. A sepulchral pall hung over the facility. The infirm elderly residents, either slumped in wheelchairs or upright-ish with the assistance of walkers, moved torpidly and aimlessly about. Most of them had frozen on their faces that permanently startled look of people who have suffered strokes, or are dosed on so many medications they're tranquilized into another universe, appearing as if they don't know where or who they are.

Just as the Xanax kicked in, I found my way to my mother's tiny, claustrophobic room and stepped inside. Cluttering it were a desk, a TV in the corner, and a bed positioned diagonally against one wall. Between the bed and wall was the portable toilet she used at night. I looked away when I noticed that the previous night's contents had not been emptied.

When she heard me enter, my mother gave me a backward look from her desk, where she had a view of the freeway out her only window. I came around and placed a hand on her shoulder. After her stroke she had stopped coloring her hair and it was now a slate gray. Her mouth sagged on the left side where the paralysis had crippled her. Early pictures of her revealed a woman who bore a remarkable resemblance to a young Ingrid Bergman and, if one looked hard enough, you could still color in vestiges of a once beautiful woman, now wizened by a stroke and old age. She didn't look anything like the actress who played my mother in the movie, but then the actor who played me was a far cry from how I looked then, too.

"Hi, Mom."

"Miles!" she said, almost as if she hadn't expected me.

"Come on, let's go."

"I've got to go to the bathroom."

"We don't have time for that."

"I have to go," she said. She grabbed the right handrim and started windmilling her one good arm and rolled herself past me into the bathroom. In the reflection of a wall mirror I witnessed her hoisting herself up out of the chair and plopping down on the toilet. She slid down her loose-fitting, elastic waist-banded sweat pants and stared blankly into space.

Impatient, I glanced at my watch.

"I didn't think you were going to make it," she said from the bathroom.

"Hurry up, Mom, we've got to move."

"Don't make me nervous," she said, "I won't be able to go."

I shuffled in place, tapped my foot with annoyance, glanced frequently at my watch, felt my phone buzzing incessantly in my pants pocket, all the while plagued by the image of an irate Melina racing up the freeway in her new Lexus to intercept us, reclaim Snapper, and harangue me into infamy. Hell, call the cops and have me arrested for grand larceny!

"Come on, Mom, come on," I exhorted. "Time's a wastin'."

"I'm coming."

I heard her transfer herself back into the wheelchair and I turned to her. "Are you excited?"

"Oh, yes," she said.

I hustled around behind her, grabbed the steering handles and pushed her toward the door.

She threw me an alarmed backward look. "Do you have my clothes?"

"Yes. Joy bought you all new duds."

"Do you have my pills?"

"Yes." We were out in the hallway now and rounding the corner by the nurse's station.

"Did you get Snapper?"

"Oh, yes, we got Snapper."

"Oh, that's such good news," she said, relief washing over her.

The head nurse, Yvonne, a stout woman of Eastern European descent, emerged unexpectedly from one of the patients' suites and strode toward us. She stopped when she saw us approaching, so I brought my mother and myself to a halt so as not to arouse her suspicions.

"Going upstairs for lunch?" Yvonne asked, glancing at her watch. "It's a little early."

"No, my son's taking me to Wisconsin, you son of a bitch!" my mother said in a tone of righteous indignation.

From behind her, I shook my head emphatically no. "We're going out to eat. She's not in a good mood."

"Evidently," Yvonne said, her occupationally impervious bearing the only obstacle between my mother's freedom and re-incarceration in Las Villas de Muerte.

"And," I added, sub rosa, "talk about maybe relocating her somewhere else."

Yvonne nodded, as if my words had vouchsafed a ray of sunshine to her depressing job. "That's a good idea," she said compassionately, moving around us and on to some other pressing obligation.

As she went past, my mother bellowed, "Screw you and your damn home! Your food tastes like crap!"

"All right, Mom, cool it. Or I'm going to wheel you back into that room with that shitcan next to your bed and never visit you again."

That shut her up. She flopped her favorite blue Gilligan's Island hat on her head and braced for the new beginning ahead.

I pushed my mother forward. Halfway to the elevator I glanced back over my shoulder and glimpsed a circumspect Yvonne standing imperiously, broad and mammoth as a linebacker, arms stapled against her chest, glowering at us.

Jack and Joy had the side door open and the pebbled ramp on the lowrise floor extended out to the sidewalk when I finally made it out of the facility, the iPhone still buzzing in my pocket like a whoopee cushion. Hurrying, I pushed my mother up and in and backed her where a seat normally would be positioned and set the hand locks. Snapper leapt up into her lap and my mother and the impish Yorkie fell into a bawling and tongue-licking reunion.

Jack and I climbed into the front and Jack turned the engine over and started off. He glanced back at my mother. "Hi, Mrs. Raymond. Remember me? Jack."

"Jack? How are you?"

"Excellent. We're going to drink a lot of good wine."

"Oh, I hope so," my mother said.

Jack laughed and steered us toward the blessed liberation of the interstate.

I looked into the back. My mother, after mawkishly reacquainting herself with her dog, finally noticed Joy sitting next to her and broke into exultations of happiness.

"Oh, Joy, I'm so glad you're here. I didn't think you would make it."

"It's okay, Mrs. Raymond," Joy said in her soft, slightly Tagalog-accented voice. "I'm here."

"Oh, I'm so glad to be out of that place," my mother blubbered from the back.

"We're going on a vacation, Mom."

She crooked her arthritic index finger at the ceiling as she was wont to do and said through squinted, teary eyes, "I'm so happy."

"I don't want you to be crying all the time. It's going to be a long trip if that's all you do. Okay?"

"Okay," she said, stifling her tears.

I leaned toward Jack and whispered, "I wouldn't put it past that hot-blooded Brazilian to call the cops on us. So, we've got to motor. Although

I doubt the cops would put out an APB on a dognapper, especially one she just finished having sex with."

"How do the cops know what we're driving?" Jack said.

"Good point. I'm a little discombobulated," I said. "Inauspicious start to the day, if you know what I mean."

"Amen, brother, amen. Why don't you just call her and tell her what the deal is?"

"Are you kidding? She's probably over at Las Villas right now telling the head nurse the story. I mean, I hope she's just resigned to the fact that it's my mother's dog and is only storming around in her house. I hope!"

"People get pretty emotional about their pets," Jack countered.

"Yeah, I know." I gave another backward glance to my mother. She was still kissing and hugging Snapper.

A surge of relief suffused me as we arced back over the curving onramp onto I-5 and burned rubber north. I rooted an envelope thick with twenty-dollar bills out of the glove compartment and reached it back to Joy who eyed me questioningly. "As promised. One week, in full, your plane ticket and something a little extra, you know, for personal expenses and stuff." She nodded, then slipped the envelope into her purse. "And thanks again for agreeing to come, Joy."

"It's okay, Mr. Raymond."

"And don't call me Mr. Raymond. I'm not as old as your dad."

My mother took notice of the envelope. "How much are you paying her?"

"None of your business, Mom."

"Whatever it is, it's too much," the girl born in the Great Depression cried.

"Whatever it is, it's not enough." I locked eyes with Joy and mouthed: *Don't listen to her.*

Jack steered the car into the middle lane. I rummaged under the front seat, coming up with the '07 Sokol Blosser Pinot Noir Goosepen I had already uncorked and stowed, filled two plastic cups and handed one discreetly to Jack. "Let's keep it exactly at the speed limit, okay?"

"Okay."

"And let's keep our voices down. My mother may be an invalid, but she's still sentient."

"I am not an invalid!" my mother spoke from the back over the roar of the engine.

"We weren't talking about you, Mom."

"Yes, you were!"

I lowered my voice. "See what I mean. And if she asks you what's in that cup, you say it's water, or she's going to want some."

Jack nodded, sipped the Goosepen and smacked his lips. "Man, you've got the good stuff."

"This is awesome juice. Teeth-blackening. Huge mouthfeel. I'm getting excited."

"Can't wait until we get up to Oregon. That's going to be fun."

I smiled. "Christ, it feels good to be underway, doesn't it?"

"Hallelujah," Jack said, toasting me.

"How did you get Melina to give you Snapper?" my mom asked from the back.

I turned around and faced her. Snapper was curled up in her lap, panting contentedly. I decided that it had been the right thing to do, regardless of the perfidious methodology. "It wasn't easy, Mom."

"Did you have to give her money, too?"

"No, I gave her something better than that," I said, the wine rekindling a return to my former humorous self.

"What was that?" my mother wanted to know.

"I promised I would give her a sperm donation. She wants to have kids and my seed is in high demand right now."

My mother laughed at this. So did Joy.

Jack, also laughing, happy to see that my previous dyspepsia had been unknotted into the old Miles Raymond he knew, kept the Rampvan at the speed limit. And the sippy cup never far from his lips.

As we shifted from the 5 to the 405 and continued to blaze a northerly trail, Joy turned her attention to my mother and was helping her with her *San Diego Union* crossword puzzle. Snapper had apparently already forgotten about Melina and his Alpine chalet and blood sausages, or whatever she spoiled him with, and had fallen asleep. Jack and I, cast at last on a river of sanguinity, slowly drank.

chapter 5

W e rode through LA as the vast city hummed with cars and their harried drivers scurried helter-skelter in every direction to make a living, or a name, for themselves. It was refreshing not to get off at the 10 Freeway and be heading back to Santa Monica and my own minefield of worries.

Jack and I kept our sippy cups half full. Somewhere inside me I realized we were rolling the dice, but both of us had built up such a tolerance to the grape we needed the medicating libations to maintain our sangfroid. As long as we kept it under control I believed we could manage it. And there was no way I was going to get Jack or myself to go cold turkey on the trip.

My mother's voice piped up from the back. "What're you drinking up there, Miles?"

"Just a little water, Mom."

"Oh, that's a lot of horse muffins," she retorted. "I bet it's wine."

"Okay, just a little, uh, Pinot. Jack and I have had a long morning," I said in a rising tone, over the roar of the engine.

"Can I have a glass of wine, please?"

"Mom, you have to wait till we get to Buellton. We have a nice dinner planned for you. You'll get two glasses of the finest Chardonnay"–her favorite variety and the only one she would ever drink–"I don't want you passing out on me, okay?"

"I'm not going to pass out," she bristled.

"Let's wait until Buellton."

"It's not fair that you get wine and I don't."

"Mom, in an hour, we'll be at the Marriott and I'll open you the finest Chardonnay and I'll get you straightened out, okay?"

"It's five o'clock." She was a five o'clock drinker like her first-born, Hank. She never took a drop before five, but right on the dot, she had a glass, then, until her stroke, quite a few more.

"I know it's five, Mom, but now that you're out of Las Villas the imbibition rules have changed. We may go wine tasting in the morning, we may not start until late. We're on a whole new schedule now."

"I'm nervous."

I turned and looked her squarely in the eyes, hoping to dispel her apprehensions. "Jack, Joy, and I are going to take care of you, okay?"

"Okay," she demurred. "You promise?"

"Yes."

"Phyllis," Jack roared. "You're in good hands."

I shot Jack a look as if to say, *Let me handle this.*

I turned back to my querulous mother. "When we get up there, we'll get freshened up, and hustle you out to dinner ASAP."

"That's good news. You promise?"

"I promise. I don't want you coming down with the vapors."

My mother chuckled at the word *vapors.* "Oh, I won't," she said. "I don't get depressed like you, Miles."

"No one does." To quiet my mother I produced a CD folder from the drinks console and selected Harry Belafonte's *Greatest Hits*, slipped it into the CD player and adjusted the volume. At the sound of Belafonte's mellifluous voice, and the first of his sappy hits, I watched my mother's reaction. When she heard her favorite musician start singing his signature track, "The Banana Boat Song," she tapped her index finger against an imaginary object and said, "Oh, Harry. He was fantastic."

"Are you happy, Mom?"

Her eyes pinched closed and it looked like she was going to start crying again. "This is the best day of my life."

As the lyrics came in over the melody, Jack sang boisterously along, his voice a shockingly beautiful baritone:

Daylight come and me wan' go home
Day, me say day, me say day, me say day
Me say day, me say day-o
Daylight come and me wan' go home

Work all night on a drink of rum
Daylight come and me wan' go home
Stack banana till de mornin' come
Daylight come and me wan' go home

Come, mister tally man, tally me banana
Daylight come and me wan' go home
Come, mister tally man, tally me banana
Daylight come and me wan' go home

When the chorus started up, Jack raised his voice and sang in a booming tone, turning frequently to serenade my enchanted mother:

Lift six foot, seven foot, eight foot bunch
Daylight come and me wan' go home
Six foot, seven foot, eight foot bunch
Daylight come and me wan' go home

My mother broke into song only when Belafonte sang, "Daylight come and me wan' go home." There was something sad in the way she croakily harmonized with Harry's dulcet crooning, as if "The Banana Boat Song" was going to become the anthem for the last journey of her life.

In the smog-choked Valley, we merged onto the 101 and continued north in the direction of Santa Barbara, moving against the prevailing traffic and making good time. The sun began to bend off to the west and the blue sky was striated with apricot-colored clouds that looked like gigantic pennants suspended in deep space.

"Are you going to call Maya when we get up there?" Jack asked.

"I don't know," I said. "She was kind of cold to me on the phone the last time I spoke with her. I guess when the movie came out I sort of went off and did my own thing and... Plus, she's not going to move to

LA because she's got her own little boutique winery thing going, and I'm certainly not going to move up there because all I'd do is get drunk and pick up groupies at the Hitching Post."

"What's wrong with that?" Jack asked.

I smirked and shook my head. "I'm sure it'd get old real fast. Then, in no time, I would become a local joke. I'm trying to move on, Jackson. I'm trying to shed this past, but it keeps pulling me down."

Jack, no doubt eager to discourage my introspection, tacked: "So, Terra's really doing lap dances in Reno?"

"That's what I gleaned, yeah. You drove her into a life of prostitution, Jackson."

"No, I didn't."

"You had that girl's head turned totally around during that crazy week."

"She had *my* head turned totally around. I almost blew off the wedding."

"Which, in retrospect, might have been the best thing that could have happened to you."

"But then I wouldn't have had Byron," he said, a little wistfully.

"I've got to go to the bathroom," my mother barked from the back.

"All right, Mom," I said. "We'll take the next exit." I turned to Jack: "This is going to be a pretty frequent occurrence. She takes some powerful diuretics for her edema. Just so you know."

"That's cool," Jack said. "If Phyllis's got to go, she's got to go." He turned around and, his mood lifted by the wine he'd been sipping, said to my mother over the music. "All right, Phyllis. Pit-stop coming up. Time to rinse a kidney."

In Ventura, I directed Jack to a turnoff I was familiar with and he braked at a gas station mere yards from the off-ramp. Joy slid open the side door and, after I had pulled the ramp out from the undercarriage, wheeled my mother out. Snapper leapt out of the van and took off running.

"Snapper! Snapper!" my mother screamed. "Get back here!"

Snapper, hearing her familiar voice, came to a sliding stop, lifted his leg and urinated on the tire of a parked car, and then sprinted back, panting excitedly.

My mother turned to Joy and reproached her. "You can't let him out like that. He has to be on his leash."

"I'm sorry, Mrs. Raymond."

"Mom, it wasn't her fault. She was hired to take care of you, not Snapper."

"He could have died," she cried. Snapper was now back in the van with the door closed and his bladder blissfully relieved.

"Well, everything's fine now. Just relax, Mom, okay?"

"Okay," she said. "I'm sorry, Joy."

Joy, ever patient, wheeled my mother off in search of the service station's bathroom.

I maneuvered the van next to one of the pumps and took the pit-stop opportunity to top off the tank. Jack had wandered off and lit a cigarette, a nasty habit he had broken at Babs's behest, but now was back to chipping away at.

As I refueled, I noticed Joy emerging from the bathroom and discreetly lighting a joint. She took a couple puffs off it, then disappeared back inside the bathroom. Once we had done our business and sated our various vices, we all congregated back in the van and continued up the 101 in the direction of the Santa Ynez Valley.

The sky colored a darker shade of blue as we passed through Santa Barbara and drew closer to the destination of our journey's first leg. Hugging the 101, and directly off to our left, the immense Pacific, with its mottled white-caps, took on the appearance of crumpled tin foil struck by bright light. Eventually, the 101 curved away from the ocean and, just before the town of Buellton, we bore through the same tunnel the characters had in the movie.

"Life imitates art," I mused to Jack.

"I hope not," Jack said, drawing laughter from me.

As we crested the Santa Ynez Mountains and coasted the final few miles toward Buellton, night was just starting to descend. As always, whenever I came to pay a visit, the valley, with its beautiful rolling hills and unpolluted skies and swaths of vineyards, brought me a certain serenity.

Jack pulled into the Marriott, which fronts the 101, and I got out to check in. The clerk at the reception desk recognized my name and was all atwitter. On the desk were stacks of the *Shameless* wine map, a tourists' guide to many of the locations in the movie. The local chamber of commerce had quickly pounced on its notoriety in a shameless run of greedy self-promotion. The young, blushing woman assigned us two adjacent rooms on the top floor. I went back out to the Rampvan. The air bore a slight chill now and I was feeling refreshed, looking forward to dinner and wine at the Hitching Post.

I approached Jack, smoking, and said, "Okay, here's the deal. They don't allow pets. So, you're going to put Snapper in this tote bag I brought. In it you'll find a sweatband. I want you to put that over his snout so he doesn't start barking his fool head off."

"Okay," Jack said, dropping his cigarette to the asphalt and extinguishing it with a twist of his shoe.

"We'll get my mom settled in and then we'll head over to the Hitching Post."

"Sounds like a plan."

"Check this out," I said, handing him one of the tourist maps.

Jack glanced at it. "These fuckers were all over this one with their PR, weren't they?"

"This place has changed forever, I'm told. A friend of mine came up a couple of months ago and said it was a madhouse at the Hitching Post. But we have a table."

"Excellent."

Joy wheeled my mother from the van as Jack and I hauled out the bags. A bell captain loaded them onto a luggage trolley. As Jack stayed back to park the van and sneak Snapper inside, I escorted Joy and my mother to their suite.

"You okay, Mom?"

"Oh, yes."

"Not too tired to go out to dinner?"

"Oh, no."

"Because we could order in for you."

"No," she said sharply. "I want to go out. I want to live. I don't care if I die choking on a nice big T-bone steak!"

I laughed. "That food in Las Villas was pretty bad, huh?"

"Oh, you don't know. That would have killed me before my heart gave out."

I laughed and gave her shoulder a little squeeze. We were all in an ebullient mood, the way being in a picturesque new setting with star-riddled skies and foreign smells gives one the sense of newness, discovery.

Joy and my mother disappeared inside their special handicapped room.

Inside my expansive room I opened another one of the Willamette Pinots, an '08 Bergström, and poured two glasses in the Riedel sommelier's glasses I had brought along for the trip. Wineglass in hand, I drifted

out onto the small concrete patio and took a seat in an all-weather chair.
The 101 traffic roared in opposing directions on the other side of the large swimming pool that glowed turquoise in the encroaching dark. I would have preferred a B&B in the middle of nowhere, but my mother felt more comfortable in the concrete wombs of the more corporate hotels. With her infirmity, it was probably a prudent course. My thoughts strayed. After a half a glass of wine, an unadulterated peace invaded me, rushed in and cushioned my soul. It had been a tough road to this penthouse suite. My journey was by no means over, but I felt like I had crested some kind of professional hill and now, if nothing else, was enjoying the ride back down to the quotidian sphere.

A few minutes later, there was a knock at the door, accompanied by a familiar booming voice. I let Jack in and poured him a glass before he commandeered the bottle and we repaired to the patio. In reverential silence, we watched the sun lower to the horizon and slip lyrically away to the other side of the world.

"You got Snapper in okay?"

"Yeah," Jack said. "Fucker bit me." He glowered at his finger and then shook it.

"That's why they named him Snapper. Chomp chomp."

"Great," Jack said. "Thanks for the warning. Ten days with that little lap shark, huh? I might have to petition for a raise."

"You're already overpaid," I said. "That wine in your glass is worth a double sawbuck alone."

He drained his Riedel and said, "Good. In that case, I'll have another."

From where we were seated we could see the sign for the Days Inn where we used to stay. "There's the Windmill," I said, gesturing and nostalgically calling the place by its former name.

Jack looked over. "Oh, yeah. Those were the days."

"I like Windmill Inn better. Sort of more appropriate for the kitschy Solvang motif."

"Yeah, I agree," Jack said. "Man, it seems like yesterday we took that trip."

"Yeah," I said, reflecting back with him. "Remember that time I came back to the room and you and Terra were going at it like marmots?"

"Don't remind me," Jack said. "That chick was smoking hot. I've never had better sex in my entire life."

"It's probably because you were about to get married and you knew that it wasn't going to be anything serious."

"I don't know," Jack said. "Yeah, probably it wouldn't have lasted." He turned to me and said with a grimaced expression, "She's really a stripper in Reno?"

"That's the scuttlebutt in the tasting rooms. People up here know what everyone's doing, who they're fucking, how much they're drinking. I've got to be careful."

"Terra's not in the wine business anymore?"

I shook my head. "Pussy for cash. That's the word."

Jack visibly winced and shook his head, no doubt a succession of prurient images suddenly menacing him. "Man."

"You're lucky you didn't get crab lice and pass 'em to Babs."

"The chick was follically challenged. What would crabs clamp onto?"

I laughed. "And you were going to blow off your wedding and were trying to inveigle me to move up here with you and start a winery! Fuck, man, you had flipped your pons."

Jack sipped the Pinot he had refreshed his glass with, smacked his lips and furrowed his brow. "I said that?"

"Yeah. And you were fucking serious. I mean, I knew you were out of your coconut, but you presented it to me in a way that was so genuine I was almost swayed by your lunatic logic."

"Hmm," Jack said.

"I mean, new pussy does that. When I had the affair that broke up my marriage I was so out of my mind over this stupid little nothing D-girl it wasn't funny. I mean, I thought I was behaving reasonably normally, given the crazy circumstances, but in retrospect I was out of my freaking gourd. New pussy is like the call of the Sirens, Lorelei beckoning sailors to their doom."

"Yeah," Jack said. I sensed that he was traveling back in his mind to what wrecked his marriage; a trace of lament and remorse had crept into his voice. "Yeah. New pussy. They ought to put a warning label on it."

"Like that would do any good. God really fucked us with that one, didn't he? Gave us this turbo-charged sex drive to ensure the propagation of the species, but didn't count on modern civilization and the fact that we don't need it anymore. But here we are, stuck with it. It's driving us crazy."

The orange bled out of the sky and the empyrean purpled. Owing to the scarcity of ambient light, stars broke out like fireflies on a summer night in the Midwest and coruscated in the darkness. I kept flipping my iPhone over and over in my hand like a deck of cards. "I think I'm going to call Maya and invite her to the Hitching Post."

"Excellent idea," Jack said. "See if she has a friend." I looked over at Jack and he met my dismayed expression. "Or maybe not."

"Or maybe not. Jesus. That's an understatement." Shaking my head to myself, I found Maya's number in my contacts and pressed Call. After five rings her voicemail intercepted the call. I listened to her familiar sultry voice until the beep sounded. "Hey, Maya, it's Miles. I'm up here in Buellton. Going to head over to the Hitching Post in a bit. You're welcome to join us if you're free. Would love to see you and catch up. Take care." I turned to Jack. "She was probably sitting there staring at her phone."

"I doubt it," Jack said. "I'll bet you she shows."

"Uh. I don't think so."

Jack suddenly held his wineglass up to his face. "What's this wine we're drinking? It's delicious."

"It's an '08 Bergström." I didn't bother to recite the vineyard because Jack didn't care. I upended some more into my mouth. "It is good, isn't it?"

"Excellent."

"These Willamette wines are fucking impressive."

There was a soft knock at the door. I got up from my chair, crossed the spacious room, and answered it. It was Joy. A shower and a change into a black sleeveless dress had left her positively transformed. Her bloodshot eyes betrayed a few more hits of pot and there was a suppressed giggle evident in her otherwise diffident expression. "Your mom's all ready."

"Okay," I said.

"She wants a glass of wine now," she said.

"I bet she does." I went into the portable refrigerator and produced a bottle of Chardonnay, uncorked it, poured a glass, then went next door to placate my mother who, if she didn't get her evening glass, would be unappeasable. I found her out on the patio with Snapper resting in her lap. I handed her the half-glass of Chardonnay. She sipped it and a smile broadened across her face.

"Oh, I needed that," she said.

I pulled up a chair next to her, placed a hand on her shoulder and gave it a squeeze. "How're you doing, Mom?"

"Fine." She sipped her wine with relish. Her endlessly shifting mood changed like the stock market.

"Excited?"

"Oh, yes."

"It's going to be a zoo at the Hitching Post tonight. Sure you want to go?"

"Stop asking that," she reproved me.

"Sure you wouldn't like to go somewhere more quiet?"

"No."

"Okay. Just checking."

"Do you have to put that sweatband over Snapper's nose?"

"Mom, if management finds out we've got a dog in here they'll kick us out. Do you want to stay at the Motel 6?"

"Oh, no," she said, laughing.

"Or in a tent at a campsite?"

"Don't joke me."

"All right then, stop your bellyaching. Enjoy your wine."

I rounded up our gang for a night of food and wine plundering. We abandoned Snapper to the room with the sweatband around his snout, climbed into the Rampvan and rode the short distance over to the Hitching Post. The parking lot was so full it was difficult to find a place to park. Something I had never seen before: a crowd of maybe twenty people clustered around the entrance waiting for their names to be called. The four of us threaded our way through them and went in the front door, my mother spearheading the charge in her wheelchair. The noise level inside was deafening. The maítre d' exclaimed: "Miles! Good to see you."

"Nice to be back at the scene of the crime," I shouted to her over the noise. I ducked around the corner and glanced into the bar. They were four deep! Packed in like sardines in a tin. Again, something never witnessed before at the Hitching Post, at least not by me. *Shameless*, like the maudlin *Field of Dreams*, had turned one of its key locations into a tourist-groupie magnet, drawing fans from all over.

I said to the maítre d' (whose name I was blanking on), "Jesus, I've never seen it like this before."

"It's your doing, Miles. You changed it all."

"I didn't. The movie did. But, whatever..."

She smirked at my modesty.

"I hope my lifetime certificate is good for four."

"For you, the moon!"

We were escorted like royalty to a large center table. A chair was hauled away so Joy could slide my mother up to her place in her wheelchair. Jack took a seat and leaned back, hands behind his head, beaming, sizing up the possibilities. I got up to go to the bathroom. Jostling through the throng at the bar I cast about for a sign of Maya, but didn't see her through the arms raised to get the attention of the beleaguered bartenders.

When I came out of the bathroom, a valley winemaker recognized me and leapt up from his coveted stool. "Miles. Good to see you." He embraced me.

"Hey, Dick, how's it going?" I shouted over the din. "How're the grapes shaping up this year?"

"It's going to be a good vintage. Here, you want to try something?" He motioned to the bartender who, seeing me, gave me a thumbs-up and quickly produced a wineglass and waved to me over the crowd. Dick poured me a half-glass from an unlabeled bottle he had with him. I took a sip and sloshed it around in my mouth.

"Pretty powerful juice," I said.

Dick, a little high on the stuff already, raised a hand in an effort to get everyone's attention. "Hey, everyone," he announced, "this is Miles Raymond. The guy who wrote *Shameless*."

"Dick, Jesus," I said. "I don't need this."

Dick had known me before the movie took off. "Have some fun with it, Miles."

Heads turned. Within seconds, the crowd imploded on me. Cocktail napkins and business cards and matchbooks were thrust in my face for me to sign. I did my best to accommodate everyone, thinking that maybe it wasn't such a good idea to have come to the most celebrated location in the movie. But then I had a lifetime free certificate, so.... As I expected, a couple of attractive women wormed their way close to me. Women who wouldn't have paid attention to me when I used to be a habitué of the unknown, unprepossessing joint this had once been. At the mention of

Shameless it was as if ten years of wear-and-tear had been magically effaced from my true age. One of the women thrust a business card into my hand and said loudly, "Call me, Miles. I'm at the Days Inn." Drunk out of her skullcap, she put her mouth next to my ear and whispered lewdly, "I want to fuck you into a coma." She backed away and waited for my reaction.

"What's your name?"

"Patricia."

"Patricia. I'll take the coma, but not the fuck. Thanks."

"Oh, don't be such a wet blanket, Mr. Famous Writer."

I backed away through the crush of bodies.

"See you at the Days Inn later maybe," she shouted over the din.

I just smiled wryly at her and finally broke free from the autograph hounds and elbowed my way back into the main dining room. A special magnum of the Hitching Post's signature Pinot, the Highliner, had already found its way to the table and Jack was filling glasses for everyone. My mother wasn't really a fan of red wine–she said it was sour. So I summoned our waitress over–it wasn't Maya, of course–and ordered her a glass of Alma Rosa Chardonnay, which I knew she would like.

"Where'd you go, Miles?" Jack asked.

"It's fucking nuts in the bar. Some winemaker recognized me so I had to sign some autographs." I produced the business card from my front shirt pocket. "You want to get laid? Here you go." I handed Jack the card.

Jack glanced at the card. "Massage therapist. Shiatsu. Thai," he read aloud. "Nice." He smiled broadly. Things were picking up after the afternoon's deplorable dognapping episode.

"She's staying at the Days Inn. You can pretend she's Terra."

Jack smirked. "Dude, she wants you. Not me."

"Tell her Miles sent you as his crackerjack replacement. I'm sure she'll do you."

Joy absorbed this badinage with bemusement. She was so shy and inexpressive it was hard to know what she was thinking.

As my mother jubilated in her Chardonnay, I said to Joy, "How do you like the wine?"

"I like it. No aftertaste."

"No aftertaste? That's it? Try another sip. Move it around in your mouth." I sudsed the wine in my mouth to demonstrate.

She took another miniscule sip and tried to replicate what I had shown her. "It's good. No aftertaste."

"Okay," I said, resigning myself to the fact her drug of choice was something you smoked, not drank.

The restaurant's affable owner, Frank Ostini, bedecked in chef's whites and wearing his iconic pith helmet, materialized at our table. His teeth shone white under his bushy moustache. He extended an arm and said, "Miles. Good to see you."

I took his hand. "Likewise, Frank. Place is hopping."

"Quadrupled the business."

"When're you buying your yacht?"

He laughed, obviously elated in the flush of a windfall that had he had his way, would never have happened.

"Remember when you tried to shut the film down because you thought the script romanticized over-imbibition?" I needled him.

"I do. Thank God they talked sense into me."

"I mean, come on," I teased. "You're not in the mineral water business. Jesus. What were you thinking? Half the people up here are wine drunks."

He scowled a moment at my jibe.

"By the way, thanks for the magnum. Highliner's tasting better than ever."

"You're welcome. Can I take your orders?"

"Mom? What would you like?"

"I want a big steak."

I gestured to my mother. "Frank, this is my mother. We're headed to the International Pinot Noir Celebration in McMinnville, Oregon and then I'm taking her to Wisconsin and turning her over to her sister."

Frank placed a caring hand on my mother's shoulder. "Nice to meet you, Mrs. Raymond."

Tears formed in her eyes. "My son's a big success."

"Oh, that's for sure," replied Frank. "Huge." My mother nodded, trying to ward off the tears. Frank squatted down next to her. "How would you like your steak?"

"Well done," my mother replied. When we were growing up she cooked the shit out of everything, believing all meat was tainted with trichinosis.

Jack, Joy and I placed our orders and Frank, after showering me with more compliments, disappeared back into the kitchen.

My mother, tears still glassing her eyes, pointed a finger at me. "I always knew you would make it. Your father thought you were a loser, but I believed in you."

"Thanks, Mom. Good to know Dad had thrown in the towel on me." For a moment I grew wistful thinking about him. My father had wanted me to drop my artistic aspirations and come into the family business, selling commercial coin-op equipment to laundries and apartment complexes. Instead, I had moved to LA, where I had struggled mightily to find a toehold in the film business. I had borrowed heavily from him—and others—and though they had come through in my destitute years they had all urged me to get a *real* job. Now that my ship had come in, his untimely death—a massive stroke while he was undergoing a triple bypass had plunged him into an irreversible coma—weighed heavily. He would have been so proud to see me gain this level of recognition. It would have vindicated me in his eyes, effaced years of often-mutual animosity over the fact I hadn't used my college degree in the pursuit of something that would pay the bills. Well, I was paying the bills now! I remembered having to appear alongside my poor mother in front of a medical ethics board at a V.A. hospital and implore them not to let my father waste away on life-support. They agreed to pull his feeding tube, but, even then, it was three agonizing weeks before he officially died. It took a toll on my mother, and she suffered her devastating stroke less than a year and a half later. I looked over at her. She was ecstatic to be out of Las Villas de Muerte, sitting in a lively restaurant and drinking her treacly Chardonnay, and my heart went out to her. Hell, if she croaked on this trip, would that be the worst thing that could happen to her?

Jack refilled my glass, hoisting me out of my reverie. "What's up, dude?" he asked, noticing I had dropped out of the conversation.

"I don't know. I was just thinking what a bizarre little household we are here. You're like my dissolute brother; Joy"—I patted her on the head—"the sister I never had and always longed for; and my mother, well, my mother. We're the ultimate dysfunctional family."

"You're getting sentimental, Miles," Jack said.

"No, I'm not."

He shot me the look that said I was waxing specious, but shook his head and smiled.

The various courses came and we dug in. From time to time we were
interrupted by someone wobbling over to the table to have me autograph
something–cocktail napkins being the most popular. With her half-
necrotic brain, my mother didn't really comprehend what it all meant.
She just knew that I was the center of attention, and that I had accomplished something momentous, the magnitude of which was lost on her.
Joy, appearing prettier and prettier the more Pinot I consumed, would
drop her gaze into her lap if I tried to make eye contact. Being in the
Hitching Post, with all these people fawning, she understood that I was a
celebrity of some ilk, but she seemed embarrassed by all the attention.

Near dinner's end, my iPhone beeped. Wrestling it out of my pocket,
I saw a notification for a text message. The text read: *I'm at the Clubhouse
if you want to have a drink-M.*

"Who was that?" Jack asked, noticing my eyes narrow and my brow beetle.

"Maya. Wants to have a drink."

"Are you going to meet her?"

"Yeah. Why not? Can you get Joy and my mom back to the Marriott?"

"No problem, dude." He fingered the business card in his hand.
"Hmm. Patricia. Sounds promising."

"Why's that?"

"Starts with a 'p.'"

"You fucking dog, Jackson."

After dinner I shook more hands, declining numerous importuning
offers to hang out at the bar or decamp to another location for more wine.
We gathered ourselves back in the Rampvan and took off.

Jack dropped me off at the entrance to the Clubhouse Bar, the cheerless
watering hole at the former Windmill Inn. A major scene in the movie
had been shot there and I was expecting another crowd, but when I ambled inside the place was relatively sedate. A few stragglers sat at the bar.
A couple of locals, who looked like they would stab you to death for an
hour's pay, were shooting a game of pool.

I found Maya seated exactly on the same stool Jack and I had found
her on years before when we met her here for a drink. A glass of red wine
stood on the bar in front of her. Next to it was a bottle. Maya wouldn't
stoop to drink the paltry, and poorly chosen, selections on the Clubhouse's
list, so she usually brought her own and paid a corkage. Now that the

Hitching Post was overrun every night, she likely preferred the solitude of the Clubhouse.

"Hi," I said.

"Hi," she said, forcing a smile. She hadn't changed much, but too many cigarettes and too many hours under the hot sun in her vineyard had conspired to produce crow's-feet that crinkled at the corners of her large eyes. A dye job had lightened her hair, and it looked like she had lost a little weight since we had last seen each other.

I corkscrewed down on the stool next to her. We didn't embrace, we didn't kiss cheeks, we didn't even shake. A tension had to be bridged before we could touch each other, so much had gone down since our meeting, the movie's coming out, and my meteoric rise to my odd version of fame. Circumspection ruled over the short space between us as we tried to read each other through the subtlest of inflections.

"What're you drinking here?" I said, reaching for the bottle on the bar and turning it so that the label faced me. "Ne Plus Ultra Wines. This your label?"

"Yeah," she said.

"I like the name," I said. Then, in what I thought was a humorous tone, I added, "I taught you that word, didn't I?"

"No, you didn't," she said caustically. "You're such an asshole, Miles. Besides, it's not a word, it's a phrase, you philistine."

"That's true," I quickly back-pedaled. "You're right." She turned away from me. "But," I teased, "I believe I used it in my novel to describe what it was like to have sex with you."

"Yeah. And now the whole valley knows what it's like to have sex with Maya."

"Sorry. I write from personal experience."

She rolled a tongue over her front teeth. There was palpable hostility in that space between us now.

The bartender broke away from a baseball game on the overhead TV that had mesmerized his weary, brain-dead soul, and came over. "Would you like a glass?"

"Or you want me to drink straight from the bottle?"

Mirthlessly, he slid a glass from an overhead rack and set it in front of me. Maya proudly poured it half-full with her maiden Pinot. I took some into my mouth and sloshed it around like a wine professional. Maya expressionlessly waited for my assessment, no doubt braced for a trenchant critique.

"Where're the grapes from?" I asked.

"This new vineyard north of Clos Pepe. First vinifiable harvest."

"Nice," I said.

"Nice?" she jumped on me. "That's all you're going to say?"

I took another sip. "It's more than nice, Maya. It's elegant. Like you." She forced a smile. "And I appreciate the fact you're going for something not so highly alcoholic. More Burgundian. Not one of those Syrah-laced Pinots that Bruno used to make."

"Thanks," she said.

"How many cases did you produce?"

"Only about a hundred." She glanced at the bottle. "You really like it?"

"Yeah. I do. And not just because you made it, either. Makes a lot of these other valley Pinots pedestrian by comparison."

She laughed. "Put it in your next book."

It was kind of an odd sensation, after the scene at the Hitching Post, to have Maya hustling me. "If I write one, I will, I promise."

She nodded. I nodded. We sipped her wine in silence. We were, as usual, avoiding talking about our history. Uncomfortable, I looked around the Clubhouse.

"It's refreshing to see that the *Shameless* insanity hasn't gripped this place in its steel vise. The Hitching Post looked like something out of *The Rocky Horror Picture Show*. I mean, I actually heard people quoting lines right out of the movie."

"I know. You ruined it for all of us. I can't go there anymore. It's so crazy, Frank's thinking of closing it one night a week and only letting locals in."

"He should. Pour free Highliner. Be a goodwill gesture to the community."

"So, you're up here with your mom and Jack the asshole and..."

"And my mom's caretaker. Oh, and my mom's nasty little dog."

At the picture of the four and a half of us Maya just shook her head. "How's it going so far?"

"So far okay. One day down. Nine to go." I smiled. "I brought plenty of wine."

Another silence descended. We sipped. The bridge still needed another section. I wondered if more wine would complete the construction.

"How's your new boyfriend?" I ventured.

"We're just dating," she said, her voice still serrated with an undertone of rancor.

"Dating seriously or...?"

Maya simmered at the question. Then she picked up her glass and tossed the wine in it into my face. She swiveled off her barstool and strode outside. I forearmed the wine from my face and glanced in the direction she had fled. Maya hadn't left. She was standing under the portico, a match illuminating her face as she lit a cigarette.

After a moment I got up slowly off my barstool and sauntered outside. I stood next to her. She wouldn't meet my gaze. A chill had crept into the air, and it wasn't just the ocean breezes.

"I'm sorry," I said. She glared at the burning end of her cigarette, as if studying it. "Can I bum a cigarette?" She handed me her pack of American Spirits. I fingered one out and stuck it between my lips. She flicked a lighter aflame and I inhaled it until it glowed red. We warily observed each other out of our peripheral vision. The passing traffic on the 101 was light. Stars dotted the clear night sky. I should have been feeling on top of the world, but instead I was feeling a sinking despair. Women with whom I had a history often made me feel this way. If I'd gone to a head-shrinker I'm sure he would have pointed out that this was a pattern with me: throw myself headlong into something, get high on wine and wax all passionate and romantic and tell them what they longed to hear–and actually feel it, too!–then wake from the hangover and gradually push them away. That's what I had done with Maya, and now, out here in front of the Clubhouse Bar, where we had shared a number of wonderful times–God, I remember once kissing wildly and not caring who saw us–there was a tension as ugly as a barbed-wire fence.

"No one ever taught me how to deal with success. I'm sure you can be taught. I haven't dealt with it well. I've alienated a lot of people. You know, obviously I have intimacy issues. And all the wine has clouded my judgment." I took another drag on my cigarette. "And so I'm sorry that I blew you off and went off on..." I faltered, "...on this crazy, hedonistic journey to nowhere. I liked myself better before the movie, if you want to know the truth."

She stamped out her cigarette, spit smoke, and looked at me for the first time with her dark, brooding eyes. "So did I," she said. Then she reached

both hands up and grabbed my head as if catching a hard-thrown football.
She brought her mouth to mine in a savage kiss. Her voluptuous lips
smashed against my face in a torrent of fury or passion or longing or some
other emotion volcanically brewing inside her, taking me by surprise. She
finally withdrew her mouth, but still clutched my head in her hands as if
she were going to crush it. "I want to hate-fuck you so badly, Miles." She
brought her lips to mine again and kissed me like she wanted to devour
me, not make love to me. "But I'm not going to give you the satisfaction."
With that, she pivoted in place and started off. Ten paces away from me
she stopped and turned. "You know, Miles, I liked you so much better
when you were a pathetic, pathological lying loser who couldn't get his
novel published and couldn't get laid. You're a different person now. So
fucking full of yourself." She shook her head disgustedly, then strode over
to her black Jeep Cherokee, turned the engine over and roared off.

Desolate, I walked back into the Clubhouse. Maya's half-empty bottle
still sat perched on the bar. I poured a glass, debated calling Jack–I could
guess where *he* was!–but decided against it, not wanting to get shanghaied
into a long night at the Hitching Post.

I paid the corkage, tipped an obscene $100 so the bartender could in-
vest in a new shirt, and left. Walking along a deserted stretch of 246 in
the direction of the Marriott, I considered what a contemptible, smug
jerk I had become, what a little gust of fame had engendered in me. And
all it took was thirty minutes with Maya to evoke it. I missed her. I had
her and I let her go. Now, like my marriage, it was over. No going back.
God, I was miserable. I didn't know what I had been expecting when I
came to the Clubhouse, but I got hit upside the face, and it hurt. Hurt.
Made me think of a line Kafka wrote in a letter to his Czech translator,
Milena Jessenska: "You are the knife that I twist into myself." Is it why I
couldn't love without always wanting to run away?

I stopped on the 101 overpass, jackknifed over the guardrail and stared
at the red and white rivers of traffic. Naturally, Maya had been hurt by
my pushing her away when the movie hit. I'm sure it wasn't too difficult
for her to go on the Internet, punch my name into Google, and find photos of me with different women at premieres and film festivals and awards
shows. She'd heard me profess my love for her enough times to believe it.
And now the only way she could express her deep-seated–and legit–re-

sentment was to invite me for a drink, kiss me *hatefully*, then give me the middle finger and walk off forever. I felt lousy.

The 18-wheelers rumbled under me, heading north and south to drop-off destinations. A part of me wanted to join Jack and get obliterated, and another part of me just wanted to return to my hotel room and reflect on everything condemnable I had become.

I started off again slowly, my legs heavy. Here I was in the valley I had done a bit to help make famous and I was suddenly all alone, anonymous. It was a stark reminder of the future that awaited me. Fatalistic, okay, but I knew in my gut it was true.

The walk past a McDonald's and a Motel 6 and a 4-plex showing Hollywood's dregs was depressingly lonely. (Had I fantasized that Maya and I would laugh it all off and have a wild night in the bedroom? What a fool I was, I thought, for being so oblivious of how I had hurt her.) The hotel lobby was lonely. The slow-moving elevator–come on, already! Down the corridor back to my room. The room was lonely. I poured a glass of Pinot and lay on the bed. My cell rang. I was hoping it was Maya, but it was Jack. I didn't pick up. A minute later I received a text message: "It's happening, dude! It's on!" I closed my eyes and fell into a disquieting sleep.

Jack barreled in around four a.m., complete with slamming door and thundering footsteps. He was loud and drunk and laughing, filling the room with his presence. He turned on the light, annoying me.

"Jesus, Jack," I said, jerking upright.

He found his wineglass and helped himself to a healthy pour. "Man, it was wild over at the Windmill." He whistled. "Fucking chicks, man." He pointed his glass at me. "They really wanted to meet you."

"They didn't want to meet me, they wanted to meet this shell of a man I've become," I said, still irritated by the glaring light and Jack's barely pre-dawn arrival.

Sensing my peevishness, he said, "How'd it go with Maya?"

"Ever heard of hate-fucking?"

"Heard of it. Not quite sure what it is. Probably how Byron was conceived."

"She said she wanted to hate-fuck me, then she flipped me the bird and split."

"Fuck, man, why didn't you go back to the Hitching Post?"

"I was tired. And a little drenched with Maya's maiden bottling. Did you get your nut? Pour me a glass, will you?"

Jack was happy to oblige. "Yeah, I got my nut," he said, handing me the glass he had refreshed. "I think I promised her and her friend that we would take them wine tasting today. Hit all the locations in the movie."

"Well," I sighed, "that's not going to happen."

"No, I suppose it isn't."

We stayed up talking and drinking until raw dawnlight was visible through the curtains, then split an Ambien and conked out.

chapter **6**

When I woke, there were eleven messages in voicemail, all from my mother. Suspecting she might call, I had muted my cell phone so that I could get some sleep.

As Jack snored, I showered, climbed into fresh clothes, and stepped into the corridor. I found my mother parked outside her door. She raised her one good arm toward the ceiling and demanded in a rising tone, "Where were you? I was so worried." She started crying.

I squatted down in front of her. "What's wrong, Mom?"

"I thought you'd gotten arrested."

"I was out with an old girlfriend."

"Did you sleep with her?"

"Mom! Jesus."

"You could have called. We say goodnight before I go to bed. You scared me."

"I'm sorry. I accidentally had my ringer off. It won't happen again. Didn't Joy take you down for breakfast?"

"No, I was so sick with worry I couldn't eat."

"Well, that's ridiculous," I said, rising to stand upright.

Joy, hearing our voices, opened the door. The piquant smell of marijuana preceded her. She rubbed her eyes with her small hands fashioned into fists, looking sleepy-faced.

"Good morning, Joy," I said. "You don't look like you slept much."

She combed the hair out of her face with her hand. "Your mom's tooth was hurting."

I looked down at my mother in quiet alarm. "What's wrong with your tooth?"

"It's fine," she said curtly.

"Joy just said it was bothering you last night."

"It's fine this morning."

"Are you sure?"

"I'm hungry," she said.

I faced Joy. "You didn't take her down for breakfast?"

"She wasn't hungry earlier. She was upset about you."

"Well, let me find Jack. Why don't you two go down to the restaurant and we'll join you in a minute?"

"Hurry up," my mother barked. "I'm starving."

I went into my room and found Jack lounging on the bed in a courtesy bathrobe, sipping a glass of Pinot. He toasted me silently, a salacious grin on his face.

"Let's go down and get some breakfast before my mom flips out. Then we'll do a little wine tasting on our way out, you fucking degenerate."

"Now you're talking my language," Jack said, rolling off the bed.

Jack—prospect of a late-morning wine tasting and a night of hot sex elating him—pulled himself together in record time and we took the elevator down to the windowless, bottom-floor, catacomb-like restaurant. We found my mother and Joy seated at a table for four. I would have elected to go elsewhere, but with my mother's infirmity, this was easier.

A waitress appeared with two laminated menus and handed them to Jack and me. I glanced at my mother, who was massaging her lower right jaw.

"Is that where your tooth hurts, Mom?"

She dropped her hand immediately. "I'm fine," she said. "It's just a little sore."

I looked at her skeptically. "Have you had trouble with it before?"

"Oh, it comes and goes," she said in a blithe voice.

"Maybe we should take you to a dentist?"

"No," my mother said sharply. "They'll hospitalize me."

"For an infected tooth?" I asked in disbelief.

"Yes. Everything has to be done in the hospital. And I'm sick of hospitals."

"Okay. Okay. Relax. Jesus. If it blows up on you we'll just tie a string around it and do it Afghani style."

Everyone laughed, including my mother. An RN before her marriage, she had a bit of the macabre in her.

Her and Joy's breakfasts came as Jack and I ordered. My mother must have been famished. She demolished a four-egg omelet in minutes, while diminutive Joy picked at a semi-circle of fruit festooning a bowl of cereal she left untouched. She was a wisp of a girl and I could see why.

Jack's and my meals came–dreadful scrambled eggs and overcooked bacon. We scarfed the grub down. We were on the same page, eager to get on the road and to a few select wineries before we headed out of town.

When we had finished we packed up the van, watered, fed and peed Snapper, climbed in and sailed off on leg two of our voyage. It was a beautiful blue-sky morning. We drove six miles north on the 101 to the Highway 154 turnoff in the direction of Foxen Canyon Road. A meandering two-lane country road, the Foxen Canyon Wine Trail–as it's known–evoked pleasant memories of sojourns I had made here years before, often alone, in search of respite and escape from the depredations of my then-life. Anxiety had me in its perpetual grip as I rode in search of wine and the emollience it brought about in me. It was different now. I appeared to have firm footing on the ground beneath me: career, money, women if I wanted them. And unlike my old Honda Accord with its worn shocks and rusted muffler, the Rampvan glided along the road like the automotive equivalent of a hydro-foil. Almost overnight, everything had changed.

I wrested myself from my reverie and found Jack with the *Shameless* wine map unfolded in front of him on the steering wheel. I'm sure he, too, was trying to do what I had done years before: escape. But from the frown on his face I could tell he was besieged by all his worries–dwindling job opportunities, absentee fatherhood, burgeoning waistline–and, in silent communion with his unspoken woes, I felt sorry for him. He'd brought it on himself, of course, with his wanton, unbridled ways, and I'm sure he wished he could rewind the last five years and plot things differently. But Jack was a guy who always lived his life forward, not retrospectively and in remorse like me.

Suddenly, he stared laughing. "This is wild, Miles. A map to all the places we used to go. Bizarre."

I glanced into the back of the Rampvan. Joy's head was resting on her shoulder and she was staring trancelike out the window at the bucolic countryside with its iridescently green undulating grassy hills, contented cattle, interspersed by the symmetrical grids of vineyards, all basking under the genial canopy of a limpid, baby-blue sky. Next to her, my mother cradled a panting Snapper in her lap. Now and then she rolled her tongue around her lower right jaw and winced.

I turned to Jack and said in a lowered tone, "We're going to have to do something about my mother's tooth."

Jack threw a backward glance at my mother. "Yeah, it's going to base-ball on her one of these days. I tried to blow off an impacted molar once a long time ago when I was dead broke. I woke one morning and looked like Brando in *The Godfather*. Fucker hurt, too."

"What'd you do?"

"Took a pair of pliers and yanked it out. Stuffed some cotton in and went hillbilly until I could borrow some money to get a bridge."

I laughed uproariously.

"True story," Jack said.

About fifteen miles up the Foxen Canyon Wine Trail I instructed Jack to pull off onto the dirt shoulder and brake to a halt in front of a dilapidated, barnlike structure: Foxen Winery's utterly and deliberately unprepossessing tasting room. It had looked like an abandoned building when Jack and I first visited, years before. Until the film was released, we would have been the only patrons at this early hour. But times had radically changed and now there were already five other cars parked haphazardly and at oblique angles around the charmingly (now!) decrepit shed. With their lineup of exquisite wines, the ramshackle tasting room was an oenophile's dream, rising up out of nowhere like a Saharan oasis.

Jack and I extended the ramp and Joy wheeled my mother out.

As Joy was getting her things together, my mother looked all around and said, "Where are we?"

"There's a dentist here, Mom. Okay, his license has been revoked and his instruments are a little rusty, but his rates are reasonable. He's going to get this tooth out. No hospitalization."

For a brief moment, she looked thunderstruck, believing me. Then the delayed synapses of her compromised brain started firing and she snapped, "Stop joking me."

"You'll like this, Mom. You wouldn't believe it, but they've got some great wines in here."

"Oh, that's such good news," she cooed as our dysfunctional little contingent crossed the short distance over the dirt and into the tasting room.

There were about a dozen wine aficionados sampling Foxen's product when we bulldozed a path up to the bar. The young tasting room manager smiled at me.

"Miles! How are you? Haven't seen you in a while."

"Hi, Susan," I said. "Beautiful day."

"It is," she said. "It always is. Wow. What a surprise!"

I opened my hand and gestured to my mother. "This is my mom. She's going home to Wisconsin."

"Hi, Mrs. Raymond," Susan said.

My mother nodded, at a loss for words.

"She needs a taste of Chardonnay," I said. Turning to my mother, I said, "Don't you, Mom?"

"Oh, yes," she said. "I'm on vacation!"

Susan laughed and poured a half glass of their '08 Tinaquaic Vineyard Chardonnay–an austere wine–and handed it to me. I nosed it, then passed it to my mother.

"Chardonnay, Mom. But very different from what you're used to. Meaning, more than seven dollars."

"Oh, stop it," she said.

"What would you like, Miles?" Susan said. "Pinot?"

"No, Susan. We're still in the brunch mode. How about a little of that Chenin Blanc?" I turned to Jack. "A little white Loire, big guy?"

Jack flashed a 1,000-watt smile at the very cute, brown-haired, green-eyed Susan and said, loud enough for everyone to hear, and embarrassing me in the process: "I'll have whatever the *Shameless* guy is having."

As Susan poured us generous dollops, mutterings arose from the others in the tasting room. A guy in his thirties, clutching a copy of my novel, was staring at me. He flipped it over to look at the thumbnail shot of the author. It was five years out of date, but I'm sure the bloodshot eyes and slightly bloated countenance didn't completely efface the fact that I was the same guy. He weaved his way through the patrons.

"Are you Miles Raymond?" he asked.

"No, I'm his twin brother. I'm just trying to get some free wine and some star-struck pussy."

He reared back and laughed. "You're him! You've *got* to be him!"

"Guilty," I said, silently praying he wouldn't grope me.

He extended his hand and I shook it affably. "It's a real pleasure to meet you," he said, in the stentorian voice of someone who has been drinking too much. He turned to his cohorts. "Hey, everyone, this is Miles Raymond. The dude who wrote *Shameless*." Everyone's attention was suddenly riveted on me. The hoi polloi closed ranks and converged. The drunk who had recognized me thrust book and pen into my hands.

"Have you read it?" I asked, pen poised over the title page, trying to conjure a funny inscription.

"Three times," he said. "I loved that scene where they go out with the boar hunter. Why wasn't that in the movie?"

"I don't know. I think the director's afraid of guns or something."

Two attractive women, whom I pegged to be not just lesbians, but lovers, were next. I scribbled my John Hancock across their *Shameless* winery tour maps. Others had me sign bottles of Foxen wines they purchased. I got machine-gunned with a lot of the familiar questions. In the midst of the blizzard of queries I noticed my mother holding up her glass and beseeching Susan for more, going unnoticed in the stampede over her to get to me, sunk as she was in the crowd in her wheelchair. I plucked her glass from her hand and reached it across to Susan, who poured her their '08 Bien Nacido Chard.

I handed that to my mother, then said to Joy, "How about you take her outside in the sun? I'll be with you in a bit." Joy nodded assent. "But watch how much she drinks. She can be *really* sneaky." Joy nodded knowingly, already onto my mother's guile whenever wine was present.

When I turned back to the crowd Jack was regaling by far the most beautiful woman in the room with stories about himself and his exploits as inspiration for Jake. Her eyes grew moony as she gazed adoringly up into Jack's florid face.

I whispered into Jack's ear: "We have to be in Paso tonight."

Jack whispered back to me: "Just getting a phone number for a return visit, short horn. Relax."

"I don't want you doing her in the Rampvan."

Jack looked at me and grimaced. "That's high school, dude. I'm disappointed you would think that of me."

I set my glass on the bar in front of Susan and spoke sub rosa: "Jack and I would love to try a couple of those single-vineyard Pinots you've secreted from the marauding masses." Susan giggled. "How can we finesse this?" I said, flirting shamelessly. "A dozen books? A quiet, romantic picnic?"

She leaned over the bar and said in an undertone, "Just don't say anything, okay?"

"Okay, Susan. Work your magic. Legerdemain is the operant word."

Susan disappeared into the back. I squeezed Jack's shoulder and he swiveled his head toward me. "We're getting the good stuff. Pretend it's the entry level, okay?"

"You're the one who's going to pontificate and blow our cover."

"And it's your job to stop me," I said, already a little high from the Chenin Blanc, and mockingly brandishing a finger at him.

Jack winked at me. We were getting tipsy and having a good time. It was only a hundred miles to Paso Robles, our next stop on the itinerary, and we had plenty of time to squander. I had planned it that way.

Jack put his arm around the woman he was making eyes at and drew her into our vinous cabal. "Laura, this is the famous Miles Raymond."

I made a face and shook my head. "Not really," I said.

"Yes, but you wrote *Shameless*," she said, unable to disguise her excitement. She was no more than 5'5", a brunette with shoulder-length hair that shaggily framed an olive complexioned face. Her smoldering black eyes and Salma Hayak eyebrows matched her dark brown tresses and I caught myself glancing down at her cleavage, more than visible in her summery tank top.

"Laura," I said. "You have such a lovely, exotic accent. What's your nationality?"

"Spanish," she replied.

Jack nudged my shoulder, as if I needed any coaxing.

"Spain," I said. "How come the women there are the most beautiful in the world?" I was instantly enamored.

She blushed red. Jack smiled. If Laura was mine, he was certain, in his inimitable way, to flush out her friend. Women never go wine tasting alone. Uh-uh.

"Miles?" Susan hollered. I turned and stepped toward the bar. She slid two half-full glasses of red my direction. "Sea Smoke," she said conspiratorially. "Sold out."

"Thank you, Susan," I said. "You're a sweetheart. I'll put you in my next novel."

"Yeah, right."

"No, I will, I promise."

"Well, just make sure I keep my clothes on. I don't want you describing something you haven't seen."

I must've already been a little looped on the Chenin Blanc because I raised my glass and said, "That could change between now and then."

Susan laughed a throaty laugh and turned back to the buzzing crowd. She raised the volume on her voice. "Anyone need anything else here?"

Half of them raised their glasses and shouted, "Yeah!" It wasn't even noon and the party was in full swing.

I edged past an elderly couple I guessed to be the owners of the grotesque RV parked out front. The man said, "Loved the movie."

"Thank you," I said.

His wife, a loose-limbed chubby already half in the crapper, piped up: "Where do you come up with these ideas?"

I tapped a forefinger to my temple and raised my glass of single-vineyard Foxen Pinot. "Between here and here lies the Rubicon of the imagination," I replied grandiloquently, as I was wont to do when I got a little wine in me. They regarded me strangely and clearly didn't know what to say.

I wormed my way back to where Jack was. More people had filtered into the tasting room. Those who were there when we arrived hadn't left, my presence conferring on Foxen's modest little facility the aura of something grander than the other tasting rooms in the vicinity.

I handed Jack his glass of Pinot. As he raised it to his mouth I put my lips close to his ear and said, "Sea Smoke. Single vineyard. Sold out. 148 cases."

Jack worked it around in his mouth and weighed in. "Awesome."

"An orgy of flavors," I said. When I turned to look at the lovely Laura, the anticipated friend was standing next to her, a smile emblazoned on her face. She had long honey-hued hair that straddled a face freckled with light brownish spots. Big-boned and gangling, close to six foot; the divisions of the spoils, if Jack and I had elected to journey there, *and* if the women were willing, became patently obvious.

"Hi, I'm Carmen," she said, thrusting out her long, elegantly fingered hand.

I took it in my mine and held it for a meaningful moment. "Hi Carmen. I'm Miles."

"I know," she said excitedly. She turned to her friend and they giggled.

I swiveled my head and whispered into Jack's ear: "Laura."

"I figured," he said. "Now that you have the upper hand you get the dark meat, is that the deal?"

I laughed. "You need that Amazon to find your dick under that gut. Laura would have to be a contortionist to get that silly little thing of yours inside her."

"You're having fun with this, aren't you, Homes?"

I slapped him on the back. "You can dish it out, but you can't take it."

Jack smirked. "So, what's the plan, Stan?" he said. "A little shuttle dick-plomacy?"

"No," I said. "Let me take care of it."

Jack laughed because it was such a glaring anomaly that I would be taking care of anything that had to do with the arranging of who, where and when.

A finger tapped me on the shoulder and I turned. Joy held up an empty glass. "Your mom would like some more."

"How's she doing?"

"Fine."

"She getting slurry?"

"She's okay, I think."

I held up my mother's wineglass so Susan could see it. I held my thumb and forefinger an inch apart to indicate how much, then jerked my thumb to the open door where my mother was parked outside. She smiled and nodded. I passed the wineglass back to Joy and she took it over to Susan for the refill.

"So, Miles, what's your next book about?" Laura asked, batting her eyes.

I took a sip of the Pinot, which was really luxuriant, silky and herbaceous, and considered her question. "Well, I always write in the first person. So, I'm thinking about writing a book about a guy like Martin who meets this beautiful girl from Spain in a tasting room and throws it all away to go off with her."

A wry smile creased her pretty face. "Yeah, right," she said.

"Or maybe not," I tacked, afraid suddenly of alienating her with my lame flirtatious banter. "I don't know, Laura. Honestly? I'm kind of blocked." I shrugged. "So, what brings you to the Santa Ynez Valley?"

Carmen held up the *Shameless* map. "We are doing the tour of your movie. Which we both *loved*."

"Oh, yeah? All the way from Spain, huh?"

"Yes."

"You know, my friend Jack here is the inspiration for the Jake character," I said, clapping Jack on the shoulder. Quid pro quo, as it were, for hooking me up with Maya years ago.

"Yes, he was telling us *all* about it." Carmen turned to Jack. "Did you really cheat on your fiancée just before you got married?"

"Pure fiction. Right, Miles?"

"Well... yeah, it's fiction. The real Jake would never cheat, Carmen. He's a one-woman guy."

Carmen and Laura looked at each other, their glance acknowledging that I was surely being facetious.

Laura said, "Well, we have to fly back home tomorrow. Do you want to go wine tasting with us?"

Jack widened his bloodshot eyes at me. "Well," I started, "unfortunately, we're taking my mom, who's in a wheelchair, up to Portland, then on to Wisconsin to be with her sister, so..." Jack's shoulders visibly sagged. "But, hey, we're heading up to Paso Robles this afternoon. I've got an event there tomorrow at Justin Winery," I added casually.

Jack looked fixedly at me like I was about to blow it, utter something alienating, grow all nasty and snobbishly erudite about wine and prompt them to hightail it.

"Where's Paso Robles?" Laura asked, flashing her dark eyes at me and making my knees weak.

"Eighty miles north of here. Gorgeous place. Beautiful winery."

Jack chimed in: "We're heading to the International Pinot Noir Celebration in Oregon." He placed a hand on my shoulder, pressed his ruddy cheek next to mine and added for maximum effect, "Miles is the master of ceremonies."

"Wow," exclaimed Laura. She was looking more beautiful with every sip of the startlingly delicious Pinot, helping me–God bless her!–to bury the harsh, if justly deserved, rejection by Maya. "What does a master of ceremonies do?"

"I think he gives an opening speech," I said, "then they strip off all his clothes and send him loose through the vineyards and the participants chase after him brandishing Dijon clone cuttings and he becomes like Cornell Wilde in *The Naked Prey*."

Laura erupted into knowing laughter.

"You've *seen* that film, Laura?"

"I'm getting my degree in cinema at the University of Barcelona."

"Really, no shit?" Now the needle on her attractiveness was climbing past ten! "Criticism? Writing? Production?"

"Directing."

"Reeeeeaaaallly?" I said, the wine hyperbolizing my speech. "And you thought *Shameless* was pretty good, huh?"

"I think, sorry for my English, it's a minor masterpiece."

"Well, thank you, Laura." I turned to Jack. "Jesus, this day's getting off to an auspicious start."

Jack looked anxious as to where I was going with this. I think the arcane film reference had him a tad concerned. Laughter warred with worry.

"Well, sounds like quite a trip," Laura said, referring to something I had evidently said and already forgotten.

"Would you two beautiful *señoritas* like something a little more exciting in your glasses?"

They both thrust their wineglasses at me and chorused, "*¡Sí, sí!*" Loved it! Fuck, man. Maya, you are so yesterday!

I ferried their glasses over to Susan and set them on the table. "Could I get a little more of the Sea Smoke, sweetheart?" Ever since the film had been released their tasting room business had gone through the roof. You couldn't get into their wine club, even if you begged.

"No prob, Miles," Susan said. She set the glasses under the bar, discreetly filled them halfway up, and set them in front of me.

"Thanks."

"And don't write in your next book that I did this."

I laughed. "Maybe I'll play god and have everyone take their clothes off and start having sex."

"No!" she exclaimed. "It's already too crazy in here. I used to have a stress-free life."

"All right," I said jauntily. "Back in a bit for another hit."

I carried the Pinot back to the girls and passed the glasses into their waiting hands. Jack went out to check on Joy and my mother. I leaned my head in to the two Spanish girls. "Single vineyard. Very sought after by Pinot *vignerons*. Highly allocated," I murmured in a tone to let them know they had entered my inviolable world and were drinking something spectral. "Just don't let it out."

We sipped Foxen's Sea Smoke studiously.

"Oh, wow," said Laura, raising her eyebrows. "It's very different from what we've been drinking."

"This is nice," Carmen chimed in, a little too loudly.

I tapped a forefinger to my lips. "Stick with me," I said, winking conspiratorially.

A few moments later, Jack reappeared at my side.

"How's my mom doing?" I asked.

"Gal loves her wine."

"I know. Speaking of which. We need to be freshened up."

"Indeed we do," Jack said. He slung his arm over my shoulder and rubbed his beard against my cheek and slobbered, "You are awesome, dude. Awesome!"

I handed him my glass. "Tell Susan we want to try the Sanford & Benedict."

"Sanford & Benedict," he echoed. "Aye, aye, captain." Jack blustered his way through the crowd and bushwhacked his way to the bar.

"We're going up and up," I said to the two Spanish girls, adding, "Until we touch the edge of the vinous empyrean."

They laughed at the silly trope, though who knows whether it translated? I made a quick mental note to go light on the polysyllabics, wine having the unfortunate effect on making me go supercilious.

A stocky man in his thirties, red-faced, wobbling in place, picked up one of the spit buckets from the bar. Susan shouted at him, "Hey, hey, HEY!"

But the guy, with Neanderthal forehead and manifesting all the physiognomic characteristics of fetal alcohol syndrome, was on a mission. He staggered over to me, hoisted the dump bucket high over his head and shouted: "Shameless!" Then he threw back his head like a spooked horse and upended the contents of the bucket over his florid face. He wiped the spilled wine from his face with both hands like windshield wipers run amok, and grinned the grin of a farm-boy idiot. There was a brief, almost hushed, silence before the packed tasting room started hooting like a crowd of soccer hooligans.

Susan, accustomed to puerile imitations of that scene in the movie, had already, via cell, summoned help. Minutes later, in the ruckus that followed, a burly young man hurried in; his heavy work boots thundered on the planked floor. It wasn't hard to discern who the tasting room miscreant was–the guy's yellow shirt now looked like some hippie tie-dyed rag–and the vintner aide went right up to him, wrestled him into a half nelson and spun him around. "All right, pal, you've had a little too much."

When the Spit Bucket Upender tried to break free of the hold, a scuffle ensued. Some of the other wine appreciators in the tight quarters were jostled and spilled their wine on their companions' attire.

Jack handed me the two glasses that Susan had refreshed and said, "Sanford & Benedict as ordered," then hustled over to help the somewhat outmanned vintner aide. They arm-wrestled the Upender outside into the blazing sun and forced him to the hot dirt-and-gravel shoulder. The vintner aide gave him a stern upbraiding, and Jack, for good measure, booted him in the ass a few times. Upender's equally inebriated girlfriend got upset and started flailing her tiny fists at Jack. Jack grabbed her by both wrists and practically lifted her up off the ground in his attempt to calm her down.

"Rape! Rape!" the Upender's girlfriend screamed. "Rape!"

"You should get so lucky!" Jack shouted into her hysterical face.

"Jack's a man of action," I explained to Laura and Carmen. "He doesn't like violence."

Two more workers from the winery appeared to help roughhouse the obstreperous couple into their car. One of them reached into the Upender's pocket and stripped him of his car keys. "I'll call you a cab!"

Jack lumbered back into the tasting room.

Behind the bar, Susan resumed her duties. She wagged a finger at me. I shrugged, but she smiled to show she was kidding.

I turned back to Laura and Carmen, shaking my head. "Jesus. What's wrong with these people? Can't they hold their mugs?"

"This happen a lot?" Laura asked.

I lifted my glass of Sanford & Benedict and said, "The power of words."

They laughed until their cheeks were rosy as uncooked saffron and their eyes watered.

Jack extended his hand and I returned his glass. He looked at his forearm with an expression of disgust. "Fucking chick scratched me."

I examined his injuries. The arm was raked pretty good and fresh blood marked the wounds. "Not as bad as when Terra went after you."

"Let's not go there, Homes," Jack said, glancing over at Carmen to see if she was eavesdropping, the minor language barrier affording us some latitude.

"Excuse me, girls," I said. I zigzagged over to the bar and whispered to Susan, "Can I have that bottle of the S&B? I'll pay for it. I think I need to get out of here. For your sake *and* mine."

She produced the bottle, with alacrity, from below the counter. "On the house."

"Thanks, Susan. Sorry if I caused a stir here. Jack was the one who blew my cover."

"We're always glad to see you, Miles."

I picked up the bottle, turned and caught Jack's eye and motioned with my head to the outside deck.

Jack said something I couldn't catch to Laura and Carmen, and the two of them smilingly trailed him out to where I had indicated.

I placated the circle of people who had surrounded us by signing a few last autographs, then canoed my way through the treacherous straits of the burgeoning mob and outside, to join Jack and the Spanish girls. The wind had freshened, the sun was blazing in the cloudless sky, and hawks and turkey vultures were now swooping in baleful circles homing in on otiose rodents. I set the bottle on the wooden balustrade and Jack instantly grabbed it by the neck and refilled the girls' wineglasses. I stood behind Laura and, without thinking, splayed my fingers and combed them through her silky dark hair. She gave me a backward smiling glance, which I took as reassurance it was okay I had touched her.

My hand resting on her bare shoulder, I asked Jack, "Hey, where's my mom?"

Jack gestured with his wineglass to a knoll overlooking one of Foxen's splendiferous vineyards. I panned with his arm. Just over his extended wineglass, I could make out my mother sitting in her wheelchair, signature Gilligan's Island hat on her head, a glass of Chard glinting in her hand, appearing positively at peace with the world. Scampering around her was Snapper whom, I could hear, she frequently admonished.

"Where's Joy?"

"I don't know," Jack said.

"Excuse me a sec." I set my S&B on the picnic table and traipsed up the hill to where my mother had been wheeled. About twenty feet short of her I paused. She was staring out over the vineyard, nodding her head up and down, unaware of my presence, swimming in her stroke-addled, hypnagogic netherworld. There was something sad about her sitting there all alone. Then, too, she was out of that mausoleum, Las Villas de Muerte, she had before her a gorgeous view, not to mention a cold glass of artisanal Chardonnay, while reposing under the soothing sun. All her peevishness had been replaced by a profound serenity, the likes of which I hadn't seen since that moment she had gone out like a light on a dimmer switch and almost died.... She was going home.

Not wanting to startle her, I made a gingerly approach. "How're you doing, Mom?" I squatted to her eye level.

She turned her arthritic neck as far as she could manage, and a sad smile creased her face. "Marvelous," she said. She raised her wineglass as if saluting the abode of God, which was no doubt soon to reclaim her. Her face grew merry. "I'm flying with the angels. Whoo!"

I laughed. "It's a beautiful view you've got here."

"I know."

"What're you thinking about?"

She sipped her wine. "About how lucky I am to have you for a son."

I hooked an arm around her shoulders and said, "Well, I didn't like seeing you so unhappy in that place."

"I was going to die there."

"I didn't know what else to do, Mom."

"I know."

"I know you had a stroke and things are different, but I'm taking you home."

"That's such good news."

"Do you miss Dad?"

She lifted an arm at a forty-five degree angle and pointed a finger at the pristine blue sky. "Oh, yes. He's up there somewhere." She nodded to herself. "We had a pretty good marriage."

"Where's Joy?" I asked, eager to get off the subject.

"Oh," she said in a trilling voice. "Off smoking her Mary Jane somewhere." A look of sudden alarm clouded her face and she hunched forward, shouting, "Snapper! Snapper! Get back here."

Snapper had ventured down the hill in pursuit of a blue jay who was toying with him, dive-bombing and nipping at him, then elevating out of his reach. Several times he leapt up in the air, yipping excitedly, the cackling bird barely eluding his jaws. Hearing my mother's admonitions, he jerked his small box-shaped head in her direction and mindfully sprinted back to her.

"Okay, Mom, I'm going to go back down to the tasting room. You all right? You want to go?"

"No, I'm fine."

"If you need a little more wine, just ask Joy, okay?"

"Okay."

"We're on vacation," I said magnanimously.

"Oh, yes," she exclaimed.

I straightened up and started off. Halfway down the narrow road, I heard my mother cry out, "Joy! Joy!" I looked back and saw Joy materialize out of nowhere and minister to my mother. She took my mother's empty glass and headed in my direction. I waited until she caught up with me.

"Your mom wants more wine."

I laughed. "Oh, yeah. One glass and the trapdoor springs."

"She said you said it was okay."

"You have to monitor it, Joy," I said. "Okay?" But what I was really thinking was how I could keep my mother occupied while I figured out what to do with the Spanish girls.

We started down the hill together. I walked deliberately slowly because her stride was only half that of mine. "Give her whatever she wants. Within reason. She's had a hard life."

"Okay."

"You don't drink wine, huh?"

She shrugged.

"You like pot, huh?"

She smiled. "I drink wine some time."

"I can't smoke pot. Makes me too self-conscious."

"I have a medical marijuana card," she confided.

"Oh, yeah, for what? Just to get pot?"

"No," she said in a chastising tone. "I had a bad accident. A car ran over my foot. I was in the hospital for three months. At first they wanted to amputate it."

"Really? That's awful."

"I had like ten surgeries," she amplified. "I couldn't walk for six months. I stayed with my sister."

"So, are you still in pain?"

"Not when I smoke," she giggled.

I didn't know whether this was a positive or negative admission, but I was a little looped, so I squeezed her shoulder. "Well, you're doing a great job, Joy. We're going to hang out here another hour, then hit the road." I bent my head down so that I was looking into her eyes, but she averted her gaze. "Everything going okay?"

She grew a quizzical look and just nodded. When we reached the tasting room, I said to Joy, "Tell Susan you're with me and you'd like a glass of the Viognier. Make sure you get an ample pour."

"Okay."

"My mom will sleep it off on the way to Paso Robles." I patted her on the shoulder and sent her on her mission.

I returned to the deck where Jack and the two Spanish girls were seated around the picnic table. The wine had gone to my head and I was in an uncharacteristically touchy-feely mood. I eased down next to Laura and bumped my shoulder affectionately against hers. "Hey, Laura."

"Hey, Miles."

Her womanly nearness made me feel warm and fuzzy all over. I lifted my glass and saluted Jack. A beaming Jack toasted me back. Carmen, it seemed, had wriggled closer to him on the opposite side of the picnic table. I sensed that a colloquy between her and the lovely Laura had been conducted, in the event we should prove to be amenable to additional festivities. By their laughter I concluded we pretty much could do as we pleased. But I needed more time, and more wine, to suss this one out. Marcie would

have a hematoma if I canceled on the Paso event, but I'd bailed before–often
last minute with a crucifying hangover and a pack of lame excuses–"Brother
just went in for emergency triple bypass surgery" her current favorite.

I sipped my wine. The noise from the tasting room was resounding.
Cackling laughter would occasionally shear away from the thrum of inebriated voices. Twice I was interrupted by people demanding autographs.
I was surprised by how many people had brought my book with them,
reading passages as they traipsed from tasting room to tasting room. They
wanted to know if I was going to be at the Hitching Post later so we could
continue the party. The more I drank the more Laura's face seemed to glow.
This was my time, I thought, feeling my shoulder warming against Laura's.
Jack was right. Why hold back? I glanced up at the knoll where my mother
was basking in the sun just as Joy reached her and handed her a glass of
golden Viognier. My mother wouldn't know it was Viognier, but she would
know it tasted outrageously good. I suddenly found myself saying, "So,
you girls came all the way over from Spain just to do the *Shameless* tour?"

"We did," Laura said.

It flashed on me that I was repeating myself. I set my wineglass down
and slid it a foot away. "And where are you staying?" I asked.

They answered in unison, "The Windmill Inn."

"Oh, Christ," I said. "You really are doing the tour, aren't you?" I tried
to sound jokingly sarcastic, but Jack wasn't convinced. He frowned at me,
gave me the stink eye, fearing I was about to alienate them with my irrepressible sardonic wit. To allay his fears I added, "It warms me to the cock-
les of my heart that my words could have such a salubrious effect on such
lovely women from so far away."

Jack evidently had no idea what to make of *salubrious*, and my tone of
voice may have come off a tad disingenuous, or a little too mocking, so
he went on the mend. "What Miles means to say is that he couldn't be
more happier at this point in his life. Right, Miles?"

"Exactly," I said in a rising tone. "Could not be a scintilla more happier." But Jack had nothing to worry about. The Spanish Laura was exactly
my type. "So, Carmen, what do you do back in...?"

"Barcelona," Carmen said in her Catalan pronunciation so that it came
out sounding like "*Bur*-celona." "I work for an architecture firm doing
their, how do you say, their gardens and plants..."

"Landscaping?"

"Yes," she said. "But it's environmental. Good for the land."

I poured some more wine–where had it gone so quickly? "God, a woman who works the earth with her mind! Is there anything sexier, Jack?"

Jack smiled. "Nope."

"You know, it's too bad we have to be up in Paso Robles and you girls have to fly out tomorrow."

Now Jack frowned. "They don't fly out of LAX until late tomorrow, right, ladies?"

"It's a red-eye," Carmen said.

"Well, then maybe the two of you would like to come up to Paso with us." Relief washed visible over Jack like a thunderstorm bursting over a desiccated floodplain. "We're staying at this great little bed & breakfast. There're only four suites, and they're amazing, and I'm confident I can get you into one."

Jack was nodding nirvanically like a bearded Buddhist. The girls were making intense eye contact, locked in a dialogue whose language was composed of darting eyes and subtle birdlike expressions.

"Okay," Laura said. "That sounds fun."

"Great," Jack said.

I straightened from the bench. "Laura? You want to take a stroll with me and check out the Pinot grapes?"

She leapt to her feet. I held out my hand and she took it in hers. "Grab your glass." I raised my eyes to Jack. "Hold down the fort, Jackson."

"Will do, *Capitán*." He tented his forehead with one hand and mock saluted me.

I seized the near-empty bottle of the Foxen Pinot and escorted Laura away, toward my lair of drunken erotic fantasies. Over my shoulder I said to Jack, "Susan'll give you another bottle. Try their dry-farmed Cab Franc."

"We'll see you in a bit, Miles," Jack said, waving and smiling.

I ushered Laura down into one of Foxen's vineyards. Out in the open, away from the shelter of the main winery and the tasting room, the cooling wind off the ocean rustled the flora and cooled the perspiration that had our clothes sticking to our skin. It was late July and the gnarly, trellised and netted rootstocks, abundantly leafed out in canopies of shimmering green, rose above us as we descended between rows. Clusters of fruit the

size of a girl's fist hung nestled in the leafage, promising an autumn profusion. In the next two months they would swell to twice their size and
ripen to a dark blackish-purple, ready for harvest.

I didn't know what I was going to do with this girl. She was barely
thirty, more than a decade my junior. She had journeyed 6,000 miles to
visit the locations in the movie, spurred by a vivid imagination that the
film inspired, wanting to see where it all happened in reality. I sensed that
she was looking for romance and that, in her mind, it was her felicitous
fortune that she had stumbled upon the author of the book that had inspired her vacation. For a moment I felt what it must feel like to be a rock
star after an electrifying set.

"Do you have a boyfriend back in Barcelona, Laura?"

"It's LAU-ra," she corrected.

"LAU-ra. I love that pronunciation."

"No."

"No. How come? You're so beautiful." She was.

She shrugged. "I'm too busy."

"You're not gay, are you?"

"No. I tried it once, but I didn't like, forgive me my English..."

"Lobster nibbling?" I attempted to joke, but it didn't translate.

She looked at me strangely and I tried to maintain.

"So, you want to make movies?" I inquired, quickly shifting the subject.

"Maybe. Be the female Almodóvar?"

"Do you like his films?"

"He is a genius."

"I agree," I said. "What about Buñuel?"

"More than genius. A god."

Christ! "Hey, if I came to *España*, would you show me around?"

"*Claro*! You should come. It's a beautiful country. You speak *castellana*?"

"*Muy poco.*"

She smiled shyly."

"All right. I'm coming. That's not a threat. It's a promise." I pointed
my wineglass at her for emphasis.

We had reached the end of the vineyard grid. A patch of wild fescue
beckoned and I plopped down on my butt and elbows, the sky a vertiginous swirl of blue and drifting wisps of indolent clouds. Laura coiled

down next to me. I poured us both more wine. She sipped it with evident pleasure. I inquired whether she drank a lot of wine and she said she did, she loved wine. But since Pinot Noir wasn't indigenous to Spain and because *Bourgognes rouges* were too expensive she rarely drank any. "But this tastes a lot like our Riojas," she remarked, studying the wine in her glass.

"You know," I said, "some wine historians contend that when phylloxera decimated France in the mid 1800s and destroyed most of their vines, they took the Pinot rootstock they salvaged to Spain, where it flourished and was renamed Tempranillo."

"Oh, yeah?" she said.

At a momentary loss for words, I said, "So you like Almodóvar, huh?"

"Yes. He is a true *auteur*."

"*Talk to Her* was a brilliant film."

"I think I like his earlier films better. More..." She fumbled for words.

"Risk-taking?"

"Yes. Risk-taking."

Our eyes locked. Totally high on the Foxen grape, I said, "I'd like to write you a film, Laura."

"Really?"

"When I come to Spain. Maybe we'll write it together."

"I think you're drunk, Miles."

I sipped more wine. "Drunk on you, Laura." I leaned in and kissed her. Her lips were soft and pliant. We set our wineglasses down. Then we kissed again, this time more ardently. "I think you're the most beautiful woman I've ever been within five feet of."

"Now, I know you're drunk."

"No, seriously. And I've met Penelope Cruz."

"Really?"

"Uh-huh. I mean, she's pretty, but your beauty is... unique, *muy especial*. Okay, so I *am* a little tipsy."

She laughed and we kissed again. Then we stared meaningfully into each other's eyes. She really was extraordinarily beautiful. I wanted to make love to her so badly, maybe because I was still smarting from Maya's rejection, but I feared if my move was too aggressive it could blow the whole Paso plan. And that I would never hear the end of it from Jack.

I tore away from our lovestruck gaze and cast my eyes over the trellised vineyard. I could make out my mother, still parked atop the knoll with her glass of wine and frisky dog. She seemed content so I returned my attention to *LAU-ra*. "I can't believe we met," I whispered into her ear before kissing it lightly. "Do you think it's fate?" I nuzzled her ear again and spoke mellifluously into it. "Maybe I wrote my book so that a woman like you would come to me from somewhere faraway and make me deliriously happy." I actually meant it when I said it, even if all the wine had disinterred a romantic fantasy I pathologically kept hidden from women.

"Maybe," she said. She picked up her glass and took a sip. I sipped mine. The sun beat down on us. A native raptor cawed overhead. We locked eyes again. I wanted to say, "I really want to lick your pussy," but, instead, I quoted a line of poetry from memory: "'I seek in my flesh, the tracks of your lips'."

"That's Lorca," she cried.

"Yes. One of my favorite writers."

We kissed again, this time more passionately. She set her wineglass aside and lay down on the wiry grass. I eased myself on top of her. Her chest swelled and I wondered if she wanted me to take her then and there. Slowly, with my eyes fastened on hers–rejection be damned!–I unfastened the top button of her jeans. She made no move to protest. Wordlessly, very slowly, teasingly, I undid the other four until her panties were revealed, shockingly white against her light brunette skin. She fell silent. Her face was frozen into a kind of compliant smile. She may have been floored by my romantic patter, or she may have, well, just wanted to get laid in a vineyard. Then she looked up at me. In her unblinking eyes there was yearning, an attempt to read me, and perhaps a scintilla of danger stirred with lust. I stared into the dark passageways of her eyes as I concomitantly slid my hand into her panties, forded her silky-haired pussy, found the wet crease in her thatch of wiry hair and carefully everted it. Again, without receiving any remonstration.

"You're so wet," I said in a susurrus voice.

She smiled, threw her head back, then collapsed her arms and lowered herself to the grass and surrendered to my desires.

I massaged her clitoris with my forefinger until it swelled like the flesh of a raw mussel. She shut her eyes against the advent of pleasure. A gust of wind clattered the leaves of the Pinot rootstock and freshened our bodies. I kissed her. "You taste like *tapas*, Laura."

Her body rocked with laughter. "Oh, yeah?"

I kissed her lightly again, my left hand still gently massaging her clitoris. "Scampi. Pickled olives. Smoked paprika. Saffron. Seafood. Paella." In-between kisses: "I make an amazing paella."

"You do?"

"Yeah. It took me about fifty botched attempts to perfect it."

"You cook?"

"I love to cook."

We kissed again, this time more passionately, our lips deliquescing. I could feel her chest swelling, surrendering to me. She *was* a beautiful woman. Perhaps the most beautiful woman I had ever kissed. It made me want to kiss her that much more. I gently pushed my finger inside her and she moaned. I obliterated her moans with more kisses. My cock grew hard and struggled to escape my tight pants. I deftly unbuckled my belt and unbuttoned my jeans and swiftly brought her hand to my fleshy rudder. She squeezed it artfully. Her whole body leapt up into mine as if her soul were a succubus inhabiting me in my dreams and tyrannizing my unconscious. I awkwardly rode her tank top up to her neck and redirected my mouth to one of her exposed breasts. She had been blessed with dark, sexy nipples, the color of squid ink, and I could feel them distending against the flicking of my impious tongue. Her chest heaved against mine. Unrepentant, I licked a trail to her belly button. Her hand lost purchase on my cock and it staggered in the air like a sword stabbed in stone. I wriggled her jeans off to just below her knees and bifurcated her legs. I dissolved into her pussy. Her small hands reached for my head and clutched it forcefully as if fearing I would decamp for more conventional expressions of licentiousness.

"Pour some wine on me just like your character did in your book," she said, startling me.

I looked up at her. "Really? That's so cliché, Laura."

"I don't care. I want you to lick wine off me. *Por favor.*"

Her *por favor* made me laugh. I reached for the bottle, scrabbled to my knees, my cock still leaping around like a boom cut loose from the rigging, and straddled her pussy. Like a cellarmaster decanting the finest aged Burgundy, I tilted the bottle until just a trickle streamed into the Tastevin of her bellybutton. She giggled, as if undergoing some kind of pleasurable torture. I traced a trail of wine from her navel along the gloriously faint line of dark hair to the nearshore of her abundant pubic hair, then to the headwaters of her wetness.

She laughed all the way during the teasing liquid journey. When the bottle was emptied, I fell on her again with an unquenchable thirst for both the sexual thrill that the wine inspired and the vertiginous thrill of her midday al fresco nakedness. All, it appeared, because one day I dared to write a book that I thought for certain would capsize my "career."

"Oh, God, Miles. That feels so good!" Her voice rose and her spine arched and her thighs tensed and quivered. "Don't stop! Please."

I had no intention of stopping. Sex in the out-of-doors, especially with someone you just met, whether it be on a deserted beach accompanied by thunderous surf or in a ripening vineyard emitting its floral piquancy, is about as torrid as it gets. It was, that is, until I heard a faint, but familiar, cry.

"Snapper," the distant voice sounded. "Snapper," my mother wailed from atop the knoll. "Snapper! Come back here!"

Sensing something amiss, I hoisted myself up off Laura and clambered to my feet. I tented my forehead, shielding it from the sun, my cock hard as a hammer. I could make out my mother hunched over in her wheelchair, her arm extended toward the vineyard at the bottom of the grassy hill, calling frantically for her dog.

"What is it?" Laura asked, whiplashing from the cunnilingus interruptus.

"My mother," I said.

I didn't see Joy anywhere in sight and my mother continued to yell at Snapper, who was running around in crazy circles, chasing another taunting blue jay. Suddenly, in a moment of utter foolishness engendered by her stroke, she released the brakes on her wheelchair, clutched the handrim with her one good hand and dislodged herself from the precipice and started down the hill! In her demented determination to reclaim her pet, she picked up speed and charged down the slope, looking surreally like some handicapped Soap Box Derby contestant on a collision course with a trellised row of grapevines instead of a finish line.

"Holy shit!" I cried.

Laura scrambled to her feet. "What?"

"My fucking mother!" Bent at the waist, she was now halfway down the hill, trailed by a funnel of dust. I pulled up my pants and took off running, buttoning them as best I could manage in a full headlong sprint toward God knows what calamity. I ran tangle-footed along the perimeter of the vineyard until I came approximately to where my mother had launched her kamikaze pursuit of her uncontrollable dog. Careering into the vineyard, I ran up between the Pinot rootstock, the foliage slapping at my arms. "Mom? Mom? Where are you?" I called out.

I emerged on the other side, but didn't see her. When I looked around I saw Joy diagonally navigating the knoll in a frantic descent, slipping and falling on her ass a few times. I walked along the vineyard rows calling out my mother's name. About a dozen rows down from where I'd emerged I heard whimpering.

"Oh, Snapper, you make me worry so much," my mother was cooing to her incorrigible pet.

I found her about ten feet into the vineyard and closed in on her hurriedly. "Mom, Mom, are you all right?"

Strangely, as if in a dream, she lifted her wineglass, which she had tucked between her thighs, and took a sip. The wine had sloshed out on her death-defying plunge down the hill and she was more dismayed to think that it was empty than that she could easily have been maimed in the brakeless ride. "Can I have some more, please?" she said, squinting her eyes against the sun, utterly oblivious of what had just happened.

"Are you all right?" I said.

"I'm fine."

"What'd you do that for?" I implored.

"Snapper was running away."

"Jesus, Mom, you could have killed yourself!"

"Then you would have gotten your trust fund."

"There's no trust fund left, Mom. Doug spent it all!"

"I don't care if I die," she said petulantly. Or, possibly, truthfully.

"Well, I do. Not on my watch." I patted her Gilligan's Island hat. "I was worried. You freaked me out."

"I'm sorry."

"Do you want me to cut your wine allotment?"

"Oh, no."

I stared angrily at the panting Snapper and brandished a reproving finger at him. "It's your fault, you little devil. Do it again and I'm going to have you euthanized."

"Don't say that," my mother screamed. "He's all I've got."

I looked at her, incredulous. "Mom, *I'm* all you've got."

"You're not always there for me."

"What're you talking about? Okay, so maybe we weren't very close when I was growing up, but that doesn't mean I'm some heartless bastard. I'm fucking taking you back to Wisconsin."

"Because you want to get rid of me! And watch your language."

"Want to get rid of you? If I wanted to get rid of you I wouldn't have called 911 when you had your congestive heart failure. You had died, Mom, and gone to heaven. I made that call and they brought you back. I'm the reason you were sitting on that beautiful knoll with an expensive glass of wine in your hand a moment ago." I shook my head. "You think I wanted to go on this journey? Take you and Joy and Snapper all the way to Wisconsin? If you thought about it for one second–if *I* thought about it for one second–you would have to conclude I had one foot in the loony bin!" I lowered my voice to a more conciliatory register. "And all I ask is that you not do crazy shit! Otherwise I'm going to have to lock you in your hotel room with Joy and that"–I pointed at Snapper–"stupid animal."

"He is not stupid," she said, breaking into tears.

I exhaled a sigh and knelt in the dirt beside her chair. "Look, Mom, I know only half your brain is working. But that pretty much sums up half of the people in this country. Especially those nincompoops in Washington. So, to me, you're almost normal. I mean, what possessed you to release the brakes on your chair? You could have gotten a WUI?"

She looked at me quizzically. "Huh?"

"Wheelchairing under the influence."

She chuckled. "Oh, no."

"Look, Mom, we have a long way to go. I want to have fun on this trip, just like you. I'm doing my best. Okay?"

"I know," she said, suddenly contrite.

"So, no more reckless wheelchairing or I'm going to turn this thing around and deposit you back in Las Villas de Muerte."

"I'll be good."

"Okay."

Joy found us in the vineyard. Seeing my mother none the worse for wear, she searched me for an explanation.

"She's okay," I told her.

"I'm sorry. It's my fault," she said matter-of-factly.

"It's not your fault, Joy," I said.

My mother crooked her forefinger at me and said, "What's that on your face?"

Remembering suddenly the wine-infused cunnilingus, I wiped my mouth with the back of my arm a couple of times to tidy up.

"And how come your buttons are undone?" my mother asked, jabbing her finger at my crotch.

I glanced down and noticed that I had managed only half the fly on my jeans. I quickly remedied the oversight, but not before a bedraggled Laura materialized in the vineyard, running her fingers through her straggly hair.

Snapper, sniffing something that made him–and hetero men everywhere in the world!–go crazy, ran up to her and started leaping up and trying to get a closer whiff of her forbidden, and now redolently ripe, fruit.

"Snapper. Stop that," my mother scolded.

Snapper darted back to my mother, lifted his leg and urinated on her wheelchair, then leapt up into her lap with the agility of a bullfrog.

"Mom, this is Laura. I met her in the tasting room."

"Did you drink from the wine bucket?" my mother screeched.

"No, Mom. I didn't drink from the spit bucket. I spilled a little wine when I saw you flying down the hill. I still can't believe you did that." I burst out laughing at the recollection of my mother hurtling down the knoll in her wheelchair in her death-defying pursuit of her dog. "Jesus–fucking–Christ. If you want to commit suicide, let's go to a gun shop and put you down properly!"

Laura and Joy exchanged raised eyebrows, unaware that my mother and I were comfortable with this sort of macabre badinage.

"Watch your language," my mother reproached. "He's watching." She pointed to the hot blue sky.

I looked up where she was looking and said histrionically, "Sorry, God." Then I looked back down at her. "All right, let's get you back." I clutched

the handlebars on the wheelchair and spun her around. It took the
strength of all three of us to push her back up the hill. Now and then it
felt like a Sisyphean effort and, yes, admittedly, a part of me secretly
wished she had gone in peace, wineglass in hand, soaring heavenward with
her imaginary angels. But the woman had the proverbial nine lives of a
cat. She had survived two marriages, three rambunctious sons, a pulmonary embolism, a massive cerebral infarct, and arrhythmic heart attack,
and congestive heart failure. She was one tough old bird.

Gasping for breath, we finally reached the crest of the hill. I let a still-
shaken Joy take the reins. Laura and I hung back. When they were out of
view Laura wrapped both arms around me and hugged me tightly. Sometimes interrupted sex can make a woman cleave to your body in anticipation of deferred gratification.

"Will you come to Paso Robles?" I asked in an undertone. "I didn't
mean to be so forward. You just really turn me on."

She looked up at me with ardent eyes. "We said we would."

Relief suffused me. "Great. Because I really want to get to know you
better." I kissed her to demonstrate that I meant what I said. And I did.
"Plus, we have some... unfinished business."

Laura laughed, and we kissed again. "Okay, Miles, we come to Paso."

chapter 7

We decamped from the carnage at Foxen, leaving Susan an outrageously generous tip, and headed north in the direction of Paso Robles, meandering along the serpentine two-lane Foxen Canyon Road. The prevailing afternoon winds had sprung up and the local raptors were out tracing black, foreboding circles in the sky. More vineyards in full bloom fled past us like film through a sprocketless projector that would not turn off. In the rearview mirror I could make out the royal blue Toyota FJ Cruiser, Laura and Carmen aboard, right on our tail. It hadn't been much of a decision for them. We were all high on wine and once I convinced them that they'd have no trouble making their midnight flight out of LAX the next day, they were up for more adventure.

In a low voice so my mother and Joy couldn't hear, I told Jack about going down on Laura in the vineyard and her nearly coming just at the moment my mother careered down the hill. Jack laughed so hard tears reddened his eyes.

"How was she?" he asked.

"Fucking hot." I lowered my voice even more. "She's got hair all down the inside of her thighs. Positively animalian." I raised my voice again. "Plus, she knows a lot about film and literature. Super-bright chick."

"There you go," Jack said.

"Yeah, but she lives in Spain."

"You like Spain. Maybe after this trip you should move there, shack up with her, and write that next book you're all brain-crippled about."

"I told her I wanted to come. But I didn't tell her about my flying issues. How am I going to get there? That's a fourteen-hour sustained panic attack."

"I'll fly with you, dude."

"How about you and Carmen? Is there a spark there?"

"I think the chick wants me," Jack said, a self-satisfied grin archly planted on his face. He patted his stomach. "Despite the belly."

"She wants Jake."

"Jake. Jack. Who gives a shit? What's your line: 'sometimes reality is more fiction than fiction'?"

"Yeah." I motored down my window. The air was warm, and fragrant with the odors of the indigenous flora. I shot a backward glance and found my mother with her head cocked to one side, fast asleep, lightly snoring, the wine having served as anesthesia. Joy sat dutifully next to her, her eyes trained out the window, enraptured by the passing countryside. Snapper lay in the shape of a comma on the rubber-matted floor, napping by his food bowl.

"Why don't we pull over?" Jack suggested. "Laura can ride with you and I'll ride with Carmen."

"Better if my mother doesn't know they're coming with us to Paso."

"Dude, she already knows. She may only be firing on three cylinders, but half an engine still puts her in the upper twentieth percentile."

"I don't want you pulling over and hitting tasting rooms and doing Carmen on some country road and then losing the trail."

"I know where we're going," Jack, pussy on the brain, argued. "And I'm not going to do her in the car. What do you think this is? A frat party?"

"It's only a few hours to Paso. Let's just mellow out until we get there."

Jack produced two plastic cups, defiantly poured them half-full out of the bottle he had cadged from Foxen and handed one to me. It tasted divine. And I desperately needed divinity after my mother's headlong plunge toward oblivion. I could just see the headline: "Author's Mother Perishes in Freak Wheelchair Vineyard Accident—Wine Involved."

"Don't let my mom see it," I whispered to Jack.

"No problem, short horn."

Jack glanced out the rear window. "Chicks are right on our tail."

"Did you think they were going to ditch us?"

"It's happened."

We wended our way back to the 101 past an apparent infinitude of lush green vineyards and rollercoastering rangeland. There was something so pacific in these untrammeled vistas that an unaccustomed serenity fell over me.

We finally reached the freeway. I exhorted a grumpy Jack to cork the Foxen and stow the sippy cups under the seat. We peeled off on the north onramp and sped in the direction of Paso Robles, Laura and Carmen right behind us, as if their Toyota were on an umbilical cord connected to our Rampvan. God, I thought, a little Pinot in the mid-afternoon, a woman who is a vision of pulchritude *and* desires me, blue skies, nowhere to be, no clock to punch, no baleful employer, my best friend in the world next to me cracking me up and laughing again as if he–we!–had no cares in the world... why wasn't I happy?

"This celebrity thing is weird," I muttered to Jack, growing philosophical.

He turned and looked at me. "How so?"

"Well, I was nowhere, nearly homeless, as you know, and suddenly one book, one movie, and I'm hoisted to some ethereal plane where everything seems sort of Barmecidal."

"What the fuck? Jesus, Miles, you should have to go one week and only use words with less than three syllables."

"Fewer. But don't tell me you don't know the meaning of *Barmecidal?*"

"Bar, definitely. Homicidal. I'm getting there!"

I laughed. "Anyway, means the illusion of abundance. Barmecide was a nobleman in *The Arabian Nights* who served an imaginary feast to a beggar."

"Why?"

"To mess with his head. Same reason rich people do most of the shit they do."

"Asshole!" Jack snarled.

"Anyway, I'm just worried I'm at that illusory feast and soon I'm going to be that indigent beggar. I'm already dreaming about it. My unconscious is fatalistically conditioning me for The Fall!"

"Just go with it, Miles. Try to enjoy the moment and not get all tangled up in your fucking intellectual psychoanalyses."

"I'm trying to. But I'm wondering if I'm getting away from my true self. I mean it's sort of an out-of-the-body experience to go into these

tasting rooms that the movie, instigated by me, made famous, and see
all these amateur wine enthusiasts with my book, crammed together
swilling like they're on the eve of the Apocalypse. Then doing all kinds
of crazy shit like that guy back at Foxen." I shook my head to myself.
"Then you meet some pretty girl and a half-an-hour later you're licking
her pussy in a vineyard. It's like something you would make up to impress
your friends at a party or something and no one would believe you."

"Well, believe it," Jack said. "Because it's all happening right now."

"But we both know it's fleeting. Look at you. Seven years ago you were
a hot TV director, and now look..." I cut myself off, not wanting Jack,
who was feeling momentarily liberated from the onuses of his life, to sink
into a miasmic depression.

"I'm a loser now, is that what you're saying?" Jack countered in a voice
tinged with hurt.

"No. You're the same Jack, but your circumstances have obviously dramatically changed. And mine will, too. This won't last forever. You know that."

"Well, you can choose to enjoy it while it does last, or just let all this fun
pass you by and then five years from now regret that you didn't partake."

"Yeah, but my overriding question is: am I losing the person who created all this celebrity in the first place? You know my famous adage: what
you're doing is what you're becoming..."

"... And what you've done is what you've become. Yeah, yeah, yeah.
Boo-hoo."

"Yeah, but tell me, am I becoming just some wine whore? Propped up
to promote a product? You think it's enviable–and I suppose in some ways
it is: the women, the hard-to-find artisanal wines suddenly there when you
want them–but I'm afraid the ground is foundering under me. And I'm
afraid that I'm medicating myself with wine to numb myself to all these
concerns. I mean, I should be back in Santa Monica writing right now."

"Miles. Look in the rearview mirror." He adjusted it for me. "What do
you see?"

I could make out LAU-ra and Carmen laughing and bouncing up and
down to music we couldn't hear. "Happy girls."

"Hap-py girls! Ex-actly! Fun, Miles." He closed his hand into a fist and
rubbed it against my unshaven cheek. "Have you forgotten our little conversation the other night?"

"The live-for-the-moment lecture?"

"That's right, dude. Live for the moment. Because all your brilliant Jungian insight isn't going to mean shit when that blood clot rockets to your brain."

I nodded, unconvinced.

Jack tacked. "And this trip isn't without purpose. You're doing a very humanitarian thing. You're taking your poor mom to live with her sister."

"My poor mom who didn't even want to have kids," I reminded him.

"Whatever. She needs you now. And you're coming through, man. I wouldn't want to be in that place where she was living. That's no life. You're fucking saving her from a fate worse than death."

"I guess," I said, the wine starting to wear off and a low-grade depression burrowing into me like a pernicious corn weevil. "But all the women. I mean, I could be sleeping with a different woman every night."

"Why don't you?" Jack said.

"Because that's not what I'm looking for. It takes a lot of effort. Plus, I'm worried I'll get jaded. I sometimes wonder if I'm only going to be able to get off if I start doing some really kinky shit to them like that famous actor whose name we won't mention who could only get off by peeing on them in showers and then masturbating on their faces."

"Who was that?" Jack asked.

"Sorry, Jackson. I can't really divulge the name because it would compromise the woman who was the recipient of his kinky fantasy."

"I don't really want to know anyway." He looked at me and mused, "How the hell did we get to golden showers?"

We rode in silence for a while. I glanced back several times at my mother and Joy. My mother was still snoring in her chair. Snapper, in tune with my mother's wine-induced slumber, slept at her feet. When she had been released from the hospital after her stroke and returned to her condo, her dog had kept her company in the desolate stretches when she was all alone. In the process she had so anthropomorphized the little monster she was practically married to him.

"How're you doing, Joy?" I asked in a voice low enough not to wake my mother, who would immediately clamor for a pit stop.

Joy turned and looked at me. "I'm fine."

"Are you having fun?"

She pointed out the window with one of her diminutive fingers and said, nodding, "Beautiful scenery."

"Central California. Yeah, it's very beautiful. Still somewhat undiscovered. I bet you could find work up here easily. You're really good at what you do. And I appreciate your patience with my mom." I pointed a finger at her in mock reproof: "But you've got to be a bit more vigilant with that little devil there." I shifted my gesticulation to Snapper, whose ears suddenly straightened and his eyes popped open—as if he heard *and* understood me!

"I will," she said. "I promise."

In the tiny town of Templeton, just south of Paso Robles, following our trusty GPS, we took the Las Tablas Road turnoff, rode a few miles, then hung a right on Vineyard Drive, a winding stretch of ten miles that coursed tortuously through beautiful, opulent vineyards and towering trees, until we came to Justin Winery, a beautiful tract of wine property. A lot of money had been poured into the place by the owners, who I was informed were out of town. Their palatial estate stood sentinel on the highest knoll. All it was lacking was a moat and guards patrolling with automatic weapons and they could have weathered a natural disaster, swilling the finest wines and guffawing at the chaos the world had been plunged into. My kind of life!

Jack and I tumbled out of the Rampvan. Joy roused my mother, who spluttered awake, and then wheeled her out after Jack and I had dutifully extended the ramp from the van's undercarriage. Behind us, Laura and Carmen braked to a halt, climbed out of their rental and stretched their hands, fingers splayed, to the sky. Their armpits were shaded with hair. I glimpsed wild boar stampeding in their dark eyes.

Laura came up to me. "It's so beautiful here, Miles."

"Not as beautiful as you... LAU-ra." I raked a hand through her lustrous dark hair. "I'm so glad you decided to come."

She smiled. It *was* beautiful. All you could hear was the sonorousness of birdsong emanating from the wooded surroundings. The atmosphere was a hothouse of redolent plant smells and the hum of an ungoverned insectary. It was a sweltering afternoon, but I could already begin to feel the cooling air rushing in from San Simeon, streaming off the chilly Pacific. I felt refreshed, rejuvenated, invigorated. God, it felt good to be out of LA.

"Mom, this is Laura–whom you met–and her friend Carmen. They've come up to see me speak tonight," I properly introduced the lovely Spanish pair.

My mother, still groggy from the wine at Foxen, shook their hands and fortunately didn't say, in her unrepressed way, anything that would alienate them. Since her stroke, she had a disconcerting habit of expressing exactly what was on her mind, uncensored, unbowdlerized. After shaking their hands she looked all around her and drank in the beauty of Justin's property. She pointed that gnarled finger of hers at the sky, as she was wont to, and rhapsodized, "Oh, this is to die for, Miles. Why can't I move here?"

"Because you're going to live with your sister in Wisconsin."

"Oh, that's right," she said obliviously, as if she truly had just awakened to the point of the trip.

"Besides, you'd be drunk on wine all day. Because that's all they have here, Mom, is wine and more wine."

"Oh, don't make fun of me. You drink, too."

"I drink. You drink. We all drink for ice cream." Everyone laughed, giddy with the exhilaration of having landed in a new place.

"Oh, stop it," my mother said. "You're being silly now."

I looked up and noticed that Joy had drifted off and was facing toward some topiary shrubs. She took a few blasts off a joint, snuffed it out in her little Altoids tin, then returned to where we were milling around, smoke curling wispily out her nostrils, a smile tucked on her face, the mood adjustment having been effected.

"Feeling better, Joy?"

She smiled and nodded enthusiastically.

A few minutes later, a middle-aged man with graying hair and a sparse beard that seemed to only flourish around his chin came out to greet us. An amiable-seeming mixed-breed dog trailed him. Snapper, now on a leash, barked like crazy, growing defensive at the sight of the much bigger animal.

The man affably introduced himself as the director of sales and marketing and said his name was Mike. He pumped my hand. "I'm so honored to meet you, Miles."

"Nice to meet you, Mike."

I introduced our motley crew, including Laura and Carmen. As Snapper and Mike's dog continued to yelp and sniff each other's privates I pulled Mike aside and said, "I know you only have four rooms in your bed & breakfast and I realize my publicist only booked two. But there's been a little change in the configuration of our party between Bien Nacido and here. Is there any chance that one of the others is unoccupied?" I leaned close to him and said in an undertone: "When my friend has sex he's so loud I can't concentrate."

Mike chuckled as he glanced at Laura and Carmen. "As a matter of fact, we kept all four for you so you would have complete privacy."

"Great," I said, clapping my hands together. "Are there a lot of people coming to the event tonight?"

"It's sold out."

"No shit. I haven't prepared anything. Now I'm nervous."

"Just be yourself."

"Easy for you to say. If I'm just myself it could end in pouring spit buckets over my face."

"Yeah, I saw that on YouTube," he laughed.

Chagrined, I wiped a hand across my face.

Mike patted me on the shoulder. "You'll be fine."

I broke away from Mike and approached Carmen and Laura, standing off to the side, puffing Gitanes. "You're in," I said.

"Is it expensive?" Laura asked.

"It's all comped," I said. "Won't cost you a *peseta*. And dinner's on me. Wine's free. All you can drink. So, put your traveler's checks in your money belts; they aren't good here." The girls looked at each other and shrugged. God, it felt good to wax munificent instead of sneaking Ben Franklins, back when there were any to sneak, from my mother's upstairs safe.

I went over to where Mike was chatting up Jack. They bore the same bearish features and each possessed an easy sense of humor, laughing frequently.

"Hey, Mike, I think we'd like to get settled in, take a power nap, maybe have an early dinner because my mom probably will be put to bed before the show."

"No problem," Mike said. "Let me show you your suites."

Being special guests for the event, we didn't have to bother checking in. Mike called an assistant who came and helped us with our luggage.

Carmen and Laura had the clothes on their backs—and not for long, as Jack, lips pressed to my ear, wolfishly reminded me.

The Just Inn, as it's known, consists of a block of two structures with four guest suites. They're gray, wood-shingled buildings engirded by dense vineyards that, now it was the middle of late-July, were leafed out in a profusion of variegated shades of green. My mother was in heaven. I could see it in the glow of her face and it made me happy.

"Pretty nice here, Mom, isn't it?" I said.

"Oh, yes," she said, as Joy continued to push her in the direction Mike was taking us.

"See, all that money you loaned me when I was broke didn't go to waste, did it?"

"Oh, no. I always knew you were going to hit the big time."

I laughed. I was in a good mood myself. Jack was in a good mood. Laura and Carmen thought they had stumbled onto Ponce de Leon's Fountain of Youth.

Mike led my mother and Joy to the Tuscany Suite, a 600-square-foot room done up in kind of a European style with tapestried curtains and a marble bathroom. Laura and Carmen were given the Provence suite, beautifully appointed with leather-upholstered chairs, marble-tiled bathroom and a sisal rug half-covering a gleaming hardwood floor. And Jack and I commandeered the much larger Sussex suite. It was a little frou-frou for me with its canopied bed and Provençal upholstery, but I wasn't complaining. All the rooms featured beautiful stone fireplaces. And even though it was the summer and stiflingly hot in the hills, I fantasized an image of a crackling fire, a glass of Justin's finest and Laura snuggled next to me on the couch.

I let Jack carry the luggage into our suite while I accompanied my mother and Joy into theirs to make sure everything was okay. My mother would never have stayed in a place like this when she vacationed. The height of her travel accommodations would have been a Marriott—or worse. When she saw her sun-dappled room she broke into tears.

"What's wrong, Mom?"

She had trouble voicing her answer. The tears choked her words. "I feel like I've died and gone to heaven."

"Okay, Mom, the restaurant opens at six-thirty, and I know you like to eat early so you can get your wine..."

"Oh, yes," she chimed in.

"So, Joy," I said, turning to her. "Get her bathed and ready by then, okay?"

"Okay," she said.

"Are you all right?" I asked. I was constantly concerned about Joy. This trip was a big undertaking, a huge risk for me, and I couldn't afford to lose her due to apathy, or worse. But the money I was paying her was ten times what she would be making at Las Villas de Muerte, so I had that to counterweight my worries. I leaned in close to her and whispered so my mother couldn't hear. "I'm going to try to make more pit stops so you can..."–I brought two fingers to my lips to pantomime smoking.

She giggled. "Okay. Thank you."

"Come here," I said. She didn't move, so I stepped forward and wrapped my arms around her and murmured in her ear, "I know it's hard taking care of my mother. I know she can be a real bitch at times. Just ignore her. She's had a massive stroke and she doesn't mean most of what she says. She's very needy. This is a long trip, but we're going to get there, okay?"

"Okay," she said.

"So, we'll come get you around six-thirty. All right?"

"All right," she said.

Raising my voice, I directed it toward my mother. "We'll see you in a few hours, Mom. They have a terrific restaurant here with a lot of tasty Chardonnays."

"I can't wait," she said, as she stared out the window at the vineyards.

I left the room and went over to the Sussex where Jack and I were bivouacked. In the capacious suite I found Jack sprawled listlessly in one of the mahogany leather armchairs. He had already opened a bottle of the complimentary wine. I must have been a special guest because the complimentary bottle was Justin's signature wine, the Isosceles, a Bordeaux style, a gold medal winner at some wine festival, with an impressively high score of 94 from some wine magazine. I poured myself a glass, kicked off my shoes and slumped onto the couch across from Jack who looked at me, grinning, nodding, his face already florid.

"You're living the life, Miles," he said. "You are living the life."

I sipped the wine. It was massive, still young, with a walnut mouthfeel of tannins, but had a softness to it from the addition of Merlot and Cabernet Franc that made it satiny, velvety. A beautiful wine. And although

Pinot was the grape variety I was hopelessly in love with, this was a wonderful palate change.

"You know," I said, "I wondered why they invited me to speak because Justin doesn't make a Pinot."

"You're the wine dude, man," Jack said. "All wine sales, except Merlot, are going through the roof. These people owe you. You're good publicity for them."

"This is quite a setting, isn't it?"

"Beautiful," Jack concurred. "I don't know how I'm ever going to be able to go back to LA and my shitty one-bedroom in Silver Lake." He shook his head to himself at the deplorable image that had suddenly blossomed in his imagination. In an effort to efface it, he drained and immediately refilled his glass.

"So, Laura's going to be staying here with me. And you'll be down with Carmen."

"I will be down with Carmen."

"Laura confided to me that Carmen hasn't had a man in her life since her divorce, so I'd go light on the grape if I were you. You don't want to disappoint her."

"Speaking of which," he said, setting his glass down. "Do you have any more of those Vs?"

I set my wineglass down, went over to my suitcase, rooted around in my toiletries kit, found the vial of Viagra, shook out three, then walked over to Jack and slipped them into his open palm. "These are a hundred mikes, dude. You're still young. I suggest only taking a half."

Jack dropped the three blue, football-shaped pills into his shirt pocket and said, "Okay."

I returned to the couch and my Isosceles and rummaged for my cell in my pants pocket. There were four messages. One was my publishing agent in New York beseeching me to come up with a one-sheet (synopsis) proposal for my next novel. It would be too late to call her back in New York. Besides, I still didn't know whether there was going to even *be* a next novel! The second call was from the indefatigable Marcie, wondering whether I'd made it to Paso Robles "in one piece"—knowing my penchant for getting derailed at tasting rooms and canceling events last-minute she had worked hard to set up. The third call was from my older brother. He was pretty lit up, slurring badly, and would never remember that he'd made the call. The fourth was–and I leaned forward when I heard her voice–from my ex-wife, Victoria. She was just checking up on me, seeing how I was doing, wanting to know how I was "holding up." Relations had normalized between us. I had e-mailed her about the proposed trip. She thought it was pretty crazy, but since she was no longer controlling my life and colonizing my unconscious, she ended with "whatever." Now she was checking up on me! Worried no doubt that I had gotten into another one of my wine-fueled adventures that was sure to end in disaster.

I returned Marcie's call. She answered on the first ring. "Hey, Marcie, it's Miles."

"Miles. Did you make it to Paso?"

"I made it to Paso. I go on in four hours."

"Good," she said, sounding reassured. "How's it going with your mom?"

"Everything's going great. There was a little mishap at Foxen Winery earlier today, but–"

"What?" she said, cutting me off.

"I don't want to go into it, Marcie. Everything's fine. I'll make the IPNC, don't worry."

"What about the AMEX black cardholders' dinner at Per Se in New York?"

"I don't know. I know it would be good promotion for me to hobnob with billionaires, but... but the Silverseas Cruise thing with me as the enrichment lecturer, keep that one on hold. After this trip I may need to get on a cruise ship for two weeks."

"Okay," she said. "Knock 'em dead."

"I always do, don't I?"

"And don't drink from the spit bucket. You don't need *that* kind of publicity."

"I hear you Marcie. No antics. Take it easy." And I hung up.

When I looked up Jack had disappeared. I heard the shower running. Jack was lustily belting out a tune I didn't recognize. I took a sip of wine, then straightened to my feet and drifted over to the picture window. The immaculately manicured vineyards stared back at me, nonpareil in their beauty. The pre-twilight sky was streaked with cotton candy-like clouds colored orange by the fading light of the sun.

I left the Sussex suite and sauntered out into the vineyards, wineglass in hand. When I was far away from everything I sat down cross-legged in the dirt. The ripening grapes were drooping pendulously on the vines. I picked a grape from one of the clusters and bit down on it. Sour; they would need more ripening, of course, before they were ready to be harvested. Wine is so complex, I mused. Thousands of experts and hundreds of thousands of amateur experts would rhapsodize or vilify the vinification of these seemingly simple bunches of grapes. But in the end, it was just these innocuous clusters, photosynthesis, rain or no rain, cool ocean breezes, alluvial soils, that produced these epiphanies in the bottle hundreds and thousands of miles away.

I studied the wine in my glass. Held it up to the descending sun. It was garnet-colored in the glass. My thoughts drifted to Joy's foot and what it must have been like to wake in a hospital and have a doctor inform her that it might have to be amputated. I felt sorry for her, and it changed how I felt about her all of a sudden. Next my thoughts strayed to Jack. His life had changed so dramatically in the last five years. He had journeyed as far as he could go to the other side since his marriage ended and sometimes I wondered if he wasn't slowly killing himself on purpose. I had trouble thinking about my mother. It was true what I said at Foxen that we had never been close. I realized suddenly that I didn't really know her. And though her stroke had hobbled her speech, her ability to ambulate, her memory, she was still a human being and maybe there was a reason she had survived the congestive heart failure, even though at the time I had chastised myself for having called 911 and summoning the paramedics to come in and save her life.

Reflection provided me no answers to these complicated life questions, so I hoisted myself to my feet, clapped the dirt off my pants and shirt, and walked slowly back to the huddle of suites. The fading light of the sun painted them in a golden hue, drawing me toward them like a fairy-tale realm.

When I entered the Sussex suite, Laura and Carmen, looking refreshed–lipstick, make-up, wet hair–half-filled wineglasses in hand, were there yakking away with Jack.

"Miles, where were you?" Jack asked in his now booming voice, fueled by a second bottle of Isosceles which he had uncorked in my absence.

"Oh, I just took a little walk. Trying to come up with something original to say tonight."

"Here, let me refresh your glass," he said.

I came toward him and extended my empty glass. He started pouring. "Hey, hey, just a half. I've got to give a talk in a couple hours."

"Oh, right, I forgot," Jack said. Then he impishly poured another splash. "Here's so you don't get nervous."

I backed away from him and eased down next to Laura on the couch. I looked over at her. Her eyes were flashing and she wore the most beautiful smile on her face. "How's your room? *¿Muy bonito?* Like you?"

"Sí."

I leaned into her and she pressed herself next to me and all my fears and anxieties about having invited her and her friend up to Justin evaporated. "Hey, Jack, did you know Laura is studying directing at the University of Barcelona?"

"No," Jack said.

"She's made a couple of award-winning documentaries, but she wants to get into fiction features. I'm going to write her a script."

Jack, feeling happy–the wine, the girls–said to Laura, "Miles is a great writer." He toasted me with his glass. "And the smartest guy I know," he added magnanimously.

"Coming from Jack that's not necessarily a compliment."

The Spanish girls laughed. When they laughed they were happy. And that made Jack and me happy. Happiness not generally being my forte.

"Hey, I just had a brainstorm," I said. "Laura and Carmen should come up to the IPNC with us and document this trip. What do you think?"

"Brilliant," Jack said.

I turned to Laura. "What do you think?"

Laura exchanged looks with Carmen, and they shrugged at each other.

Exhilarated by the wine, I said, "You've got Martin and Jake from *Shameless*, Martin's mother in a wheelchair, and a pot-smoking Filipina caretaker. And... and a Yorkie terrier. I mean, you can't make that shit up."

Everyone laughed.

"If we had more time," Laura said.

"It was just an off-the-wall idea."

"Miles is having ideas all the time, girls. I don't think he ever relaxes that big brain of his."

I raised my glass. "That's slowly shrinking."

Everyone laughed.

"What's your next novel, Miles?" Carmen asked me.

"I don't know," I said. "Everyone keeps asking me that. Maybe I'll do a Thomas Pynchon and disappear for seventeen years."

"You're not Pynchon," Jack said.

"How would you know? You've never read *Gravity's Rainbow*."

"I've read enough to know."

"What? Like five pages?" I turned to Laura. "Have you read Pynchon?"

She nodded. "He's, how do you say in English? *Impenetrable.*"

"Impenetrable! I agree." I turned to the three of them. "I want to toast Laura and Carmen. An unexpected surprise. Right, Jack?"

"Absolutely," he said.

Fueled by the wine, I added bombastically: "Are there two more beautiful women in the Central Coast?"

Jack raised his glass. "If there are, they've had a lot of surgery."

Everyone laughed.

At 6:15, we walked over to the Tuscany suite to gather up Joy and my mother. Joy had bathed my mom and styled her hair and sprayed her with a spritz of her favorite cologne and she looked ten years younger.

"You look nice, Mom," I said. "Do you have a date?"

"Oh, no," she said. "I wish I did."

"You have Jack and me."

"I know," she said. "I'm starving... and I need a glass of wine."

"Coming up," I said. "Coming up."

Together, the six of us trooped down a path of dirt and gravel toward Deborah's Room, Justin's on-premises restaurant. It's a small, high-ceilinged space with only a handful of tables. I wondered how it sustained itself with just the four suites on the property, as it would be a long haul for anyone living in the area.

The menu was very limited, but ambitious, with just three entrées. We all ordered the prix fixe with the restaurant's wine pairing. The wine list was small, but adequately represented the world, traipsing from Burgundy to the Rhone to New Zealand to California. They started us with a '97

Bollinger *Grande Année Brut*. My mother loved champagne, but she had
never experienced a vintage one like this. It had a toasty, yeasty, chalky
quality to it and it disappeared quickly with the six of us, so we ordered
another with the first course.

Then they moved us on to their reserve Chardonnay, a big buttery,
full secondary malolactic fermented wine my mother rhapsodized as
"the nectar of the gods." As we progressed to the entrees, we moved
into the reds. I was in an expansive mood, so, from the handful of
Bourgognes rouges, I broke ranks from the pairing selections and asked
for an '02 Domaine Mugneret-Gibourg, Grand Cru, Echézeaux, an
ethereal wine that had everyone exultant except my mother, who stayed
with her ambrosial Chardonnay.

"Mom," I said, to reel her into the conversation which Jack had been
dominating with apocryphal stories from our lives that had spawned my
book. "Do you remember the time you almost burned the house down
trying to make french fries?"

"I remember," she said, her face a little slack from wine.

"Phyllis, you burned the house down trying to cook?"

"My mom couldn't cook, could you, Mom? You could resole your
shoes with her roast beef." Everyone reared back in laughter, including
my mother. "Our family dinners lasted like ten minutes. Everyone just
wanted to get away from the table."

"So, how did she almost burn the house down?" Jack said.

"Do you want to tell the story, Mom?"

She shook her head.

"She put this huge pot of oil on the stove to make fries, then she went
into the family room and had a cocktail. Then, a couple more cocktails.
The next thing you know the pot of oil had ignited and the whole kitchen
was on fire. There was so much smoke we had to crawl out the front door
on our hands and knees. Do you remember that, Mom?"

"Oh, yes," she said. "I forgot about the oil."

"Mom, you burned down half the house because you were drunk."

"That's not true," she said. Then she looked at me with a pained expression. "Why would you say such a thing about your mother?"

"I'm sorry, Mom."

"Besides. We got a whole new kitchen from the insurance."

Everyone laughed and that seemed to mollify the slight tension that had sprung up between mother and son.

I put a hand on my mother's shoulder and gave it a squeeze. "I didn't mean that, Mom," I said in an undertone.

"I was not drunk," she said.

"Okay, I said I'm sorry."

She held out her empty glass. "Can I have another glass? You made me upset."

Feeling guilty, I refilled her glass without doing battle with her. Joy glanced over circumspectly. Now, I felt doubly guilty and reached for my glass of ice water.

As eight o'clock rolled around, a middle-aged woman with short-cropped hair and a friendly smile materialized at the table and reminded me it was close to time to go on.

"All right, let's rock-and-roll, it's show time," I said, animated by the wine.

My mother had grown drowsy. She tried to inveigle "just a smidgen more" of Chardonnay, but I wouldn't let her have it. It would have been unfair to Joy, who'd have to do bedtime with my mother half in the bag. I whispered to Joy that she should put my mother down and not bring her to the event because there would be more wine there, but that *she* was welcome to attend.

Outside, the night sky was speckled spectacularly with stars. Cricket-song chirred loudly, making me realize just how far out in the country we were. Guests had started arriving en masse and the headlights on their luxury cars were blinding, spraying the vineyards and the various winery structures and lighting them up.

Jack, Laura, Carmen, and I made our way over to the winery, laughing, cracking jokes.

We entered the winery, laughing, our arms around one another like a foursome of college kids out on the town. It was the most capacious barrel room I had ever seen. In the tenebrous light its arched corridors seemed to stretch to infinity. There was a large anteroom with a movable rostrum set up for me to speak. The crowd was already near overflowing, all of them sipping wine they found at the three tasting stations set up for the event.

The Justin PR person ushered me up to the podium. The guests, most of them wine club members who had ponied up $100 to sip Justin's finest and hear me tell saucy anecdotes about *Shameless*, broke up their conversations, settled into the foldup chairs and directed their attention to the rostrum. The PR lady looked a little nervous. Had she seen the latest humiliating YouTube post? She took the microphone and spoke into it: "All right, everyone, we're ready to begin."

The attendees collectively stopped their chatter and the room gradually fell silent.

The PR lady cleared her throat. "Tonight, we have a special guest. I'm sure most of you have seen the movie *Shameless*, which has had such a tremendous impact on the wine industry." There was a scattering of applause. "And although Justin doesn't make a Pinot"–she turned and gave me a mock reproving look–"and although we do use a little Merlot in our Cabernet varietals just as they do in Bordeaux, we feel indebted to the man who finally wrote a novel that celebrated our passion for wine. So, without further ado, I offer you Miles Raymond."

As I walked to the rostrum, wineglass in hand, there was an explosion of applause. I already had them where I wanted them. I adjusted the mike. I looked down. There were Laura and Carmen and Jack seated in the front row. Laura was beaming up at me. Behind her, a sea of waiting faces. And I had nothing prepared!

"Hi everyone. Thanks for coming. I really didn't think anyone would show." Laughter. I took a sip of wine to fortify myself. It weirdly animated me. "When I wrote *Shameless*, my life was shit. My mother–who is with us here at Justin, but in bed right now–had suffered a massive stroke. My younger brother brought her back home after a three-month stint in the hospital and then proceeded in just two years to gut her modest savings." Audible groans. "I then had to leave Los Angeles and the film business to go down and care for her. It was the start of a brutal two years, during which time I weathered my agent's dying of AIDS and my being divorced–deservedly–by a loving, supportive wife. Thus the character of Martin and his remorse over a wrecked marriage. Anyway, I finally crawled my way back to Santa Monica and my rent-controlled apartment, had to take in a roommate for the first time since college"–I shook my head to myself at the memory of yet another indignity–"and started writing." I paused for another slurp of wine and barreled forward, the crowd growing blurrier and blurrier in my vision. "I wrote a novel that got me a new publishing agent. He submitted it and over the course of a year we accumulated about 70 rejection letters–thus Martin's character of the budding author who can't get published. Then, with no money, having tapped out all my friends, the wolves nipping at my heels, in a heightened state of anxiety, I wrote *Shameless*." There was applause. "Wait a second. It gets worse before it gets better." Nervous laughter followed as I regrouped. I raked my hair back off my forehead. "We went out with it to both film and publishing. The publishers hated it, wrote it off as an over-sexed screenplay." There were some groans of discontent from the audience. "And the film world turned their noses up at it. They didn't know what to make of it. Two guys go where? Do what? That's not a movie. That'll never be a movie!" The laughter resumed. "Finally, ten months after it had been submitted to him, Dmitri Anton, the director, read it and called his agent and said it was going to be his next film. My new agent got really excited. Everyone got really excited. It was leaked to the entertainment trade papers. But… it *wasn't* his next movie. He went off to do something else. But the option money allowed me to breathe a little. Still, you know," I said, pausing to take another sip of wine, "looking back, being broke and in debt with horrible credit, I learned a valuable lesson"–I found myself raising my voice like some Baptist preacher–"You *can* rise like Lazarus from the ashes of your despair and destitution!" I took another, this time, gulp of wine. I was being more personal than I had intended, but that was my wont, *and* my Achilles heel. "There's an upside to bad credit, however." I paused for comic effect. "You're immune to identity theft." Roaring laughter. "And there's an upside to being so broke you can only afford the cheapest bottle of Merlot." Another pregnant pause. "I got really expert at cunnilingus." There was kind of a collective bemused response from the audience. "I was so destitute, I couldn't afford prophylactics." The cachinnation that followed was deafening. I looked down and Laura and Jack and Carmen were laughing so hard they had tears in their eyes. "How has my life changed? Well, I don't have to drink cheap Merlot anymore. They probably wouldn't sell it to me anyway after the damage I did to their industry." More laughter. I was on a roll. "And the Pinot people owe me royalties!" Laughter now crescendoing. "But I'm not totally down on Merlot. Anyone out there with a bottle of '82 Pétrus–100 percent Merlot–I'll quaff it like a sailor on shore leave." The laughter was infectious now. It didn't seem to matter what I said anymore. I was giving them what they wanted, surprised at my ability to turn it on without a script, completely extemporaneously. "Anyway, I could go on and on about my life before and after the book and movie, but I think I'll turn it over to all of you, should you have any questions."

A forest of hands shot up. The predictable queries came in a veritable avalanche. How long did it take me to write the book? "Ten years of drinking my way through the Santa Ynez Valley, nine weeks to write it up." Reverberating laughter. Why did Martin have to steal from his mother? "In the book he was flat broke and wouldn't have been able to go on the trip; plus, his mother was relatively well off. In the movie, she was middle-class and Martin had a job, so maybe it made him less sympathetic, I don't know." Was I happy with the movie? "Well, the movie won over three hundred and fifty citations and awards from various critics and awards organizations, and was a very faithful adaptation of my work–with a few necessary compromises–so, absolutely, I got lucky." What are you going to do next? I finished my glass of wine. "I'm going to sign some books and then go back to my suite that the nice people of Justin gave me with my friend Jack–who was the inspiration for the character of Jake–and these two lovely women we met at Foxen today who agreed impromptu to join us." Finally, in a rising tone: "I don't know what they were thinking. Did they read the novel?!" Riotous, eye-watering laughter. Even Laura and Carmen were jackknifed over in their chairs.

When it was over, the Justin PR lady led me to a table that had been set up in the cavernous barrel room and sat me down. My ears were still ringing from all the hilarity and applause. I asked her to bring me another glass of wine to gird myself for the book signing. The guests formed a line. It snaked all the way out the entrance and into the night.

The signing got underway. I tried to personalize all the books by asking them a little about their lives, whom the book was for. They crowded in on me, peppered me with more questions. Spouses and girlfriends flirted degenerately. Some slipped me their business cards. Other people–vintners, people in the wine world–slipped me *their* business cards, inviting me to this high-end tasting or an event at their winery where I would be the guest speaker. Most of the cards would be in the wastebasket in the Sussex suite the next morning. Some that held promises of obscene appearance fees I would pass along to Marcie to ferret through.

The book signing lasted an exhausting two hours. From time to time, as I grew more and more inebriated, I was asked to stand and take pictures with some of the attendees. Some women, uninhibited thanks to the liberal pours, unrepentantly groped me. One woman brushed her hand against my groin and told me where she was staying in Paso Robles, then passed me a business card with her cell number scrawled on it and implored me to call her anytime I was in town. Even though Laura was hovering protectively over me and had been introduced as the woman I had brought to Justin!

When it was over and the crowd had filtered out, my hand was cramped and I was feeling a little lightheaded. All who remained were a few people from Justin, the incandescently lovely Laura, Carmen and the thousand kilowatt-smiling Jack, lit up on wine like a Roman candle. I surmised the event had been a success, but it had taken a toll on me and I histrionically slumped forward.

"Are you okay, Miles?" Laura asked, hooking an arm around my neck.

"Get me the fuck out of here." I looked up. "I'm fine. These events just take it out of me."

I said my goodbyes to the organizers and the people who had helped put the event on, and then the four of us weaved our way back to the Sussex suite. Jack had cadged some more bottles of Isosceles from the vintner and proceeded to open one the moment we bustled into the suite. The windows had been left open and a slight chill invaded the room. I squatted down in front of the stone fireplace and lit a fire that was already set up with starter paper and split logs of oak. I shuttered the windows and sat down wearily on the couch next to Laura. As if she couldn't restrain herself, as if her passion for me had been building up in her all day and had reached an apotheosis at the event, she leaned over and kissed me ardently. I kissed her back. With the relief of the evening's being over I just melted into her like emollient equatorial waters.

Jack poured everyone glasses of wine. The collective mood was borderline euphoric: the sylvan locale, the event, my well-received talk–one of which I had no recollection!–the sumptuous wine, all free of charge. I was

delighted to see everyone so elated. As the fire grew into a warming blaze
that flickered lambently over everyone's faces, the three of them reminisced over the things I had said, laughing at lines they remembered and
I didn't. These events were always a blur to me in retrospect. Little white-
water rafting trips on acid.

"Well," I interjected at one point, "at least I didn't drink from the spit
bucket." And they all laughed. "But they probably wanted me to."

"Is that true," Laura asked, "that you once drank from the spit bucket?"

"It is true. It was exaggerated in the movie and it didn't happen in a
tasting room," I lied, "but rather at a private tasting. The oenophiles were
pretty appalled, but they joked about it for a long time after so I thought,
that's got to go into the book. And I'm glad it made it into the movie. It
gets a huge laugh. I love making people laugh. Tragedy qua tragedy can
be such a downer. But if you can meld tragedy with comedy, I think that's
the secret. Tragedy is leavened and mitigated by comedy. And comedy underscored with tragedy makes it less inane."

Laura's and Carmen's expressions grew thoughtful as I digressed, per
my wont, into my intellectual analytical mode. But when I glanced at Jack
I saw only a look of unmitigated consternation. He was slowly shaking
his head. I smiled back at him. I was so loaded on wine my smile was difficult for him to accurately interpret. Laura and Carmen didn't know what
to make of our facial signals.

Jack unlocked his eyes from mine and moved his hand to Carmen's
thigh. She smiled up at the big guy, semaphoring he wouldn't be disappointed. Laura still had her arm clamped around my neck and was leaning
her head against my shoulder. A strange thought flared in my besotted
brain: I'll ask her to marry me and move out to LA. She was beautiful–I
loved brunettes–educated, cosmopolitan. Could I do any better? Best not
to propose when drunk, I cautioned myself, but I was suddenly so assailed
by the loneliness of all the one-night stands, I really did want to marry
her on the spot. I exhorted myself to pull it together, not to go down that
mawkish road, think carefully of what would be lying in wait for me the
next morning when I went, "Huh? What? Did I say that?"

Holding Carmen's hand in his bearish paw, Jack stood and said, "We're
going to take a walk. Smell the vines." Carmen rose with him.

"Euphemisms aren't necessary, Jackson."

He and Carmen both laughed. Christ, I thought, she's almost as tall as him. Thank God they're not going to be in the adjoining room!

"See you in the morning," I said, waving.

Jack winked at me and then they were gone, their shoes crunching on the gravel outside.

Laura and I started making out. Between Lethean kisses she said, "You were really funny tonight, Miles."

"I was?" I said, pretending not to know.

"Really funny," she said. "But all those women coming on to you." She shook her head. "They have no, how do you say..."

"Conscience."

"*No tienen vergüenza. Sí.*"

I kissed her briefly. "God, I love it when you speak that Catalan Spanish. It's so sexy."

She blushed, then said, "How does that make you feel? All those women?"

I shrugged. "It doesn't mean anything to me, Laura. I mean, it's flattering. But, do any of them really want to get to know me? Or do they just want to go on this little ephemeral celebrity ride, then dump me when it's over? I'm just happy to be here with you. I'm happy that you and Carmen came up."

"You mean that?"

"Yeah," I answered, kissing her softly, but meaningfully.

"I can't believe I met you. It's so unreal I'm sitting here in this beautiful place with the author of *Shameless*."

"I'm just a guy who got lucky," I said, trying to infuse some modesty into the dynamic.

"No, you're not, Miles, you're a genius."

"Oh no, not the G word," I said. "I'll never write another book. Besides, I'm doubly lucky. Look at you."

She laughed, then pulled me toward her and lashed her lips to mine. I kissed her back. Her lips were soft and full. Her ardor was palpable. When her hand groped my thigh I instinctively thought it was time to refresh our glasses. I disentangled myself from her and said, "I'm going to go to the bathroom, then open another bottle."

"Okay," she said.

I navigated an oblique path to the bathroom. I took a pee, shook a V out of its vial, bit off only half, ground it up and moved it under my tongue for quicker absorption. We were going to be having sex—and soon—and given how much wine I had consumed, I was anxious not to disappoint. Besides, I had a reputation to uphold! Couldn't have it getting back to Spain that I had failed her in the sack, I chuckled to myself.

In the kitchen, I foraged around in the little Vinotemp that Justin had provided and found, to my amazement, a hard-to-find, small-production '08 Hilliard Bruce Pinot from the Santa Ynez Valley. I couldn't believe the way everyone was treating me. Currying my favor with special bottles like this, and all the rest.

I uncorked the bottle. When I turned away from the kitchen, Laura had slithered off the couch and was lying on a faux-animal-hide throw rug in front of the fire, which was now blazing away, tendrils of flame licking the flue. During the few minutes I had been gone she had some-how managed to remove her top, her jeans and her shoes and now lay contentedly on her side, in black bra and panties, her elbow propped on the rug and her head resting in her hand, staring contemplatively into the fire. With her olive complexion, the light emanating from the fire made her appear like some odalisque in a seraglio. The cigarette she had lit—she languidly blew smoke rings with her exhalations—could have been opium.

I sat cross-legged next to her and handed her the glass of Pinot.

"Thank you, Miles," she said. She took a sip.

"This is a really special bottle," I said, sampling it myself. "Impossible to find."

"Mm, it's good," she said. "*Muy intenso.*"

"*Muy intenso*, indeed." An explosion of Pinot fruit, even to my half-shot palate.

Bewitched by the wine and the moment, I traced a hand down one of her bare arms, gawking at her near-naked body. She was small breasted, and she had this hair that overran her panties that most American men would have found disgusting, but which I found sexy. "God, you're a beautiful woman, Laura."

She smiled. Then she inhaled from her cigarette and chased it with an-other sip of the elegant Hilliard Bruce. She locked her onyx-black eyes on mine and asked, "Do you have a lot of women in your life, Miles?"

"What do you mean?" I answered evasively.

"In your speech, you talked about the women since the movie came out."

"I don't have anyone special right now, if that's what you mean."

"Are you looking?"

I sipped my wine–shaking my head every time at how tremendous a Pinot it was–and shrugged. "I know that I'm not happy with this parade of women." I looked up at her for a response. She was staring down at me with blinking eyes. Those dark, thick Salma Hayek lashes. God!

"Did you mean what you said, that it was fate that we met? That you might come to Barcelona?"

My hand glided slowly down to the furry part of her inner thigh. I was a little embarrassed suddenly that she had thrown my words up in my face. It's one thing to utter them, it's another thing to have to affirm them. Not wanting to lose the mood, I found myself saying, "Yes, Laura. I feel like there's a connection between us. An inchoate one, but one nonetheless."

Her eyes watered a little. "Because I thought it was really sweet what you said."

"I meant it, Laura." I continued to stroke her inner thighs. "But you're only here one night."

"I know," she said.

"Let's make the most of it."

Our mouths found each other's in the fitful firelight. The Viag was kicking in and my cock stiffened with alacrity. I slowly slipped my hand inside her panties and it found a Pyrenees forest dark with mystery. I maneuvered them off, and in doing so found myself between her glorious legs. Unhesitatingly and unapologetically, I licked the inside of her thighs. She lowered herself to the faux animal hide. We were back in the Foxen vineyard now picking up where we had left off when my mother's daredevil feat to retrieve her dog had rudely interrupted us.

I brought her to orgasm four times in the course of the night and the next morning, twice by licking her, twice by the fire and twice in the comfy bed. In between we shared cigarettes and sipped wine. We confabulated about our shared passions for food, wine, film, literature, travel (okay, I lied). Now and then I complimented her on her body, the taste of her mouth and the odor of her pussy. Drunk, I held nothing back. I was an open wound. Every romantic fantasy, everything I ever wanted to say to a woman sober, every dream I had ever had about being in love, it

all came out in an unbridled torrent from my deepest recesses. And every
time we started up again, despite our weariness, it was more intense, and
I found myself wanting her more and more, wanting to express it like I
hadn't done in a long time. Was it because she was leaving the next morning and I wouldn't have to deal with the psychological mess my words
and actions would have engendered? Did I really mean the things I was
saying? Or was I just so lonely for a real love relationship that I was im-
personating someone I wanted to be but was incapable of becoming?
Whatever, she let me ravish her. God, it felt good to be making love to
someone I really wanted to be making love to.

chapter 8

Sunlight poured implacably through the blinds we had forgotten to shutter. I disentangled myself from the sodden limbs of Laura and thrashed out from under the tangle of the down comforter and stepped into the kitchen, nursing an 8.8 on my own personal hangover scale: Can you walk? Check. Remember last night? Fucking A'. Some ellipses? Well, yeah. Some overly amatory things uttered maybe regretted in the dawnlight? That, too. In the refrigerator I found a bottle of a local Zinfandel rosé. Still in a semi-fugue state, I uncorked it and poured two glasses and then tasted one for cork taint (negative), for Brett (negative), and sweetness (negative). Vinified in a very dry style–unlike all those millions of gallons of white Zinfandel quaffed by lonely, horny housewives in the 1980s–it could have passed for a fine, dry Provençal rendition.

As I turned to go back to the bedroom I espied a small picnic basket with a blue-and-white checked napkin draped over it, just inside the door. I went over and lifted it up by its bamboo-woven handle. A warmth and piquant redolence emanated from its hidden contents.

Back in the bedroom I found Laura propped up on a pair of gigantic down pillows, puffing languorously on a cigarette. I handed her one of the glasses of wine. Employing my smattering of Spanish, I said, "*Pelo del perro.*"

It hit me that "hair of the dog" probably meant nothing beyond the literal in Spanish. Whatever. She thought it was funny and laughed until tears came to her eyes.

I set the small picnic basket next to her and climbed back into bed.

"What have we got here?" she said, directing her attention to the basket. She lifted the napkin, revealing two just-baked cranberry scones. Rooting around, she found a couple of hard-boiled eggs, a slab of butter, cheeses, and an assortment of charcuterie. "Oh, this is nice," she said.

"Very European," I remarked.

She picked up one of the warm scones and bit into it. "Mmm," she said. "Have a bite," she said, extending her arm and offering me the scone.

"In a minute. My stomach's not quite there yet," I said.

After a couple glasses of wine my appetite miraculously returned and we enjoyed a delicious private brunch. I reached for the bottle on the nightstand and was a little dismayed to find it already empty. And Laura had only had one glass. Got to put the brakes on, I admonished myself, glancing at a digital clock that showed that it wasn't even 9:00 a.m.

"You know, Laura," I started. "Why *don't* you and Carmen come with us up to the Willamette Valley?" She furrowed her brow at me. "I'm serious. I was thinking about it in the middle of the night. You can fly out of Portland–it's a major airport–I'll cover the penalties, you're still on holidays for another couple of weeks."

"Carmen has to be back to work."

My shoulders sagged. Then, I brightened. "So, why don't you come up with us? There's plenty of room in the van. I'll buy a digital camera and you can document our trip. I'll pay you to do it. What do you say?"

"Miles."

"No. Seriously. Last night was just so intense. I really don't want you to go. Come with us."

She laughed at the suggestion. "Miles?"

"What?"

"I can't abandon my friend."

"Why not? She's a big girl."

Laura looked at me with sad, flashing eyes, as if she were considering it. But in my hungover state I may have misread her. Flush with money now, had I alienated her by offering–boorishly–to pay her? Where was my sense of propriety? No one had trained me for success. And sometimes my munificence came off as crass. No, it *was* crass.

I set my wineglass on the nightstand, slipped on top of her and kissed her. Only a few inches from her face, I whispered, "I meant everything I said, Laura."

"Miles, it's only morning and you're already drunk."

"No, I'm not," I weakly protested. "I'm just thirsty."

She laughed a sarcastic laugh, then grew serious. "Even if I do want to go, I don't want to be with you up at some big wine festival with all these women."

"They don't mean anything to me," I found myself pleading.

"Look, we had a nice time. How do you say, *un petit romance*."

"A fling?"

"A fling. Yes." She traced a finger across my cheek. "I think you're just lonely."

I rolled off her and reached for the comfort of my wine. Staring at the wood-beamed ceiling, I said, "You're right, I am lonely."

She propped herself up on an elbow. "I had a nice time. You come to Barcelona and visit me. Then I'll know you mean everything you said."

Her words struck me like a curare dart. She was right, of course. I *was* lonely. And fragile. The sudden realization of the weight of everything involving taking my mother to Wisconsin and trying to get through every day with increasing quantities of wine. She might as well have said: You need a mother, not a girlfriend. Of course I had a mother, but…

I turned and looked at her. "Well, I tried."

"You come to Barcelona and we'll have *un gran aventura*. Okay?"

I smiled at her. She pointed at the bottle of rosé. "And you slow down. You're going to kill yourself."

Then she kissed me and I kissed her back, the way you do when your partner is on the verge of leaving and you have that sinking feeling in your solar plexus that you probably will never see each other again. We were gearing up to make love once more when we heard the front door open. Footfalls sounded in the main room. Too light to be Jack. Knowing him, and how much wine he probably had consumed, I surmised he would still be asleep at this hour.

The steps approached the bedroom door and halted. A soft knock followed. "*¿Laura? ¿Estás se despierta?*"

"*Sí*," Laura said, quickly pulling the comforter up over our naked bodies.

"*Sí, está bien.*"

Carmen pushed the door open tentatively, checked to make sure she wasn't disturbing us, then gingerly entered. Her long blond hair was in a tangled mess on her head. She looked like she had walked ten miles in gale-force winds and slanting rain from a broken-down car. As she approached she wasn't walking very straight either.

She raked the snarled strands of her mane off her forehead and pulled a hand over her face, as if hoping for some magical transfiguration of her rag doll countenance (which never materialized). Her eyes were bloodshot, and gray pouches underscored them. She looked exhausted, like she hadn't slept but a few hours.

Laura switched to English. "Are you okay?"

Carmen glanced over at me. "Your friend, Jack, he has—how do you say in English?—a lot of energy." She shook her head to herself as if she had quite a long night. "*Muy fuerte.*"

Laura turned to me and translated. "A lot of passion."

A joke about giving him some Viag crested on my tongue, but I held back, not wanting to blow Jack's cover in the event he and Carmen had become instant soul mates.

I clambered out of bed and quickly knotted a towel around my waist, went into the kitchen and, still feeling a little depressed about Laura's impending departure, deftly uncorked a second bottle and poured another glass of the rosé—a full glass!—and brought it back into the bedroom and handed it to Carmen who accepted it with alacrity. She brought the wineglass to her lips and it wasn't a sip she took, but rather a guzzle, as if she had crossed an arid region and stumbled upon an oasis in desperate need of slaking her thirst. She paused a moment, then she drained the entire glass.

"*Faltado, gracias, Miles.*"

Laura and I looked at each other and laughed.

Carmen calmed and a glow suffused her still haggard countenance. She said to Laura: "*Pienso que debemos fequir el camino.*"

Laura turned to me and said: "We should get going. We have to check out of the Windmill Inn by noon and then get back to LA."

"I understand. I've got to get my mother and gang up to Fresno today, so..."

As I waited in the bedroom, Laura and Carmen shared a shower together. They returned, looking revivified and we exchanged goodbyes. Carmen left the bedroom for a moment while Laura and I kissed passionately and hugged in that way new lovers hug to reassure each other that this won't be the last time.

"I'm going to miss you," she said.

"You won't reconsider?"

She shook her head. "I can't. It's been fun. You fly to Barcelona. I will show you good paella."

"Okay," I said, staring into her dark, blazing eyes whose meaning I couldn't read. Was she really going to miss me? Or was this just another fling? Soon to be exiled to the dustbin of memories like too many before her.

She placed her index fingers over my lips to shut me up. "Goodbye, Miles."

Then she and Carmen were gone. I showered and dressed and poured myself yet another glass of wine. Then I called over to my mother's room. She, not Joy, answered.

"Miles. Where are you? Are you in the pokey?"

"No, Mom, I'm right next door to you. Did you get breakfast?"

"Oh, yes. It was fabulous."

"How's your tooth?"

Her voice lowered and she grudgingly said, "It's okay." My mother was not one to complain of physical maladies.

"Put Joy on, would you?"

My mother, barking instructions, handed the phone off to Joy. Her high-pitched voice said, "Hi."

"Hi, Joy. How's it going over there?"

"Okay."

"How's my mom's tooth?"

"Not so good. Her mouth has swelled a little."

I swept a hand across my face. "Okay, it's only like three hours to Fresno. We'll try to get her into a dentist today and get that tooth extracted. Did you get her bathed and everything?"

"Yes."

"Good. Well, take her and Snapper out for a little walk in the garden. I'll wake Jack and we'll get on the road in half an hour. Okay?"

"Okay," she said. I hung up, feeling anxious and relieved. Relieved, because Joy was a godsend.

I called over to Jack's suite, but no one answered. A few minutes later he came lumbering in through the front door. If Carmen looked like she had been in a hailstorm, Jack looked like he had been on a month-long bender. He was wearing green medical scrubs for pants and a vanilla-white Hawaiian shirt, dappled with large pineapples. His bushy hair was a veritable tumbleweed perched atop his head. The whites of his eyes were so red he looked demonic, a denizen-escapee of some pernicious netherworld. And—I couldn't help but notice—there was a bulge evident in his crotch that looked positively frightening.

"Give me a glass of that wine," he said, frazzled.

I poured him a glass, handed it to him, and he emptied it down his throat with all the intemperance of a sot in the throes of the D.T.s. "Fucking cock won't go down," he said, a worried look furrowing his face.

"What?"

"Won't go down. I did that chick like five times last night, came every time, and it wouldn't go down."

"I mean, not even like right after?"

"No. And I had like three bottles of wine beginning at Foxen."

"How much of that Viag did you take?"

Jack's expression disorganized into one of deep concern. "I don't know, I was a little looped."

"I gave you three. How many are left?"

"None," he said.

"What?" I practically screamed.

"I took a half like you said, then I thought I should take the other half, and then, I don't know, I worried because of all the wine that I was going to disappoint this chick which, as you know, can wreck a man's ego for life and"—he pointed a finger at his temple like the barrel of a handgun—"get inside his head and never get it up again. You know what I'm talking about?"

"Jack, those were 100 milligrams each. That's the strongest they manufacture. It's for 70-year-olds who haven't had a boner in ages and you go and take, for your age, a sextuple dose. Are you out of your fucking mind?"

"I was sideways, Homes."

"I don't give a shit. You know what you've got?–and, yes, I did bother to read the fine print when I picked them up from the pharmacy."

He looked up at me, his face dark with anxiety and fear.

"Priapism."

"What?" he barked.

"Priapism. It's a rare disorder where the penis will not detumesce."

"What's *detumesce?*"

"Go flaccid, return to normal. The condition's named after the Greek god of male procreative power, Priapus. The son of Dionysus–the god of fertility, wine, and drama, which pretty much sums you up. And he's the son of Aphrodite, the god of –"

"Okay, okay, enough with the classical mythology lecture. It hurts. You'd think an all-night hard-on with a hot chick would be my ultimate dream, but it's not." He reached for his groin, grabbed his leviathan of a shaft and tried–it was almost heartbreaking to witness–to squeeze it into submission. "Man, after she left, I did the knuckle shuffle and it *still* wouldn't go away. Maybe this'll help." He finished his wine and poured another glass, starting in on it without a pause.

I picked up my laptop, already booted so I could scope Fresno hotels and typed "WebMD.com" in the URL bar. In their search engine, I typed "Priapism." I scanned the symptoms and remedies.

"Okay, it says here to give it 4-6 hours, then if it still Eiffel Towers on you, go see a doctor. They'll give you some kind of analgesic. If that doesn't work..." I stopped and I could feel my eyes widening like Peter Lorre in *M*. "Holy crap."

"What?" he said. "What?"

I read verbatim from the online medical literature: "If the medications don't reduce the swelling a scalpel is used to make an incision in the head of the penis to release the blood that's causing the irremediable engorgement."

"They cut my dick?" he cried.

"Jack. You're 42. You don't, to my blissfully limited knowledge, have an ED problem. You Hoover down 300 mikes of a powerful drug that semaphores to the brain to send all your blood to your dick. 300 mikes. That's like declaring all-out thermonuclear war on your wholly hypothet-ical inability to get aroused."

"Okay, I fucked up, okay. Just shut the fuck up, would you?"

"Oh, you're blaming me because I'm your wingman now and was just trying to help you out." I got up from the couch and strode toward the kitchen. "Let's try this," I said. I opened the freezer compartment and found a pair of ice trays. I ejected the cubes into an ice bucket that the good people of Just Inn had provided. Once I'd filled it with water I brought it back to Jack. "Here," I said. "Stick it in."

Jack untied the drawstring on his surgeon's pants–I elected not to point out the irony of his being already in ER garb–and they collapsed to his ankles. He wasn't wearing any underwear.

"Holy shit," I gasped, getting my first, and I hoped for the rest of my life last, look at the beast. It was huge, thick as a sausage, vein-riddled and crimson from all the blood that had surged there. "That's a true Louisville Slugger, Jackson. All it needs is the insignia burned in. Bonds could have broken Aaron's record without 'roids with that thing!"

"Fuck, man, this is no time for joking. I'm serious." Jack slowly guided his cock into the bucket of ice. "Jesus, Homes, this is freezing!"

"Keep it in there like maybe thirty minutes."

"Thirty minutes! My dick'll turn into a fucking Ice Whammy!"

"No wonder poor Carmen was such a wreck. She could barely walk."

"I didn't *want* to keep screwing her," Jack explained, still wincing from the ice bath now enveloping his most sensitive organ. "I was just trying to get the thing to go down."

"You think it was fair to her to turn her into a fucking human spittoon to relieve your self-induced malady?"

"I didn't know I *had* anything, asshole. I thought if I could keep coming it would finally go down like it always does. But it didn't."

I started laughing, less at the situation than at his dismayed expression. My laughter grew uncontrollable. It took hold of me as if I were possessed and the next thing I knew I was on the floor, rolling around, tears streaming uninhibitedly down my cheeks.

"It's not funny, Homes! It's not funny."

I couldn't stop laughing. My rib cage was hurting. "Three one-hundred milligrams, dude," I sputtered between irrepressible laughter. "They probably only gave that high of a dose to chimps in the experimental stages before the FDA approval." And I collapsed back into hysterical laughter.

Jack was not amused. His cock was so rigid he had to use the force of his hand to direct it downward into the ice. After a few minutes he pulled it out and it sprang upward like a flowering agave, turgid, twitching with an otherworldly life force I had never before witnessed. "Fuck, it hurts, man. Ice ain't doing shit for it."

My laughter finally subsided and I straightened to a standing position. "Put that thing away. It's only three hours to Fresno and we got to get my mom to a dentist because her tooth is getting worse. While there we'll get you to a doctor. Hopefully, it will have gone down by then." Jack pulled up his pants but the bulge was shockingly blatant. He looked like a teenager ducking into a whorehouse. "What does it feel like?"

"Like the Space Shuttle with all the rockets fired but secured to the scaffolding that won't release."

"I didn't realize you were a metaphorist, Jackson. Beautiful trope."

"Fuck you. Let's get to Fresno."

"Sure you don't want to duck into the bathroom and try to whack it off one more time?"

"Jesus, Miles. Stop joking. I've got a medical emergency here," he said in a pained voice emitted from an even more pained-looking face.

"All right. I'm sure the doctors will know what to do. If they have to slit the helmet, they have to slit the helmet."

"Don't say that, Miles, do not say that. Fucking image has me freaked out."

"Carmen must have thought you were the greatest middle-aged lover on the planet."

"Chick hadn't been laid in a year. The last two I had to lube her she was so dry."

"You know, I would have thought this would have been your dream: a perpetual hard-on."

"It's not funny, Miles. It's not funny."

"All right, we've got to make tracks. Go back to your room and pack. Take some Aspirin. Give the Louisville another ten in the ice bucket and we'll come down and get you, all right?"

"All right," he said. He turned around clumsily, holding his massive erection with both hands as if he had been kicked in the groin by a black belt in karate, and tottered out the door.

I packed and then walked the short distance over the gravel pathway to the Tuscany suite to check on my mom, still bummed about Laura's leaving, still battling a hangover, three Motrins not doing shit for my sledgehammer-pounding headache, and now facing two potential medical emergencies. When I came in I found her stationed in the center of the room, slumped in her wheelchair, her elbows on the armrests. Joy was sitting on the couch reading a trashy entertainment magazine. I approached my mother, who wore a sullen expression. The right side of her lower jaw was visibly swollen. She was fingering it as if testing it, hoping that it might go away of its own volition.

With a look of concern, I said, "We're going to get you to a dentist in Fresno, Mom. Okay?"

"No," she barked. "They'll want to hospitalize me."

"For an infected molar?"

"Everything has to be done in a hospital," she wailed.

"Why?"

"Because of all the medications I'm on."

"Well, we'll see about that." I stood and addressed Joy. I rooted the car keys out of my pocket and handed them to her. "Get packed up and get my mom in the van and I'll go gather up Jack."

She set her magazine aside, rose from the couch and accepted the keys. "Okay. We're all packed."

I don't know if it was the wine, the pressure of now having two injured parties on the road or what, but I came toward her and enveloped her in my arms. "I really appreciate everything you're doing, Joy. You're a champ." I released her quickly so she wouldn't misinterpret my gesture.

She giggled. The marijuana aroma haloed her face. I didn't disclose Jack's affliction. I doubted they, being women, would want to hear about permanently turgid penises and an explanation of the rare condition known as priapism.

I went over to the Provençal suite to check up on Jack. He was sitting on the couch, his colossal erection plunged into an ice bucket he had fashioned from the bathroom wastebasket. I tried not to laugh. He looked over at me and shook his head grimly. I placed a hand on his shoulder and said, "How's it going? Any improvement?"

"Fuck, man. It hurts." He pulled his cock out of the ice bath. It was now a reddish-blue from the cold water immersion. When he let go of it it sprang to the ceiling like a startled bullfrog leaping off a rock.

"Jesus Christ, Jackson," I said empathetically. He looked at me with his face pinched in pain. I squeezed his shoulder. "We're going to take care of it in Fresno. Fresno is going to be our city of Lourdes!"

"They're not going to slit my helmet, are they?" he said, tears springing to his eyes.

"No, man. They got fucking meds for this. With all the Viag and Cialis out there, this has got to be like LSD meltdowns in the '60s. Come on, get dressed, get packed up, let's blow this winery."

Jack, still clutching his priapic member, joined us in the van. He had a half bottle of wine with him and a full pour in a plastic cup. He tilted the bottle but I waved him off. "Obviously, I'm going to be doing the driving today, and I've already had a little bit this morning," I said in a lowered voice so my mother wouldn't hear.

I gave a backward glance toward her. She was massaging the right side of her jaw. I turned away, started the car and drove along the gravel drive-way and braked to a stop at the reception building. Inside, I asked for the PR person who was summoned by the young girl at the front desk. She came out a moment later, all smiles.

"You were great last night, Miles. Thank you for coming. Anytime you want to stay with us, just give me a call, okay?" she offered, slipping me a business card.

"I will, I promise. Thank you for your hospitality."

We drove down the winding, oak-shaded single-lane road in the di-rection of Paso Robles. We connected onto the 46-East at the 101 cloverleaf and started on the Fresno leg of our journey. When my mother learned that we were heading to Oregon she requested a detour to visit her brother Bud, whom she hadn't seen in years. Jack had had no beef with it then, but now that he was in pain, the extra stop caused him to grouse.

"Do we really have to stop to see your mother's brother?"

"Yes," I said. "It's probably going to be the last time she sees him."

"That's one butt-ugly drive, and one depressing city."

"I know," I said. "I know."

From the 46 we connected to the 41, a two-lane rural highway. We
passed through postage stamp-sized towns with eccentric names like Shan-
don and Reef Station. My mother, on a potent dose of diuretics, had to
go to the bathroom frequently. Each stop, Jack and I would hang back as
Joy wheeled her into a convenience store bathroom so she could do her
business. While she did, Joy would always pop back outside and take a
few hits from her half-smoked blunt. Jack was still in pain, the erection
wasn't ebbing, and I think he was starting to grow anxious about seeing
a doctor to get it taken care of.

"Is the wine helping?" I ventured.

"A little," he said. He glanced over at Joy who averted her gaze. "Maybe
I need some med Mary."

"Don't mix wine and pot," I advised, "you'll get the spins."

"Yeah, probably." Then, his thoughts turning to me, he observed, "You
seem a little down."

"Yeah, I was bummed when Laura left."

"You kind of fell for her, didn't you?"

I shrugged. "I guess."

"There'll be way more in the Willamette."

I turned to him and said. "Right now, for some reason, that's not a
consolation."

"Sorry." He looked away. "You really did fall hard for her. I haven't
seen you like this since the Maya period."

I stared straight out the front windshield at the desolate road ahead,
nodding noncommittally in response.

We got off Highway 41 at the I-5 junction in Kettleman City, a barren,
depressing way station with a population under 1,500. We stopped for
lunch at a joint called Mike's Roadhouse Café only because it looked a
cut above the fast-food franchises that defaced the dilapidated town. The
exterior was done in a kind of Western-style with an A-framed, wood-
shingled roof. One could almost picture horses hitched to the wood-slat-
ted fence in front a hundred years ago. The food was pedestrian, but my
mother was not an epicure and she dug into her grilled cheese with relish.
Any food consumed outside Las Villas de Muerte was haute cuisine to
her! When she slyly tried to order a glass of the house plonk Chardonnay
I nixed it and she grew sullen.

"Mom, we've got to get you to a dentist in Fresno and I don't want you stinking of wine."

"Oh, don't make fun of me," she said. "Can I have a glass, please?" she tried to wheedle.

"No," I said firmly.

"And I didn't burn the house down because I was drunk."

"Okay, Mom, okay. I embellished it a little for comic effect. I'm a writer. I do things like that. I'm sorry."

After the dispiriting lunch, we piled back into the Rampvan, crossed the I-5 and arced onto the 198, a four-lane highway that aimed us due north in the direction of Fresno. This being the middle of July, the heat was oppressive. The AC on the Rampvan blasted us mercifully with cold air while we were driving, but every time we had to make a pit-stop for my almost incontinent mother and stepped outside the air was scorching, Saharan hot. The temperature gauge on the GPS read 101 degrees, only further exacerbating Jack's irascibility—Fresno, his unabated erection, and my insistence that he ease back on the wine and shift over to mineral water. Nothing was assuaging his mood. Worse, his groin looked like he was trying to smuggle a small exotic animal through Customs.

We forged on. The passing landscape was hideous. Sere farmland and open stretches of desiccated countryside, where only the hardiest of plants survived and reptiles flourished, fled past in an apocalyptic diorama. Try as I might, I couldn't get Laura out of my mind.

In the small town of Lemoore we stopped for an umpteenth bathroom break. I let Jack take the wheel as I got on my iPhone to scope out dentists in Fresno. The plan was to get my mother's tooth extracted, get Jack into a clinic somewhere that treated priapism, check into the Marriott—where I had in my foresight booked a reservation via Internet—visit my mom's brother in the morning and then continue north.

As Jack drove, pushing the needle to 75 so we could make our milestones, I got on the phone to 1-800-DENTIST. After a series of attempts involving mostly electronic call directors and numerical options I got the names and numbers for a few dentists in the greater Fresno area. The first was leaving the office early and couldn't take my mom, his golf game at some private country club overriding an elderly woman's dental emergency. The office manager at the second place was

affable until I informed her that my mother was a stroke victim with
total left-side paralysis and would probably have to be worked on in her
wheelchair. The line went silent.

"Hello, are you there?"

"I'm sorry," the receptionist said. "I was checking with the doctor. He
says he's real sorry, but he doesn't, um, work on, um, handicapped patients."

"I see," I said, the various mounting crises, not to mention my own
depression, starting to make me come unglued. "I understand. That's cool.
Thanks. And please tell the doctor next time I'm in Fresno with my civil
rights attorney girlfriend who specializes in ADA litigation, I'm going to
FUCKING OWN HIS PRACTICE!" I punched the phone off in anger,
my frustration exacerbated by my hangover, the desolate landscape and
the creeping presentiment that we weren't going to make the IPNC in
time. I motored down my window and hung my head out for a second to
catch some fresh air, to see if that would change my perspective on everything. It didn't. Joy looked tired from another sleepless night. Jack sat in
quiet agony, surgery scenarios no doubt making him shudder. My mother
stoically nursed her inflamed molar, and I was still mourning the loss of
a woman whom Jack had rightly surmised I had fallen for. Only Snapper
seemed to have come out of the Justin leg medically and psychologically
unscathed. The air was still restaurant-kitchen hot and it practically peeled
off a layer of skin. And it was only 11:30 a.m.! I gunned the window back
up in response to protestations from the rear.

I turned around and looked at my mother. "How's the tooth, Mom?
Does it hurt badly?"

"Comes and goes," she muttered.

"That's what my last girlfriend said about me."

Joy pistoned a fist to her mouth and giggled spontaneously. My murderous sense of humor was having, I discerned, a nice little effect on her. I also
noticed that she had unbuttoned the top two buttons of her white sleeveless
blouse, revealing the fact she wasn't wearing a bra. Her dark-red nipples
could be seen clearly through the diaphanous material. I had to look away,
a woman's naked body not what I needed to be visualizing just then.

"What's the matter?" my mother croaked after eavesdropping on another failed attempt to line up a dentist who would take her. "Won't anyone see me?"

"I'm working on it, Mom, I'm working on it." I turned to Jack. "What's coming up next, Captain?"

Jack glanced at the GPS and said, "Caruthers. Another fifty long, motherfucking miles."

"Caruthers! Jesus. They probably don't have dentists there, just let their teeth rot. Anyway, let's make a pit-stop there, I need a cold beer or something to take the edge off."

"I hear you, brother, I hear you."

I phoned the final dentist on my list, a Dr. Wen-Jen Yang. When I told Dr. Yang's receptionist I was traveling with my mother and that she had what appeared to be an abscessed tooth, the initial response was very concerned and sympathetic. I decided not to go into the patient's other infirmities, hoping for as welcoming a reception. And I was confident of getting it, booking an appointment for two o'clock, the dentist generously giving up his lunch date to make room for my ailing mother. Ecstatic, I swiveled between the two front seats and said, "We're in, Mom."

Her face brightened. "Oh, that's such good news."

"Okay, here's the deal: He's a local barber, but he does tooth extractions in the back of his shop."

"Oh, no," my mom said, chuckling. Joy looked out the window, smiling a laugh, avoiding my gaze.

"I'm just kidding you, Mom. He's a real dentist. We're going to take care of that tooth."

On the outskirts of the tiny town of Caruthers we came upon the burnt-out shell of a FedEx tractor-trailer lying on its side, an automotive leviathan annihilated by a meteor. Framing the bleak foreground image of charred wreckage was the bleak countryside, which seemed to spread to some infernal infinity.

We pulled into a gas station/minimart. Joy once again dutifully wheeled my mother into the bathroom. Thank God for Joy, I thought, patient and kind with my paralyzed mother. Jack and I went inside the refrigerated sanctuary of the minimart and bought a quart of Sierra Nevada Ale. I'm not much of a beer drinker, but the intense heat of this Central Valley agricultural hellhole made the heavier alcoholic effects of wine less agreeable, though I had stowed a couple of bottles of white Burgundy in the cooler, replenished with all new ice.

Jack and I were sitting up front, discreetly sipping the cold ale in our plastic cups, waiting to go, when Joy returned with my mother. I opened the door and leapt out to help Joy, whom I was starting to worry about in terms of going the distance. It was hard work being with my mother 24/7 and I sensed she needed relief from time to time. "I'll take her," I said.

With her index and middle fingers fused, she tapped her lips several times.

"That's cool," I said. "Spark up."

"I don't want to around your mom," she whispered.

I nodded. She walked off, disappearing into the bathroom. I turned back to my mother and rolled her up the ramp and into the rear of the van. I braked her into place, slipped the ramp back into the undercarriage, and bent down to pet Snapper. The little devil was face-first into a bowl set on the hot asphalt, lapping like a camel who had just crossed the Gobi.

Remembering Jack's condition, I got back on my iPhone, called Fresno information and asked for the number of a hospital close to the dental clinic. They gave me the address of St. Agnes Medical Center, which I punched into the GPS under destination #2. As luck would have it–and we weren't having all that much recently–St. Agnes was only a few miles from Yang's office.

"All right, Jack," I said, climbing back into the driver's seat, "I found this place where they're going to take a look at your swollen Johnson. If they recommend you go into the ER and get your dick lanced, that'll be your call, okay? But I need you on this fucking trip. I can't drive all the way to Wisconsin by myself."

"I'll make it," he said. He chugged some ale, refreshed his glass, then glowered at me with an expression suggesting that if I even so much as chortled he would cold-cock me. "All right, Miles, thanks."

"I'm sure it's no big deal. There's got to be an anti-Viag med that redirects the blood back to where it's most needed. Which in your case is..."–I tapped my temple with a forefinger.

"Hilarious, Homes, hilarious."

"I'm just trying to lighten the mood. You were the one who took the–I still can't believe it–300 milligrams, not me."

"Yeah, but you were the one who gave 'em to me," Jack growled.

"Don't blame me, motherfucker," I snapped, temper momentarily flaring. "I was just as drunk, but I only took a half."

Jack shook his head disgustedly—at himself or me? I couldn't tell—and sat staring out the front windshield, no doubt regretting his decision to accompany me on this trip. The collective mood was quickly deteriorating.

After my mom had relieved herself, Snapper had hydrated, Joy had had her med Mary Jane fix and Jack and I had sandpapered our hangover grumpiness with a couple more cups of ale, the five of us got back on the road. We continued on the 198 and headed north, the arid scenery broken up now and then by beautiful orchards, beautiful as long as you were traveling in an air-conditioned car and didn't have to stop and step out into the now stifling 110-degree heat.

Past Caruthers we started seeing the first signs of urban civilization, evidenced by subdivisions erected on the outskirts of Fresno, a city of nearly half a million residents. Soon, we had forded the 99 Freeway and were in the city proper.

The Rampvan's navigation system worked wonders. The electronic woman's voice guided us confidently and faultlessly through the labyrinth of the unfamiliar city. Dr. Yang's clinic was a single-story beige stucco structure with a red-clay tile roof, a few miles from the downtown nucleus. Parking on the street, I killed the engine and punched in the address of the St. Agnes Medical Clinic.

"Look, Joy," I started, trying to sound casual, "Jack's got a bad stomach. Might be an ulcer or something, so while I'm with my mother getting her tooth worked on, I want you to accompany Jack to the hospital, okay?

"Okay."

I produced my wallet from my back pocket and handed her five twenties. "I'm sure you guys'll be done before us, so here's some cash. Get lunch somewhere."

She took the bills from me with reluctance, as if she was too proud to accept handouts. She slipped the money into her handbag and clasped it shut.

Jack turned around and, rooting deep for the humor that had abandoned him, joked, "Good luck, Mrs. Raymond. If you don't come out of surgery, it was great knowing you."

"Oh, don't joke me," my mother said.

"You'll be fine," Jack reassured her. He clamped a hand on my shoulder. "See you in a bit, brother."

"Good luck, big guy. Both of you."

I wheeled my increasingly anxious mother up a concrete path to a door decorated with six shingles advertising the dentists and periodontists headquartered within.

Inside the polar-cool office complex, styled on a Southwestern theme, replete with soft adobe tones and framed reproductions of black-and-white aerial photos of Fresno in its infancy, we followed the arrows down the hall to Dr. Yang's suite.

I opened the door and wheeled my mother backward into the small waiting room. The office manager, plump and in her thirties, with a helmet of dyed blond hair, swiveled in her chair at the sound of the door opening. Her prefabricated smile instantly transmogrified into one of alarm when she got an eyeful of the two of us. "Can I help you?"

"We have an appointment at two," I said, leaving my mother to approach the reception window. "I'm Miles Raymond. I'm the guy who called from the road and said we had an emergency situation. My mother has what appears to be an abscessed tooth."

"Uh, yes, but, uh..." she started, but found her speech hobbled by what I surmised was her alarm at my stroke-addled mother, now slumped slightly forward in her wheelchair, her Gilligan's Island hat making her look like some refugee from a war her side had lost.

I leaned my elbows on the desk and tried to cut the helmet-haired woman off at the headwaters. "Look, we're kind of desperate here. I'm taking her across country via Oregon to be with her sister in Wisconsin. Her tooth's killing her. Could the doctor please just take a look at it and see what we're dealing with?"

"Just a minute," she said nervously, no doubt fearing the imminent wrath of Dr. Yang for her having failed to ascertain fully the patient's condition. She swiveled in her chair and rose cumbrously from it. Her ass was Kansas-wide and she had to shift it sideways in order to wedge it through the doorway into the adjoining suite of examination rooms. By a surprising feat of adroitness, she was able to accomplish this without pivoting her shoulders or twisting her knees.

I turned to my mother and bounced my index finger on my lips. "Not a word, okay? I'll get you a nice glass of cold Chardonnay when we're done."

She brightened. "I'll be a good girl," she said.

Becky–in white letters on her nameplate–returned, shoehorned herself back into her chair, and said with an unwelcoming look on her face, "Okay, we'll need you to fill this out." She handed me a clipboard bearing two Xeroxed pages of medical history questions.

"Do you have a pen?" I asked.

Flustered, she fumbled for one on her cluttered desk, handed it to me and said in an unfriendly voice, "Here you go."

I sat down wearily in an uncomfortable fiberglass chair and filled out the ridiculously long form with a conspiracy of prevarication. When I was done I handed it back to her. Her foreboding expression had not changed; dark clouds had scudded across the wide sky of her hideously made-up face. As she opened the door and held it so that I could push my mother in I espied her exchanging dagger looks with the dentist.

Inside the fluorescent lit treatment room, Dr. Yang, a small man with a receding hairline, blinking behind small, round horn-rimmed glasses, greeted us defensively, as if we were the IRS. Next to him stood a statuesque woman I pegged as of Eastern European descent. She, too, wore a baleful expression. I introduced my mother and myself and Yang and I shook hands. Summoning all the professional sang-froid he could muster, given the predicament he suddenly faced, Yang bent down and took my mother's hand in his briefly, smiling through pursed lips. I think he felt sorry for her, but the inconvenience of having to deal with a handicapped person, a stroke victim on his lunch hour no less, dismayed him to the quick of his being.

Exchanging nods with his technician, he said, casting his eyes away from my mother, "We're going to have to get her up in the chair, otherwise..." He chopped himself off and held up his hands as if saying he wouldn't be able to do anything to remediate her dental woe. I think he hoped that would be the end of it, apologies would be exchanged and he and his technician and Becky could race off and chow down on some Mexican combo plates and wash them back with stiff margaritas, libations they now all desperately desired.

"No problem," I said, springing into action. I stepped across to the dental chair. "Does this armrest come up?"

Dentist and technician exchanged quick looks of petulant annoyance but, trapped in our itinerant freak show, worked up a response. The

technician came forward, wordlessly depressed a lever and raised the
padded armrest until it pointed ceilingward.

"Does the chair lower?" I asked.

Again, the technician wordlessly accommodated my request, then stood back, arms folded across her prodigious chest, waiting to see what would happen next, her countenance signaling that she expected the worst.

"Thank you," I said sarcastically. I wheeled my mother adjacent to the dental chair and braked it tight. I circled around so I was facing her. "All right, Mom," I said. "Here we go. We've done this a hundred times. Okay?"

"Okay," she said. Bravely, she raised her right hand and I clutched it with my right. Using all my strength, I hoisted her to a wobbly standing position. Behind her the dental clinic trio–Becky had joined us–exchanged wide-eyed looks of horror at what they were witnessing.

"Okay, Mom, let's turn you this way." I stepped to my left, as if leading a grotesque dance of the paralytic, and managed to get her ass balanced precariously on the edge of the adjustable examination chair. With both hands, I pushed her lower body until her backside was fully planted on the hard cushion. Then, employing both arms, with a great heave, I lifted her legs up and swiveled them onto the chair, which in turn simultaneously rotated her upper torso so that she was now lying perfectly supine. Hooking my hands under her armpits, I hoisted her up so that she was sitting properly in the chair, concluding a feat of comic maladroitness. I wheeled around to face the three of them, whose collective alarmed expressions underscored their disbelief, and said jocularly, still a little high from the Sierra Nevada and hoping to lighten their disheartened mood, "Okay, ladies and gentlemen, let's drill and fill!"

They looked at me like I had lost my mind in the Central Valley heat. I probably had. But my mother was in the chair now and there was no alternative but to go through the motions of a preliminary examination. I was silently gleeful, confident I had them by the short hairs.

Dr. Yang breathed deeply in and out of his nose like an anxious animal, then turned to his statuesque technician–I caught the nametag, Deidre, and assumed Slovenian, or Transylvanian, the pale expression she wore! They shared ominous looks.

Becky handed him the medical history chart I had filled out and he dropped it to his side without looking at it. He shifted over and gazed gravely down at my mother. "Where does it hurt, Mrs. Raymond?" My mother patted the right side of her mouth. "On the bottom?" She nodded once. "Could you open your mouth for me, please?"

My mother tried her best to open her mouth but, because of her full left-side paralysis, she had trouble complying. Yang pulled on a pair of surgical gloves and pried her mouth open as he might that of a recalcitrant dog. He inserted an instrument with a small mirror attached at one end and took a closer assay of the problem area. He visibly winced.

"Doesn't look good," he muttered. He turned to Deirdre–whom he was almost certainly banging (the image appalled me!)–and said, "Let's X-ray it."

She shot him a look like, *Are you fucking out of your mind, pencil dick?*

"Let's do it," he commanded.

A reluctant Deidre dutifully disappeared for a few minutes to get the equipment she needed for the X-rays. She returned and stood over my mother, speaking in, yes, a thick Slavic accent, "Hold your mouth open, please?"

Once again, my mother acceded to the request as best she could manage. Using dental tongs, and with some finessing, the technician managed to place a slide of unexposed negative where Dr. Yang had indicated.

"Okay, bite down, please," she instructed. My mother did as she was told. The technician rotated a flexible metal arm where the X-ray camera was mounted, aiming it where the negative had been planted. Last, she fitted a lead-lined vest over my mother's chest.

Dr. Yang motioned for me to step behind the X-ray control machine so I wouldn't get zapped. Deirdre pressed a button on the X-ray machine. The device emitted a sharp buzz. Done, the technician came forward and removed the film from my mother's mouth.

I waited by my mother's side while the dentist and his technician developed the slides in the adjoining room. I eavesdropped on them as they conferred over the pictures. Deirdre was saying something in a harsh undertone I couldn't make out.

"I'm scared," my mother said.

"It'll be all right. Hell, you've almost died four times and you're worried about a damn tooth?"

She chuckled at the mordant observation.

Yang finally rematerialized, Deirdre towering over him from behind, both their expressions even darker, if that were possible. He glanced at the chart, finding it difficult to meet my desperate gaze. "Your mother has an abscessed lower molar. All the way up the roots. You'll want to have it extracted."

"Well, let's do it," I said, growing impatient, itching for resolution and a drink.

"Your mother's taking a lot of medication," he started, scanning the chart on which I had filled out her medical history, including the cocktail of meds she was dosed on daily. I sensed in his deliberate avoidance of my beseeching gaze and his solemn tone that his heart was not really in the procedure. "I'm particularly concerned about the Coumadin, the blood-thinning medication for her clotting. This is a very high dosage." He stabbed the chart accusingly with a forefinger.

I crossed my arms and waited for the verdict.

Suddenly, he grew animated, as if all the energy he had expended to suppress his disconcertion with the appalling series of events that had ruined his lunch hour had unleashed a different personality. "This has to be done in a hospital under proper medical supervision," he said in a rising tone. "She could bleed to death," he concluded, practically screaming at me.

"We'll take that risk," I said gently.

"I won't," he said sharply. "I'm sorry. I'm not going to risk a med-mal." Now, *he* had *me* by the short hairs.

I sucked in air as deep as my lungs would expand and released it. "Look," I started, in a placating tone, "could you just give her something? A shot of Novocain? Some kind of antibiotic? Anything that might hold her over for a week until I can make arrangements with a hospital?" He stared at me blankly, in an inchoate state of rage. I thought he was going to go psychotic on me like one of those Korean assembly members who break out into fistfights if they don't agree on budget cuts or whatever. "Please," I said. "We're in desperate straits here."

Now that I had relented a little and it looked like he was going to make that lunch after all, his tone changed just a shade, back to the humanitarian he had been before he was born. "Okay, I'll numb her up a little, inject an antibiotic, give her a prescription for a painkiller. Then I suggest you just rinse it out periodically with warm salt water. It might buy her a week."

"Okay, Doctor, I appreciate it. I'm sorry I barged in on you like this."

"But this molar is going to have to come out sooner or later," he admonished. "She's got an open wound in there."

"All right," I said, growing exasperated.

I leafed absently through a magazine in the waiting room while the dentist shot my mom up with some Novo and gave her some painkillers to swallow. We left with prescriptions for Vicodin and clindamycin in my mother's hand and me $350 lighter in the wallet.

Back outside the sun was blazing. The fiery way it reflected off the streets and buildings was blinding. Even the darkest sunglasses didn't shield me from its malevolence. Jack and Joy weren't back yet so I wheeled my mother back into the lobby of the dental clinic to escape the heat. I parked her wheelchair next to a couch and slumped down into a chair. The antiseptic room felt like an oasis compared to the outside.

My mother was working her numbed jaw around as though she had a throbbing pain she couldn't ameliorate.

"How're you feeling, Mom?"

"Better," she mumbled, barely able to form words. Then she raised her good right arm, crooked her index finger and pointed it at some numinous being who was responsible for all her miseries. "I told you they would say you have to hospitalize me."

Fear struck me like a thrown dagger. We couldn't afford to hang around Fresno five days for a tooth extraction! This was absurd. Naturally, I deprecated myself, as I'm inclined in moments of stress to do, for even concocting such a trip as this. What the hell was I thinking? I berated myself. Fuck! Fuck! I inhaled deeply and let it out. "We're going to make it, Mom. I'm not going to let them hospitalize you."

"That's good news," she said, still staring at that spectral presence she saw in her damaged mental theater. Then she slowly swiveled her head in my direction. "Don't ever let them put me in the hospital, Miles."

"I won't, Mom. We can't. I'll go to a hardware store and buy a pair of pliers and do it myself."

"Oh, no," she chuckled. Then her expression changed. She was seeing and feeling something I wasn't. "No, I mean if something happens... don't let them hospitalize me, okay?"

"Okay, Mom," I said. "We'll find another dentist who'll do this. In this screwed-up economy someone's going to take a grand, have us sign a re lease of liability. We just went to the wrong guy," I said to reassure her.

"Don't let them hospitalize me. Please."

"Okay, Mom."

"I don't want to die in a hospital."

I nodded, irritated by her repeated exhortations. "Okay," I said, "I promise." Then I placed a hand on her rounded shoulder. "You're not going to die, Mom. You've survived a pulmonary embolism, a massive stroke, a full-frontal heart attack and a congestive heart failure where you *had* technically died. You've got the proverbial nine lives of the cat."

She laughed at my hyperbole. Then she grew reflective. "Remember when you were little and you had the two burst eardrums?"

"Yeah," I said, amazed at her recall. "That was painful."

"They wanted to hospitalize you, but I wouldn't let them take you."

"How come?"

"Because I was so afraid you were going to die," she sniffled.

"What's with you and hospitals?"

"I was a nurse. People don't come out of hospitals. Even little boys. They can get blood diseases, staph infections. I've seen it."

"A lot of people come out of hospitals, Mom. You did. Three times."

"I bet you wished I had died. Doug told me that."

"Yeah, well, he's the one who conned you out of all of your money, Mom. Why would you believe him? It is true that Hank and I wanted to put you on a no-code," I admitted. "And you wouldn't be here if I had. And you know what?"

"What?"

I squeezed her shoulder. "I'm glad we didn't."

She smiled at me and tears leached from her shut eyes. The day had lingered on, way too fucking long, and I was worried about making our scheduled destination.

chapter 9

Through the tinted windows of the dental clinic, the Rampvan loomed into view and braked to a halt in front of the swinging glass-door entrance.

"They're back," I said to my mom, rising from my chair. "I need to talk to Jack. I'll have Joy come get you."

I opened the fenestrated doors and it was so cripplingly hot it was like sticking my head into a bladesmith's forge. Joy emerged from the passenger side, produced a flame from a small disposable lighter, took one urgent hit from her half-smoked joint, snuffed it out in her little Altoids tin, then walked up to me.

"My mom's inside," I said.

"Did they take out the tooth?"

"No. But they gave her some Novocain, and antibiotics. If it starts hurting, we'll find another dentist." I jerked my head in the direction of the clinic. "Fucking dentist was an asshole. But, she's fine now. I've got to have a private word with Jack, so go inside and keep her company for a few minutes. Okay?"

"Okay."

"Get Snapper out of the back and take him in with you. That'll make her happy."

"Okay."

She gathered up Snapper from the back, leashed him, and then disappeared inside the clinic.

I climbed into the passenger seat and found Jack behind the wheel, his normally florid face drained of blood. Glancing down, I noticed that he had an ice pack planted on his crotch and was pressing down on it with his left hand.

"What's the verdict?" I asked.

"Just what you diagnosed, Miles. Acute case of priapism brought on by an overdose of Viag." He shook his head disgustedly to himself.

"So, what does that mean?"

"Well, apparently, there are two kinds. Low-flow and high-flow. I have low-flow, which means I have blood trapped in the... erection chambers. It's the worst of the two."

"The *worst*?" I asked with mounting alarm.

He must have been focused on what was going to happen next because he didn't amplify.

"What do they want to do?"

"I ice it overnight and if it doesn't subside, they do a procedure called an aspiration."

I nodded, feeling sorry for my friend. Even the urge to find the humor had deserted me. "An incision to release the blood?" I ventured.

"Not exactly," he said, his Ray-Bans concealing his eyes and the anguish that must have been emanating from them. "With a huge syringe they insert a needle into my cock and draw the blood out."

I visibly winced. "Fuck, Jackson. Fuck."

"And," he added, "if it doesn't go down, and I don't go through with the procedure, they told me I risk ED problems the rest of my life." He finally turned to me and said in a plaintive voice: "I'm forty-two, Miles. I've got at least a couple thousand more fucks left."

"Maybe it'll go down," I said, affecting hopefulness I didn't believe.

"I fucking can't believe this," Jack whined. "They wanted to do the aspiration right there and then."

"Maybe it would be the prudent decision," I said. "I'll go with you. I'll be with you the whole time. I'm your friend, dude. You've been through a lot of shit in the past couple of years. And I don't want to see you go flaccid for the duration if that's what you're risking. Fucking'll kill your life-spirit, man. Let's just grit our teeth and go in and man up."

He was silent a long, clock-ticking moment. "Fuck, man, a needle two inches into my cock?" He shook his head at the horrific image. "Like something out of a Wes Craven movie. This is surreal shit, Miles."

"You know what my mom says?"

"No, what?"

"She told me the drag about getting old is that all they do is stick needles into you." Jack managed a laugh. "Come on," I said. "I'm sure they'll give you a powerful local and you won't feel a thing."

Jack slammed both hands on the steering wheel a couple of times. "All right, fuck! Let's get it over with."

I climbed out of the Rampvan and went inside to retrieve my mother and Joy. After Joy had transferred my mother and Snapper into the back, I pulled her aside in the blistering heat and said, "I've got to take Jack back to the hospital. He's got a… condition that needs to be attended to. It's no big deal." She nodded. "Can you drive?" She nodded again without saying anything. "You have a California Driver's License and everything?" I asked.

She looked at me, reasonably irritated with being condescended to. "I have a car, Mr. Raymond. You saw it."

"Right!" I slapped my forehead, remembering we had met her at her car what seemed liked weeks ago. "And don't call me Mr. Raymond, Joy. Jesus."

"I can drive."

"Okay, you're going to drop us off at the hospital and then I want you to check into the Courtyard Marriott I booked for tonight. The address is already inputted into the GPS. It's not far. Jack and I'll take a cab there once they're done with him. All right?"

"Okay."

"Make sure my mom gets a glass of wine–just one!" I said, straightening my index finger for emphasis. "Take her down by the pool. And, you, take a swim or something. Relax, okay? You've been working hard. And you're doing a great job."

"Don't worry, Mr. Miles," she said.

"And not *Mr. Miles* either," I said with affected pique. "Miles. Just Miles."

The little wake-and-baker giggled.

We climbed into the Rampvan. I sat in the back with my mother who cradled a panting Snapper in her lap, petting his head and talking to him

as if he understood her and they were conversing in some polyglot stroke
victim/canine lingua franca. Joy took the wheel, moving the seat forward, while Jack, sitting shotgun, opened an ale and chugged it. Joy looked over at him before starting the car.

"What?" Jack said, dismayed by her icy stare.

"I no get DUI," she said.

"Oh, fuck," Jack said, sounding, unreasonably but not entirely without reason, peevish. He drained the bottle, handed it back to me, then smiled affectedly at Joy. "Feel better?"

Joy just looked straight ahead, turned the engine over and drove us over to St. Agnes Medical Center. She dropped us in a parking lot fronting the ER.

"Where're you going?" my mother said in a rising tone of fear. "To another wine tasting?"

"No, Mom. This is a hospital. I told you, Jack's got a minor emergency..."

"What?"

"He has a hemorrhoid that needs to be removed, okay? We'll meet you back at the hotel in a few hours. Joy'll take care of you."

"Joy can't take care of me all by herself," she wailed.

"She has, she can, and she will," I said adamantly. "Now, stop your caviling or I'm going to turn this ship around and take you back to Las Villas de Muerte." I said it forcefully, the stress of the torrid day exploding out of me.

"Don't threaten me with your fancy words," she shot back.

"Try to be cooperative. We've all got our issues here." I closed the van's sliding door on her before she could launch into more protests. I circled around to the driver's side and murmured to Joy, "Don't listen to half of what she says. The stroke changed her into someone she would be appalled to see if she were normal."

"I know," she said. "I work with them. Remember?"

"Okay. Just give her a glass of wine and she'll come around."

As Jack and I got out of the van, my mother, ill-tempered that I was abandoning her, yelled, "I hope your butt feels better, Jack."

Jack, not exactly looking forward to the aspiration, shot back, "Thank you, Mrs. Raymond." He cupped his hands around his mouth and added in a rising tone, "I hope you enjoy your afternoon in your wheelchair!"

My mother flipped him off. Jack looked at me, shaking his head. "What the fuck's up with Phyllis?"

"She thinks you're a bad influence on me."

"Oh, *I'm* a bad influence on *you!*"

"Just ignore her, man, okay, she's had a bad day."

"Oh, *she's* had a bad day?" Jack raged. "She's got a fucking little abscessed molar and I'm about to let some asshole Fresno doctor plunge a needle into my dick!"

Joy drove the Rampvan off. I hooked an arm around Jack and pulled him toward the entrance to St. Agnes's ER. "Come on, man, it's going to be fine. You'll be back in action by the time we get to the IPNC where there're going to be tons of hedonistic chicks drunk on wine." That didn't seem to cheer him up.

Jack just gritted his teeth and let himself be escorted into the ER.

Inside, after Jack re-acquainted himself with an admitting nurse who had evidently seen him earlier, the doctor who had examined him was re-summoned. He was a young, nerdy-looking man with black-framed glasses and the pallor of those who rarely see the sun.

"Let's just do the aspiration, Doc. I don't want to risk not being able to achieve an erection the rest of my life."

"He lives to get laid," I joked.

The doctor didn't laugh. Laughter had no place in his job description, or his training. "All right," he said. "Come with me."

After Jack's vitals were checked and some blood was drawn, the white lab-coated physician led us into a small OR outfitted with diverse medical equipment. Jack was instructed to lie on the examining table. The doctor spoke into a speakerphone and asked for a nurse. A moment later, a gorgeous, curvy black woman appeared in a crisp white nurse's uniform. She was as cheery and ebullient as Jack was disconsolate and disconcerted.

The doctor and the nurse–Latisha on her nametag–conducted a little sotto voce colloquy and I watched Latisha's eyes widen as she was apprised of Jack's condition and what the procedure was to entail.

After the doctor was finished getting Latisha up to speed on the course of action, she approached Jack. "So I understand you've got an acute case of priapism?"

"Yeah," Jack growled.

"Viagra, huh?"

"I don't really need it," Jack said, a little disingenuously. "I'd had a little too much to drink, but…"

"You wanted to impress your woman," she said, finishing his sentence. Jack laughed in spite of himself. "Isn't that our job?"

"Okay, we're going to have to strip you down, Jack, honey, and let the doctor see what he's dealing with here."

Jack reluctantly pushed his pants down. As the waistband crossed the threshold of his crotch his still gigantic cock shot upright, as if spring-loaded, and surged vertically toward the ceiling, an exotic plant growing in time-lapse photography.

Latisha reared back when she saw it and brought a hand to her mouth in an effort to suppress her astonishment. It wasn't just the size, but how the purpled veins stood out, turgid tributaries coursing down a thawing snow-capped mountain. They visibly throbbed, the mass of blood that had pooled there seeking an egress. His cock quivered in mid-air like an arrow that had just struck a tree. "Oh my Lordy," Latisha said, unable to constrain herself. "I bet that hurts."

"Fucking A it hurts, sister."

Latisha laughed so hard, her prodigious boobs shook. "Oh, I bet."

The nerdy Dr. Reid returned to the OR bearing a syringe with a needle that looked like something used on livestock or pachyderms, some beast with such thick skin it required a needle a quarter-inch wide to inject whatever meds the vet had to introduce into its bloodstream. And the syringe, itself, was nearly the size of a wine thief. Hell, a turkey baster!

Jack got a glimpse of the gigantic syringe and a look of horror clouded his face. "Holy shit, Doc, you didn't tell me you were going to use a horse hypo!"

"I'm afraid, Jack, after re-looking at the CT scan, that so much blood has pooled into your genital chambers that we're going to have to go in a little deeper."

"How much deeper?"

The doctor held his thumb and forefinger about three inches apart, then, recalibrating, widened it to four.

"Shit. All right," Jack grumbled, accepting the doctor's explanation, "let's get it on."

The doctor turned to Latisha. "Go ahead and numb him up," he said.

Latisha approached the procedure table. With surgical-gloved hands she squeezed an analgesic from a silver tube onto her index finger. Then she spread it over the head of Jack's penis, moving in slow circles around the opening. "Tell me when you can't feel my finger anymore, okay?"

"Okay," Jack said, staring at the ceiling. "You know, sister, if you used your other hand for support, you might get better coverage," Jack suggested in a lame attempt at a joke.

Latisha giggled, but kept up the application of the analgesic as the harried doctor waited, no time for banter, testing out the syringe. Now and then she would glance at Jack's terrified, ghostly-white face, waiting for an answer.

Finally, Jack said: "I think it's pretty numb now, sister. Roll over and let doc take over."

She laughed and backed away from Jack's turgid member.

The doctor said to her, "Have tape and gauze ready, Latisha."

"Right away, Doctor," she said.

The doctor approached Jack, brandishing the mammoth syringe like some mad scientist in a black-and-white horror movie. "I'm not going to mollycoddle you, Jack. You're going to feel pain. A lot of pain. We could do general anesthesia and put you under, but you'd have to check in, stay overnight..."

"I get it, Doc. We're on the road. We don't have time for that. I made a mistake, I'll take my medicine. Let's just get it over with," he finished sourly.

The doctor locked eyes with Latisha, who nodded. Dr. Reid returned his attention to Jack's, uh, problem area. With the syringe and four-inch needle pointed downward, vertically, he could have been a toreador, his sword over the shoulders of an exhausted, slouching bull, preparing to administer the *estocada*.

He paused, saying to Latisha: "Could you steady his penis for me, please?"

Wordlessly, she came forward and grasped hold of Jack's cock with her strong right hand and held it upright–not that it was going anywhere!–in a fixed position. The doctor initiated the slow insertion. When the needle was a half-inch in, Jack started screaming bloody murder. The spate of profanity that spewed from him would have caused a Catholic archdiocese to prepare the flock for the Rapture.

"Holy motherfucking Jesus fucking suck my dick Christ THAT HURTS!"

Dr. Reid, ignoring Jack's avalanche of imprecations, kept pushing the needle down the middle of the quivering shaft.

Jack's face looked more terrified than the subject in that painting "The Scream." "Fuck, man. Fuck me. FUCK!!"

When the doctor had the needle halfway in–easily two inches–and with Jack still cursing a blue streak and his upper body writhing like someone who had been struck by a Taser–he drew back very slowly on the plunger, using his index and middle fingers. Blood blossomed in the syringe. As the doctor continued to withdraw the plunger, the blood kept rising, keeping pace with the plunger. When it was three-quarters full, a look of concern darkened the doctor's face. He kept withdrawing the plunger, but now more slowly. "God, I didn't expect this much," he muttered, trying to maintain his professional aplomb, but growing manifestly worried with each CC of blood he drew from Jack's cock.

Jack, his eyes covered with one hand, oblivious of what was going on, threw his head back and forth like some convulsing clairvoyant in the face of a vision of biblical floodwaters drowning the earth.

"Have you ever done one of these aspirations before?" I asked the doctor.

"No," he said, his voice tense. Without looking at Latisha, he said, "You'd better get the gauze ready." Latisha nodded. When the plunger reached the end of the syringe the doctor stopped. It become apparent that he didn't know what to do next, as if he hadn't been trained for the complication rapidly arising–so to speak–in this procedure. As the blood threatened to burst the syringe I noticed that instead of withdrawing the plunger he was now pushing down on it as if fighting an inexorable current, a tsunami in microcosm. "There's a lot of pressure," he said in an even more anxious voice. "I'm going to have to take it out, Latisha. You got the gauze?"

"Yes, Doctor."

Dr. Reid furrowed his brow as if debating the repercussions of the evasive maneuver. But before he could act, the plunger launched itself out of the syringe, a small, albeit powerful, projectile. Freed of its obstruction, blood pumped out of the syringe in a thick arcing stream. Dr. Reid freaked. "We've got a bleeder! WE'VE GOT A BLEEDER!"

A more composed Latisha intoned, "Take the needle out, Doctor, so I can staunch it."

With blood spattered all over his hand and the sleeve of his white lab coat the doctor withdrew the needle from Jack's penis. A thin stream of blood geysered out of his cock and spray-painted the white foam ceiling panels, splotching them red–Bansky would have been impressed. Latisha had a thick layer of gauze ready and was desperately applying it to Old Faithful. The fabric was quickly impregnated with blood. Another nurse, a slight blonde, came rushing in and visibly stiffened once she got a horrific eyeful of the Grand Guignol scene. A red light was blinking on a monitor. Latisha and the blonde nurse began an emergency relay system with the gauze. The blonde would assemble a compress, Latisha would apply it, the blonde would discard the blood-soaked gob and prep a fresh one. They worked swiftly, expert blackjack dealers in a crowded casino.

Jack finally ventured a look. He started screaming.

That's when I left. I staggered down the fluorescent-lit corridor, passing the human flotsam that litters the hallways of medical facilities, until I found a bathroom. I went straight into one of the stalls, knelt down and vomited. Vomited until it felt as if there was nothing left of my stomach.

I clambered to my feet, wobbly, ready to faint, flushed and left the stall. Still queasy from the aspiration gone haywire in the OR, I walked slowly back, hoping that things had been resolved, that Jack's cock had been tied off or something. Amputated and cauterized. Anything!

I craned my neck around the doorway. The room had quieted. Latisha was finishing taping up the head of Jack's cock, which, miraculously, now lay semi-flaccid on his hairy gut.

I entered the OR on tentative steps as if the room were booby-trapped and approached the doctor, shakily removing his surgical gloves. "How is he?"

"It was touch-and-go there for a while. He had a lot of blood in those chambers."

I looked at Jack and nodded. His face was spectrally pale and seemed frozen in a monochromatic grimace of dread. I placed a fraternal hand on his shoulder. "How're you doing, big guy?"

Without moving his head, Jack said in a frogged voice, "I don't know."

"He lost a fair amount of blood," the doctor explained. "About what he would donate in two visits at a plasma center. So, be careful. Fainting is a concern."

Latisha and I pulled Jack's trousers back up and tied a knot with the drawstring. Carefully, we maneuvered his hulking body off the surgery table. With his arms slung around our shoulders we stutter-stepped him down the linoleum corridor toward the exit, a tranquilized bear re-released into the wild. He was unsteady on his feet and I wasn't sure he could manage on his own.

In the lobby Jack had to sign some release forms before they would let him go.

He managed to Latisha, "Thanks, sister."

"Oh, you're welcome, honey."

"Thanks, Latisha," I chimed in.

"That's what we do here," she said. "We save penises." I laughed. Jack wanted to, but didn't. She smiled, showing a big white toothy mouth. Then she turned and walked off.

I helped sit Jack down on one of the waiting room chairs. He looked enervated, beaten down. I flipped up my iPhone, navigated to an app that guides you to local taxis, typed in Fresno, was quickly connected to a Yellow Cab dispatcher and told him where we were and that we were ready to go.

I closed my phone and turned to Jack. "How're you feeling?"

"How do you think?" he snapped, returning to life. "Fucking needle halfway up my dick, dude!"

"I was there, remember?" There was a silence. Gathered around us in the remaining chairs was a gallery of faces frozen in various states of anxiety as they awaited news of their progeny, spouses, siblings and sundry loved ones. "How long are you going to be out of action?"

"When the bleeding stops." Jack held up a plastic bag filled with gauze and tape. "I guess we'll have to get Joy to do this."

"That wasn't part of her job description," I said. "Can't you do it yourself?"

"I suppose I have no choice," he muttered.

"Well, at least it's gone down. The worst is over."

"Yeah. The question is: Will it ever come back up?"

I chuckled. Through the tinted-window exit I saw our Yellow Cab brake to a stop. "Ride's here," I said to Jack. "Can you stand on your own?"

He rose wobblingly to his feet. He staggered in place a bit, but ventured a few steps on his own with me just behind him in case he fainted. He threw me a backward glance. "I think I'm okay," he said.

Outside, the sky was marbled with periwinkle blue and orange clouds as the sun slipped down on its ladderless arc. The heat had abated slightly, but it still had to be in the low nineties as we made our way toward the cab. I opened the back door and helped Jack clamber in. It would probably take him no more than a day or two to find his sea legs. I hoped. Prayed, too, that he wouldn't use this as an excuse to bail on me.

The cabbie knew the way to take us to the Courtyard Marriott on East Shaw, which proved a short, five-minute drive. The Fresno version was like all the others: stucco facade, three stories, antiseptically clean, utterly characterless and soul-destroying. The kind of place my mother loved. The cabbie left us under a marquee in front of the lobby. I walked Jack in, still a little unsteady on his feet, got him settled in a chair, and hit the check-in desk.

We rode the elevator to the third floor and padded down a carpeted hallway to our room. The security card, as usual, took a couple tries. I gently shoved Jack inside. "I'm going to check on my mom and Joy, get the keys to the van and go down and get us one of those Foxen Chards I have on ice and bring you a glass."

"Now you're thinking," Jack said.

"I've got your best interests in mind."

"Without me, you'd never make it to Wisconsin."

"Fucking A, brother."

He disappeared inside our room and the door automatically closed behind him.

Footsteps approached the door of the adjacent room when I knocked, then stopped. The door didn't open. I assumed Joy, with her characteristic circumspection, was eyeing me through the peephole.

I knocked again. "Joy, it's me, Miles. Open up."

The door opened. Joy smiled, but remained silent, her face expressionless. I entered their spacious, handicapped suite. Two double beds, neatly made up, faced a large-screen TV. My mother sat parked on a tiny patio overlooking the pool that, in the deepening twilight, glowed turquoise. I came up behind her and placed a hand on the nape of her neck. She managed a quarter turn, all her arthritic neck would allow.

"Miles. I thought you'd left," she said in the deranged, paranoid manner she just couldn't seem to shake.

I dragged a patio chair over next to her and sat down. "Where would I go, Mom?"

"I don't know. Back to those girls you enjoyed some kind of hanky-panky with."

"All right, Mom, let's not get into my personal life here, okay?"

She smirked. "Jack didn't have hemorrhoids. I'm a nurse."

"He's got a bleeding ulcer."

"Oh, no," my mother said. "Because of me?"

"No, Mom. Because he had a kid and got divorced and is out of work..."

"And because he drinks too damn much!"

"And probably that, too. But from you and me, that's a bit like the pot calling the kettle black, isn't it?"

"I only have two glasses. I'm not an alcoholic," she retorted defiantly.

"No one said you were, Mom. But it's amazing how tenacious you are in getting me to pour you a third–and sometimes a fourth. If I left you alone with a whole bottle, I'd bet it'd be gone."

Her face grew angry. So, she sat there stony-faced and stared down sullenly at the pool. "I've had a hard life. I raised three kids. I deserve my wine."

"I know you do, Mom. Anyway, speaking of which, I'm going down to the van and get a bottle and bring it up and pour you a nice cold glass. How does that sound?"

She was still peeved, but at the thought of a cold glass of Chardonnay in her hand and the relief it would bring her, she instantly softened. "I would like that, please."

"Okay, Mom, I'll be right back. And I apologize for what I said about your wine. You're a grown woman and you deserve as many glasses as you want. Within reason."

"Thank you," she grumbled.

When I turned back to the room, Joy was missing. A moment later the door opened and she came in, reeking of reefer.

"Where are the keys to the van, Joy?"

She went over to her purse, fished around in it for a moment, and handed them to me.

"Could you do me a favor?" She waited. In a lowered tone so my mother couldn't hear: "Could you roll a nice blunt for Jack? He had a little surgical procedure and, well, it might be good to medical marijuana him a bit."

"Okay." Finally, she dropped the cigar-store Indian expression and giggled.

I went out and found the van, which stood out in the lot with its dirt-streaked sides. Joy had been thoughtful enough to have the valet haul up our luggage. I opened the cooler and un-submerged one—ah, screw it, two—bottles of Foxen's single-vineyard Chardonnay. They were icy to the touch. Perfect accompaniment to this hot weather and overall miserable day of asshole dentists, incompetent doctors, blistered landscapes and the baking hellhole that was Fresno.

With my key ring corkscrew, I opened one of the bottles as I walked down the corridor, back to the adjoining rooms. Joy let me in after a knock. I held out the open bottle and said, "No more than one glass, okay? We're going to go out to dinner later. You can have as much as you like, of course. If she wants to go down by the pool, take her down, all right? But without Snapper."

"I know," she said. "I brought him up in your mom's satchel. I put the wristband over his nose like you said."

"That's great, Joy. You're an angel."

She smiled. Then she took the bottle from me. I turned to walk away. "Oh, Miles?" I turned back. She handed me a thick joint and I took it from her.

"Thanks. Powerful stuff?"

She giggled. "Good for sex."

"Oh, okay," I said, a little taken aback. "I don't know if that's in the cards this evening for Jack but, hey, the night's young."

I found Jack reposing on one of our room's double beds. With the Riedel stemware I had fetched from the car I poured a healthy amount and held it out to him. He held out his hand, but I pulled it back out of his reach. "If you start feeling woozy, with the Vicodin and shit..."

"Just give me the goddamn glass and stop talking to me like I'm some infant."

"Not to mention the two pints of blood that you lost in the OR."

"I didn't lose it! The fucking quack lost it!"

"Whatever, all I know is that ceiling looked like a Jackson Pollock."

Jack didn't laugh. He squeezed his eyes shut and pinched his temples in annoyance. "Okay, Miles, I'll pace myself."

I handed him the glass, then poured one for myself and stretched out on the adjacent bed. After a few meditative sips, I remembered the joint in my front pocket. I rooted it out and then casually flipped it over to the other bed. Jack looked down at his side where it had landed. "Present from Joy. Medical Mary Jane. Might take your mind off your injured pecker."

"Thanks," Jack said. "I'll fire it up in a minute." He shook his head. "Man, what a day!"

I sipped my wine. God, it tasted good. Not over-oaked. Excellent balance. My spirits were lifting. "Tomorrow, Mendocino. You're going to like that place."

"Chicks?"

"Nah, it's just a beautiful B&B over this cove. Great place to chill. If you're feeling better we'll do a little wine tasting. It's expensive, but it's sort of a treat for my mom who, once I dump her in Wisconsin, I probably won't see a whole lot of anymore. Hell, maybe never. Given her condition, she's probably not long for this world."

Jack shook his head solemnly. "Yeah, I don't know how she hangs on. She can be a mean fucking cuss."

"She's a tough old bird, that's for sure."

"I didn't realize it was going to be this much work."

I whipped my head in his direction. "What? Are you going to bail on me?"

"I'm not going to bail on you. I've been on location shoots way more brutal than this detail." He drank resolutely, as if to efface those memories. "I just don't know why we had to detour through Fresno."

"Jack. I told you. She hasn't seen her brother in ages. It seemed the humane thing to do. I didn't promise this was going to be *all* fun and games."

Jack switched on the TV and channel-surfed until he found a baseball game. I broke open my MacBook, logged onto the hotel's Wi-Fi and went Google-ing for nearby restaurants. I found a place just down the street that looked like it had a decent wine list and a prosaic enough menu that my mother would find something to order. It wasn't cheap, but it had been a tough day for everyone and I reasoned that a relaxing meal in a comfortable, homey environment might elevate everybody's flagging morale.

"Okay, Jack, why don't you take a shower and let's go eat."

"I'm not really hungry," he groused, refilling his glass, his hand clutching the bottle like a dead chicken.

"Come on, Jack. I need you to pull it together. You know my mom likes to eat early and be put down early, so we're sort of on her schedule until she's in bed."

"All right," Jack said. He hauled himself heavily off the mattress and staggered toward the bathroom. A few minutes later I heard Jack cry out in pain. "Ow. Shit. Ow. Shit." I surmised that he was un-bandaging his wound. The shower started running. There were more cries of pain as the hot water hit his wounded manhood.

After Jack had showered and redressed his member, I showered and put on the best clothes I had brought, as the joint apparently had a dress code. I don't think Jack had brought a sport coat with him, so I implored him to put on his nicest shirt, and he grudgingly complied.

We gathered up Joy and my mother. Joy had styled my mother's hair and dressed her in her finest apparel: sweat pants and a red cotton blouse. Joy looked the best of all. She was wearing a sleeveless black dress with a V-neck that revealed her surprisingly ample cleavage. Before we left the room I had Joy affix the elastic wristband on Snapper so he wouldn't bark his head off. As my mother implored me to take it off, I worried that the little imp would probably figure out a way to paw it off, then start really barking. So, for different reasons, I acceded to my mother's importunings. Now, everyone was happy! Jack got his dick fixed, Mom got some novo and meds for her infected molar, Joy was no doubt dreaming of lobster, Snapper had avoided being muzzled, and I, well, was the ad hoc, de facto ringmaster of one *fucking* freak show!

We piled into our handicapped-equipped van and rode down East Shaw Ave., a three-lane road bounded by desolate office complexes, car dealerships and sundry Americana franchises. A temperature gauge on a Chase Bank electronic board read 97 degrees.

"Five-thirty and it's 97," I said to Jack.

"It's a fucking hellhole here," he spat.

"Tomorrow we'll be back in wine country and in three days the International Pinot Noir blowout. All your troubles and worries will be assuaged." I looked over at him and winked. "And your big guy might be back in operation."

"I hope so," Jack said.

Fleming's Prime Steakhouse & Wine Bar is a chain restaurant with some twenty locations scattered around the country. Inside, it was pleasantly cool and nicely appointed with wood-paneled walls, carpeted floor, damask-covered tables and built-in maple wine racks. Yellow, half-moon chandeliers hung from the ceiling, lending the main room a warm and welcoming feeling. There were no windows, by design—who would want a street view of hideous-looking Fresno, California? We were shortly enwombed in another world. We could have been anywhere, I thought. And quickly ran through a couple of piquant fantasies!

We were led to the center table by a goateed man in a black suit, white shirt and tie. He pulled a chair away to accommodate my mother's and chivalrously slotted her into her place. A black-bound wine list was handed to me. Another man soon appeared at our side. Wordlessly, he set menus in front of us. Then, with hands clasped behind his back, bending forward slightly at the waist, he said, "Hi, my name's Christopher and I'll be your server tonight. Can I get anyone anything to drink?"

Before my mother could say anything, I consulted the list's by-the-glass selection. "My mother's going to have a glass of the Picket Fence Chard."

"Excellent choice," replied Christopher.

"And the three of us are going to share a bottle of the Bergström Pinot."

"Very well, sir," Christopher said.

"And bring us some ice water as well."

He nodded, pivoted, and disappeared almost as quietly as he had arrived.

"How's the tooth, Mom?"

"Good," she said.

"Those Vicodins will get you to Wisconsin," I joked.

"Oh, no," she said. "I don't need any more drugs!"

We all laughed, including a grim-faced Jack. I knew once he got a little more wine in him his humor would return from the dead.

The waiter brought my mother her glass of Chardonnay, which she wasted no time in raising to her lips. I pointed at Joy to get her attention. Then I panned my extended finger to my mother's wineglass and shook it slightly so Joy understood: keep her monitored. Joy nodded, accustomed now to the semaphore. The waiter presented the Willamette Pinot for approval and then proceeded to uncork it.

"Are you from out of town?" he asked.

"We're going to the International Pinot Noir Celebration," I said. "Up in Oregon."

"Willamette Valley. Beautiful there. I went once. Great three days... what little I remember of it."

Jack and I shared a laugh.

Jack said, "Miles is Master of Ceremonies this year."

"No kidding," said Christopher, as he sniffed the bottle to determine whether it was corked. Deciding it was fine, he poured a dollop in a Pinot-specific Riedel wineglass. I nosed the wine, but didn't taste it.

"Why don't you try it?" Jack asked.

"The professionals never taste it, they just sniff to see if it's off." I turned to Christopher. "It's fine. Ramp us up."

He poured Joy's wide-bottomed, narrow-lipped Pinot-specific stemware about a third full. "So, how'd you get to be Master of Ceremonies?"

"Oh, well..." I started, not sure I wanted to go down that familiar road.

But it didn't matter because my mother blurted out, "He wrote *Shameless*."

Christopher stopped in the middle of pouring for Jack and turned to me, his expression now one of wide-eyed shock. "Are you joking? You wrote *Shameless*?"

I hung my head and nodded. I was tired; I didn't want the fawning that was sure to ensue. "Yeah," I said, a little weary already at the inevitable consequences of my admission–especially to someone who obviously knew his wines.

"I loved that movie," he effused. "It's one of my favorites of all time. In fact, it was required viewing for our entire wait staff here."

"Really?" I said. "So, they all drink from the spit bucket now, huh?"

He laughed and thrust out his hand. "It's a pleasure to meet you...?"

"Miles. Miles Raymond." I took his hand and shook it.

"Wow, we don't get many celebrities up here in Fresno," he said, flushing red and grinning broadly.

"And for good reason," Jack interjected, unable to hide his sarcasm.

"I'm not really a celebrity. I'm just a sadsack writer who got lucky."

Christopher cocked his head to one side and smirked at my modesty,
not believing it for a second. "I'll bring you your water," he said. "And
it's a pleasure to meet you, Mr. Raymond."

"Miles, please," I said.

He glided away. My mother, her glass now half drained, donned her
reading glasses and opened her menu. She scanned it a moment, then let
loose a kind of owl cry. "Woo. It's expensive."

"Who cares, Mom? Order whatever you want. It's been one long hell
of a day." Jack and I locked eyes and exchanged a meaningful look that
only underscored my words.

"Rusty would never take me to a place like this," she said, still staring
goggle-eyed at her menu, referring to my father.

"He was a cheapskate, wasn't he?"

"Oh, yes," my mother said. In a singsong voice that had only mani-
fested itself since her stroke, she added, "All I did was cook, cook, cook.
We never went out. And when we did it was pizza." She made a face,
looked at me over her rectangular-lensed glasses and said, "That's what
killed him. All that damn pizza."

We all laughed and sipped our wine. The Bergström was nice, well balanced,
a lot of ripe fruit, not too alcoholic. I turned to Joy: "You like the Pinot?"

She nodded enthusiastically. "No aftertaste." This had become her de-
fault response every time I asked her about the wine.

"Anything else?" I prodded.

She took another sip, let it swash around in her mouth a bit, then pro-
nounced. "Tastes a little like hashish."

"You would know," my mother said without looking at Joy.

Joy glowered at her.

"All right, Mom, can it, or I'm wheeling you back to the Marriott and
ordering you pizza." I turned to Joy. "Hashish, huh? In all the winespeak
I've heard over the years, and that includes melting asphalt and cricket
legs, I've never heard anyone compare a wine to a cannabinoid."

My mother, who was ignoring us, set her menu down, reached for her
wineglass and simultaneously announced, "I'm going to get the biggest
goddamn steak they have. To hell with Rusty. I don't care if he's mad at
me," she added cryptically, as if my father were a reproachful presence
hovering over her.

"You get the biggest colon-buster you want, Mom, okay? I don't think Dad's going to come down and snatch it away from you."

"I wouldn't be so sure," she shot back.

Everyone laughed, including Joy.

"And I want to take the bone back to Snapper."

"Absolutely, Mom. That's why they call them doggie bags."

My mother ordered the prime bone-in rib-eye with the classic Caesar to start and a baked potato side. Joy, a finicky eater, demurely ordered a shrimp cocktail appetizer and Fleming's house salad.

"Is that all you want?" I asked, incredulous. She shrugged. "Come on, Joy, it's on me. I'm flush with cash. Do you like seafood?" She nodded. I turned to Christopher. "Bring her the Australian lobster tails," I said grandly.

"Oh, no," Joy said. "That's too expensive."

"Not at all, Joy," I said. "You've been doing a yeoman's job. Hasn't she, Mom?"

"What's *yeoman* mean?" my mother asked.

"Someone who uncomplainingly does hard, thankless work."

Jack and I ordered meat and fish respectively and Christopher disappeared.

"I'm not thankless," my mother barked.

"No, but sometimes you're thoughtless. Joy's doing a great job, isn't she, Mom?"

"Oh, yes," she cried out, the wine having momentarily liberated, however evanescently, the last vestige of human decency in her. "Without Joy"–tears suddenly sprang to her eyes–"I wouldn't be able to get to Wisconsin."

"Mom, please stop crying," I said firmly.

She squinted and bobbed her head up and down, staring into her thoughts. "Oh, this is the best night of my life."

"That's what you said last night."

"And it was until you brought up the fire."

"I've already apologized for that, Mom. But, you remember when Hank burned down our vacation place in Baja?"

"Oh, yes. I remember. Rusty was so angry with him."

"Do you know how that happened?"

"It was a propane leak."

"No, Mom. He was getting the generator out. He'd been drinking all the way down, the moment he crossed the border. It was out of gas. So,

he filled it up, but he was so drunk he sloshed gas all over the garage floor.
Then, when he pulled the starter cord, a spark ignited."

"Oh, no," she said.

"Oh, yes," I said. "There's a pattern here in the Raymond family."

My mother grew reflective. "I didn't know that," she said.

"Obviously, Hank lied because Dad would have disowned him."

"That's true." She looked up at me over her glasses. "Why do you have to bring up all this bad stuff?"

"What does it matter, Mom?"

"I don't want to remember the bad stuff," she cried.

"I'm sorry. I just thought you might like to know the real story."

"No, I'm not interested," she snapped. "I just want to enjoy my wine." Tears sprang again to her eyes. "And these last few days I have before you abandon me at my sister's."

"I'm not abandoning you, Mom. I'm taking you where you said you wanted to go."

"I know," she said. She nodded some more, adrift in a world of her own creation. "Could I have another glass of wine, please?"

"With your dinner, Mom. Remember, you're taking a lot of meds and we've still got a long way to go."

"I know. You've all been so good to me." And tears watered her eyes again.

The food could have been deemed delicious, if you were partial to that kind of cuisine. I couldn't believe my mother, devouring her mammoth steak, Caesar salad *and* the jumbo baked potato, fully loaded. Joy nibbled at her lobster guiltily, knowing that it had set me back over $40. Jack and I got a second bottle of Pinot—hell, we were only a mile-and-a-half straight down the road from the hotel, so why not get a little tipsy? My mother tried to inveigle a third glass of the Chard, employing her sad clown expression oh-poor-me-I'm-in-a-wheelchair routine, but I reproved her, "Mom, you've already had two glasses, and you had one back at the hotel."

She held out her glass like a little kid, cocked her head coquettishly to one side and said, "Please. One for your mother, who raised you..." Tears welled in her eyes.

"You are un*fuck*ing believable," I said, not swayed by her weak shot at emotional blackmail. "You're going to get a nomination this year. Best performance by a stroke victim who wants a fourth glass of wine."

Everyone laughed. Except my mother. Her lachrymose charm suddenly changed into a flash of anger. "Oh, damn it, don't be like that to your mother. I'm not a child."

Christopher, who was hovering over us, awaiting the verdict, glanced back and forth between us as if he were mid-court at a tennis tournament.

I turned to him and said, "Give her a half a glass."

I don't know whether Christopher was being charitable or had put in the wrong drink order because he brought my mother a full pour. She was in heaven. But wasn't I being a hypocrite with the two bottles of wine, not to mention the one Jack and I had pounded at the Marriott? And Joy was still on her first glass, so there were extenuating circumstances here for sure.

During the course of the sumptuous repast, some of the wait staff and kitchen crew came over to shake my hand, congratulate me, and then have me sign autographs on menus and cocktail napkins and even the sleeves of their chefs' uniforms. At one point, sweating like a factory worker, the chef himself, rotund with a florid face–a walking myocardial infarction!–emerged from the kitchen and pumped my hand. "Wine sales are going through the roof because of you," he proclaimed, a bottle or two to the wind himself it seemed.

"Well, the movie did that," I said, all modesty. "I just wrote the blueprint."

"It starts with the book, doesn't it?" he said in his booming voice. "How's the food?"

"Marvelous," my mother said, a half-chewed chunk of rib-eye clearly visible.

Everyone laughed. Periodically, Joy would have to remind my mother to wipe the left side of her mouth. Now and then Joy would do it for her, occasionally having to retrieve pieces of semi-masticated food that had fallen onto the napkin in her lap.

After desserts, one of the wait staff–a pretty, sylphlike brunette beauty–came toward me, bent at the waist and whispered in my ear, "After we close, we're going to have a little celebration. It's one of the waiters' birthday. We'd love to have you as our special guest. We're going to open some awesome bottles." I was a little bit–well, more than a little bit–drunk, but I could have sworn she added in a lower, more brazen, tone: "You can have anyone here you want, Miles."

"I'll think about it," I said, feeling jaded. "Thanks for the invite."

I paid the tab, which totaled well in excess of $500, tipped obscenely so they wouldn't gossip that the author of *Shameless* was a piker, and rose from the table with my anomalous troop.

As we went out the front door, the brunette vixen brushed by me again and said, "See you back here a little later, I hope."

Without breaking my stride, I smiled at her a little affectedly, but said nothing, and trailed my dysfunctional family out into the still torrid night.

The valet brought the Rampvan up and opened the doors and helped everyone in. I must have slurred a little because he said, "Sure we can't call you a cab?"

"We're just a mile down the road, at the Marriott. I'm sure I'll be fine," I said, enunciating carefully.

Out of Fleming's drive-up, the direction I needed to go was left, but that would require crossing a double-yellow line. Looking right, I could see I was going to have to go pretty far before I could turn around. There were no cars on the road and the weeknight Fresno cityscape was deserted. I executed the left and headed in the direction of the Marriott.

Halfway to the hotel I could make out the big green-and-red, garishly lit neon sign. Everyone was laughing about something Jack had said when, checking my rearview mirror, I caught the flashing colored lights–red, white, and blue–of a cop. They must've been flashing awhile, because a few moments later I heard the shrill WHOOP WHOOP as an audio reminder, followed by a stentorian voice on a bullhorn: "PULL OVER TO THE SIDE OF THE ROAD." The megaphone-amplified voice was followed by another WHOOP WHOOP.

"Oh, fuck, just what I need."

"Keep it cool, Homes," Jack said.

I complied with the order, switched off the Stevie Wonder CD Jack had put in and had been singing to, and waited. A uniformed officer–Fresno PD? County sheriff? I couldn't tell–slowly approached my side of the car, right hand riding his holster. I motored my window down and manufactured a smile. He was in his thirties, mustachioed, a young Steve McQueen look-alike, his face set in a perpetual snarl. He was wielding a baton-sized flashlight, which he directed contemptuously into my eyes.

"Can I see your driver's license and registration, sir?"

I reached around for my wallet and fished it out of my back pocket, fumbled with the plastic inside card holder, while Jack rooted around in the glove compartment for the rental agreement.

The cop shined his light on the license once I handed it over, then back into my face. "Are you aware that you made a left over a double-yellow?" he casually asked as I passed along the Avis folder.

"No, I didn't see it," I said. "We're not from here, we're passing through."

"Where're you coming from?"

"Well, we started in San Diego and we're headed to Oregon." I shrewdly stopped myself before elaborating that we were headed to the International Pinot Noir Celebration–what a bonehead mistake that would have been!

"I meant, where're you coming from tonight?"

"Oh," I said amiably, "we had dinner over at Fleming's."

"Have you been drinking, Mr. Raymond?" he asked, expressionlessly.

"A couple of glasses of wine over, I don't know, three hours, that's all. We're staying down the road at the Marriott." I pointed through the windshield toward the three-story stucco structure lit up like a fabled sanctuary, but felt myself receding with every passing second into the encroaching net of a DUI.

"Would you mind stepping out of the car, please?"

Without protest–indeed, with the cheerful readiness born of fear–I opened the driver's side door and climbed out. I can't remember, but I may have stumbled a bit on the little step-up assistant, just enough to give him pause. I stood out in the dank Central Valley night air, the radio from the cop's cruiser squawking a cacophony of overlapping voices issuing from various disembodied dispatchers. I was sentient enough to envision a night in jail awaiting a morning arraignment while Jack, Joy, my mother and Snapper were holed up in the Marriott, my mother's tooth worsening and Jack and Joy's patience strained to the cracking point.

"I'm going to give you a field sobriety test, sir, because I have cause to believe you've consumed more than you've said, that you're impaired and quite possibly over the legal limit."

My instinct was to protest. But I've learned over the years that arguing with cops and getting obstreperous in such situations only exacerbates things. Besides, I reasoned silently, monosyllabic cooperative answers would give him less chance to analyze my clearly hobbled speech. "Okay," I said meekly.

"I want you to look straight up at the sky" he demonstrated briefly–"and remain like that for thirty seconds. Okay?"

"Okay." Shuffling my feet, I tried discreetly to widen my stance, having learned from my years playing golf that a solid base was important for a successful swing. I slowly tilted my head upward ninety degrees, and stared at the sky. I don't remember whether I swayed, but the thirty seconds felt like an eternity.

Next, he said, "Now I'd like you to stand on one foot and hold that for ten seconds."

"Oh, the flamingo part of the test," I joked.

He remained poker-faced.

I cocked the knee on my right leg and lifted the foot off the ground. That was a mistake; it would have been much easier to balance myself on my right side than my left. I tried, but I couldn't make the full ten seconds and had to plant my right foot back on the ground lest I fall mortifyingly into a heap onto the asphalt.

"Mr. Raymond, I believe you're over the limit." He looked at me, awaiting a response. I could see that he was vacillating on the question of arresting me.

"Look," I started, in as calm a voice as I could muster, "I've got my mother, who's in a wheelchair, and her nurse, and a friend who's just undergone a very invasive medical procedure, we're taking my mom to Wisconsin to be with her sister." I held open my hand and motioned toward the ethereal Courtyard Marriott, less than half a mile from where we, cop and celebrated author–reputation about to be tarnished–stood. "We're just staying right down there..." I cut myself off.

I sensed my rambling plea had ever so slightly swayed him. "Stay put," he commanded. He walked around to the passenger door on the van and rapped on the window with his flashlight. I was praying Jack wouldn't fall out of the cab and launch into his desperate actor routine and get us *all* thrown into jail.

Through the window I could make out Joy sliding open the passenger door, then returning to her position next to my mother. The inside of the back was lit up now with the overhead lamp, but the cop still sprayed his flashlight around, trained no doubt in its intimidating effect. I was hoping he wouldn't poke around in the ice chest and find the bottle of Puligny-Montrachet I had been chilling for Joy, Jack and me. I also prayed that the dramatis personae, especially my paralyzed mother, to greet him when the door was opened would move him to a more compassionate verdict.

Suddenly, my mother cried out, "Don't arrest him! He's my son! He's taking me home to Wisconsin. Please don't arrest him!" This was followed by a brief silence. Before she started ululating: "I can't breathe. I can't breathe! I can't breathe!"

Fresno's finest, disconcerted by the sight of my mother and the shrill sound of her wailing, backed away from the passenger compartment and wordlessly circled around the front of the Rampvan, all the while directing the beam of his flashlight inside, then back to where I, sweating bullets, had remained standing, raking my hair with my fingers in anticipation of the worst.

"What's wrong with your mother?" he asked.

"I don't know," I said, genuinely worried. "Tonight was her birthday dinner. She takes a lot of meds. She might need her nitro patch."

As my mother continued to caterwaul, "I can't breathe" from inside, the cop switched off his flashlight, reached in through the open window and removed the keys from the ignition. He dangled them tauntingly in my face and said, "Consider yourself lucky." Then, he wound up like an outfielder trying to throw out a runner at the plate and hurled the keys over the van and into a forest of bushes that fronted some faceless corporate office structure. So far I didn't even hear them hit the ground.

"Thank you," I said meekly.

"Now, go see what's wrong with your mother," he admonished. "Call 911 if it's an emergency. Happy birthday, Mrs. Raymond," he called out grimly through the open window of the van, then marched back to his cruiser, entered it, slammed the door shut, threw it into drive, executed a curving U-turn across the double-yellow and vanished into the Fresno night.

I rushed around to the back. My mother had her hand planted on her chest. Joy was stroking her hair. Jack had his head telescoped halfway into the back. "What's wrong, Mom? Are you okay?"

She stopped her crying almost as abruptly as she had started and spoke in a voice clear as a bell, "Is he gone?"

"Yeah. What's up with the histrionics? You could have gotten us all thrown in the pokey."

"You told me to fake a panic attack if we ever got pulled over."

I coughed a laugh. Then, everyone, including Joy, started laughing.

"You are awesome, Mrs. Raymond," Jack said, beaming. "Thinking on your feet, you wily gal."

My mother smiled like a little girl hearing praise for her winning science project. "I'm not as dumb as you think."

"We don't think you're dumb, Mom."

She crooked her index finger and pointed it skyward. "I saved us all from going to the pokey."

Everyone laughed again. Tremendous relief had washed over the entire van. It had been a long, murderous day, and the last thing we all needed was for me to be hauled in and booked on a DUI.

I gave my mother a little squeeze before climbing back behind the wheel to confer with Jack. "Fuck, man, that was close."

"I hear you brother, I hear you," he said, also greatly relieved. Jack, seeing me make no move to start the vehicle, said, "Let's go."

"Fucking cop threw the keys out there."

"What?"

"Just wound up and chucked 'em. I think sort of in that direction." I pointed to the office complex edifice. Jack glanced out the window. "There's no way we're going to find them till it's light."

"Don't you have a spare?"

"No. They only gave me one set."

"Fuck," Jack said. "And you didn't think to make –"

From the back, my mother yelled, "Why aren't we going? I want to get back to Snapper."

I turned around. "Mom, the cop threw our keys away. We're going to have to have to hoof it back. Okay?"

"That bastard!" my mother said.

"All right, let's get out," I said.

Everybody climbed out of the Rampvan. Jack retrieved the Montrachet out of the cooler and the motley four of us walked and rolled the short distance back to the Marriott, Joy leading the way pushing my mother, Jack and me trailing in a solemn silence. To passersby we must have looked like a straggling band of survivors, all that remained of a vanquished army.

Back in our room, Jack and I, wineglasses in hand filled with chilled white Burgundy, lying on our separate queens, were reminiscing about the brush with the law when we heard a meek knock at the door. I got up to see who it was.

Joy was standing there, still in her sleeveless black dress. She looked pretty cute. I saw Jack take indecent notice, molesting her with his eyes.

"Hi, Joy. How's it going?" I said.

"Good. Your mom wants you to come in and say good night."

"Would you like a little glass of wine while I, uh, tuck my mother in?" She nodded up and down.

Jack leapt up from the bed, found a fresh wineglass and poured her more than she probably wanted and brought it over to her.

"Thanks," was all she said.

"I'll be right back." I would have cautioned Jack against even the possibility of laying a hand on Joy, because I knew he had been fantasizing about putting the moves on her since we got on the road. But with his manhood now a disabled veteran, there wasn't much to worry about.

I went next door to my mother's room. She lay supine on the bed, propped up on two pillows, the covers over her. Snapper, snuggled up next to her, perked up his little elfish ears and looked at me threateningly for a moment, growled, drawing his lips back to reveal his fangs.

"Oh, Snapper, it's just Miles coming to say good night. You be quiet." Snapper's ears folded down to a floppy position and he closed his eyes.

I eased down onto the edge of the bed. "How's the tooth, Mom? I saw you rub your jaw a couple times at dinner."

"It's fine," she said sharply.

"Did you rinse out with warm salt water like the dentist advised?"

"Yes," she said.

"But it's still bothering you, isn't it?"

"A little," she allowed. "But I don't want to be hospitalized."

"No one's going to hospitalize you, Mom. Okay?"

Her face suddenly grew introspective. I could see she was trying, in a bold effort to articulate what she was thinking, to assemble words that were darting around erratically in her stroke-damaged brain. "I mean," she started. "I don't want to go to the hospital for anything. I'd rather just die."

"Well, sometimes you don't have a choice, Mom."

She grew confused, as if she didn't comprehend that she didn't have indomitable control over her destiny. "They can't take me if I don't want to go," she said naively.

I didn't want to get into an argument with her; I wanted to get back to my glass of Montrachet, which I purposely didn't bring over to my mother's room because it would have taunted the demonic alcoholic force that slumbered latent inside her. So, I patted her on the shoulder and said reassuringly, "No one's going to take you to the hospital. And certainly not for an abscessed tooth."

"Oh, that's such good news," she said, genuinely relieved.

"That dentist we saw today was just playing it by the book. We'll find someone in Portland with a little more liberal mindset."

"Just don't tell them I'm on Coumadin," my mother advised in a sudden flash of wisdom.

"Good thinking. I won't. That was a mistake."

She nodded to herself while stroking Snapper's back.

"You'll be in Wisconsin with your sister pretty soon, Mom," I said.

"That's good."

"You're glad to be out of Las Villas de Muerte, aren't you?"

"Oh, yes. Every day someone would die in there. It was so depressing."

I nodded empathetically, at a loss for words.

"I appreciate you doing all this for me, Miles," she started before tears hampered her speech. "I know you're busy and a big deal now with your book and movie, but I'm worried about your drinking."

I didn't like having to hear about something I knew myself was getting out of control, much less from my stroke-addled, Chardonnay-guzzling mother. "That's why I brought Jack, to help with the driving."

"He drinks more than you!" my mother exclaimed.

"Well, we sort of tag team it, Mom. He drinks when I don't and I drink when he doesn't."

Knowing I was playing with her, she forced a laugh. Then the tears started up again. "I just want to make it to Wisconsin without you getting thrown in the pokey," she blubbered.

"Don't worry, Mom."

"Okay," she said. I rose from the edge of the bed. She cocked her head toward me and said, with reddened eyes, "Give me a kiss good night."

"Mom," I said, standing over her. "You know we don't do that."

She looked puzzled, groping desperately around in her whorled memory for the meaning of my words. "But we could start now," she insisted softly.

My mother had been a dutiful, but unaffectionate, mother, probably because she never had wanted to bear children. The three of us were not breast-fed and we never hugged, as far back as I could remember. When I got to the VA Hospital to pull the feeding tube on my comatose father after a triple bypass had gone haywire and rendered him a vegetable, I remember hugging my mother once he officially was declared dead. I remembered, looking at her in the Marriott's queen bed, how foreign her rounded, overweight body had felt in my enveloping arms as we silently commiserated my father's grim departure. I realized only then that moment that we had almost never touched. Headshrinkers had later theorized that this was probably the reason I had such difficulty with intimacy with women: Victoria, Maya, others, and all the one-night stands.

I leaned over the bed, squeezed her shoulder and said, "Good night, Mom."

"Good night, Miles."

I left her suite feeling sad. My mother, all alone in her hotel room. My mother, all alone in her condo when my brother went to part-time care. All alone in Las Villas de Muerte, staring at her TV, waiting, waiting, all the time she once told me, for one of her sons to come and take her for a drive.

Getting to the other room, I was assailed by the stink of some serious weed. Joy and Jack were passing a joint and laughing. Joy, who had a wicked giggle—which was nice to see for a change!—was sitting daintily on the edge of Jack's bed. Jack offered the joint to me, but I shook my head.

"Doesn't mix with wine for me. I get the spins. Plus, it makes me extremely self-conscious. If I thought about where we were, this quartet of ours and all the shit that's happened, I'd have a nervous breakdown."

Jack and Joy laughed, a kind of rolling laughter engendered by their being stoned.

I found my wineglass, moved to refresh it with the Montrachet, but only a dribble came out. "Jackson, you killed the fucking bottle."

"Relax, dude, there's another one in the mini-fridge."

I squatted and extracted a bottle of Justin Chardonnay. Opening it with my trusty key ring corkscrew, I poured a healthy splash. "Anyone else?" I said, holding up the bottle.

Joy shook her head in a tight no.

Jack said, "I'm good, brother."

I lay down on the adjoining queen and sipped the wine. Joy extinguished the blunt in her Altoids tin, and rose. "I should get back to your mother."

"No, stay," Jack said. "Phyllis's fine."

"I've got to give her her meds and take her brace off." She crossed to the door.

"All right, Joy, sleep well," I said.

"Thanks for the herbaceous adjustment," Jack said, raising his glass.

The door closed, leaving Jack and me alone. We sipped our wine in silence. Outside, someone dove into the pool and splashed around. Room service pushed a heavy cart clinking with dishes past our door.

"How's your cock?"

"It's fine," Jack said. "The needle hole isn't very big and it's stopped bleeding."

"Good. I was worried about you in that OR."

"The question will be when I take it for a test run. Will it rise to the occasion? Will it hurt...?"

"Will you come blood instead of opalescent seed?"

"Homes. You've got a way with putting horrific images in a person's mind."

I laughed. "That's why they pay me the big bucks."

"Fuck you, Homes. You just got lucky."

"Do you believe that fucking cop? Half a mile from the hotel, old woman in a wheelchair, no one on the fucking road, and he was on the verge of getting the cuffs out. Jesus! What the fuck's up with law enforcement these days?"

We fell into silence again, then Jack said. "If you want to take a cab back to that joint and do that waitress, that's cool, man."

"Nah. I considered it, Jackson. I mean, she's pretty cute and everything, but they're going to be going nuts until the wee hours and you know restaurant people, they're some of the most intemperate, degenerate souls in the world. We got to find the keys to the car and do some motoring tomorrow." I turned to him. "And, in deference to your injury, I wouldn't want you to be here all by yourself imagining me pounding some pretty girl on the floor in one of their private rooms, the two of us dousing each other's genitalia with some exalted Bourgogne *rouge*."

"Well, that's generous of you, Miles. Even if you are full of bullshit."

"Yeah, I was bullshitting you. I'm just tired. And I'm growing weary of the one-night stands."

"But you liked that Spanish chick, didn't you?"

"Laura," I said, pronouncing it phonetically. "Yeah. Smart girl. Passionate as all hell. Grandfather's some kind of famous lit professor in Spain. Knew Lorca personally or some shit. Mother's a painter. Hell, my dad sold Laundromats and my mother was a nurse. Imagine having artists as parents? I'd be so much further along in my career if I had."

"You can't think about shit like that," Jack said. "So, you liked her?"

"Yeah. I really liked her." I sipped my wine and grew contemplative, journeyed back to the Just Inn and Laura naked on the fake animal rug in front of that romantic fire. "You know, I don't mean to get all maudlin and shit, but I think I'm reaching the point I'm just tired of sleeping alone, or watching the chick leave while I'm nursing a hangover and trying to recollect how it all came to happen that a naked woman was in my house or hotel room. It gets dispiriting. It'd be nice to have someone who, you know, got me. Knew when to leave me alone, had a career of her own, paid her half and didn't expect me to support her..."

"And knew when to suck your dick," Jack finished.

"And knew when to fellate me. Absolutely."

"You might have to lower your standards a little bit," Jack mused.

"I'm not going to lower my standards. I don't want to wake up next to somebody who starts babbling about subprime mortgages or how to pull the perfect double espresso."

"So, what about Maya? She's smart. You guys can go on and on all night about wine."

"You know, too much baggage, too many scars. And do I really want to live in an area I helped make famous and fall headlong into that hedonistic crowd? Fuck, man, I'd never write another word again in my life, Jackson."

I heard gentle snoring. Cocking my head in Jack's direction, I saw that his head had drooped to one side. I rose, went to the dresser and found

an extra blanket and draped it over him. Next, I slowly untied his tennis
shoes and removed them from his malodorous feet. He snored away. I
slipped out of my clothes and climbed into the other bed. Maybe because
we had been talking about her, my thoughts turned to Laura. I could see
her face punctuated by those blazing black eyes and those red lipstick-col-
ored lips, hear her Catalan accent...

chapter **10**

Early the next morning I roused Jack from a deep slumber to help me go look for the keys. He grumbled a bit, but I inspired him to take a shower and get dressed so that we could get the visit with Mom's brother over with and get back up into wine country.

"Okay, now you're talking my language," he said.

While Jack showered I got on the computer, tinkered around with Google maps, and then charted our day's itinerary–assuming, I thought ruefully, no one came down with priapism, we weren't arrested for a DUI and none of us had to make an emergency dental visit.

A heavy blue sky greeted us as Jack and I walked out of the Marriott, donned our sunglasses and made our way down East Shaw in the direction of our abandoned vehicle. It wasn't even eight o'clock and I estimated the temperature to be in the upper 80s. By the time we got to the van we were drenched in sweat, shirts sticking to our backs.

We searched the area where I calculated the officer had thrown the keys, a vast parking lot bordered by a dense hedge interspersed with trees. The sun beat down mercilessly as Jack kept muttering, "fucking cop," and "why didn't you have a spare made, Miles? That was idiotic!" I theorized at one point that the key ring could be up in the branches of the trees, to which an exasperated and hung over Jack responded, "Let's just call a fucking locksmith."

"It's 8:30, Jackson," I said, "there's no locksmith on call right now. Let's just give it another hour."

"Fucking cop!" Jack yelled, his hangover and sore pecker gripping him like twin lobster claws. "Why didn't he just leave them down at the station? Asshole."

We fanned out again and continued our search for the hurled set of keys. Like trapped flies, we zigzagged this way and that, bent at the waist, scouring the area for the proverbial needle in the haystack. To passing motorists we must have looked like a pair of LSD-tripping hippies anachronistically lost in time. After a futile hour of looking we trudged back to the idled Rampvan, a grousing Jack eager to get back into the rhythm of the road. As we approached the van, something glinted and caught my eye. I stepped closer and zeroed in on the object. I jackknifed forward and burst out laughing.

"What's so fucking funny?" Jack said.

"Check it out," I said, pointing and motioning for him to come over. I was still laughing, more out of relief than mirth.

Jack stalked around to the back of the Rampvan where the keys sat perched on the rear bumper, sparkling like a diamond bracelet under the malefic, blindingly bright sun.

"Fucking cop faking a throw, Jesus," he said disgustedly. "Must have gotten a good chuckle out of that one."

We climbed inside and I started up the motor. It was a reassuring sound. I turned to Jack: "What a joy to hear that engine turn over and feel that AC," I said somewhat giddily.

"Fucking A, brother. Fucking A." He clapped his hands together. "We're just lucky this baby didn't get boosted."

"Or towed."

"Or towed."

Back at the Marriott, Joy brought my bathed and groomed mother to the lobby and we made our way over to the Courtyard Café. A typical corporate hotel breakfast spot: green carpeting, Naugahyde chairs, cheap wood tables, Styrofoam-paneled ceiling and large plate-glass windows letting in way more light than Jack or I cared for in our current condition. While Joy pushed my mom through the buffet, which she insisted on, Jack and I ordered from the a la carte menu, too hung over to deal with the congested line of predominantly corpulent Courtyard guests pigging out at the buffet in an apparent state of permanent insatiety.

After we had ordered, Jack, unshaven, asked the teenaged waitress, "Can I get, like, a Bloody Mary from the bar or something?"

"We don't have a bar, sir," she said.

"Jesus, what kind of a hotel is this? No bar? Wow."

I leaned across the table and said to Jack, "We've got at least another bottle of Foxen Chardonnay in the cooler. Let's just get through this breakfast."

Jack looked unappeased. "I need a drink, man."

"I know you do. So do I. But, let's just ride it out and let my mom have her breakfast, okay?"

"And do we really have to go see her brother Bud who she hasn't seen in fifty years?"

"Yes, we do."

"It's fucking hotter than a blast furnace here."

In my peripheral vision, Joy came rolling my mother back to the table. "Jack, I'm paying you good money on this trip, right? Money you need, right?"

"Yeah," he admitted reluctantly.

"You've been getting laid, you've been drinking wines way out of your price and palate range, and feasting like Lucullus. Let's just slow down a little; we've got a long way to go yet." Jack grew sullenly silent. "How's your...?"

"The bleeding's stopped but it still hurts like shit where he stuck the needle."

"I'll bet. He sunk that fucker in deep. Take a couple Vikes, it'll take the edge off."

Jack uncapped his vial of painkillers and popped two. Joy pushed my mother into the empty space at the table where a chair had been removed, and lifted the tray of food my mother had selected from her lap. Jack looked like he was going to hurl when he got an eyeful of her spoils.

"Jesus, Mom, are you going to eat all that?"

She shrugged like a shy little girl. Maybe it was because she'd had parents who went through the Great Depression. Or the fact that my father was so parsimonious that she took any opportunity for gluttony at someone else's expense, as if to spite him.

She damn near ate it all: the waffle with butter and maple syrup, the Denver omelet, the two pieces of toast slathered with butter and strawberry jam, and the three greasy-looking pork links. Jack and I, our stomachs unsettled from all the wine, picked desultorily at our scrambled eggs.

Joy daintily, and slowly, picked at a bowl of granola topped with fruit and
a dollop of yogurt. Now and then I couldn't avoid noticing that my
mother was working the abscessed tooth with her tongue.

"How's the tooth feel this morning, Mom?"

"It's okay," she said.

"Think you can make it to Portland? I've got connections up there."

"Oh, yes. *No problema.*"

"Are you looking forward to seeing Bud?"

Her eyes half-shut with tears and she nodded.

We finished up breakfast, retrieved Snapper, and converged on the
Rampvan, getting the AC fired up. I punched in Bud's address on the
GPS and let the monotone, English-accented feminine voice guide me to
where he resided.

My mother's brother, whom she earlier admitted had fallen on hard
times, lived in a three-story heap of weathered brick adjacent to the Fresno
freight yards. The asphalt lot was weed-fissured and badly buckled in sections, having surrendered to erosion and lack of the necessary funds to re-
pair it, and the white lines had long since faded to ghostly reminders of
parking spaces. They didn't need many because it looked like most of the
residents of the Ponderosa Hotel were pensioners, lone men subsisting on
meager fixed incomes in squalid shoebox-sized quarters, each with one
window and one mattress and one hotplate to his name.

We all clambered out of the Rampvan. It was hot out, the kind of hot
that envelops you like an equatorial prostitute in an un-air-conditioned
motel room. Nearby, an anaconda of a freight train, most of the flatcars
loaded with felled and exfoliated trees, lay still in the intense sun.

I got behind my mother, took the handles of her wheelchair and turned
to Jack and Joy, "I'll take her up."

"All right," Jack said, sipping a Sierra Nevada he'd squirreled away in
the cooler, massaging his hangover. Joy fingered her tin of marijuana, no
doubt itching to light up. Snapper, tethered by his leash, was jumping up
and down and barking, straining for a run.

I rolled my mother over the bumpy asphalt toward the entrance. The
Ponderosa must have been built in the early 1900s, when there were no
ADA laws, and I had to turn her around and dolly-bump her up the short
flight of concrete steps to the entrance.

The dusky, mote-swirling lobby reeked of disinfectant. The threadbare wall-to-wall looked like it had absorbed its share of urine and vomit and God knows what else. A gray-haired desk man with a cadaverous face, fissured as the asphalt outside, sucked on a cigarette as we approached the tiny reception cubicle. A tarnished antique hand bell rested on the desk. Alerted by footsteps, I turned and watched an elderly man, stooped over, obviously drunk, stagger out the door and into the blinding sunshine like some kind of prehistoric bird with a maimed wing.

"We don't have any rooms to let," the man said in a sinister growl, taking a hit on his cigarette and setting it in an ashtray where it smoldered.

"We're here to see Bud Kuchta. What room is he in?"

"Bud? 311."

"Thank you."

I turned my mother away and pushed her down the ill-lit hall that looked like one of the rejected set designs from *Barton Fink*. Rejected because it was *too* depressing.

My mother's wheelchair barely fit in the creaky elevator, which I imagined being winched up by a pair of bald, tattooed men, it shuddered and shook so much in climbing just two floors.

We came out into another dimly lit corridor with more threadbare carpeting and that same rank smell of industrial-strength disinfectant.

We came to a halt at 311. I let my mother knock on the door. A cigarette-hoarse voice called out from behind the door, "It's open."

I turned the burnished brass knob and pushed open the door, my outstretched arm reaching across my mother's shoulder. We were welcomed—if that's the right word!—by a small rectangular room scarcely more commodious than a prison cell. To the left lay a gray-and-white patterned mattress with no linens, just a filthy army blanket. To the right was what amounted to a tiny kitchen with a shelf fashioned out of a 1x6 board nailed crudely to the wall and lined with cans and cans of food. A hotplate rested atop a miniature refrigerator. Jaundiced sunlight streamed through yellowed and rent curtains illuminating a space petrified with dust, a room that hadn't had a proper cleaning in years.

Bud sat slouched at a wooden desk by a dirt-streaked window, staring out at the freight yard. He was a hollow shell of a man in his seventies with a pallid complexion, thinning gray hair and a fragilely emaciated

body as if he didn't get much nourishment, and certainly no exercise. An
unfiltered cigarette burned between tremulous fingers. Next to an ashtray
overflowing with butts, an uncapped pint of Popov vodka gleamed in the
sunlight. I positioned my mother in the middle of the room, which placed
her very close to her long-lost baby brother. I couldn't imagine what must
have been going through her stroke-addled brain.

"Hi, Bud," she said.

Slowly, as if it hurt, Bud turned to face us. I wasn't sure whether he
was happy to have the company, or if seeing his sister after fifty years only
reminded him what a squanderingly lousy mess he had made of his
wretched life. Then, too, he was seeing his sister for the first time after
half a century in a wheelchair, a victim of a stroke. The mutual sibling
dereliction was both pathetic and heart-rending.

Bud croaked in a barely audible voice, "Hi, Phyllis."

I pushed my mother a little closer. "This is my son, Miles."

"Hi Bud," I said. "It's nice to meet you."

He nodded without meeting my gaze or offering his hand to be shaken.
He reeked of tragedy. If there was a scintilla of life spirit left in him it was
buried so deep it would have taken an earthmover to excavate it.

Uncomfortable at this moribund reunion, I backed away from the
chair. "I'll leave the two of you alone. Come back in an hour. We've got
to get on the road, Mom."

I walked out of the Ponderosa Hotel as if Death himself, with scythe
and monk's cowl, were stalking me.

I found Jack leaning against the Rampvan, amber bottle of ale clutched
in hand, lit cigarette dangling from his lips, checking his messages. Joy
had wandered off with Snapper toward the rail yard and its labyrinth of
rusted tracks. Holding him by the leash, she stood silently, dwarfed by all
the freight trains resting inanimately in the distance, awaiting their marching orders. The sun was starting to climb into the sky and the asphalt
baked from its intensity.

Jack clicked off his phone and looked up at me, the beer having cheered
him up. "Mom meet Bud?"

"Pretty grim in there," I said, shaking my head. "Pretty grim."

Jack cast a backward glance at the dilapidated hotel. "Looks like I've
got a shot at getting on this reality show," he said.

"Oh, yeah?"

"Yeah, Rick left a message. Said they need an A.D. So, it's not directing, but..."

"That's great," I said. "When would you have to start?" I asked, worry creeping into my voice.

"I don't know, I have to call him. Don't worry, Miles, I'll make it to Sheboygan. I'm sure it doesn't go until the fall."

The depressingly desolate freight yard and the brief encounter with Bud foundered me to a level of despair I hadn't experienced since before the sale of the novel. I rummaged in my pocket for my cell, scrolled through my directory, stopped at Laura. I had saved a picture of her I had taken and now her youthful, smiling face with those luminous eyes was boring straight into the emptiness of my soul. I scrolled to her name in my contacts and tapped it. After five rings I got her voicemail.

"Hi, LAU-ra. This is Miles. I just wanted to *habla* you and see if you got back to *Bur*-celona okay. I miss you. Call you again."

Jack, eavesdropping, remarked, "You really miss her, or you just keeping the fish on the hook?"

"No. I miss her. I've never made it with a European before. I got to get out of this California rut. These aerobicized, surgically enhanced bleached blondes experimenting with polypsychopharmacology. Neurotic nut bags. Laura's the real deal. Plus, she's got this beautiful silky armpit hair and that turns me on."

Jack laughed. "So, are you going to move to Spain?"

"I'm going to move somewhere. I need a whole change of venue, Jack," I said morosely, the visit with Bud bumming me out and eliciting a rainbow of surging emotions around my current state and my uncertain future. "I'm sick of this monster I created. Drink. Fuck. Drink. Fuck. I need to get back to my true self," I concluded, nodding affirmation of my newfound resolve. "Not that I'd even recognize it. But hey, depressing visits with broken-down uncles can have a salubrious effect on one."

"Salubrious?" Jack said. "We all need some salubriousness."

"Salubrity."

"Fuck you."

Joy rejoined us with a panting, happy Snapper. We waited a clock-ticking hour, confabulating desultorily, before I returned to the mausoleum of the Ponderosa Hotel to reclaim my mother.

I re-entered Bud's room to find the two of them awkwardly embracing,
brother jackknifed at the waist like someone with scoliosis, sister extending
her one good arm across his emaciated torso. Likely due to the fact that
the pint of Popov was nearly empty, Bud seemed in a markedly more upbeat mood. Wrapping up his goodbyes with my mother, he lurched toward me like a human scarecrow and pulled me down into a bony hug.
The stench of booze and the sour smell of someone who rarely showered
discharged from his pores. It was the malodorousness of death. "Take good
care of my sister," he effused. "She's a saint. A real saint."

"I will," I said, a little confused at his transformation. Perhaps my
mother was a saint?

"Bye Bud," she croaked through a shroud of tears. "Get on that train
and come visit Alice and me."

"I will, Phyllis, soon's you get settled in," a florid-faced Bud said, waving goodbye, smiling through his eroded landscape of a face.

In the elevator I said, "Your visit really cheered him up, huh?"

"Oh, yes," she said. "He's lived a hard life."

"How come I never met him?"

"We never knew where he was most of the time. He was homeless. Rusty
used to get so angry when he would call collect and then ask for a handout."

I flashed on a memory of my parents having gotten in an argument
after a phone call that seemed to unnerve them. I remembered asking
them what was wrong, and all my stoic, Czechoslovak mother's having
said was: "Your Uncle Bud needs help."

"Oh, yes," she said now. "He used to call all the time." Tears leached
from her eyes. "I'm so glad he's got a place to live."

I wheeled her out of the flophouse, backed her down the short flight
of concrete steps and bumped her across the buckled asphalt parking lot
back to the Rampvan. Family-reunion mission accomplished. As Joy took
the reins I said to Jack, "Get thee to a winery!"

"Amen, brother. Amen."

We loaded everybody up and took off, Jack at the helm. I admonished
him to go light on the beers, that we had a ways to go to the Sonoma Valley, where we planned to stop for a late lunch and a little wine tasting–at
"primo Pinot properties" I exulted to Jack–before getting at last to the
end of this leg of the trip: picturesque seaside Mendocino.

Freed from the depressing Ponderosa Hotel and the desolate freight yard, we were all happy to be back on Highway 99 and bearing north, putting the miles behind us. I continued to worry about my mother's infected tooth and making it all the way to Wisconsin where she could get it properly taken care of before it exploded on her, but other than that an amicable atmosphere of calm pervaded the Rampvan.

Half an hour out of Fresno, a green highway mileage sign read: "Merced 18 mi."

I turned and faced my mother and said excitedly. "Mom, we're going through Merced."

"That's where you were born," she said.

My father had been briefly stationed at Castle Air Force Base in Merced when we were young. My memories of the small town were fragmented into snippets of blurry, indistinct images because we'd moved away when I was three. The story, as told by my father, was that he was grounded and didn't want to have anything more to do with the Air Force if he couldn't fly. So, he took early retirement with no benefits, which always struck me as a little implausible. But after he died and I had moved my mother into the assisted-living facility I sifted through her personal belongings to see what was worth saving. In one of the many boxes they'd had in storage, I found a file. Inside it, I discovered yellowed pages typed by someone on a manual machine, presenting a radically different account of why my father had left the service. According to these documents typed up by some anonymous party, my father, drunk on his ass in the Officers' Club, had cold-cocked a senior officer (a full colonel no less!) and put him in the hospital with a broken nose. He narrowly averted a court-martial by agreeing to a dishonorable discharge. When my mother regained some of her sentience following her stroke, I questioned her about the information in these official documents. After some hemming and hawing, she grudgingly admitted it was all true. She'd no doubt been sworn to secrecy, so as not to besmirch the family name and vitiate the esteemed image the children erroneously held of their charismatic father.

"You remember what street we lived on, Mom?"

"Oh, yes," she said, her memory remarkably lucid when it came to long-ago events and places. "East Alexander. 727." She pointed her right index finger to the ceiling to ward off tears. "I always remembered it because that's my birthday."

"Do you want to stop and see the old place, Mom?"

"Oh, yes. Please."

I turned to Jack, already scowling at the prospect of another sponta-neous detour. "Half an hour, tops," I said. "It's where I was born."

"It's cool," he said, a second ale having sanded the ragged edges off his hangover.

At the off-ramp for Merced we pulled into the first gas station. I punched 727 E. Alexander into the GPS. Jack returned from the conven-ience store with some Red Bulls–his preferred transition beverage–and Joy wheeled my mother out of the bathroom and back into the Rampvan, her reddened eyes indicative of her being–and justifiably so!–stoned out of her coconut. Jack fitted the ramp back into the undercarriage and settled into the passenger seat, popped open a Red Bull and sucked on it thirstily.

"Where's Snapper?" my mother asked, rapidly growing alarmed.

"Where's the little guy, Joy?" I said.

"He was in here."

"He's not in here!" my mother shrieked. "Oh, no!"

I leapt out and frantically looked around. Across the street I spotted Snapper lifting his leg against a car in front of a Denny's. I sprinted across the busy street and called out his name. Ears pricking up at the familiar timbre of my voice, he came running, leash trailing behind. I grabbed it and scolded him like my mother would: "Snapper. Don't go running off like that. Bad dog." I gave him a little rap on the head and he whimpered. Christ, I thought, now *I've* anthropomorphized him!

I returned the incorrigible escapee to my mother who took up the re-proaches where I had left off. Then, as if her dog were not responsible for his mad dash across the busy intersection, she turned her splenetic angst on her nurse. "You have to watch out for Snapper, Joy."

"I'm sorry."

"You smoke too much Mary Jane," she shot back viciously. "That's why you forget."

"Okay, Mom, okay," I said sharply, anxious to quash the enmity building in the back of the van. "He's back. Everything's cool. Now, just calm down."

My mother returned her attention to Snapper. "Oh, Snapper, why do you make me worry like that? Huh? What would I do without you?"

I turned the engine over and started out of the Shell station, following the audio directions issuing from the GPS. A couple of times I glanced in the rearview mirror. Joy had her head turned away from my mother and was staring out the window, as if transfixed by the landscape. But that landscape had nothing transfixing about it. It was clear Joy resented being chastened by my mother. In my solipsistic way I hadn't given much thought to all the hours they had spent together and how my mother probably–no, for sure–treated her like a slave on a plantation she ruled over as dynastic matriarch. Because Joy was shy, and because the pay was so generous, she remained uncomplaining, but I worried about my mother's belittling treatment of her. Worried that the emotionally repressed Filipina was going to explode.

Merced is a city of fewer than 100,000 residents. It's blisteringly hot in the summer and cold in the winter. Mostly lower middle-class, it boasts a large Asian population. The residential area looked pretty rundown, and included a lot of RV and trailer parks that were pictures of bitter communal neglect.

The GPS finally guided us to our destination. I braked to a stop in front of a single-story stucco structure. I rolled my mother out while Jack and Joy, who had no interest in this stop–in fact, were grumblingly annoyed by it–remained inside the air-conditioned van.

My mother and I parked ourselves on the sidewalk before the house that she and my father had once owned and where I had spent my earliest infancy. The front yard was a riot of weeds and unwatered grass, parched brown by the punishing heat, littered with discarded toys, so much flotsam on a polluted waterway. A cheap, inflatable pool, bone dry, sat like a massive, turquoise carbuncle in the middle of the desiccated lawn. In the driveway was parked an old, rusted Datsun pickup, its bed piled high with unrecognizable junk parts salvaged from God knows where.

"Do you remember the time you ran away at night and we found you sitting on the railroad tracks?" my mom said, staring at the dilapidated house.

I had a vivid memory of it, in fact. I remembered running on the tracks, across the street, as if wanting to escape. "Yeah, I do."

"We were so worried," she said. "We thought a train was going to come and kill you. Why do you think you did that?"

"I don't know, Mom. I've actually told four headshrinkers about that to get their interpretation."

"You've been to four shrinks?" she asked.

"Well, five, if you count the biofeedback guy." I paused, and journeyed back in the impressionistic memory. "One shrink, a woman, said that maybe there were problems in your marriage, and maybe I was, in my preconscious way, trying to commit suicide." I looked down at my mother. Her face had grown ominously dark all of a sudden as if I had disinterred something unpleasant from *her* memory bank.

"I've always wanted to ask you something, Mom..."

"What?"

"When we were little, you went away for a year, do you remember that?" She receded into a stony silence.

"Dad said that you had to, for work. What was the real story?" Her expression was devoid of affect.

"Did you have a nervous breakdown or something?"

"No," she replied harshly.

"Where'd you go? Huh?" I tried to make light of it. "Take the cure?"

"I want to go back." With her one good arm she tried to wheel her chair away from me, but a wheel was stuck in a crack in the sidewalk.

"What's wrong, Mom? It was a simple question. It was forty years ago. What does it matter?"

"I want to go. Take me back."

"Okay. Okay." I got behind her chair, one wheel of which she was still trying to dislodge from the sidewalk crack. "Are you sure you don't want to go up to the door and knock and see who's living there?"

"No!"

I rolled her back to the van. "I didn't mean to upset you, Mom. It was just something that I always wondered about."

"I don't want to talk about it!"

"Okay." I massaged her shoulder but she shrugged my hand away.

"I think you'll like Sonoma a lot better," I said.

As I wheeled her up the ramp into the back, she stuck to her petulant silence. Jack glanced from my mother to me, uneasily. "What's going on?"

"Nothing. Personal." I threw a backward look at my mother. She avoided my gaze.

Inspiration lit up my mind like a flare as I roared away. "Jack, see if you can pull up the address for Domaine Carneros." A beautiful, chateau-styled winery that specialized in champagne, but did nicely vinified still wines as well. I remembered their outdoor restaurant as lovely, with panoramic vineyard views under creamy blue skies. And the food was scrumptious.

I punched the address Jack gave me into the GPS, was gratified with the news that, a mere 150 miles away, we could easily make lunch. After the punishing heat of Fresno and the white-trash environs of Merced, and the frostiness of the exchange with my mother, Domaine Carneros would be an ethereal transition. Moods, I reasoned–especially my mother's fickle ones–would be quickly ameliorated. I prayed! Invoking the deity. After begging for absolution for my transgressing soul. LAU-ra. You will be my anima. You will rescue me from this morass without my having to resort to the latest SSRI. I chuckled.

"What?" Jack said.

"Nothing. A little private tête-à-tête with myself." I snapped my fingers. "Hey, I've got a brainstorm. Go to the Domaine Carneros Web site and see when they close for lunch, then call them and book a reservation for whatever's their last seating. Have you figured out how to do that on your iPhone, big guy?"

"I can do anything," Jack said. "Except fuck!"

I laughed.

"It's not funny."

We rode the 99 north through Modesto and other landlocked dystopias where lives were squandered and wrecked by low-paying jobs and futureless aspirations of a mostly soul-crippling nature. Jack got through to Domaine Carneros's number and made a reservation for two o'clock.

"An hour-and-a-half there, we should have no problem making Mendocino," I calculated out loud. "And from there, just a day's run up to the IPNC. Jack, did you know that the Willamette is planted in 2/3's Pinot?"

"I know. You already told me."

"Sorry. Anyway, most of it is so small-production it never gets out of the state. You're going to be drinking some really great stuff."

"I'm looking forward to it. Looking forward to getting off the road for a few days and cooling our heels."

"Amen, brother, amen."

We arced off the 99, hooked back onto I-5 and headed toward Stockton, where my mother made me stop so she could relieve her bladder.

"I'll take her in, Joy," I said, hoping to diffuse the no-longer latent animosity hanging over the two women like a poisonous gas.

Joy just nodded.

Jack went into the convenience store for a pack of cigarettes and more Red Bulls as I wheeled my mother into the bathroom. In the handicapped stall, I held out my right hand for her to grasp and hoisted her out of the wheelchair.

"Pull my pants down," she instructed, the tinge of hostility for asking her those personal questions sharpening her words.

I worked the polyester slacks down to her knees. I was shocked and mortified to see she wasn't wearing any underpants. "Don't you wear underwear, Mom?"

"No. It's too hard to go."

Averting my glance, I swiveled her until she was plopped on the toilet.

A moment later I heard pee tinkling into the bowl. When she was done, we reversed the maneuver and got her back in her chair.

As I wheeled her out of the bathroom, I said, "I didn't mean to bring up anything uncomfortable back in Merced, Mom."

"It was a long time ago," she said enigmatically. "I'm hungry."

"Lunch is soon," I said.

Back in the cool of the van, Jack offered me a Red Bull.

"I hate that shit. Tastes like industrial waste. Give me one of those waters." I turned around. "Anyone need anything back there?"

Joy remained mute, as was her wont. She had her eyes glued on the scene out the window.

"I'm fine," my mother said.

"All right. Domaine Carneros in an hour."

A little ways up the I-5 we veered left on rural Highway 12 in the direction of Napa. The scenery improved dramatically. Parched fields surrendered, first, to lush, green rollercoastering farmland, then finally to vineyards cooled by the prevailing winds streaming over the chilly waters of San Pablo Bay. Highway 12 turned into the two-lane 121 and bent north toward Yountville, and Domaine Carneros. A few wispy clouds had amassed in the deep blue sky, a half-hearted threat of a late-afternoon thundershower.

We pulled into the parking lot at Domaine Carneros, a gorgeous parcel of vinous acreage. We were a little early so we decided to sample some of

Domaine Carneros's finest before eating. Jack and I definitely needed a libational adjustment and I was positive a little bubbly would pacify my mother's unrepressed peevishness.

As we trudged up the concrete path to the winery, the tasting room loomed before us, a grand above-ground grotto, its sloping facade decorated with an abundant arbor of intertwining ivy.

Inside it was cool and the musky smell of all things wine-related greeted our senses. We bellied up to the bar which was manned by three pourers. Open bottles glinted on the oak-paneled surfaces, interspersed by spit buckets. This being a weekday, it wasn't too crowded–maybe four or five samplers of Carneros's exquisite champagnes, Pinots and Chardonnays.

I turned to the three of them and said in a lowered tone: "Mom, Jack, don't mention the movie or the book, okay? I just want to enjoy my wine in anonymity for once."

They nodded in agreement.

I handed one of the pourers my credit card. He placed four tasting glasses in front of us and poured into each a dollop of their Pinot Noir Rosé–lovely, dry, perfumed, *and* pinkish-hued. After tasting through a couple of their low-end champagnes and a Chardonnay, we journeyed to their Pinots.

"Are you sure you don't want to try this with us, Mom? All you ever drink is white. Maybe it's time to light the other pilot."

She scrunched up her face and shook her head no. "I don't like red wine." She held out her champagne flute and pleaded, "I'll have a little more champagne, please."

After a series of samplings that seemed to elevate everyone's spirits we climbed a short flight of stairs to The Restaurant Patio. Round, white-clothed tables, shielded from the sun by large blue-and-white umbrellas, were arranged on the terrace overlooking the vineyards, just as I remembered. I flashed back to fifteen years ago, when Victoria and I honeymooned up here to go wine-tasting. We splurged on the posh Sonoma Mission Inn, laughed and drank our way through the Sonoma Valley, dreaming of the films we would make together. We made them. They went unrecognized. And the marriage foundered on the shoals of artistic failure. As the Maître d' seated us, removing one of the chairs so that Joy could wheel my mother up to the table, I tried in vain to shake the image of Victoria and me and that youthful, starry-eyed time, to stave off a bout of melancholy that the alcohol only exacerbated.

We were handed lunch menus and a wine list. As everyone perused the menus I turned my attention to the wine list. When our waitperson, a slim guy in his twenties with thinning blond hair, appeared I said, "Bring us a bottle of the '99 Vintage Brut, will you? And some water."

A few minutes later he returned, and expertly uncorked the champagne, bearing down on the heavily pressurized cork as it emerged from the neck of the bottle. When it neared the top, he gently bent it sideways, producing just the slightest, barely audible, *pfft*.

"Nice," I said.

"Can't let those bubbles escape." He poured us all around. "It's all about the bubbles."

I held my flute out to the center of the table and proposed, "Let's have a toast." All three extended their glasses. "First of all to Jack–a little under the weather for reasons I won't elaborate on–for accompanying us on this journey and sharing the driving. My best friend, the only one I can divulge my deepest secrets to, and vice versa." Everyone clinked glasses with Jack. "To Joy, who has taken on the thankless task of caring for my cantankerous, sometimes racist and demeaning moth–"

"I am not," my mother chopped me off mid-word.

"...who forgets, because of the devastating brain injury she suffered, that we do have her best interests in mind, won't abandon her–unless she becomes a total pain in the ass!–and merely hope she will stop her caviling and caterwauling." I placed a hand on my mother's shoulder and gave it a squeeze. "But we still love her." The tears once again sprang to my mother's eyes and she nodded like some sad Buddha figurine come to life. "A toast to you, Mom." We all clinked glasses with her, even Joy, who had borne the brunt of my mother's ill-temperedness. "And, finally, to me, for opening up my wallet and funding this roustabout freak show. I've had my doubts, I admit. Sometimes I wake in the middle of the night and think I've gone AWOL from the reservation, but if we can get my mom to Wisconsin to be with her sister and have some fun along the way, then it'll all have been worth it." I thrust out my glass and circled it around the table, as they clinked theirs against mine.

The lunch menu was small, but eclectic and had something for every-one. The view was bucolic and peaceful, the surrounding countryside a merciful remove from the brambly dessication of Central California. The irritability that seemed to be fomenting with the detour to see Bud and the house where I grew up, the personal contretemps between my mother and me, had evaporated. We were in the heart of wine country now, with cold, wondrously tasty vintage champagne, cooling breezes, lush greenery, and life suddenly seemed, for once, haloed with pleasantness. After a single glass of champagne, I broke the bank on a bottle of Chandon's Carneros Pinot, a rich, jammy one that had Jack exulting and smacking his lips. My mother, of course, liked the fact that we had abandoned the champagne in the ice bucket to her. Joy, as was her preference, drank abstemiously.

Once sated on the kitchen's terrific offerings, we left the table and headed back to the Rampvan. Jack, popping a Red Bull and arguing that he was fine, commandeered the wheel.

"Just keep it at the speed limit, okay? We don't need a reprise of last night."

"Hey, I wasn't the mental midget who did a left on a double-yellow, short horn."

"Okay. Guilty." I punched in the address of the B&B in Mendocino and the Brit-accented woman's voice transformed us back into direction-less robots.

A little high on wine, I said to Jack, "I wonder what the chick who does the GPS voice looks like?"

"Yeah, I'm starting to get horny for her."

I laughed. The wine-buzz had raised our moods. We were past the halfway point and now it was going to be wine and more wine all the way to the Willamette.

With less than two hundred miles between us and Mendocino I tai-lored the route options to take us through the picturesque Sonoma Valley, hoping that the dramatic change of scenery would continue to elevate our collective mood as we bore down on the Willamette Valley, where the three days off the road would certainly rejuvenate us all.

As we drove through the increasingly wooded landscape on a tortuous single-lane road flanked by vineyards and orchards and wineries, Jack an-noyed me with his frequent requests to pull over for "a little taste."

"Let's just wait until we get up to Anderson Valley," I said, as we fled by yet another quaint sign, complete with arrow pointing down a dirt road. "I'll take you to Ridge and we'll pound some awesome Zins."

"All right. I'm going to hold you to it."

In the back my mother had fallen asleep, her head listed to one side. Joy was leaning against the window, hypnotized by the traveling terrain. She looked lonely, far away from where she had grown up.

"Were you born in the Philippines, Joy?" I asked.

She nodded yes.

"Your parents?"

She nodded, her eyes still trained out the window.

"Any brothers or sisters?"

"Two. Sisters."

"What do they do?"

"One's a doctor. The other's an architect."

"Oh, really. Where do they live?"

"You ask too many questions."

"I'm just trying to get to know you. We've still got a long way to go."

"They're on the East Coast," she said evasively.

"What about your parents?" She made a face as if hoping I would stop. "Are they still alive?"

"My father's dead."

"He must have died young."

She nodded, bent her head toward the window and lost herself once again in the fleeting verdancy.

I turned back to the windshield. With all the wineries we were passing I was jonesing for a drink. "You know," I said to Jack. "My mom's crashed out. We're coming up on Gary Farrell. We should run in and get a quick taste. Used to be a great winery."

Jack turned to me and smiled broadly. "You've got your ESP working now, Homes."

As the sign for Gary Farrell came into view, I wordlessly signaled Jack to make the left onto a narrow asphalt road. We climbed through towering trees that dappled the steep acclivity. I told Joy, my voice lowered so as not to wake my snoring mother, that we were going to go in for a little taste, that I had a few friends to say hi to, and would be back shortly. She nodded, a flicker of disapprobation in her expression.

"I'd invite you, but if she woke and found us gone, she'd freak out."

Joy gave another nod, still looking peeved.

"Plus, you can..."–I pressed my middle and index fingers together and tapped them against my lips. She looked down and giggled.

Gary Farrell is nothing less than one of the finest New World *vignerons*. However, he had sold out to a corporate entity, so the jury was out on the recent vintages which didn't bear his signature. The winery, constructed of stone and wood, is set in a grove of majestic redwoods. His tasting room is nonpareil: you enter through heavy wood doors with a triangle arch into a large room that is all wood and glass. There's no bric-a-brac for sale: no T-shirts on display, no corkscrews with his logo, no superannuated tomes on wine. Just a long, lacquered, crescent of oak that serves as the bar, in an octagonal building perched atop a hill that reigns over Sonoma. The tasting room's austerity, combined with its spectacular, sweeping views of the Russian River Valley, always makes me feel like I'm floating weightless in some rarefied realm.

As if on cue, the lone tasting room manager, a middle-aged ash-blonde, drifted over, welcomed us to Gary Farrell and then asked, pro forma, which tasting we wanted to do: the Premiere or Limited release, which was $5.00 more. Naturally, we chose the latter.

"I'm really interested in your Pinots," I said to her.

"Oh, you must have just seen that movie, *Shameless*." She laughed. Her ruddy face looked like Mrs. Santa Claus.

Jack rolled his eyes; he knew what was coming next.

"Well, actually... I wrote the novel it was based on." This was my problem. Get a little wine in me and I unleashed the beast. After ten years of hardship and rejection, and less than a year's success, I still craved the attention.

Her eyes widened and her head thrust forward slightly. "Really? You're kidding, right?" she asked skeptically, as if I were lying in hopes of some free wine.

I leaned my elbows on the bar and telescoped my face close to hers and said *sotto voce*, "Tell you what. Let's play a little game. If I can prove in less than a minute, without making a phone call, that I wrote the novel, will you pour us through all of your Pinots? And then when I get home from my trip I'll sign books for everyone here and ship them to you."

She ruminated a moment, contemplating breaking established tasting-room protocol, then decided, if I was for real, the new owner likely wouldn't mind. "Okay, you're on."

I rooted my wallet out of my back pocket and produced a piece of paper folded into quarters, unfolded it, and handed it to her. With both hands she held it up to her eyes. She was looking at my lifetime free certificate from the Hitching Post. In the lower left corner was hand printed: "Miles '*Shameless*' Raymond–Thank you!"

"So, if I go broke," I joked, "I can park a trailer someplace near the Hitching Post and eat and drink gratis the rest of my life."

"You're Miles Raymond?" she asked, incredulity mixed with the celebrity excitement factor.

"Yep. I am," I said, immodesty now rising–and not always flatteringly! "So, can we get started on those Pinots? My friend and I have a thirst that needs slaking."

"Well, I guess. After all, you won the bet. It's such a pleasure to meet you."

I handed her a credit card. "Put whatever number you want on it, I don't care."

She pushed my Amex back. "Our Pinot sales have gone through the roof since that movie came out. We owe you, too."

"Well, thank you for your generosity...?"

"Debbie."

"Nice to meet you." We shook, and she knelt down, reemerged with the first bottle, set it on the bar and uncorked it. She poured us liberal dollops.

"I've got to go into the back to get some of our library wines."

"Do you want to see our library cards?" Jack, also pretty lit up, joked. Debbie laughed.

"That would be nice. We'll make sure no one in here throttles the bottles," I tritely rhymed.

She tittered, still giddy at having met a demi-celeb, and disappeared.

I turned to look at Jack, laughing his head off. "Miles, you are something."

"You think Oprah ever pays for a dinner? Chick's a billionaire and she never forks over. Get it while you can, right?"

"Fucking A, brother," Jack said, draining the first Pinot, a Carneros selection sourced from ten different blocks in the Ramal Vineyard. He moved the wine around in his mouth, puffing out his cheeks in the process. "Tasty."

"This guy just makes really fucking awesome Pinots," I said. "Blackberry, raspberry, cedar, cigar, it's just got it all," I rhapsodized.

Debbie returned with four bottles. She proceeded to uncork all four, then lined up an argosy of Riedel stemware and set to pouring. Next up was a Pinot from the Hallberg Vineyard, Russian River Valley. Another perfectly decent, if not stellar, wine. Didn't appear the wines had suffered much in Gary's absence. Or was I losing my palate?

As Debbie went off to attend to her more pedestrian–God, I've become such a *fucking* snob!–customers, Jack and I resumed our conversation. Now and then I would catch a subtle gesture from Debbie, and customers' heads turning to get a look at me. They probably fantasized I'd be some nerdy goateed drunk when, in fact, I was 6'1", with a full head of hair, and in pretty decent shape, when I wasn't on a jag.

"So, what really happened with you and your mom back in Merced?" Jack asked, popping my balloon and bringing me back to reality with a thud.

I told him about my mother's leaving the family when I was eight, my dad's attempts to take care of us, the fear the experience had engendered in me, and the cathartic relief when she returned. "There was never any real good explanation for it, so I finally asked her, and she got all bent out of shape." I sipped my wine. "I'm sure she just wants to forget whatever painful period it was."

"How do you know it was painful?" He winked at me.

"Oh, come on, man. She had a nervous breakdown. Probably from having three boisterous boys back-to-back." I reflected for a moment. "I guess because we were never close growing up, and because this is probably the last time I'm going to spend any time with her I was just curious. Maybe it'll shed new light on why I'm so fucked up, why I became a writer, I don't know. It's a chapter missing from my life, a lacuna with no explanation. But..." I threw up my hands. "If she doesn't want to talk about it, that's cool. I don't want to be stuck in the car for another week with her hating me for bringing it up."

"Amen, brother. Amen."

I rooted my iPhone out of my pocket and said to Jack, "I'm going to call Laura."

"Miles's in love," Jack incanted like a kid on a school playground.

"No, I'm not. I just like her."

He bumped his shoulder against mine. "You miss her."

Just as I was about to dial her, Jack grabbed the phone from me and cut the call. "Don't D&D, man."

"I'm not drunk."

"Hey." Jack pointed a finger at me. "I don't want you to say things you're going to regret."

"Give me my phone back," I said. Jack handed it to me but, taking his advice, I slipped it back into my pocket.

"Smart, Homes."

"You're right. I was feeling mawkish. This is where Victoria and I honeymooned."

"All the more reason, man. Your life is going great. Do–not–go–there."

Debbie drifted back over and asked how we liked the Hallberg. We told her–well, I told her–it was "splendiferous." She noticed that the bottle was down to half, but didn't seem to mind. In fact, she poured herself a taste, professionally sampled it and spat, and agreed, "Yeah, it's holding up nicely." She uncorked another bottle and poured us liberally again. "This is from the Rochioli Vineyard."

I perked up and said to Jack, "Incontestably one of the finest Pinot vineyards on all of the Pacific Coast."

Jack and I sampled. He liked to smack his lips. I liked to work it around in my mouth before swallowing.

"God, this is nice," I said, reaching into my lexicological memory bank for something more expressive. "Velvety, satiny, not a hint of meretriciousness."

"I concur," Jack said. "Without the purple prose."

I laughed, set my glass on the bar and slurred to Debbie: "I'd like to revisit this most marvelous libation."

She chuckled, pouring both Jack and me some more. "Would you mind signing some autographs?" Debbie asked.

"No. Absolutely. Bring 'em over. Let's have a Pinot blowout," I said a little bombastically, heedless of my mother and Joy, waiting in the baking Rampvan.

Debbie broke away from our cabal and went to the other customers, edging closer to Jack and me.

"So," I said to Jack, while savoring the Rochioli, "I think I'm really emotionally ready to meet someone, settle down. Not have kids or any of that baggage–no offense–but someone to hold onto in the middle of the night when the creepy crawlers rise portentously from the mire of the collective unconscious to assail me. That's what I'm looking for."

"Can I make a suggestion?" Jack said.

"Sure."

"*Portentously, collective unconscious*. No."

"Yeah, I guess I've always been my own worst enemy. I just love words. There's got to be a beautiful woman who loves words... and sex... and food. And, being adored by a devoted man who won't run around on her." I pointed my empty wineglass at him.

"Hey, don't go there, either," he warned. "I'm sure Victoria would have a good laugh over that one."

"Touché. But, no, seriously, I wouldn't do that again. Too much pain."

"Yeah," Jack replied, suddenly downcast. "Tell me about it."

From the far end of the bar, Debbie parallel-walked with an elderly couple, leading them in our direction. As Debbie poured us yet another ineffable Pinot from the library selection, the senior-citizen couple, big grins plastered on their faces, came over to greet me, congratulate me, ask me questions I had fielded hundreds of times since the movie's release. They importuned me to sign bottles with one of those permanent marker pens in inks that coruscated gold and silver. I was happy to oblige.

As we continued drinking, more tipsy wine tasters ambled over, some of them Gary Farrell Winery employees. Soon, Jack and I were in the middle of a starstruck huddle of wine lovers. Answers to their questions made them laugh, often uproariously. More single-vineyard Farrells were poured. I was losing sense of time, but all the wine and adulation had me inured to its consequences. At one point I glanced at my watch and realized over an hour had passed. I poured myself a glass of water and drained it. Then another in an effort to whiplash back into a more sentient, and sensible, being.

"We've got to go, Jack," I whispered. "Or we'll never get out of here."

We broke away from the now boisterous crowd and walked unsteadily out. The bright sunlight beat down on us at an angle through the towering

redwoods. In tasting rooms I can never tell how tipsy I am. But once I'm
outside, the awareness factor of my inebriation is greatly magnified. Everything looks and feels different. The surrounding flora seems to quiver. Colors are riotously iridescent. Sounds are louder; birds in the trees seem to mock you. All sense of reality is swamped. Anything out of the norm might happen!

We traipsed down the path to the parking lot. When we got to the Rampvan we found my mom inside, but not Joy. Glancing around, I saw her sitting with her back up against the trunk of a tree, arms crossed against her chest. She didn't look happy.

"I'm sorry we took so long," I apologized.

She pursed her lips and pouted, her visage set in what one could characterize only as suppressed rage.

"You okay?"

She rose from the pine needles and climbed wordlessly back into the rear of the van. I turned to Jack and shrugged. "You all right to drive?" I asked.

"I'm fine," Jack said. "Unlike you, I know how to pace myself."

"Which is why I signed you up for this duty."

"I'm not your factotum, fucker. I'm your friend. Remember?"

"Right." Had I really become that pompous? That condescending? Jesus! Once we were underway, I glanced surreptitiously into the back. Joy was looking away from my mother and my mother was looking away from Joy. Something was wrong.

"What's going on?" I asked.

Neither said a word. A shark-filled moat had been dug between them.

I turned back and slid old Harry Belafonte into the CD player. He, if anyone could, would mollify my mother. What had gone down between them now? I wondered. Most likely my mother had disparaged Joy over something trivial and Joy had finally reached the boiling point.

Jack steered back onto the main road and continued north toward Mendocino. It was a sinuous rural route, but Jack, a seasoned over-the-limit driver, negotiated the turns deftly. The passing landscape was gorgeous. I could have been in heaven with the wine buzz I had going on, but the tension in the back was malignant; it easily traversed my wine buzz semi-euphoria.

Amid my ruminations, my mother shrieked, "I didn't take your damn money."

I whipped my head around. Joy was frantically rooting around in her oversized purse, her small hands moving furiously inside.

"You took it," she accused my mother. "You took it."

"What?" I said. "What's going on?"

"My money's gone," Joy cried. "Your mother steal it!"

"I didn't take it," my mother wailed.

"Well, somebody took it," Joy accused, her face cemented in a pout. "I didn't lose it."

"You lost the envelope with the money and the plane ticket?" I asked, incredulous.

"No," she said. "I did not lose it. But it's not here." Like one cat fighting another, she rummaged through her purse again in a flurry of motion, before coming to an abrupt halt and announcing, "It's gone."

I turned to Jack, and stared circumspectly at him.

"Hey, don't look at me, dude!"

I wheeled around to face the raging conflagration. Joy wore an expression that was, if anything, even angrier. My mother stared away from her, out the window. "When did you last have it?" I asked Joy.

"This morning," she said without inflection. "Your mom took it." She pounded her armrest. "This is the only place I leave my purse!"

My mother flung her head in Joy's direction like a sick horse and hurled the full force of her fury at her: "I did not take your money, you dirty Filipina. You're probably trying to get more money from my son because he's rich now!"

Joy's anger was barely contained within the small frame of her body and the tightness of her expression. She looked ready to explode, or self-defenestrate to exit the vehicle, but there was nowhere she could go. Even Snapper was agitated by the acrimony and was leaping up and down and barking.

"Mom," I said, "Jesus fucking Christ, apologize to her."

"They're all dirty," my puerile mother said. "I fought against them in the war!"

"We fought the Japanese, Mom," I shouted, "not the Filipinos! They were on our side! Where's your sense of history, you old coot! What's

going on in that intracranial wonderland of yours, huh?" I calmed slightly.
"Apologize to Joy."

"She wants more money," my mother said. "She's complained to me all the way."

Joy swiveled her head swiftly and said sharply to my mother, "I *have* not!"

"You have, too," my mother retorted.

"You lie," Joy said.

"And you smoke too much Mary Jane! *That's* how you lost your precious money!"

Joy crossed her arms again and stared at a middle distance that must have looked like hell.

"Stop it! Stop it!" I turned to Jack. "Pull over."

"What?"

"Pull the fucking van over!"

Jack steered the car onto the dirt shoulder and braked to a halt. He kept the engine on to keep the AC running. We needed a lot more than the factory air at this crucial juncture!

Before I could clamber out, Joy had already slid open the side door and fled the incendiary atmosphere of our now poisoned Rampvan, purse in hand.

I approached her. She wouldn't meet my eyes. "You're positive it's not in your purse?" I did my best to intone it as a question, not an accusation. She just brushed past me.

A few yards away, me worried that she was contemplating–no, attempting!–escape, she whirled around and angrily jerked her purse open with both hands for me to inspect.

"I trust you," I said, not venturing a look.

"I don't complain about money!" she said, the pout still disorganizing her face.

"And you're sure you didn't take it out at Domaine Carneros?"

"No!" She crossed her arms once more in defiance.

"Okay, okay," I said in exasperation. "Let's find it." I climbed into the back of the van, starting to scour it for the envelope I had handed Joy back in San Diego. Vehicles whizzing past caused the van to shudder, making me realize just how close to the speeding traffic we were. As I scavenged around in the back my mother sat in a stoic silence. Just outside the door, Joy stood with her arms still wrapped around her tiny torso, the buffeting wind from the passing vehicles whipping her hair like a mop. Jack, still up front, didn't come out. Right, let me sort it all out, while he chugged an ale and wished it all would go away.

There was no sign of the envelope where they had been sitting so I climbed over into the back luggage compartment and rummaged around there. Why it would be back there I didn't have a clue, but I wanted to make it look like I was getting to the bottom of the imbroglio. As I searched and searched I began to wonder about Joy's version. I didn't know her all that well. Was she putting on an act? Surely she knew by now that she had me by the short hairs. If she left I would be royally fucked. But what an actress she'd have to be! And was she capable of such mercenary monstrousness? But why would my mother take Joy's money? She knew she was being totally taken care of, cash-wise, wine-wise. Something was screwy. And all the Pinot coursing through my now-raging bloodstream wasn't helping me sort it out. I wanted to kill myself, but too many people depended on my not going down that dark, once familiar, road.

Suddenly, my mother screamed, "Snapper! Snapper! Get him, Joy, get him!"

Joy didn't move. She stood stiff as a small tree, facing the sky over the vineyards in the distance, as if she had gone deaf.

I turned to see a flash of Snapper, leashless once again, madly chasing a roadrunner up the dirt shoulder in a reckless pursuit. Joy ignored my mother's entreaties. Sensing the urgency, I took off in a trot after the little four-legged imp. Suddenly, I heard the shrieking squeal of tires as a black town car careering around the dangerously twisting road, bearing down in the opposite direction, slammed on its brakes, desperately trying to stop. Smoke poured from its fishtailing rear. Sprinting in the direction of the pandemonium, I heard one sharp yelp and saw the small body of Snapper propelled to the side of the road. He lay on his side, barely moving. I was the first to get to him, but I was afraid to touch him. Snapper was shaking uncontrollably, whimpering in agony, his eyes still showing a semblance of life. He clawed at the asphalt and tried to drag himself toward me. Once he righted himself I could see that one of his hind legs was dragging, unable to support him. The driver of the town car, a middle-aged man in a black suit, white shirt and dark tie, trotted over, effusively apologizing, almost on the verge of tears.

As I petted Snapper's head, the town car chauffeur said, "I wouldn't touch him."

"We've got to get him to a vet. They're not going to Medevac a dog!"

I slid my hands under Snapper and lifted him up and cradled him in my arms. His skin was so badly torn on his right hind leg you could see bone. Blood was everywhere, and he looked like he might go agonal.

Two couples in their thirties, clearly inebriated, to judge by their stumbling exit, disgorged from the hired town car and shambled over. The men's faces went horrorstruck when they saw Snapper. One of the girls wept. From the Rampvan, my mother's paroxysmal caterwauling was weirdly like a colicky infant. Jack, evidently unable to bear her uncontrollable anguished cries, stepped out of the driver's side and lit his first cigarette in two days, his vow to quit shattered by the sudden tragic turn of events. Joy, her expression still hardened with suppressed rage, stared balefully at me. What next? she must have been thinking.

"Look," I said to the driver and the two couples. "It's not your fault." I started back down the road as they showered me with offers to help, anything, they felt so bad seeing Snapper slipping into unconsciousness in my arms. "I highly recommend a stop at Gary Farrell."

They gawked at me strangely. I turned my back on them and walked with heavy heart back to the Rampvan.

I said to catatonic Joy without looking at her, "Let's try to be cool. None of us wants my mother totally freaking out on us. You sit back with her. I don't want her to see her dog, okay? We'll deal with the money issue, I promise. If we don't find it, I will give you all of it, the full sum, in the morning. One crisis at a time." Finally I looked at her. "Okay?"

"Okay," she said. Joy, the godsend. She'd assimilated the gravity of the situation and agreed that missing, or stolen, or whatever, money was now the least of our mutual concerns.

In the car my mother was bawling hysterically. "What happened to Snapper? What happened to Snapper?"

Joy sat next to her and remarkably made an effort to comfort her, the contretemps over the money momentarily set aside. "It's going to be okay, Mrs. Raymond, it's going to be okay."

Jack looked over at Snapper in my arms and a thundercloud scudded across his face. "Oh, Jesus."

"Get going. We've got to find the nearest vet."

"Where's that?" Jack said. Quickly sobering up, he pulled back onto the one-lane rural road.

Bless you, Steve Jobs! I thought. Thank God for the iPhone. I reached once again into my pocket. "I don't know where," I said. "I hope close."

"Where's Snapper?" my mother kept crying over and over.

"I've got him up here, Mom. He's had a mishap. He's a little shaken up, but he's going to be okay."

As my mother wept hysterically I logged onto my Google app. "Fuck," I said out loud. "Nearest town of any size is Clearlake."

"How far?" Jack asked, clearly unnerved by Snapper's tormented whimpering.

"Just a sec." I opened up our position, then typed in Clearlake, California. "Fuck. Fifty miles. I give you permission to speed."

Jack stomped the accelerator. I tapped Clearlake on the screen, punched in Find, then typed in "vet clinics." Three popped up, indicated by tiny red pushpin icons. I tapped on the closest one and the address and phone came up in a drop-down.

I touched the icon to dial the number. A receptionist answered. I told her what had happened and how far away we were. She told me to bring him in, they would be expecting us. I heaved a sigh as I hung up.

"He's going to be okay, Mom," I said, trying to reassure her even though the little devil was totally limp in my arms now, breathing rapidly and more and more shallowly, his beady little eyes starting to drift up into his head.

As we approached Clearlake, employing the iPhone's own GPS navigational instructions, I directed Jack to the Lakeview Veterinary Hospital. It was late afternoon and the sun had burnished the dreary town in Titian hues of brown and gold.

Jack braked in front of the hospital, a squat structure in a faux Spanish-style with a red-tile roof and a flesh-toned adobe facade, and killed the engine. "Keep everyone in here," I murmured to him so my mother wouldn't hear.

No luck. "I want to go!" she shrieked in an ear-piercing cry.

"No," I said sharply, then wormed out of the Rampvan with Snapper.

I hustled into the vet clinic and approached the receptionist's desk with Snapper's little life ebbing away in my arms–I could feel it. Death breaches all barriers.

My waxing philosophical was interrupted when I was met by the image of a girl with a pierced lower lip, manning the main reception area. She was used to emergencies hurtling in the front door and rose the moment I came in, registering the dark expression on my face.

"I'm the one who called a half hour ago. He was hit by a car. He's in bad shape."

The receptionist cupped a hand to the side of her mouth and called out down a hall. "Amy! Amy! It's the HBC!"

"What's that?"

"Hit by car," she decoded.

A moment later, a woman in her forties, wearing a blue scrub top, plodded heavily into view. "Oh," she said when she got her first eyeful of Snapper. "Poor thing."

She reached out her arms and I gently handed Snapper over to her. She turned and I followed her down a linoleum-tiled corridor past some small exam rooms into a larger treatment room.

"Shahar! Shahar!" Amy called out.

Amy laid Snapper tenderly down on his side on a blanket spread out on a stainless steel examining table. His right hind leg was splayed out, his breathing was still shallow and rapid, his gums graying. His whimpering had by now gone almost inaudible, as if he were sinking into quicksand.

A moment later, a woman in her thirties with dark, shoulder-length hair and a pretty round face, appeared, her countenance betraying apprehension. Her nametag read: Shahar Ariel, D.V.M. She ignored me, her concern drawn immediately to Snapper's condition.

Dr. Ariel spoke rapidly to the technician. "Let's get oxygen, an IV catheter, and give him some morphine."

I was distraught now. Tears might have begun to well in my eyes. "He was hit by a car. It was bad," I heard myself repeating over and over. The accident must have adrenalized me and processed out all the Pinot; I suddenly felt totally lucid.

Amy fitted a small conical oxygen mask over Snapper's snout while Dr. Ariel tried unsuccessfully several times to insert a catheter into the dog's left front leg. "It's hard on these small animals," she muttered, then finally, triumphantly, she exclaimed: "Got it!" She turned to the technician and said, "Let's get the fluids going, Amy. Quarter shock dose." She looked up at me and explained, "We're trying to stabilize him. He's been hurt pretty badly."

"Do your best," I said, tears streaming down my face now. "It's my mother's dog. She's had a stroke. She's out in the car in a wheelchair," I found myself blubbering.

It took Dr. Ariel a moment to process all I had said. It must have sounded so apocryphal, and she glanced up at me with a puzzled expression. Then she went back to business. As the technician inserted a thermometer into Snapper's rear, she drew a syringe from a vial, filled it with a clear liquid, and injected it into Snapper's leg where she'd managed to find a vein for the IV. In seconds he seemed to have quieted, his shiverings quelled by the narcotics. (I've got to get some of that shit, I thought ruefully, hoping humor would pull me out of my agitated state.) From a plastic bag with quarter-inch tubing running down to where the catheter had been inserted into his leg a clear electrolyte solution began its gravity flow into Snapper's bloodstream.

Dr. Ariel petted the dog's head a moment and said, "Poor little guy. Are you hurt, huh?" Snapper tilted his head in the direction of her voice. Very gently, she moved him so that he was positioned upright. Amy stepped in and held a mask over his snout to convey the oxygen. Dr. Ariel conducted a very thorough physical examination. Her eyes widened perceptibly when she looked closely at his right hind leg. "That leg's badly injured." She sucked in her breath, continued muttering. "Serious de-gloving."

"What's that?"

"Lot of skin missing. Not sure there's enough for it to grow back. We might have to amputate."

"Oh, Jesus," I said.

"The leg's gone anyway. There's no feeling. It looks like there's nerve damage." She continued to feel around. She removed the thermometer, then pinched his anus with some oversized tweezers. "Good anal tone."

"Beg your pardon?"

"Hopefully the neurologic damage is limited to the leg, not the spinal cord," she explained. She looked at the thermometer. "96.5. He's hypothermic, but that's to be expected." She came around to the nose and

said to Amy, "Take the mask off for a sec, will you?" Amy pulled the mask
away, but kept it close. Dr. Ariel bent forward, lifted his lip, then touched
his nose and studied her fingers. "No blood in the nostrils. I was afraid of
blunt head trauma. He's a little shocky, gums a bit muddy, but nothing
specifically indicating brain damage."

"Good," I said.

Amy returned the oxygen mask to Snapper's snout as Dr. Ariel put the
earbuds of a stethoscope hanging around her neck into her ears and listened to his heart. "Heart rate's elevated. Indicative of pain or shock... or
blood loss. I hope not for the pup's sake." She moved the stethoscope
again on Snapper's rib cage, cocked her head to one side and listened.
"His lungs sound a little rough, but not bad, considering...."

She continued conducting a full examination, pressing on his internal
organs to assay the damage inflicted on them by the speeding town car.
Then she said to Amy, "Go ahead and lay him back down on his side.
And give him another dose of morphine." She turned to me. "What's this
about your mother and a stroke? I'm sorry..."

I narrated our situation as quickly as I could manage.

Dr. Ariel looked down at Snapper. "His right leg's seriously injured. I
don't know if it's going to heal. If there's neurologic damage, or too much
tissue damage"–she turned her gaze to me–"it's going to have to come off."

"Will he recover?" I asked.

"He could. We have to do some more tests, make certain that we're
not dealing with a broken back or"–she shook her head grimly–"serious
organ damage, in which case...."

"It'd be best to euthanize him?"

"I'm not ready to make that call. My first reaction is that it might
just be the leg and some soft tissue injuries. If that's the case, then he
might recover."

"How long?

"If we have to amputate, and he does recover..." She pursed her lips
and calculated in her mind. "He's not going to be going anywhere for a
minimum of a week."

"We have to be in the Willamette Valley in two days, then from there
we're heading to Wisconsin where I'm dropping my mother off with
her sister."

Dr. Ariel nodded.

I looked down at Snapper. The morphine had calmed him, but he didn't look very well. "Maybe it would be best to put him down."

Dr. Ariel didn't reply right away, so I faced her. She was staring up at me, her dark eyes burning. "Is that what your mother would want?"

My Adam's apple rose and fell. Was I just looking for the easy out?

"Because if you do authorize us to kill him, I'm going to want to discuss this with your mother and give her the option of being with her pet when I do it. And it's my obligation to inform her that her dog might live."

"I understand. I was just, um..." I chopped myself off and fanned open my hands. "We've had a couple rough days, and now this."

"Why don't you go have a talk with your mother? We're going to do some quick X-rays. And blood work."

"Okay."

"Come back in an hour." She locked her dark eyes onto mine. "And bring your mother."

I glanced down at the badly injured Snapper and swallowed a walnut without the benefit of saliva. "All right," I muttered. I reached down and petted Snapper's head and walked away.

I made my way out of the veterinary hospital with a heavy heart, moving as though I were wading through hip-deep water.

Outside I found Joy leaning against the van. She was rotating the dial on an iPod, earbuds plugging her ears, and didn't hear my approach, lost in her own world. A world I could only imagine was far less pacific than the one she had entered a mere four days ago.

Jack, his head drooping out the passenger-side window, had found a beer somewhere and was discreetly sipping it. "What's the verdict?" he asked.

In a lowered voice so my mother couldn't hear, I said, "He's pretty fucked up."

"Is he going to live?"

"I don't know. But the vet doesn't want to put him to sleep."

"What is he, some right-to-lifer? Make the poor critter suffer."

"It's a *she*. And she thinks that he has a chance. But, rest assured, he won't be continuing on. And we won't be staying on."

Jack twisted his bull neck and cast a meaningful backward glance at my mother. "What're we going to tell Phyllis?"

"I don't know."

"Just tell her he bit it."

Disgust invaded me like a bite of bad food. "I'm not going to lie to her!" I said in a forced whisper. "Besides, she's going to want to say good-bye. And he's not unconscious. Jesus, Jack."

"Okay, okay," Jack said irritably. "I'm just saying that dog's been a problem since oh-one-hundred hours."

"You don't have to remind me." I inhaled deeply. "I got to talk to my mom."

Jack took the cue, opened the door and spilled out. "I'm going to take a walk." He shambled off. I was positive he was hoping he would find a dark bar he could tuck into.

I glanced up at the sky. It was deep blue, except for a high-flying jet that was making a serrated white wound, as if ripping the heavens into two. The symbolism did not go unnoticed.

I opened the side door. My mother's weeping had subsided. She seemed resigned to the worst. "How's Snapper?"

"He's alive." I pulled out the ramp, hopped into the back, turned my mother ninety degrees and pushed her out. Joy threw a quick glance, but made no move to assist us, her expression still malevolent.

I wheeled my mother up the sidewalk until I found a cinderblock ledge where I could sit. We didn't look at each other. Passing cars muffled our mutual anguish. "Snapper's right hind leg was crushed. The doctor's not sure surgery can fix it. If that turns out to be the case, it'd have to be amputated."

"Oh, no," my mother said. She sniffled, bravely fighting a heavier avalanche of tears.

"On a sunnier note, there's no evidence of head trauma, she doesn't think there's life-threatening bleeding in the lungs, and she's pretty sure there's no spinal cord injury. If there were…"

My mother finished what I had trouble voicing. "We'd have to put him to sleep."

"That's right."

"You probably wanted to put him to sleep."

I raised my voice. "It was a consideration, Mom. But the vet talked me out of it. What you have to understand, though, is that we're not going to be able to stay here while Snapper recuperates–if he does." I looked at her. She was nodding to herself, bearing the bad news with shocking equanimity.

"We have to move on. We can't afford to stay in–what's this place? Clear-lake?–for a week or longer until he gets better."

"I know," my mother said. "We might as well pronounce him dead," she added, her bitter anger flashing.

"Don't say that, Mom."

"If we have to leave poor Snapper here, then I'm never going to see him again."

I trained my gaze on the passing cars. More than once it occurred to me that a headlong run into traffic had its benefits. I rose to my feet and word-lessly got behind my mother. "Let's go say goodbye to Snapper," I said.

My mother reached her right hand up to steady her hat on her head. "Does he look bad?"

"Pretty bad, Mom. Do you still want to see him?"

"Oh, yes." She raised her right arm and pointed her finger at the sky. "I want to say goodbye. In case he dies."

We stopped to inform Jack that we were heading back in to bid farewell to Snapper.

"That's good," he said, sucking on his second beer.

"Do you want to come in?"

"Not unless you really want me to."

"That's okay." I glanced over at Joy. She caught my gaze for a moment, then looked away, her expression a harbinger of things I didn't want to think about just then.

Jack held the door open for us and I wheeled my mother inside. The receptionist wore a somber look of concern, waved *Hi*, but didn't vocalize her sympathy. We pushed on down the corridor into surgery. Snapper was lying on his side, the oxygen mask affixed to his snout, the IV drip needled into his foreleg. He seemed to be resting.

"Oh, Snapper," my mother cried. "Why are you so naughty, huh?"

Dr. Ariel entered, looking at a fresh X-ray. She stopped when she saw my mother.

"This is my mother, Phyllis," I said.

She squatted down so as to be at eye-level with my mother. "Hi, Phyllis."

"How's my Snapper?" she inquired through tears.

Dr. Ariel set the X-ray aside and grabbed my mother's paralyzed hand with both of hers. "Your dog has had a bad accident."

"I know."

The vet looked up at me as if saying, *Should I continue?*

"My mother was an R.N."

"Oh, yes," my mother chimed in.

Dr. Ariel cleared her throat. "Snapper's right hind leg has sustained serious soft tissue injuries. The good news is there are no broken bones. The hip was dislocated, but we got that back in place. But I'm concerned about permanent nerve injury and the potential of severe tissue death from compromised circulation. Crush injuries can be bad. They don't declare themselves immediately. So we won't know how bad for a few days."

My mother's gaze was fixed on the conked-out Snapper. She just nodded through the doctor's explanation and didn't interrupt.

"I think your son told you there's no evidence of head trauma. And although there might be mild pulmonary contusions, I'm going to go out on a limb and say there's no serious bleeding there. Except for that leg, there's no indication of nerve injury."

"That's good," my mother said.

Dr. Ariel let go my mother's hand. "If the leg doesn't improve... we would have to amputate."

"Oh, no."

"But I'm not ready to make that call yet."

My mother reached her hand across her chest and patted Snapper on the head. "Oh, Snapper." At the sound of her familiar voice, his eyes fluttered open, but they had no focus. He looked halfway to the grave to me.

Dr. Ariel rose. "I'll leave you with Snapper."

I drifted off to let my mother have as long as she wanted with Snapper. In an adjoining surgery area, a large dog was lying on its side. I watched a male vet in his fifties with salt-and-pepper hair performing oral surgery on the anesthetized animal. In another room I saw stacked cages with convalescing dogs and cats, the source of the animal cacophony that had greeted me on my entrance.

After a few long minutes, I returned to the treatment room. Dr. Ariel was comforting my mother, who was inconsolable. I saw her glance at her watch. I shot a look at mine. It was a little after five o'clock and I had noticed coming in that the vet clinic's hours had said 8:00-5:00. And though I'm sure they felt empathy with my mother, Snapper was probably only one of a half a dozen animals that had come in on the verge of death that shift.

I went back to my mother. "Mom, we have to go. They need to close."

Through squinted eyes still brimming with tears, she implored Dr. Ariel, "Is he going to die?"

"I don't know, Mrs. Raymond. We'll know a lot more in a few days. But for now, he's stabilized." She motioned the technician over. "Let's get him in the oxygen cage, Amy."

The technician wordlessly removed the IV tubing, but left the catheter in his leg. I sensed the presence of someone else in the surgery room, turned and found Joy standing at the entryway, duty no doubt overcoming rancor. "Hi, Joy." She came forward. "Could you take my mother back to the van?"

She nodded, got behind my mother, turned her slowly and wheeled her away.

"Goodbye, Snapper," my mother said plaintively. Then, as if he were already doomed in her mind, "I'm going to miss you."

As I held back in the treatment area, I worried about what kind of effect Snapper's dire condition would have on my mother. There were other worries as well: the imbroglio over the money; the infected tooth, which had started to distend, alarmingly, the right side of my mother's jaw. The Vicodins were ameliorating the pain and the warm saltwater rinses were keeping the infection at bay, but it was going to blow up, and if I had to hospitalize her and wait five days we'd be fucked. And she would never forgive me.

Dr. Ariel returned to the treatment area in her street clothes. She held out her hand. "I'm sorry," she said.

I shrugged. "What can you do? These things happen."

I could see it was depressing her, too. "So, you're traveling?" she asked.

"Yeah. We're taking my mother back to Wisconsin." I told her why and where I was taking her, about the International Pinot Noir Celebration, who Joy and Jack were and what their roles were and... okay, who I was.

"You wrote *Shameless*?" she said, barely able to conceal her excitement. "I loved that movie. It's everyone's favorite movie here. Are you joking?"

"No," I said. "Would you like a couple autographed copies of the book?"

"Yeah!" she said, "I'd love one."

Amy reappeared after taking Snapper away. "He's in the oxygen cage. His heart rate's still a little up, but it's normalizing. Do you want me to continue the morphine drip?"

"I think so," she replied.

"Okay."

Dr. Ariel's face brightened into a smile. "Guess what, Amy? This guy wrote *Shameless*. The wine movie? Remember, we saw it together?"

Amy's mouth opened agape. "No way."

I raised both arms, hands splayed open. "I confess. I'm the culprit."

"That's like one of my favorite movies of all time," Amy added. "I bought it on DVD and I don't even ever buy DVDs."

"Thank you," I muttered humbly. "I just wrote the novel. There were a lot of talented people involved."

"Yeah, but it all started with the book," Dr. Ariel said charitably.

"Speaking of which." I raised my index finger and said, "Excuse me, I'll be *right* back."

I strode briskly out of the clinic. Joy had parked my mother on the sidewalk, where she stared down the street, lost in grief. Jack was sitting up front in the Rampvan, listening to *his* music, sipping another ale–and needing one! Joy had coasted off in the direction away from my mother and was half concealed behind the clinic's facade, puffing on a joint–and needing one. I went around to the back of the Rampvan and grabbed five copies of *Shameless* from the case I had brought on the trip for seduction and goodwill promotional purposes.

Back inside the hospital, Dr. Ariel and Amy–now also in street clothes–were waiting for me in the reception area. Alerted to my minor celebrity presence, the male vet who had been performing the oral surgery on the brindled monster of a dog also materialized, wearing an ear-to-ear grin. I autographed and personally inscribed books for all of them, including the pierced-nose receptionist. They peppered me with some of the usual questions and I dispensed my usual funny, by now rote, answers that had them all in stitches. In short order, the funereal mood had been supplanted by one of congenial hilarity. I'm sure if vets took tragedy home with them after each day's work they'd all commit suicide in the first year of practice.

The male vet thanked me profusely and disappeared back into the bowels of the clinic, no doubt to wrap up the oral surgery on the mongrel.

The technician and the receptionist also thanked me, then departed. That left me alone with Dr. Ariel. She was looking at me with the widest smile. For a moment I thought she was flirting with me. Which, if true, played right into my hand.

I shuffled in place, and spoke haltingly. "Um, Dr. Ariel..."

"You can call me Shahar."

"Shahar. That's such a pretty, lyrical-sounding name."

"Thank you."

"Being a writer, I'm always on the lookout for unusual names. If I ever have a character who's a veterinarian, I'm going to use it," I flirted back.

She smiled demurely and angled her gaze to the floor.

"Shahar." She looked up at me. "I've got a completely off-the-wall question for you..."

"Okay," she said, waiting, accustomed to strangers soliciting free medical advice.

"My mother has an abscessed lower molar."

"Yeah, I noticed her cheek puffed out a little and I was wondering about it."

"Well, anyway, since she's on a blood-thinning medication, this dentist in Fresno wouldn't pull it because he said she could bleed to death. He said it had to be done in a hospital."

She blinked at me, waiting for the other shoe to drop.

"I'm just curious, is that really true? I mean, do you know...?"

"Well, the medication she's on, which I'm assuming is Coumadin, only reduces the clotting. They probably want to wean her down a little bit. But hospitalization for a tooth extraction seems a little extreme."

"That's what I thought."

"I mean it's possible," she warmed to the subject, "that in weaning her off she develops clots and has another stroke... or heart attack, or pulmonary embolism, and they would want her in a hospital in the event of an emergency. They're probably just erring on the side of caution." Her look confirmed that "caution" should be interpreted as "lawsuit aversion."

I nodded, coughed, clearing my throat. "Shahar, we're on our way out to the middle of America and I'm just worried about that tooth. We don't have time for a five-day hospital stay or whatever for an abscessed molar."

She gave me an intent, but not prohibitive, look.

"I'm just curious." I held up my hands in mini-surrender. "For the sake of argument. Could a vet do a procedure like that? Say you were out camping with your boyfriend and he woke up with a baseball mouth and you were his only hope between excruciating pain and relief," I rambled nervously. "I mean, I saw the guy in back doing dental work on a... um..." I stopped myself, fearing I had crossed the line into the ludicrous.

"Yeah. Probably." She chuckled. "But we wouldn't. We'd lose our license."

"But you *could* do it? Hypothetically, of course."

"If it's just a tooth extraction, yeah. I do it all the time. Can't be much different on a human."

"You do dental surgery yourself?" I asked, feigning surprise.

"Yeah. Most vets are trained to."

I inhaled deeply and exhaled slowly, sighing an emanation of seeming hopelessness. What did I have to lose? "If I offered you a thousand dollars–cash–to pull my mother's tooth, would you?"

A laugh shot out of her pretty face.

"I'm dead serious," I said. "With this Pinot festival, I'm looking at another week before we get her to Wisconsin. If that thing blows up on her, I'm royally screwed. I can't afford to hang around for God knows how long while she goes into the hospital." I paused. In desperation, I upped my offer: "I'll give you two thousand. Cash."

"Yeah, you kinda said that already." Dr. Ariel grabbed my sleeve and pulled me aside so our voices wouldn't carry down the corridor. "I wouldn't take your money," she said. "That would make it only more unethical."

"I mean if you were me and it was your mother and you were in this situation, with your training, would you pull it?"

She wouldn't admit it, so she said, "that's hyper-hypothetical, Mr. Raymond."

"Miles. If something went wrong, I wouldn't sue you in a million years, you know that. Can you imagine? Author of book becomes hit movie takes addled mother to vet clinic..."

She laughed, clearly in spite of herself.

"I mean, *Radar Online, TMZ, Smoking Gun*, hell, *The New York Post*, I'd be right up there with Lindsay Lohan!"

"I'm not worried you'd sue me," she chuckled, "but, um..." She looked off. I could all but see how she was wrestling with her conscience.

"I mean, what are the chances she's going to bleed to death because of a routine tooth extraction? Come on?"

She shrugged. "Minimal. I don't know. I'm trained in oral surgery, but there aren't a lot of canine patients on Coumadin."

I continued to plead my seemingly ridiculous, but strangely rationalized, case. "But you, yourself, just insinuated that weaning her off the Coumadin might be just as dangerous. She's in a lot of pain. Won't even *go* into the hospital–for anything!–unless I force her. And that's if we had the five days to spare, which we do not. I mean, how long does it take to pull an abscessed tooth? Ten minutes?"

"It depends," Dr. Ariel noted, "on how loose it is."

I clasped my hands prayerfully together and pressed them histrionically to my heart. "Her dog's just been in a horrible accident. And now this damn tooth business. I don't know how much more her heart can take, Doctor. If I can just get her to her sister's relatively in one piece, I'll be a happy man." I let my hands unclasp and dropped them from my chest. "Not that my happiness is any of your concern."

Dr. Ariel rolled her tongue across her upper teeth and continued to wrestle with her conscience. I waited, never once taking my eyes from hers. She gave a quick backward glance, then said in a lowered tone, "Why don't you come back in an hour when the clinic's closed. I'll take a look at it, see how bad it is... But I'm not going to promise anything."

Still a little high on all the wine I had consumed at Gary Farrell, I stepped forward and embraced her. She allowed her arms to find my back and hugged me in return. We disengaged ourselves. It had been a long day for both of us.

"Okay, Doctor. I'll see you in an hour or so. Thank you so much."

I walked out of the clinic before she changed her mind. When Joy saw me, she went to my mother, unlocked the brakes on the wheelchair and pushed her back up into the Rampvan. Jack, seeing them approach, climbed out of the cab and pulled the ramp out. When they were in, he pushed the ramp back into its undercarriage sleeve, slid the side door shut and turned to me. "What's the plan, Stan?"

"Well..." I started, staring off. I clenched my teeth and made a strange face. "This has been a pretty wacky trip, wouldn't you concur?"

"Pretty wacky. A lot of drama." He polished off his ale and set the empty on a brick retaining wall. "So, what's happening?"

"I know you're going to think I'm crazy."

"Miles," he cut me off. "That went out the window years ago. *Think*? You are, dude. We both are. Welcome to the club."

"Yeah, well, it only gets better."

Jack waited.

With an expressionless face, I said, "I asked the vet if she'd pull my mom's tooth."

Jack's mouth opened but he was rendered nonplused. A moment passed and he disintegrated into laughter, the kind of laughter that had him jackknifed over and turning in corkscrews. He laughed so hard it actually caused him to sit down on the concrete in an effort to regain some semblance of sanity. When he looked up at me, his eyes were red with tears and his face florid with disbelief.

"We're supposed to come back in an hour," I added, poker-faced.

"A vet's going to pull your mom's molar?" He tumbled into laughter again.

"No," I corrected him, "she's going to take a look at it, see how bad it is."

Through irrepressible laughter he managed, "You're going to take your stroke victim mother, your own flesh and blood, the woman who gave birth to you, into a *vet* clinic for a dental procedure?" He laughed so hard he fell backward from his lotus position and lay on the sidewalk like an upended tick, arms and legs flailing as he laughed straight up at the limitless sky.

"Jack," I reasoned, "if she has to be hospitalized we're going to be stuck in the middle of Bumblefuck, California, for a minimum of three days. Maybe longer. We've got to get that fucker out."

Jack just couldn't stop laughing. I rooted my iPhone out of my front pocket and tapped the maps app. Using Lakeview Veterinary Hospital's address, I located our position. With another tap, I enabled businesses and services to be displayed by those tiny, red pushpin icons. The restaurants near the vet clinic weren't particularly appetizing as I cursor-ed over them. Mostly franchise fast food. But I did find one place that was only two miles away, right on the lake, and I desperately wanted to get a couple glasses of wine in my mother before the hoped-for oral surgery.

The Main Street Bar & Grill is really a misnomer, as the establishment sits on the banks of Clear Lake, the largest natural lake in California, rather than on a street. The décor was nothing to write home about, the menu your basic California beach fare, but at least they had a wine list, and, amazingly, featured a Steele Chardonnay (Dupratt Vineyard, located in the nearby emerging viticultural region of Mendocino).

"We've only got an hour, so figure out what you want," I said to everybody.

My mother's chin hung on her chest. She was still palpably distraught. "I don't want anything to eat," she said, shutting her menu.

"I'm sure you'd like a glass of wine."

She started to decline that too, but her brain chemistry changed magically and she said unenthusiastically, "Yes, I could use one."

When the teenaged waiter returned, we ordered up. I told him we were in a hurry and didn't want the pampered treatment, not that we were going to get it in this backwater simulacrum of The Chart House.

The wine came. The waiter was having trouble with the whole uncapsuling and uncorking, so I grabbed the bottle from him brusquely–I guess I needed a glass as badly as my mother and Jack!–deftly opened it myself and poured everyone around. "Don't be pissed off," I said, "I tip fifty percent."

He looked at me like I was Rasputin.

My mother's mood seemed to soften as she got some wine coursing through her bloodstream. Now and then she would raise her crooked index finger ceilingward and say, "I know you're not going to let my Snapper die." Her invocation of the deity was both lugubrious and borderline funny, but no one dared to laugh.

The pedestrian food arrived in gluttonous mounds of cheap carbohydrates and overcooked protein. Jack and I ate greedily. My mother had nothing and Joy wasn't touching her order of salmon at all.

"You're not hungry, Joy?" I leaned over and whispered in her ear, fueled now by desperation, "I'm going to get all your money back together first thing tomorrow morning. I don't care if you lost it or my mother stole it or what, but you have to try to forgive my mother–she lives in another world. She says things she doesn't mean. In a week this trip'll be over." I squeezed her shoulder, but I understood more from her frosty, non-reaction. It wasn't a matter of her worrying about whether the money would be replaced, but that her character and pride had been impugned.

An hour on the dot, we were back at Lakeview Veterinary Hospital. I instructed Joy to stay with the car as Jack and I went up to the entrance with my mother and I knocked.

"What're we doing back here?" my mother wondered aloud, utterly discombobulated. "Is Snapper coming with us?" she asked in all seriousness.

"No, Mom, we just thought you might like to have, you know, one last visit with him before we head out of town."

"In case he dies, you mean?" she asked fatalistically.

"Come on, Mom, don't be like that."

Dr. Ariel opened the door and wordlessly let us in. We trailed her single-file down the darkened corridor, back into the bowels of the clinic. The clamorous barking and wailing dogs, sequestered in cages, heard our approach. Dr. Ariel directed us through the treatment area into the surgery room in which I'd observed the huge mixed breed get his teeth worked on. I parked my mother next to the stainless steel exam table.

"We're going to have to get her up on the table and lay her down," the doctor said matter-of-factly.

"What're they going to do to me?" my mother asked. "Where's Snapper?"

Shahar turned to me, realizing I hadn't told my mother about the vet-turned-dentist second act of the drama.

"Mom, that tooth has to come out. The dentist in Fresno wouldn't do it because of the Coumadin. This kind doctor is willing to look at it, and if it isn't a big deal, she might do you a favor and yank it"–I snapped my fingers–"like that!"

"I said I would look at it," Dr. Ariel reminded me.

"I know, we're playing this by ear."

"A vet?" my mother asked, her expression a quilt of puzzlement.

"She's trained in oral surgery, Mom. In India, amateurs do it on the streets with rusty pliers. Do you want to go to the hospital?" Even for me, that was low.

"Oh, no, I'd die there."

"Then let's do what the doctor tells us, okay?"

"Okay."

"Come on," I said to Jack. "Let's do this."

Jack came over and stood next to me. "This is wack, man," he said, chuckling.

"Material for my next novel," I quipped.

"No one would believe it."

"Sometimes reality is more fiction than fiction." I turned to my mother and extended my hand. "All right, Mom, here we go."

"Oh, I'm scared."

"Come on." I grabbed her hand before she could offer it. I got her arm extended and then hoisted her up out of her wheelchair against her continued expostulations that she was going to fall and my repeated assurances that she wouldn't. Somehow sensing the urgency of the situation, she pushed off her right leg and I negotiated her unsteadily to her feet. With Jack's help, I rotated her so that her butt was touching the edge of the exam table, but not resting on it. I said to Jack, "We got to get her up."

"Roger that."

We each took a thigh and hoisted her up and onto the exam table.

"Mom, you've got to cut back on those desserts. Jesus."

She laughed. "Oh, don't joke me."

From her sitting position it was easy to swivel her ninety degrees and lay her down. As we did, Dr. Ariel placed a folded towel under her head. Then she went quickly to work.

"Hi, Mrs. Raymond. I'm going to look at that tooth that's hurting you, okay?"

"Okay. How's my Snapper?"

"He's fine. We've got him in an oxygen cage. He's stabilized."

"Oh, that's such good news. I can't thank you enough. Even if you are Jewish."

"Jesus, Mom! Watch it with the appalling racial slurs. Christ!" I turned to Dr. Ariel. "Don't mind her, she's... whatever."

"Open your mouth, please."

My mother obeyed, opening it as wide as she was capable. As Jack and I stood off to the side, Dr. Ariel, employing an instrument with a small mirror, poked around in my mother's mouth. She turned to me and said, "It's pretty inflamed."

"Let's take it out, Shahar. What is it? Five, ten minutes? We'll be gone."

She sucked in her breath. "You know I could lose my license for this."

"And I would never get another book contract to save my life. And the wine world would unanimously disown me. I'd be on the street or in a loony bin for having told such a whopper to the authorities. Do the best you can. If it bleeds too much I promise I'll take her to the hospital and say I tried to do it myself. Please, Doctor. We're at your mercy here."

Dr. Ariel wasted no time now that she had decided to perform the dubious procedure. "I want to give her a local. This could hurt," she muttered. She opened a drawer and removed a syringe and a small vial of clear liquid. She plunged the needle of the syringe into the vial and withdrew a precise amount of what I assumed was Novocain. "I'm just going to numb you a bit, Mrs. Raymond."

My mother was stoic. She bravely held her mouth open as our voices were drowned in the unrelenting din of yowling dogs.

Dr. Ariel gave the injection. My mother let out a little cry when the needle pricked her gum, her face stricken with fear. "Let's just give it a few minutes," Dr. Ariel said to no one in particular.

Jack found a plastic chair and slumped into it and drew a hand across his haggard face. I remained standing next to Dr. Ariel. "I really appreciate this."

"I consulted an M.D. friend while you were gone. Keep her off the Coumadin for two days, okay? Until the bleeding subsides."

"All right."

"Watch for swelling in the ankles. If they start to puff up, resume the Coumadin. If they remain swollen you'd better take her to the hospital."

"I'm not going to the hospital!" my mother yelped.

"Don't worry, Mom," I said sharply. "You're not going to the hospital. Okay?" I turned to Dr. Ariel and said in a barely audible tone. "She doesn't like hospitals. She thinks she's going to die there. Ironic for an R.N., huh? Isn't it, Mom?"

"Oh, yes. I saw so much death!"

Dr. Ariel returned her attention to my mother. She touched the right side of my mother's lower jaw and asked: "Can you feel that?"

"No," my mother said.

"Okay, then, we're ready to start." Dr. Ariel sorted through her drawer and produced a thick-handled instrument with a flattened end. She turned back to my supine mother, whose expression now displayed a kind of frozen mask of fear. As the vet attempted to loosen the infected tooth, my mother's whole body noticeably stiffened. Dr. Ariel worked rapidly to push the gums away from the abscessed tooth. As she did, my mother's right leg violently convulsed.

"Jack," I implored in a rising tone, "hold her leg down!"

Jack, laughing a little, sprang to his feet and clamped both hands down on my mother's right ankle, lashing it to the table. As if all the energy were shunted to another part of her body, her right arm started slapping like the furiously beating wing of a dying pterodactyl. I clutched it with both hands and secured it. She was suddenly a right-sided paroxysmic creature as Dr. Ariel, ignoring her patient's physical reaction, continued to work on dislodging the infected tooth. She exchanged the tool she had for another thick-handled one with a clamp at the end controlled by a pliers-like apparatus. She gripped down on the tooth, grimaced slightly and, with little effort, pulled the molar. She held it triumphantly up in the jaws of her clamp for all to see, proud of her work. Relief washed over everyone. For totally different reasons. There should have been applause!

Moving quickly to staunch the blood, Dr. Ariel produced a vial filled with yellowish powder from her lab coat pocket. With her index finger she tapped out a small amount into the open wound. "This is Yunnan Pai Yao, an herbal coagulant," she explained.

"You practice alternative medicine on animals?" I asked.

"Yes. Mostly acupuncture, but also some herbs," she said as she picked up a tiny sponge from a medical tray table with a pair of dental tweezers and planted it where the tooth had been. "This is a Vetspon," she explained. "It'll disintegrate after a few days." She gave one last cursory examination of my mother's mouth and said, "It's barely seeping, hardly bleeding at all."

Jack let go of my mother's leg and I held her hand in mine. Her violent shaking had now subsided and she looked more bewildered than anything as she lay there trying to process what had just happened.

"How do you feel, Mom?"

"I don't feel anything," she garbled.

"We got it out. No hospital. Thanks to Dr. Ariel here."

"That's such good news!"

"Try not to use my full name if this becomes a popular anecdote," Dr. Ariel said sardonically.

"I'm sorry. Dr. X."

She smiled a laugh.

Jack and I carefully transferred my mother back into the wheelchair. Getting her off the examination table and back into her chair was easier because we now had gravity on our side.

Understandably eager to lock up the clinic and make this grossly ob-jectionable procedure disappear from her consciousness, Dr. Ariel cleaned up and put her canine dental instruments away. That done, she faced me and said, "Good luck, Miles."

"Thank you, Doctor. If I'm ever down-and-out and need a vasectomy I'm coming to you."

She laughed. "How about if you're in town again you take me out to dinner?"

"It's a promise," I said.

She went from vet coquette to deadly serious. "If she starts bleeding, you're going to have to take her to a hospital. But I think she'll be okay."

"Thanks again." I stepped forward and gave her a hug and she hugged me back. "Bye."

Jack took hold of my mother's wheelchair handlebars and pushed her out of the clinic with me trailing. We rolled her up the ramp into the van and resumed our familiar positions in the cockpit. Jack turned the key in the ignition.

"Hold on a second," I said. "I want to figure something out." I went to my iPhone's APPs and brought up Google maps. I surveyed the upper half of California. The original plan was to have cut over to the coast and stay at a beautiful B&B in Mendocino. But now that it was approaching night, and realizing that we had to be in the Willamette by the following evening, I altered the itinerary. "I'm going to cancel that reservation in Mendocino," I said to Jack. "It's going to be a fucking nightmare drive on those narrow roads at night and we're going to have to leave first thing in the morning anyway and won't get to enjoy the incredible scenery. So, I think what we're going to do..."–I tapped my location on the iPhone–"is hit I-5 and just go straight to Redding."

"Whatever you say," Jack said. "Just get me to Wisconsin, O Lordy," he sang.

I laughed as I typed Redding into the car's GPS, and said, "Let's hit it."

We pushed out of Clearlake under a cloudless, indigo-stained sky. We looped onto rural Highway 20 in the direction of the interstate. The monochromatic brown of the flat farmland, its crops already harvested, bordered us on both sides on the deserted road as we journeyed on, a little worse for wear but, we had reason to hope, our troubles behind us.

I turned around and checked on my mother. Joy had given her a Vicodin, per my instructions and she seemed in a narcotized daze. I whispered to Joy, "Don't give her the Coumadin tonight, okay?"

"Okay," she said.

"In the morning I'm going to go to a bank and get you your money." She remained silent. "I don't know what happened to it–maybe it fell out of your purse, I don't care–but I'll replace it in full, okay?"

"Your mom steal money from me," she said in a rapid machine-gun burst. She crossed her arms tightly against her chest.

"Okay, Joy, look. I'm replacing the money. I looked all around in my mom's purse and I can't find it. But, you've got to let it go until we make it to Wisconsin."

"And I didn't kill her dog!" she snapped at me.

"He's not dead. And no one's blaming you."

"Your mom is." She impersonated the excoriating voice of my mother amazingly well: "'You let him get out. You're a dog killer.'" She shook her head disgustedly, angled her face away and stared out at the featureless landscape and darkening sky.

"I'll talk to my mother. I will read her the riot act. But she's had a stroke and it's hard to control what comes out of that mouth of hers. You have to treat her like an invalid, Joy. You can't take anything personally. Please. For me."

Joy offered no reply, just went on staring out the window, the hardened look cemented on her face.

I turned back to the windshield and got out my iPhone. I called the B&B in Mendocino and canceled the reservation. Naturally, given how the day was unfolding, I got hammered by an unsympathetic innkeeper who billed me 50 percent for the canceled night. I tried to reason with her that I was traveling with my mother and that her dog had been in a horrible accident and that she, herself, had to have an emergency tooth extraction, but the innkeeper didn't give a shit–probably thought I was fabricating wildly (and who wouldn't with that wild tale?)–and was totally intransigent.

"Well, you know what," I said after I had clearly lost in my pleading. "I'm a professional writer, and I do a lot of writing for travel magazines, and I was thinking about doing a piece for *Travel & Leisure* on what a great B&B you have. But now I think I'm going to my heavily trafficked Web site and blog that we stayed at your joint and that it was crawling with vermin. Bitch." I ended the call before she could respond. "There went five clams," I said to Jack. "Fucking trip's getting expensive," I spoke ineffectually to the windshield, thinking about the $350 a day it was now costing me to keep Snapper on life support, replacing the five grand that Joy had either lost, my mother had stolen, or... Joy had... I didn't want to think about it. I didn't want to believe I was traveling with an unscrupulous person and had made her responsible for the care of my mother.

I turned my attention back to my iPhone and went in virtual search of motels in Redding, as unmemorable countryside flew past like film in a high-speed projector.

"Pretty slim pickings," I muttered while scrolling through the possibilities. "But we're going to be in late and out early, so who gives a fuck, right?"

"Boy, I could sure use a glass," Jack said. "This has been some mother-fucking day. This makes *Shameless* seem like an episode of *Little House on the Prairie*."

"Let's wait until we get there. It's only another 100 miles."

Jack just gritted his teeth and gripped the steering wheel as if he were in a race against time. I turned back to the information microcosm of my iPhone and decided on the Holiday Inn. It was Redding, California, city of nothing except heat and proximity to the Sacramento River, so of course there was availability when I inquired. I booked two adjacent rooms, read a credit card number over the phone, and ended the call.

I swiveled around to check on my mother and Joy, anxious now every time. My mother had awakened from her Vicodin-induced slumber and was sitting in a stony-faced silence as if a part of her soul had been ripped out in the middle of a bad dream. Joy's face was still fixed in recrimination. Jack just looked beat, needing a shower and a shave and an air-conditioned, fully stocked bar. And I secretly fantasized a handgun.

It was close to 10:00 p.m. when we finally pulled in to the hotel. The recently-opened Redding Holiday Inn was nicer than advertised—pool and Jacuzzi and clean, spacious rooms—but given the saturnine gloom of the collective mood, soured as it was by the sequence of acrimonious and horrific events, we might as well have been at the Motel 6 with its claustrophobic spaces, threadbare towels and scratchy, semen- and menstrual-stained linens.

His hotel being mostly empty, and seeing my mother slumped forlornly in the wheelchair, the desk clerk upgraded us to more capacious suites, one of them outfitted for the handicapped and the other the honeymoon suite complete with a pink, heart-shaped tub. I worried about leaving Joy alone with my mother for fear the bickering would be rekindled, but I desperately needed a hot shower and a couple glasses to come down from the late afternoon's woeful, albeit comically surreal, events.

After reinvigorating showers, Jack and I split a bottle of Anne Amie Pinot Noir rosé, another outstanding Willamette Valley wine. It hit the spot with its refreshing, strawberry lusciousness and cold, bracing acidity.

"Hundred-percent Pinot Noir," I remarked. "Usually, rosés are made from Grenache, but this surprises me. Man."

Jack smacked his lips. "Tasty. We are drinking well on this trip, my friend," he said, the wine producing an immediate effect on our querulous moods.

"You hungry?" I asked Jack. "It's going to be a drag to find a restaurant at this hour."

"Let's just order some room service," Jack said, rummaging around in the nightstand drawer for the hotel directory. He flipped to the restaurant menu, but quickly closed it shut. "Fucking room service ends at 9:00."

"Maybe I'll go down the hall and get us some candy bars and chips from the vending machine."

"Fuck that, Homes," Jack exploded. "And I don't want to get back out on the street looking for some fast food joint."

I saw that Jack, too, was growing unappeasably irascible and ready to close ranks with Joy over my incontinent, frequently lachrymose, and downright bitchy mother. The trip, like so many vacations people plan, wasn't unfolding as one's imagination fantasized when slouched in the comfort of one's home, combing through brochures and surfing the Internet. Cross-country trips in the summer with my brothers and parents, ensconced in a small camper lashed to a 3/4 ton Ford pickup, had been ordeals. All I remember was driving and driving and driving and impatience to get home. "Well, tomorrow we'll be in the Willamette Valley at this great B&B," I said. "Bivouac for a couple of days. We won't have to worry about driving because the IPNC has buses that take the participants on the winery visits."

Jack nodded sullenly. He was worn out, no doubt calculating how far we still had to go to get to Wisconsin, and the catastrophe that leg of the journey with my difficult mother and her procession of needs could turn out to be. "I look forward to this IPNC," he said unenthusiastically. "I'm going to get *fucked* up. Then I'm going to try out my new pecker."

"And I look forward to hearing the results."

Jack raised his glass in a mock salute.

"Well, at least we got the tooth out."

"We got the tooth out," Jack aped. "Can't wait until she has the heart attack. It'll be like *Weekend at Bernie's* all the way to Sheboygan."

"And–I shouldn't say this because I'll probably be struck by lightning–we got that fucking nightmare of a dog out of the equation. Though thank God he's alive. We would never have heard the end of that."

"I think it would have been better if you'd put him down," Jack said without remorse.

"Yeah, but you wouldn't have been the guy in there with my mom while they gave the little critter the pentobarbital. I mean, she breaks into tears enough as it is. I can only imagine the blubbering if we had had to euthanize him."

"Why the fuck did you bring him?"

"I don't know." I sipped my wine, reflected. "I thought it would keep her occupied. Also, I worried that she'd be lonely in Wisconsin without him."

That shut Jack up.

"How're you feeling down there, big guy?" I asked in a whiplashing shift in inflection.

Jack reached his free hand to his cock and squeezed it through his jeans. "It's not too bad," he said. "And I had a pretty promising little junior erection this morning."

"Good." I sipped my wine. "How long did it last?"

Jack lolled his head in my direction. "Fuck you, Homes." Then he turned his head back to the muted baseball game. "Unfortunately no receptacle."

I laughed and continued to work the Anne Amie.

"Are there going to be any chicks at this IPNC?"

"I'm sure there will be. There're nearly a thousand participants. Totally sold out."

"Probably mostly married, huh?"

"The husbands are going to be bombed and passed out on Pinot. The wives will come out and play." I pointed my glass at Jack. "And there's no better fuck than a married woman."

"Amen, brother. Amen."

"But I'm sure there'll also be pods of female oenophiles–their husbands and boyfriends fornicating back East–looking for some fun. Throw in all-day wine tasting, my undeserved celebrity, I'll hook you up, Jackson. Don't worry."

"Good. 'Cause this thing's like a spill off a horse. You got to get back in the saddle as soon as possible, otherwise you'll never ride again."

"You'll ride again, big guy," I said, slithering off the queen-sized bed and standing. "I'm going to go check on my mom, send Joy here, split 'em up."

"Excellent idea! That's a time bomb waiting to go off."

"Keep her company, okay?" I stopped at the door and shot Jack a backward glance. "And don't try to seduce her and see if that healed member of yours is back in operation."

"Fuck, man, I'd split that little Filipina in two."

"Plus, Asians scream. And they don't care who hears. Get my drift."

"Aye, aye, captain."

"I'm going to stay with my mom until she goes to sleep, then maybe we can go down and take a whirlpool or a swim or something."

I went next door and knocked. Joy answered, her face still enshrouded in a dark cloud. "Why don't you go hang with Jack, smoke some herb, I'll sit with my mom until she falls asleep, okay?"

"Okay," she said.

I gave her shoulder a squeeze. "You'll have your money back in the morning." The lovely rosé must have gone to my head because I added, "And I'm going to give you a thousand dollar bonus because of how shabbily my mother has treated you. All right?"

She nodded, then looked up at me with her face clenched in a scowl. "I did not steal money, and I did not kill dog," she stammered.

"I believe you, Joy. Okay?" I said, exasperation in my voice. "And the dog isn't dead."

"That's what your mom say."

"She's had a massive stroke, Joy." With my hand I clutched the left half of her head and said, "The whole left side of her brain is gone. Dead tissue."

She blinked, shook free from my grasp and went next door to be mercifully entertained by Jack.

I came into my mother's suite. She was lying on her back, remote in her right hand, watching the local news on TV. She muted the TV when I dragged over a chair next to her and sat down. I glanced at the muted TV: raging conflagrations fueled by Santa Ana winds, charred and mangled interstate pile-ups, abducted children.... "How you feeling, Mom?"

"Okay. Tired."

"Did Joy give you your meds?"

"Yes," she said without looking at me.

"I'm sorry about Snapper."

"She murdered him."

"No, she didn't, Mom."

"She might as well have," she pouted. "I'm never going to see him again."

"You don't know that," I snapped. "And you've got to stop this right now," I reproved her, hating to have to scold my mother as if she were a child. Which she, essentially, was. "Joy was not responsible for the accident. There was an argument and I tried to stop it and Snapper took advantage of the situation and scampered out. *That's* what happened. If it's anybody's fault, it's mine."

Her face hardened like a dried stone fruit, but she held her tongue.

"Let me see where your tooth was pulled." Still depressed, she wouldn't open her mouth right away. "Let me see it, Mom. Because if it's bleeding I'm calling 911."

At the mention of hospitalization, she opened up. Using the tips of the fingers of both hands, I pried her jaw wider, turned her toward the nightstand lamp and peered inside the cavern of her mouth. The Vetspon and the herbal powder must have been working because, to my infinite relief, I saw no evidence whatsoever of bleeding. "It looks good, Mom. Do you taste blood when you swallow?"

"No."

"Good."

"Snapper's going to die," she said, still fixated on her pet.

"If he does, when we get to your sister's we'll get another dog to replace Snapper."

She hoisted her head and looked up at me like an old judge about to deliver the sentence. "That'd be like if your kid died and I said I would get you another one from an adoption agency."

"Okay," I said, holding up both hands in emotional surrender, "okay. Not that I would know, but I guess I misspoke."

A silence descended. My mother wouldn't look at me. There definitely was something missing without Snapper in the room, cuddling up to her on the bed. I've never had pets, never wanted pets, but their inevitable anthropomorphization by their owners only made their loss that much more grievous and I could empathize. Somewhat.

"Are you glad you came, Mom?"

Her mood completely changed like a mercurial thunderstorm, "Oh, yes."

"Good. I'm glad."

"I know you're busy, and I do appreciate everything you're doing for me. I'll try to be a good girl."

"All right, Mom. We need Joy. Just bear that in mind before you tee off on her again. When you yell at her, think about this: you're giving me a panic attack. Remember that time at the V.A. Hospital when I had to leave you and go into the ER?"

"Oh, yes. I was scared."

"*You* were scared? I was the one crying and calling out for Mother Mary and Jesus. I thought I was having a heart attack."

"Oh, no."

"Oh, yes."

"But you're better now?"

"Yeah, but once you've had one of those, it never leaves your memory. It lies like a slumbering beast." I pointed my finger at her, hating to be a scold to my parent. "Think about me, Mom. Don't always think about yourself."

Her chin slumped to her chest. "I'm sorry you have to replace the money."

"We can't lose Joy, Mom. The goal is to do whatever it takes to get you to Sheboygan. Things don't always go as planned. I mean, who would have thought a veterinarian in some podunk town would be extracting your abscessed molar?"

My mother laughed a gravelly laugh. "Your dad would have liked that story."

"Oh, yeah?"

"Yeah, he loved the bizarre." She nodded to herself as if conjuring the image of her dead husband and holding it in her imagination. "And he loved his wine at night." She kept nodding. I was glad she had shifted her thoughts to something other than her badly-injured dog and, in her confused mind, that supposed devious-minded, scheming Joy. She went on nodding until her lids drooped and the remote slipped from her limp hand. I picked it up and switched the TV off. In a few minutes she was snoring. I turned off the nightstand light, rose from the chair and quietly slipped out the front door.

I found Jack and Joy passing a joint and laughing about something, probably the tooth extraction at the vet clinic. I knew Jack was ripped because his voice boomed when he said, "Miles! You're back!"

"Shhh," I said, raising an index finger to my lips. "She's asleep. I don't want to wake her. But the tooth looks good. No bleeding I can see."

"Excellent," Jack said, not really interested–probably hoping I *would* have to hospitalize her so he would be relieved of his co-piloting duties.

I said to Joy, "You should probably go back."

Without protest, she packed up her little tin of skunky-smelling buds, Zigzags and half-smoked joints and left the room in her typically wordless comportment.

When she was gone, Jack said: "Hey, Miles, do you know what O.F.W. stands for?"

"Yeah. Overseas Filipino Worker."

"No. Outstanding Fucking Woman." He drained his wineglass. "That chick's cool. Ever done an Asian?"

"Once. Never again."

Jack, his libido evidently on the rebound, said, "You could have that chick if you wanted."

"I don't want to do my mother's nurse. What're you, crazy?"

"I bet she's hot," Jack sang, drawing out each syllable.

I did my best to ignore him.

"You want to hit the Jacuzzi?"

"Nah, I'm tired. It's been a long day." I slipped out of my pants and peeled my shirt off and got into bed.

"What're you wearing your underwear for?" Jack wanted to know.

"I don't know, I just..."

"Man, you don't think I haven't seen your pecker before." I could tell he was pretty drunk by now. "Remember that time at that wine event, you got so sideways I had to hold you up and take your pecker out so you wouldn't pee your pants."

"All right, Jack. All right. Unless you want me to start bringing up all that shit with Terra up in Santa Ynez and how you almost blew off a wedding to a society girl by getting all obsessed with some tasting room manager who's now a meth-addicted slattern in Reno, I suggest you can it." I switched off the light, plunging the room into darkness. I heard Jack wrestle out of his clothes. Soon, he, too, was snoring.

I lay awake staring into the darkness. The reflection from the pool formed sinuous Rorschach shapes that shifted and changed in a silent aqueous dance on the white acoustic ceiling. I tried to analogize the amorphous images to life, but failed to find expression. I worried I was drawing further and further away from my writing, like a boat with a blown engine at the mercy of strong currents. It's the last thing I remember before toppling disquietingly into darkness.

chapter 11

B right sunlight poured through the diaphanous drapery and exploded our suite into white. Jack was still asleep when I emerged from the shower. I glanced at my watch: already 8:30. My trusty iPhone zeroed in on a nearby Wells Fargo that opened at 9:00. I roused Jack, who spluttered awake, as if plucked out of a fairy-tale world of beautiful nymphs and great ogres only to discover himself in a hospital with his limbs in traction.

"Wha-, wha-, what?"

"Get up, Jack."

"Where are we?"

"Redding. And it's going up a degree every five minutes and I want to get the fuck out of here. I've got to go to the bank. I want you to shower quickly, pack up, take our bags down to the lobby and meet Joy and my mom for breakfast. I'll join you in an hour, tops."

Jack pulled a hand over his face as if some bit of prestidigitation would magically transform him into a prince, then, coming fully into consciousness, said, "All right."

At the open door, I threw him a backward glance, admonishing, "I'm sure my mom's already up, so don't make them wait, okay?"

I closed the door on him before he could answer.

Unlike the parched and desolate-looking Fresno and Merced, the modestly-populous Redding is nestled in a valley surrounded by picturesque mountain ranges. It's not as aesthetically condemnable as the former two. As I followed the GPS instructions to the Wells Fargo branch, I noticed how the city itself was lush with foliage. Still, it was mind-bendingly hot.

I withdrew $10,000 in cash. No fewer than three bank employees were involved in the transaction. First, it couldn't be done (the teller); then I needed to show three IDs (the supervisor); then I needed to sign my signature on a score of documents. Then, that still not sufficient to get my hard-earned cash, I had to wait while my home branch faxed a copy of my original signature up to this Redding branch I had wandered into unshaven and dressed like an artist who probably wasn't one. Since the original signature card was dated by fifteen years, and since I had drunk thousands of bottles of wine in the interim, my signature had deteriorated alarmingly. Eventually, after much hand-wringing, they went back into their vault and brought out the cash. The supervisor, nervously looking around at the other customers waiting through this interminable transaction, actually asked whether I wanted to call someone for a security escort.

"This isn't Vegas, Stu," I said, reading the name off his ID plate, irritable that they had dragged this out so long. "Just give me the ten Gs and I'll take my chances with the local recidivists."

He threw me a suspicious look, then counted out–with deliberate slowness–the hundred Ben Franklins.

Back at the Holiday Inn I found Jack, Joy and my mother chowing down in another corporate-looking dining room–green carpet, fake wood tables, disc-herniating chairs, insipid food prepared by minimum wage earners with little or no cooking experience, and dilatory service.

By ten o'clock we were back on I-5, barreling for Oregon. Jack said he felt refreshed and wanted to drive the first half of the final leg to the Willamette Valley. I agreed to take over for the second half and guide us into the B&B the nice organizers of the IPNC had booked. Having only 400 miles to cover, even with my mother's frequent pit stops, we should easily make it by five, I calculated–barring another calamity!

Thinking of Joy and worried about rekindled acrimony over missing money and comatose pet, I turned around and said, "Would you like to sit up front?"

She smiled expressively for the first time in two days and nodded.

"Because it's a tough transfer up here, Mom. And I'm not going to sit in your goddamn wheelchair," I barked back, mostly for Joy's benefit.

"Oh, you're no good," she shot back.

I ignored her—which was getting easier to do—and slipped through the wide opening between the two front seats, letting Joy pass by on her way to the front. She retrieved an iPod from her purse and plugged the earbuds into her elfish ears. A few minutes later she was bobbing up and down, elated to be separated from her cantankerous charge. Elated not to have to stare in a single direction to avert her gaze. And that, going a long way toward mollifying my rising anxiety, made *me* elated.

"How're you holding up, Mom?" I asked, in an effort to win back her allegiance.

"I'm fine," she said. "I miss Snapper."

"I know. But he's not with us for now. Life goes on, isn't that what you always told me?"

"Oh, yes."

"Can I see the tooth again?" This time she turned to me unhesitatingly and opened her mouth as wide as she could. I craned my neck forward and looked into her mouth. The Vetspon had already disintegrated and I could make out the lacuna left by the extraction. A nice scab looked to be forming, in a vivid, dark magenta. "Looks like normal coagulation."

"That's good news," she said, and closed her mouth.

"No hospital."

"No, no hospital."

Within a minute, she had dozed off. I made a mental note to instruct Joy to start weaning her off the Vicodin. Given my mother's addictive personality, and her total lack of self-control, the last thing we'd need, if we even made it to Wisconsin, was to detox her from a synthetic opiate.

"Hey, Jack, what about a reality TV show where they try to get stroke victims hooked on Hydrocodone to go cold turkey?"

Jack flashed me a wicked grin, happy to see I hadn't lost touch with my sarcastic self.

I tapped Joy on the shoulder. She popped the earbuds out and turned to me. I handed her an envelope thick with one-hundred dollar bills. "Six thousand. Payment in full, with a bonus. As promised."

She took the envelope from me and diffidently said, "Thank you."

"You're doing a terrific job under adverse circumstances." I couldn't stop myself from tacking on, "Don't abandon us."

"Okay," she said.

"I also bought you a little present." I handed her a money belt I had purchased from a travel supplies store I passed on the drive back to the motel from Wells Fargo. It took her a moment to grasp what it was. She broke into a girlish smile. "It's a money belt, so"—I pointed to my dozing mother and whispered—"she won't steal from you again."

"Thank you," she said. Then she turned back to the view framed in the windshield, reinserted her earbuds and resumed bobbing to the music, whatever it was. Probably Dengue Fever.

North of Redding, I-5 snakes through the sometimes-majestic Cascades. The passing landscape grew ever more densely timbered as we tunneled our way through tall pines and colossal redwoods. Even in late July, the highest peaks were snow-capped.

I didn't know whether it was because Joy had taken my mother's diuretics out of the pharmacological lineup or whether the absence of Snapper made her less anxious, but even once she reawakened she was able to hold off on the next pit stop until we reached Grants Pass, a small town just over the state line.

A sit-down lunch would have been a protracted affair, so we took the first off-ramp and then pulled into the lot of the first supermarket we came to. As part of my strategy to defuse the burgeoning tension, I let Jack stay with my mother as Joy and I went into the store to buy sandwiches and drinks.

When we returned Jack was sitting in the passenger side, talking excitedly on his cell phone. He concluded his call and said, "It's looking good, brother. It's looking good."

"The reality show?"

"Yeah. It's a go. I don't know how many episodes they're going to shoot, and I'm just AD-ing, but at least I'm back in the game."

"That's great," I said, handing him a sandwich and a brown paper bag clinking with some local handcrafted ales.

He pulled one out and smiled at me. "Thanks, Homes. I see you're looking out for me."

"I'm looking out for everybody," I said exasperatedly, opening it for him with my all-purpose key ring corkscrew/bottle opener. "I'm starting to feel like a fucking headshrinker." I handed Jack his beer. "Could you do me a favor?" I asked.

Jack looked up at me with a mouthful of turkey sandwich.

I whispered, "Could you sit in the back and let Joy sit up here with me? As much time as I can keep them apart until this tension eases I think will pay dividends down the, uh, well, road."

"No problem," my wing man mumbled through the half-chewed mess, that cold beer in his hand already improving his mood.

I piloted us back onto the interstate. Just out of Grants Pass we spanned the scenic Rogue River and seemed to cross the threshold into another world. Suddenly, we were enwombed by jagged, forested mountains whose hillsides were slashed by indolent, molten rivers and gurgling creeks. At this altitude the temperature had dipped at least ten degrees, and the change was having a salutary effect on our beleaguered, road-weary party. That, and the fact that we were coming to the end of the first leg of our greater journey and would all be able to kick back for three days before pressing on for Wisconsin.

We made one pit stop in Eugene, and another in Salem, where we left I-5 and hooked up with rural highway 221. As soon as we got off the free-way we were back in the heartstoppingly endless verdure of wine country, right in the middle of the famed—and to some, fabled—Willamette Valley. Vineyard after vineyard property rippled over gently sloping hills. It had been a wet spring and the summer greenery of the profusely leafed-out rootstock was everywhere in evidence. The waning afternoon sun slanted through the pines and painted a filigree of gold light over the unblemished landscape. We'd all, including Joy it seemed, had our psyches readjusted with our emergence into this preternatural world. We had reached nir-vana, our own collective perception of Shangri-la. Nothing could deter us from three days of fun and exploration. Surely, this was the disposition change I'd been praying for.

"It's beautiful," my mother announced when I informed her we were almost there. "Gorgeous."

"Amen, Mrs. Raymond," Jack concurred, drinking in the vineyard landscape, and another fresh ale. "Amen."

"I told you guys." I turned to Joy and asked, "What do you think?"

She nodded excitedly, hypnotized by the countryside. Doing the seven-hour drive up front, away from the withering looks and excoriations of my mother, as well as the re-infusion of cash, had undoubtedly mitigated the damage to her pride. And it was nice to see my mother undergo a change of personality, her ululations over Snapper having grated on us and turned this dream trip into a bummer, now mercifully abating.

We arrived at the Willamette Valley's Brookside Inn Bed & Breakfast. Set in a wooded enclave, the B&B rose up like some enchanted, fog-enshrouded dominion of a wayward princess. Sunlight rayed through towering trees, casting long shadows across the luxuriantly green, pristine piece of land. As we bumped across a planked bridge that arced over one end of a private pond, a fish leapt clear out of the water and swallowed an insect, disappearing with a splash beneath the charcoal-gray surface.

Our tires came to a crunching stop on the narrow gravel road at the front of the main house, a beautifully renovated two-story structure constructed of wood and stone. We piled out, weary, but relieved. The quiet was positively deafening, the air redolent of nature in all its glory. Everyone just gazed around in awe of our sublime environs.

"We made it to the Willamette, god damn it!" I proclaimed, arms aloft in supplication to a god I didn't believe in smiling down on us.

As I walked up the short flight of steps to the front porch, the owner came out and greeted us.

"Miles Raymond?" He was a big man, in his early sixties.

"That would be me."

"I'm Bruce. I see you made it."

"Yeah, it was quite a journey," I said with irony in my voice, too mentally exhausted to elaborate.

"Why didn't you just fly?"

I turned and waved my crew up. Jack pushed my mother and Joy trailed to where Bruce and I were standing. I pointed to my mother in the wheelchair. "Uh, well, we're taking my mom to Wisconsin after the IPNC."

Bruce looked confused.

"It's a long story." I gestured to my mother. "Bruce, this is my mother, Phyllis."

Bruce bent forward to greet her. "Hi, Phyllis. I'm Bruce."

My mother arose from her spellbound state that the surroundings had induced in her and said, "Nice to meet you."

"We're going to take good care of you."

"Oh, that's such good news." She crooked her index finger and pointed it skyward. "It's beautiful here," my mother said, emotion cracking her voice.

"Yes," said Bruce. "Every day is paradise."

A gigantic black Newfoundland rose, as if on cue, from the planked porch where he was napping and padded over to my mother and nuzzled his huge head against her chest. She hooked her good arm around him and let him lick her face until it looked like a glazed doughnut. "Oh, you're a nice dog. I lost my Snapper." She burst into tears.

"He's in an animal hospital in Northern California," I clarified for our host.

"Oh, that's a shame," Bruce commiserated. "I guess you've had a hard trip, huh?" he said. He turned to my mother. "I'm sure you miss him."

"Oh, yes," she said.

"Mom, stop crying, please."

"Okay." She turned to Bruce and smiled coquettishly. "Can I get a glass of wine?"

Bruce looked at me and I shrugged, as if: why not?

"Well, come on in everybody," he said affably. "Welcome to the Brookside Inn."

The main sitting room, known as The Great Room, was bigger than my rent-controlled house. It had a high pitched ceiling with wood crossbeams, and comfortable lounge chairs in front of an enormous stone fireplace, where the proprietor had thoughtfully got a modest fire going. Floor-to-ceiling windows, divided by oak beams, looked out onto the surrounding property and all its profuse greenery. Jack parked my mother next to the blazing hearth. The Newfoundland, having made a new friend, lay down next to her.

Bruce soon came out of the adjoining kitchen with a cold glass of white and handed it to my mother, preoccupied with petting the dog. "Here you go, Mrs. Raymond. It's a local Chardonnay."

"Oh, thank you," she said, greedily accepting the complimentary refreshment. Her eyes squeezed shut and she held her glass, to the extent her infirmity permitted, aloft. "The angels must be looking out for me!"

We all laughed.

Jack and Joy found chairs and practically collapsed into them. Bruce motioned me to follow him into the kitchen—rustic and featuring an antique stove. A small dining room with more floor-to-ceiling windows was dappled with shadows from the nose-diving sun. On the other side of the kitchen sat a small alcove the inn had converted into an office. A middle-aged woman rose and approached.

"This is my wife, Susan," Bruce said.

"He does the cooking and I do the accounting," she said.

"From the looks of this place, you make quite a team." I reached for my wallet, flipped it open and fingered a credit card.

Bruce held up both hands. "All been paid for by the IPNC."

"I thought so. Was just checking. Didn't want you to think I was a piker."

"And a lot of wine has been arriving for you."

"We're not too much in the habit of hosting celebrities," Susan remarked.

"Well, if it gets us all free wine, who's complaining?"

"Shall I show you your rooms?" Bruce asked.

"You know what? We've just come four hundred miles today. Could you do us a favor and uncork one of those Pinots, pour three glasses? Plus a couple more if you two are ready to get the evening going. I think we're just going to chill in your splendiferous sitting room there, get our sea legs."

"Of course," said Bruce as he disappeared out the back.

"Nice to meet you, Susan. You have a truly lovely place here."

"Thank you."

In The Great Room, Joy sat nestled in a chair as far from my mother as possible—and behind her! The friction between the two had not, alas, yet abated. But I felt confident that Joy would stick it out with the six thousand in hand.

I plopped down across from Jack. "Libations are en route."

"Excellent."

Bruce returned shortly with an open bottle. He set it, along with three Pinot-specific Riedels, on the table that centered the room. He poured and handed around to Jack, Joy, and me. Then he held up the bottle and showed me the label. "This is an '08 Ayoub from just down the road. Mo Ayoub is a small-production, artisanal maker of only Pinot Noir. No more than a few hundred cases of this stuff. Never gets out of Oregon." He added with a crinkly smile, "We like to keep the good stuff here."

I sipped and studied. The wine was bursting with all the variety's telltale, *sui generis* characteristics. "Mm. Nice," I said to Bruce, who had remained in the room, waiting for an evaluation. I took another sip. "Really nice."

"His small vineyard is all red volcanic soil. You get a real mineral thing going on in there. Can you taste it?"

"Yeah, it's just all over the map, coming at me from every direction. Big, rich. Nuanced notes of nobility," I deliberately alliterated, mimicking the purple prose of so much ridiculous winespeak.

"Glad you like it," Bruce said, chuckling at my hyperbole. I had switched, without necessarily intending to, into the Martin West persona from *Shameless*.

Changing back into the real me, I turned to Jack, "What do you think, big guy?"

"Oh, yeah, notably nuanced," he mocked me. He took another sip and sudsed it around in his mouth, extending the impersonation. "And definitely not tighter than a nun's asshole. And it's certainly not *fucking* Merlot!"

Bruce and I laughed. The party was revving up. We had three unfettered days, sans driving, and the mood was positively buoyant.

"This is my friend, Jack. He inspired the Jake character."

"Oh, yeah," Bruce said. "That must be quite a compliment."

"Well," Jack said in his stentorian voice. "It is and it isn't. I mean, how would you like it if every woman who you met, once she found out you were the prototype for Martin's womanizing accomplice in this guy's"—Jack jerked a thumb at me—"overrated novel, said, 'Are you really such a motherfucking, lying, cheating asshole?'"

Bruce and I laughed again. Joy, who admitted to having neither seen the movie nor read the book, stared at us blankly.

"But it is true, Bruce," Jack said, "that I like the ladies." He extravagantly toasted pussy as yet unexcavated and smiled wryly.

"Well, I think you're going to have no trouble finding a few women up here who, for a couple of days at least, take off the wedding rings."

"Hear, hear," Jack said. Bruce was apparently of a liberal bent. And rumor had it that at the IPNC, if you fell in with the wrong crowd–which Jack and I were prone to do–things could get dangerously out of control.

My iPhone rang. The number was unfamiliar, but the area code was local, so I answered it, "Hello?"

"Miles?" a woman said.

"Yes, this is he."

"Hi, I'm Julie, coordinator of the IPNC."

"Of course. Hi, Julie."

"You've arrived?"

"We have arrived. Just a few minutes ago, in fact. And we're off to a great start. Bruce has poured me one terrific Pinot." A bit of an exaggeration, admittedly, but I loved its earthiness, its expression of *terroir*.

"Well, you're going to be drinking a lot more over the next three days."

"Our livers are ready."

She chuckled. "So, you're coming to the salmon bake tomorrow night, right?"

"Of course. Aren't I supposed to be doing a book signing?"

"That and more. We've got four hundred copies all set to go. You'd better be there."

"Four hundred? Jesus. I don't know if my writing hand'll hold out."

She laughed. "Okay."

"And thanks for picking up the tab here. It's beautiful. And thanks to all the vintners who sent me wine."

"They love you up here, Miles. We're sixty-five percent planted in Pinot, so your book and movie did a lot for everybody in the Valley."

The cellular meet-&-greet done, I poured Jack and myself another glass of the opulent Ayoub. When I turned to Joy I saw she still had a good bit left. She tapped two fingers to her lips in our familiar code.

"Apparently, there's no smoking allowed anywhere on the property, Joy." She drew an expression of disappointment. "As soon as we finish this wine, we're going to check in, then go out to eat. I'll make sure to stop somewhere so you can get an adjustment."

She cracked a smile at the euphemism. I wondered whether I should just say, *stoned out of your fucking gourd?*

Jack and I killed the bottle in very little time. My mother tried to inveigle a second glass of the Chard, but I waved Bruce off and said to her back, "Mom, we're going to check in, then go to a restaurant. You can have two glasses there, okay?"

She raised her index finger. "Oh, that's such good news."

Bruce assigned her The Rogue Suite, a ground-floor handicapped room in the Carriage House, a separate structure across the expansive lawn. It was a small, but pleasant, room facing the garden. Surmising quickly that Joy wasn't going to be sleeping with my mother in its queen-sized bed, I asked Bruce to have a foldout brought over.

As he left to see to that, I noticed that Joy was assaying the bathroom–where most of her duties were performed. It had a handicapped bar above the toilet and three wall-mounted bars in the tub. The room's doors were wide as well.

"Are you going to be okay in here?" I asked her nervously.

"I think so," she muttered, intently focused on the handicapped apparatuses.

"Look, if you ever need any help transferring her, just call me."

She turned and faced me. "I did one night and you were passed out. Your mom had fallen and I had trouble getting her back in the chair. I had to call the night clerk."

I felt guilty. "That was at Justin?"

She nodded reproachfully.

"I'm sorry." The extent of Joy's duties was just now dawning on me. "She's very heavy."

"Well, if you're worried about transferring her to the tub for her bath, then hand-bathe her."

She crossed her arms against her chest and looked at me. "You mom doesn't like hand baths."

"Well, she doesn't have any fucking choice, does she? And if you have any problems with her, call me on my cell–I'll wake up eventually, and I'll come right over. I don't want you two to start arguing again. Okay?"

"Okay."

"I want this to work. I want you to have fun. So, get the old coot ready for dinner. Jack and I'll come get you."

She looked pleased. Specious or otherwise; hell, I didn't have time to care.

I plodded up the narrow flight of stairs to the second floor. Bruce had me booked into The Astoria, the most spacious suite in the Carriage House. Jack was checked into the McKenzie, a smaller suite, but then I didn't think we'd be spending much time in the rooms anyway, and the time we would we'd likely devote to drinking in my designated crib.

In The Astoria I discovered–to twin feelings of horror and delight!–a veritable cornucopia of local Pinots cluttering the tables and the night-stands and even spilling over to the floor. The bottles sprawled everywhere! An oenophile's Christmas.

"Christ!" Jack exclaimed when he got an eyeful of this embarrassment of riches. "Holy moly."

"Man," I said to Bruce, who had come in to check up on us. "They're really rolling out the red carpet."

"Well, to be honest, they're hoping you're going to write about the IPNC. Or, better yet, put it in your next novel."

"Yeah, if I'm sober enough. And not in a morgue all Prince purple." Jack and Bruce guffawed. "Besides, I can't be bought."

"Oh, bullshit," Jack boomed. "Before *Shameless* you would have sold your mother's wheelchair for salvage."

"It did occur to me," I confessed.

Bruce and Jack had a hearty laugh over that one, too.

"Do you know a good, casual restaurant close by?" I asked Bruce.

"Tina's. I took the liberty of making a reservation. Otherwise you'd never get in because of the IPNC."

"Thanks. Gee."

"That's what we do here, Miles. We think ahead. I'll give you the address."

"Nah, it's fine." I held up my iPhone with its myriad apps. "I'll get it here faster than you can write it down."

"Okay," Bruce chuckled. "I'm a bit of a Luddite when it comes to all that gadget stuff." As he said this, he casually reached into his breast pocket and pulled out a card. *Tina's*, in a nice cursive. Address, phone, and even a little schematic map on the back. "In case the network is down." He left.

I stood there, feeling like an idiot. It wasn't the first time. Or maybe it was the first time I was suddenly, humiliatingly conscious of it.

Jack found a corkscrew, among the many and sundry the winemakers had left us, uncorked an interesting bottle he pulled at random, and poured two glasses into an unmatched pair of the several dozen Pinot-specific, logo-embossed glasses with which our local hosts had also gifted us. I picked up the bottle Jack had selected and looked at it. All it had for

a label was a strip of masking tape, hand-lettered with a Sharpie: "2009
Harper Voit Strandline Pinot Noir. Barrel Sample."

Jack nosed it, and took in a generous mouthful. His expression ranged
from curiosity to plebian exultation. "Mm," he said. "This is awesome,
dude. Get some of that down your gullet ASAP. Monster."

I smelled the bouquet and it struck me flush in my olfactory glands
like a vinous haymaker. In my mouth it was inky, plush, gorgeous, almost
savage, a wild ride of pepper, black cherry, cedar, and Cuban cigar–the
full three-act structure so many Pinots lack. "Wow," was all I said.

"Told you."

I passed the bottle to Jack. "This is a fucking barrel sample. Hasn't
even been released."

"Man, this is good."

"Fuck. I'm getting excited."

"Me, too."

"God, I'm glad we got off the road."

"Amen, brother. Amen." He held out his glass and we toasted. I wanted
to hug Jack just then, but that wasn't how we rolled.

"All right, let's shower up, and go eat." I picked up the Harper Voit
and corked it. "We'll take this with us, and another one."

"Oh, that's such good news," Jack drawled as he headed out my
suite's door.

I hadn't checked my messages all day. One from my book agent, but
it was now Friday night and I wouldn't have to return it until Monday.
Next from Marcie, wondering whether we had arrived. (I'd call her back
later.) Next one I had to replay twice because the voice was scratchy and
indistinct. Laura! *LAU-ra.* She had gotten home safely and was saying rapidly in broken English that she had had a lot of fun and hoped I would
honor my promise and come to Barcelona. There were two threatening
ones from Yvonne at Las Villas de Muerte informing me I needed to sign
discharge papers and pay some kind of penalty. Then a really, really vitri-
olic one from Melina about Snapper. Should I call her and inform her
that Snapper was in intensive care? Maybe shake her down for the bill?
Damn pettifogger would probably drag me into civil court and get a judgment against me for mental anguish. Fuck an attorney once, but don't
fuck her twice. When would I ever learn my lesson?

When I emerged from the shower, Jack was back, lounging in the lone chair, still luxuriating in the massive Harper Voit. His hair was wet and uncombed and he had on a blousy white shirt with the tails flying out over a pair of black acid-washed jeans. He looked like some hillbilly who had just gotten off the bus from Arkansas seeking fame and fortune in Tinseltown. I changed into my uniform of black T-shirt and blue jeans and Patagonia mock bowling shoes.

After half-killing the Harper Voit, Jack and I plodded downstairs. Joy and my mother, primped and in a fresh change of clothes, were waiting anxiously.

"I thought you went off drinking," my mother grumbled.

"Don't start in on us, Mom. I'm not that much of a degenerate."

Jack pushed her outside and we all clambered into the Rampvan. I punched the address for Tina's into the GPS and we rolled away. The tiny town of Dundee was just a ten-minute drive on tree-shaded roads. The collective mood was happily pacific, reminiscent of when we had started off. Which seemed like weeks ago!

Tina's proved to be a small, cottage-style place, painted red, its eaves festooned with a string of white lights as if the restaurant existed in a perpetual Noel. Inside, it boasted a homey, open feel, with a democratic arrangement of tables and a wood-burning fireplace. Thanks to Bruce, and his intimation that there was a "celebrity" in the party, we were seated at a center table. The place was hopping–IPNC attendees I surmised by all the bottles they had brought.

A pretty waitress slapped a wine list on the table. Jack and I had brought over one of the housewarming presents–a Van Duzer 2008 Estate Pinot–to back up our half-drunk Harper. On the wine list, I was delighted to find a Soter sparkling brut rosé. Even having not tried a Willamette sparkler, I nonetheless had a hunch my mother and Joy would like it.

When the Soter was poured into proper flutes for all of us, I raised mine. "Here's to our making it to Oregon and the International Pinot Noir Celebration."

Everyone clinked glasses and took sips. This was a beautiful, austerely dry, one-hundred-percent Pinot bubbly.

My mother, tears forming, raised her glass for a toast. We waited until her lachrymose spell had passed. "Here's to Snapper."

We all solemnly toasted Snapper.

"May he make a quick and full recovery and find a good home," I added.

"Home is with me," my mother retorted. Any argument to the contrary would have evoked her wrath.

"Home is with you, Mom." No one at the table, even she, believed it.

Menus arrived posthaste. The fare, the house crowed, was sourced as much as possible from local farmers and ranchers. The eclectic offerings included seafood, lamb, duck, steak, rabbit, and a wild mushroom risotto.

After the starters I had the waitress open the Van Duzer. A year older, it was a more balanced wine than the Harper, more complex, with a weighty mouthfeel of blackberries and hints of spice. Jack and I exchanged appraising looks. He was nodding, I was shaking my head, both in amazement at the pornographically good wine.

"We are drinking fine, my friend," I said. "We are drinking fine."

We plowed into our entrees. Jack and I abandoned the Soter sparkler to Joy and my mom, the latter hogging it. After the mains we ordered a selection of their shockingly sumptuous desserts. My mother enjoyed what I supposed might be her last orgasm over the nectarine-blueberry fruit cobbler. Feeling magnanimous, I ordered a bottle of Amity Late Harvest Gewurztraminer, a viscous, slightly treacly dessert wine I didn't much care for. My mother, however, had never in her life tasted such an elixir. Snapper seemed all but gone from her mind when she exulted over the Gewurtz: "Nectar of the gods."

"What about you, Joy?" I asked.

"Mm," she nodded enthusiastically. "Good." The girls liked their sweet shit, I thought. Fucking diabetics.

The bill was knee-weakening–and not comp-ed.

chapter 12

I woke to the incessant ringing on my cell. Blinking my eyes into focus, I picked it up.

"Are you up, Miles?"

I groggily noted two empty bottles of wine, whose contents I had no memory of drinking. My head pounded and my body felt torpid. "Yeah, Julie, I'm up."

"Opening ceremonies start in an hour. I just wanted to make sure you're going to be there."

"Absolutely."

"You'll be the last to speak. Something funny, you know. That's what they want from you."

"Okay, I'll give it the college try." I hit END, walked over to the window and drew open the curtains. On the manicured lawn separating the Main House from the Carriage House my mother sat parked in her wheelchair, head angled to the sky, basking in the sun. The coal-coated Newfoundland bounded over to keep her company. She looked at peace in this bucolic setting, even as I was feeling the extreme opposite: an infernal hangover, compounded by doubts about this madcap trip. I poured a glass of Pinot from one of several bottles left unfinished the night before and degenerately carried it with me into the bathroom. I drank liberally in the shower, desperate to quash the jimjams.

When I barged into his unlocked room, Jack was masturbating under the sheets. I backed out in a big hurry and closed the door.

"Jesus, man!" he shouted. "Don't you ever knock?"

"You're the one who always brags he never has to do the knuckle shuffle."

"My guy sustained a serious injury. I was giving him a test run. Christ!"

"Opening ceremonies in forty-five minutes. I need both of you down at the car in fifteen, Jackson."

I staggered down the stairs to the lawn, thumb and fingers pressing my temples. A vast, invisible avian population trilled in the dense enveloping thicket. The air almost trembled with pure nature–or was it my befogged perception of reality?

Approaching my mother's chair, I set a hand on her shoulder. "Did you sleep well, Mom?"

"Oh, yes."

"Did you have any problem getting bathed and everything?"

"Oh, no. I took my bath. I don't smell."

"Good. Because you were smelling pretty ripe yesterday."

"Oh, no," she chuckled.

"Oh, yes," I countered. I knelt down next to her. "So, Mom, just to remind you: we're at the International Pinot Noir Celebration. It's a three-day, all-day wine-drinking festival. These people start early and they go late. You've got to pace yourself, okay?"

"Okay. I'll be a good girl."

I straightened to my feet and caught a glimpse of Joy, moving up the gravel path leading into the inn. She'd obviously ventured out to the main road to get stoned. Shortly, a haggard and somewhat chagrined-looking Jack emerged from the Carriage House.

As we all convened, Bruce blustered out of the Main House, toting a large basket. "I didn't see you guys for breakfast, so I put together a supply of some of my hazelnut scones. You're going to the opening ceremonies, I presume?"

"Yeah," I said, accepting his offering, its piquant aromas discomposing my queasy stomach. "Thanks, Bruce. Sorry we missed breakfast. I hear your scrambled eggs are to die for."

"So they tell me. Have a great day."

Bruce looked on as we piled into the car. Giving him a wave, I punched the address of the venue into the GPS.

IPNC's kickoff was held on the green commons at the Linfield College, an old, quaint institution housed in weathered red-brick buildings, some with cupolas on their domes. A moveable podium had been set up at one end of the large grassy rectangle. Towering, gnarled oaks bordered the commons on all sides. Behind the podium the organizers had set up a three-tiered bleacher. It was packed shoulder-to-shoulder with local and international winemakers and other Willamette Valley wine cognoscenti. They were all bedecked with special orange badges. Facing the dais were nearly a thousand participants in foldup chairs, mopping their brows and fanning themselves in the strengthening sun. A heat wave had settled in over much of Oregon, and though it was only ten in the morning the temperature was already in the upper eighties, and predicted to hit close to a hundred!

I was told that there had been a number of private dinners at the hundreds of participating wineries the night before, explaining why a lot of the attendees looked slack, florid-faced, like a herd of cows headed for the abattoir.

Once Jack, Joy and my mother had been handed their badges I led them to a long, white-clothed table upon which various tin buckets overflowed with rosés and sparking wines jammed into ice, among them a few scattered whites. I poured my mother a glass of rosé and her clouded face gave way to radiant sunshine as I handed it to her. Next I filled a glass of Elk Cove Pinot Gris, while Jack, following my lead, helped himself to a glass of the same. Joy, true to form, declined. I'm sure she was shocked seeing so many people imbibing so early.

"Okay, I've got to go find the director of this orgy-in-the-making, so why don't you go find some seats? I don't think this thing will drag on all that long."

Back at the information table where we had received our badges, I was intercepted by a woman with short, spiky platinum-blond hair–Divorce? Midlife crisis?–in a simple knee-length dress, blinking with excitement. "You're Miles?"

"I am," I said.

"I'm Julie." We shook hands. "I didn't think you were going to make it. Two of our guest speakers I guess had a little too much at the Patricia Green dinner last night, you might have to carry the show."

"I'll do my best," I said, raising the Elk Cove to my lips and taking a healthy quaff.

"So," she started, leading me by the elbow, "why don't you take a seat in the bleachers and I'll get started."

Armed with my glass of Pinot Gris I wandered to the bleachers where I found a seat among some of the most famous Pinot vintners from all over the world: Burgundy of course, New Zealand, Sonoma, Monterey... Some of their ruddy, sun-weathered faces I recognized from *Wine Spectator* and *Decanter* covers. Although I had written a book celebrating their cantankerous, low-yield grape, the dirty secret was I had never until recently had the wallet to partake of their ethereal wines, especially the fabled Bourgogne *rouges*. I felt a little intimidated in their august presence.

Julie stepped up to the podium, tapped the mike to make sure it was working, and leaned into it. She welcomed us all, cracked a mild joke about everyone looking a tad hung over, paused for the laugh, cautioned that this was a three-day festival of seminars, vineyard tours, wine lunches and dinners, "So, I suggest you drink a lot of water in this heat!" To which there was a collective chorus of boos and catcalls. "Okay, and a lot of Pinot Noir, too." To which there followed good-natured derisive cheers and a lot of fist-waving from the crowd that had flown in from the four corners of the world to sample some of the finest Pinots, learn about them and, who are we kidding, get *fucked* up! Where else, I asked myself, as the sun beat down with increasing ferocity, could you consume such quantities of exquisite wine from morning to night with unbridled permission, free from dispiriting jobs, money- and energy-sucking children and, in some cases, nagging, finger-pointing spouses? This had all the Dionysian makings of a royal descent into Hades.

First up, Julie introduced one of the directors of the IPNC. Reading from notes, the portly man delivered a droning recitation of the various activities ahead, spelling out the rules and regulations we all had in the pamphlets, but no doubt hadn't bothered to read. "Let's face it," I said to the *vigneron* sitting next to me, whom I didn't recognize, "it's going to be a free-for-all whether they like it or not."

Julie retook the podium. "And, now, before we fan out into our seminars and the great Willamette Valley of Oregon, where some of the finest Pinot Noir is produced, I'd like to introduce our master of ceremonies."

She glanced down at the notes for her speech. "Eight years ago, totally broke, not even able to afford a bottle of cheap Merlot"—pause for laughter to clear—"Miles Raymond sat down and wrote a book that changed the world of wine. Most particularly the realm of one specific grape, the grape we all unwaveringly adore..." She looked up from her notes, thrust her arms in the air and shouted: "Pinot Noir!"

The cheers were so deafening that Julie could do nothing more than smile and blink until they died down. When they did, she soldiered on: "As we all know, from that book was made a movie called by the same name, *Shameless.*" More whistles and clapping and cheering. "That movie made everyone want to drink wine, especially Pinot Noir. In the year since its release Pinot sales have tripled... while Merlot sales have plummeted." More cheering. "So, without further ado, I'd like to introduce... Miles Raymond."

Still clutching my glass, I rose and stepped down from the bleachers and, as Julie back-pedaled away and clapped her hands, took over her spot behind the podium. A din of applause greeted me. Some of the attendees struggled to their feet and soon they were all giving me a standing ovation. I threw a quick backward glance to the bleachers. All the vintners and other prominent people in the world of wine were also standing and applauding enthusiastically. If they could have seen me five years before, I thought, dodging creditors, hiding from my slumlord, stealing from my mother—well, I guess they already know about that—undatable, stricken with panic and anxiety, suicidal, homicidal, matricidal, writing "career" a sullied dream. Now they were wildly applauding, some even whistling. It was as if the decade of indignities since my divorce from Victoria had all been effaced in this roar of approbation. And all the while I kept thinking: this is so fucking ephemeral.

"Thank you," I said, coming out of myself, as if surfacing in a bathysphere, in an effort to settle the crowd. "Thank you."

They finally eased back into their seats. After a few minutes it grew quiet.

I brought a fist to my mouth and cleared my throat. "I'm honored to be asked to emcee the great IPNC. Over the next couple of days I'm probably going to lose all hold on reality, so while I'm still possessed of a relatively clear mind, let me just say a few things. First, I want to apologize to the great vintners of the Willamette Valley who have been making, for the most part, trailblazing Pinots for years while my book's and

the movie's focus was on Santa Barbara County. Whose Pinots are infe-
rior." I didn't believe it, but I knew the partisan crowd would eat it up.
No sooner had I said it than there came a burst of loud applause. I held
up my hand like a snarky politician. "I'm sure I'm going to pay for that
statement, but I've had the opportunity to sample a lot of your wines–I
guess a few up here are hoping to buy some free publicity if I write a sequel"–a salvo of laughter–"but, no, seriously, I'm really impressed with
how dedicated you all are to my favorite mistress: the ethereal, the elusive,
the levitational, *ne plus ultra* of grape varieties: PINOT NOIR!" More
deafening cheering, clapping–an unrestrained explosion. When it calmed,
I finished in a rousing crescendo: "If Pinot went out of fashion, you'd
still be making it." Closing in a rising tone: "In Santa Ynez, they're such
a bunch of money-making whores, they'd probably go back to planting
FUCKING MERLOT!"

The attendees and winemakers were now stomping their feet and applauding and laughing until tears flooded their eyes. Many were jackknifed over in their chairs, clutching their guts–most quite prodigious! A
few nut cases, already half in the bag, were so apoplectic with laughter
they were rolling around on the lawn. It was a sight.

In the midst of the pandemonium, I added into the microphone in the
loudest voice I could muster: "Let's all go get FUCKED UP ON PINOT!"

I stepped away from the podium. Wine lovers swarmed me. Autographs, congratulations, questions. These were world-class Pinot-philes
and *Shameless* had christened them, showered them with fairy dust. Their
hard-to-vinify grape, usually grown in intemperate mesoclimates–beleaguered by late frosts and early rainstorms, not to mention foraging deer
and dive-bombing birds and root-ravaging boar–was now the darling of
the wine world. We had both suffered; and we had both triumphed.

When I finally broke free I rejoined Jack, Joy and my mother. "So,
we're scheduled to go on this mystery bus tour. They don't tell you where
you're going, but it's some winery. I don't know if they're going to allow
handicapped people on the bus."

"I want to go," my mother pleaded. "Please. Don't leave me all alone."

"All right, Mom, all right, stop your bellyaching."

Julie snaked through the crowd to shake my hand. "It wasn't what I
expected–all that colorful language!–but it was a huge hit."

"I'm glad. So, where're the buses? And do they have handicapped access?"

"Oh, absolutely. We have a number of special-needs attendees here," she said, glancing down at my mother.

"This is my mom, Phyllis."

"How do you do, Mrs. Raymond?"

My mother lifted her glass. "I'm flying with the angels!"

Julie chuckled.

I turned to my mother, winked and said, "You might meet someone, Mom." The old coot blushed from ear to ear.

Julie led us to the modern, streamlined buses leased from one of the local Indian casinos, ordinarily used to ferry in the poor from even farther outlying areas so they could more quickly squander their welfare checks. The sun was now hoisting itself into the blazing blue sky. A zephyr of an onshore breeze was slithering over the Oregon Coast Range and cooling our perspiring faces.

After everyone piled on our designated bus, a motorized ramp flipped open and hydraulically lowered. Joy rolled my mother on, the driver elevated and retracted it, and Joy wheeled my mother in. She had a primo seat right next to the driver, with a splendid view out the CinemaScope-sized windshield. She was in heaven. Grasping one of the overhead straps to steady herself, Joy stood next to her, dutiful as ever, a wad of cash safely in her money belt, peace restored. A couple sitting in the front row politely rose and offered Joy their seat. Joy smiled and sat down and the couple, already a few sheets to the wind, careered into the back.

The bus was full, so Jack took a seat next to Joy in the front. I wandered aft and found an aisle seat, by chance next to an attractive woman in her mid-to-late-thirties, with long straight auburn hair and an intelligent face. Instinctively, I goatishly checked for a wedding band. Negative. A crackle of electricity pulsed through me. God, I thought, I'm such a dog these days.

The bus lurched forward. Within minutes we were touring the Willamette Valley countryside on winding rural roads. Out the windows we were witness to rolling fields of native grasses dotted with indolent livestock. And vineyards and vineyards and more vineyards, many of them sweeping up terraced slopes, as if climbing a vinous staircase to the skies.

The woman next to me produced a silver flask from her handbag, unscrewed the cap and took a sip. Holy crap! My kind of gal!
Curiosity got the better of me and I broke the ice by saying, "What
is that?"

She wordlessly handed me the flask. There was no question of my being
a teetotaler–heresy at the IPNC!

I took a sip. "Hmm," I said, sneaking a second sip. "Limoncello?"

Her eyes locked on mine. "You got it."

"Late night?" I asked.

"Yeah, I was at the Archery Summit dinner. There was a lot of wine.
Oh, my God!" She shook her head and affected an expression suggesting
a wild night and a lot of drinking. "And you? What winery dinner did
you go to?"

"Didn't," I said. "Got in late."

She nodded.

"Are you here by yourself?"

"Yeah," she said. "I'm covering it for *The New York Times*."

"Oh, yeah? Wine journalist or...?"

"Wine mostly, yeah. How about you?"

"Did you... attend the opening ceremonies?"

"No, I missed them. Barely made the bus." She shook her head again,
took another snortski of the Limoncello, and offered the gleaming silver
flask back to me.

"Well... I'm the master of ceremonies," I said.

Two prolonged seconds passed as she registered what I had said. Then
her whole body swung sideways ninety degrees. "Are you Miles Raymond?"

"Yes," I said unrepentantly. "I am."

Her voice rose and the timbre changed. "You're kidding? You
wrote *Shameless*?"

"Shhh," I said, putting an index finger to my lips.

She held out her hand and I took it. "It's a pleasure to meet you, Miles."

Suddenly, she wasn't so standoffish. "You realize you're a hero to these
people up here."

I shrugged. "Hero today, gone tomorrow."

She laughed. "I couldn't help but notice you got on the bus with the
older lady in the wheelchair. What's the deal?"

"She's my mother." I filled her in as succinctly as I could on the details of our journey.

"Well, that's sweet of you," she said, a bit haltingly. "Didn't your character steal from his mother in the book–and the movie?"

"Okay, it's... what's your name?"

"Natalie."

"Natalie. It's fiction. I didn't steal from my mother in real life. Okay, maybe a dollar now and then when I was a kid to get some candy, or maybe a little more when I was in high school so I could get some pot, sure. Not hundreds like in the book." Sometimes reality and fiction got so intertwined in my wine-addled memory I couldn't tell if I was coming or going. Lying or not lying.

"I believe you."

"Could I have another shot of the Limoncello?"

"Sure." She passed me the flask. I snapped my head back and took a quick, I hoped discreet, swig. The 100-proof vodka used to make the firewater was nicely sandpapering the serrated edges of my hangover. I had a beautiful woman next to me–a writer!–we were cruising through Oregon wine country on a beautiful, if blisteringly hot, day. What could go amiss?

"You know where we're going?" I asked.

"No. It's supposed to be a mystery."

"Oh, right. I like mysteries," I said, my shoulder touching hers and receiving no resistance. She flashed a flirtatious smile, and nudged me back.

Oh, no, I thought, here we go again.

The bus's hydraulic brakes screeched, seemingly in the middle of nowhere. Everyone, as if schooled in the drill at previous IPNCs, climbed off–after, of course, my mother had been lowered on the lift.

On the dirt shoulder, a large table had been set up. A breeze was gently billowing the tablecloth, anchored by aluminum buckets impaled with uncorked bottles of an assortment of refreshing whites from WillaKenzie Estate Winery. Two servers were pouring glasses for the parched and hungover IPNC attendees. Natalie, my new best friend, flanked me wherever I went. We both got a glass of the Pinot Gris, fruity and perfect for the torrid heat, an ideal palate opener for the reds surely lying in wait.

I introduced Natalie to my Gilligan's Island-hatted mother, who was already swilling a glass of Pinot Gris.

Natalie said to her, "You must be really proud of your son."

Tears sprang to my mother's eyes. She raised her tasting glass skyward and declared through welling tears: "He's a genius."

"All right, Mom, let's not get too extravagant with our encomiums, okay?"

"Oh, get off your high horse with your big words!"

Natalie hooted at my mother's rejoinder.

Jack and Joy joined us. She wasn't drinking, but he was already on his second glass. I introduced Natalie to them, elaborating that Jack was the prototype for Jake.

"Oh, so you're the cad women see as the paradigm of noncommittal, immoral degeneracy?"

Jack brandished his glass at me. "I'll see you in court, dude."

Natalie and I touched shoulders and shared a laugh. The mood was festive, the air balmy... sexy... erotic... the wine hurtling me into that alternate universe where nothing mattered.

After twenty minutes of sipping and confabulating, our group was accosted by a man in his early fifties, in heavy work boots, jeans and T-shirt, tromping out of the vineyard, his thudding footfalls kicking up dust. He stopped in front of the forty some-odd of us and said, "Hi, everyone, my name is Rick Marston. I'm the vineyard manager. Welcome to WillaKenzie Estate Winery." There was a polite scattering of applause, and Marston swiveled a quarter-turn, gave a slow-motion pass with an arm as if he were a baseball pitcher and instructed us, "Follow me."

I turned to Joy and my mother. "Mom, maybe you should hang back here."

"No!" she fumed. "I want to go!"

"Okay. Okay." I turned to Jack. "We're going to have to push her."

"No problem."

With Joy hanging back to smoke a joint, Natalie walked next to me as Jack and I each took one of the wheelchair's handlebars and, following the trudging throng, pushed my mother up one of the loamy rows of the steeply sloping vineyard. Cresting the hill, sweating and hyperventilating, we took our place with our tipsy bus mates, who were scattered around in a loose assembly. Marston stood slightly above us and delivered a prolix and unnecessarily arcane speech about the Willamette Valley's geology while the sun, gaining strength as it climbed toward its zenith, punished us. Mercifully concluding, he led us a short distance away to a dilapidated barn, a relic fashioned out of weathered planks.

The vineyard manager stopped in front of its colossal double doors, as if deliberately trying our patience, turned and resumed his pro forma patter: "This is the cold storage facility of WillaKenzie. The grapes are picked at night and brought here to delay the spontaneous fermentation that happens when temperatures get above sixty-eight degrees. We allow them to sit for a couple of days—a process known as a cold soak—to achieve better extraction." He turned and ceremoniously opened the doors to the barn, with a folksy, "Come on inside, everybody."

Inside proved to be a sultan's oasis for wine lovers. The barn's vast, high-ceilinged interior was ringed at the walls by blue-and-white checker-clothed tables. Behind the tables stood casually attired young people, tasting room staff, Natalie informed me, from other wineries, who had volunteered their services for the IPNC. More important, the tables were teeming with uncorked bottles, tasting room stemware, pitchers of water, baskets overflowing with crackers, and dump buckets. Light that speared through the cracks in the barn made the bottles coruscate with a gleaming allure. After the arduous hike and cripplingly boring, lengthy preamble, it was all worth it.

The participants fanned out to sample some of the more serious wines of WillaKenzie. On display were also a number of Burgundies, which I was eager to sample. Natalie, who knew a lot more about wine than I did, and was particularly versed in Bourgogne *rouges*, helped me navigate my way through them, passing sometimes-trenchant judgments. "Too alcoholic," she assessed a particular one. "They shouldn't vinify Pinot at 14.9%. Ridiculous," she castigated, spitting and dumping it as if it were Pinot plonk. Then she would discover one she liked. "Here, Miles, try this. Taste the balance. Gorgeous aromatics. Crushed rose petals. Plushy." The deeper we delved the more enamored I grew. In my steadily more inebriated state, I wondered: Could this be my vinous soul mate?

My mother cleaved to her coveted Chardonnays. Jack hovered over her and kept her company, noticing how I was making tracks with Natalie. Now and then our eyes would meet through the throng and he would widen his and then smile, toasting me with his glass. I toasted him back. At one point I broke away from Natalie, who had

struck up a conversation with a Burgundian vintner–a pompous, pot-
bellied, windbag wine enthusiast with a florid face and a nose ridged
with burst capillaries–to weave a path through the crowd to where
Jack and my mother were stationed.

"How's Natalie?" Jack asked.

"Cool, man. New York chick. Beauty and brains–the *ne plus ultra*.
Knows her shit, too. Fun to learn from. I thought Maya knew a lot about
wine. This woman's got it all over her."

"Sounds like a marriage made in heaven," Jack said.

"Or one ending in A.A.," I quipped. I bent down to my mother's level.
"How're you doing, you old coot?"

She lifted her glass slightly. "Marvelous!"

"Not what you expected when you were going through the vineyard,
was it?"

"No, this is the biggest surprise of my life! I feel like I've gone to heaven
and died."

"I think it's the other way around, Mom."

"Oh, yes," she chuckled.

"Hold your mug now."

"I'll be a good girl."

I laughed and straightened up. Jack was checking out the crowd with
a raptor's keen eyesight. "See any prospects?" I asked.

Jack scrunched up his mouth and gave his head a subtle, tight shake.
"I don't do gray, Homes."

I chuckled. The crowd was for the most part pretty elderly. To buoy
his spirits, I said, "Natalie mentioned there were going to be a thousand
people at the salmon bake tonight. And a fair number of single women
your age. And younger. And drunk as skunks if it's anything like last year's
bacchanal, according to her."

"Excellent," Jack said. "It's time to test the hammer out," he said, pat-
ting his crotch.

After the mystery tasting in the cold-storage barn, we were herded back
to the bus. Everybody resumed the same seats, as if they had been assigned.
After a short drive to WillaKenzie Estate Winery proper, we were treated
to a lavish lunch, catered by one of the region's fanatically locavore chefs.
Seated at tables ringing the upstairs catwalk we were afforded a unique

view of the gravity-flow system WillaKenzie employed to transfer its wines from huge stainless steel fermentation tanks to French oak barrels.

The food-and-wine setting was almost too fairy-tale for a Pinot lover-cum-gourmand. My mother couldn't stop raving about her belly of pork in puff pastry. I took great delight in my Beef Bourguignon spilled over a delicate, parsley-infused crepe. Dessert was a warm hazelnut cake. A flotilla of wine stewards kept us drowned in the grape. I tried to monitor my mother's intake, but it was too hard, she was just having so much fun. Her good arm whipped like a flagellum for her food.

Joy was waiting in the bus when our now loud and boisterous group returned and piled back on, some staggering and tripping over the steps. Joy grew a look of silent but simmering dismay at my mother's condition: head slumped forward, badly slurred speech.

"Don't worry," I said to her, tripping over my own words, "I'll help you with the transfers."

In a fit of wordless pique, she stapled her arms across her chest, tensed her face, and gave no response.

I returned to my seat next to Natalie's. Half-drunk, my hand uninhibitedly found her thigh and squeezed it. A few seconds later, her hand found mine and our fingers intertwined, causing my heart to skip a beat. Next, like birds taking flight from on a pond without even so much as a warbling signal, their wings furiously aclatter in a synchronized rush, we were kissing like teenagers who didn't care who was looking.

chapter 13

We returned to the campus. The casino bus disgorged a precociously inebriated group of IPNC participants. Most were professional drinkers and could hold their liquor, but one middle-aged woman hurtled out of the bus's bathroom, the stench of vomit trailing her, looking like she had stumbled from the enormity of a battlefield where her faction had been horribly annihilated, her countenance that of a deathly sick cow.

Off the idling bus, I pulled Jack aside. "Look, I'm going to hang out here with Natalie a few hours. She's staying in one of the dorms. Take my mom and Joy back to the B&B, grab twenty winks and I'll see you there in a couple hours."

Using one finger and the other hand, Jack produced a vulgar gesture.

"We'll see," I said.

"What happened to Laura?" he teased.

"She's outside the hundred-mile radius."

"Ah, the hundred-mile rule. You dog, Miles."

"Takes one to know one."

Jack laughed and then wrapped me in a bear hug. "I got to be honest. I almost bailed on you. But this is awesome, this was all worth it."

"Tonight should be *pretty* interesting," I said as he released me.

"Let's hope."

"Keep Joy and my mother apart as much as possible if you can," I advised.

Jack glanced over at the two of them, and turned back to me.

"I got it, short horn. Have fun."

I dragged Natalie away from a famous–and famously garrulous–wine writer and we giggled and cracked jokes and made out while groping each other as we weaved our way to the dormitory where she was lodged.

Once inside, we collapsed in a heap onto the lower mattress of a bunk bed. Sex was awkward. We slammed against the wall, the mattress springs creaked noisily in our plundering of each other. At one point we fell off the damn thing! Having had a little too much on the mystery tour, I experienced difficulty maintaining an erection, which made the spontaneous tryst clumsier yet. In the end I opted to go down on her in a valiant, ego-saving effort to bring her to orgasm, which she muffled with a hand over her mouth. Couldn't have the others in the dormitory thinking she was some kind of wine slattern. When I remarked to that effect, she joked, "I have a reputation to uphold."

"Oh, yeah," I said as I lay naked next to her on the narrow mattress.

She rose from the bed and said, "Do you want to try something really awesome?"

"What? You've got some toys?"

"No," she giggled. She had a lot of wine samples cluttering the tiny room's small writing desk. She splashed a '96 DRC into two huge Riedel sommeliers' glasses and handed me one. The wine was luxurious, not overly alcoholic, and had a gorgeous floral finish that lingered for a seeming eternity.

"Isn't it good?" she asked.

"Yeah. So different from these monster Pacific Coast Pinots." I took another taste. Unlike most wines, this just got better and more complex the more you delved into it, yielding mysterious aromas and flavors that a first taste was insufficient to disinter. And it was sexy drinking that DRC stark naked with this savvy food and wine writer. "I should probably get back. I've got the book signing to get ready for, and if I lie around here with you and that sublime quaff I'll never make it."

"Okay, I'll give you a ride."

Natalie shuttled me back to the Brookside. At my behest she braked to a stop at the turnoff, so my mother, with her penchant for paranoia, wouldn't see a woman dropping me off in a total state of dishevelment. We kissed goodbye passionately, totally enveloped in each other, as if one

of us was headed off to the front lines. "Will you stay with me tonight?"
she asked.

"I don't know, Natalie, there's going to be a lot of women at the salmon bake, and after the book signing I'm going to have a lot of opportunities..."

She punched me in the shoulder and pretended to pout. "Oh, you'd better not," she admonished. She extended an index finger and pointed it at my crotch. "You owe me, Mr. Shameless."

We sealed the promise of a post salmon-bake salacious ravishing with another wild, slobbery kiss. "I can't wait, Natalie."

I crawled out of the car and staggered up the dirt-and-gravel road, bounding over the fairy-tale pond and emerging out of the canopy of old, gargantuan oaks into the Carriage House. I desperately needed a nap after the hot afternoon of wine, but that hope was shattered by the voice of my mother from their downstairs room, berating Joy. "You're no good," she was saying in her infantile way. "You're no good!"

A moment later, Joy stepped out.

"What's wrong?" I asked.

"Your mom. I can't handle her anymore." She irately tapped her temple with her index finger. "She has no brain! She is stupid!"

"What's going on?"

"She still accuse me of killing her dog–dog not dead," she practically screamed. "And stealing money that was mine!" In defiance of the inn's no-smoking policy she fired up a half-smoked joint and took several hits in quick succession, holding each inside her lungs before exhaling and taking the next.

"Come with me," I said.

"I'm not going back in there," she said in a staccato voice.

"Yes, you are, Joy. We're going to resolve this once and for all." I took her by the elbow and half-dragged her into my mother's suite.

My mother was parked in her wheelchair in front of the television, bewitched by some infomercial. I wrenched the remote from her hand and turned it off. Joy stood behind me at my left flank.

"Where've you been?" my mother wailed.

"Mom, I've got duties to perform up here, people I have to meet. I'm an important person."

"Oh, stop bragging," she spat.

I got right back in her face. "I want you to apologize to Joy. I'm sick and tired of this bickering between you two. Joy was *not* responsible for Snapper's accident. And she didn't lose her money on purpose to extort me. That's fucking nuts! What's going on up in that noggin of yours, huh? She's done an amazing job. Without her you wouldn't be heading to Wisconsin to be with your sister, which is what you wanted. You'd be back in Las Villas de Muerte with those moribund people waiting for the FUCKING UNDERTAKER! Is that what you want? Huh?" It was a rebuke the likes of which I had never before delivered. I stared at her with an ominous look. "Now, if you want to continue acting like a fucking child, I'm going to turn around tomorrow and ship you back. And the next time you have a minor stroke or another congestive heart failure, you know where you're going? Full convalescence. You'll become a ward of the state! You know what they do in those places, Mom, when you pee your pants? They stand you up and hose you down, then throw you back onto your cot in a room with no TV, no phone, no nothing. Is that what you want?"

"Oh, no," she whimpered, frightened by my stern–and, if I say so myself, colorful–upbraiding.

"Then apologize to Joy. Tell her you're sorry."

My mother looked down at her lap. Tears churned in her eyes. "I'm sorry, Joy. I guess I'm just a mean old cuss."

I lowered my tone: "Tell her you were wrong to demonize her for Snapper's unfortunate accident."

"I know you didn't mean to get Snapper hit by that car, Joy." She raised her head and pointed that crooked arthritic finger of hers at the ceiling. "I never should have brought him."

"Halleluiah! The only thing you've said on this entire trip that has the ring of truth!"

She looked contrite as she continued to avert her gaze.

"And you know Joy didn't pretend to lose the money? And that she had legitimate reason to believe you may have taken it? Okay, maybe she was wrong in her accusation, but she didn't make up the fact that her money was gone. She's not that kind of a person, Mom."

My mother nodded, mortified at being scolded by her son. "I'm sorry, Joy. You've been so good to me." She pointed her index finger at her temple. "I had a stroke, you know. I'm not the same. I say things I don't mean. I'm scared."

I placed a hand on my mother's shoulder and bent at the knees to be at eye level with her. "There's nothing to be scared about, Mom."

"I know," she said through her tears.

I straightened to a standing position, turned to Joy with great reluctance and said, "Please tell my mother you accept her apology."

Joy exhaled a sigh of exasperation. "I accept your apology, Mrs. Raymond."

"Oh, that's such good news," my mother said.

"Okay, I'm going to go up and take a nap. Big night tonight. A lot of single women."

My mother chortled. Joy, the weed having gone to her brain, suppressed a giggle. I pulled her out into the hallway so my mother couldn't hear and said, "If there's a problem, come to me, okay?"

"Okay."

"Give me a hug," I said. I reached my arms out and embraced her tightly and she hugged me back. I whispered into her ear: "There're a bunch of cute guys here. Enjoy yourself. It shouldn't have to be all work. This is the Miles Raymond road show. As you can tell, we get fucked up sometimes and let our hair down. Okay?"

"Okay," she said, blushing.

I released her from the hug and tottered up the short flight to my suite. Bone tired from all the female drama, I fell heavily onto my bed and closed my eyes. A moment later, Jack, full glass in hand, materialized and melted into one of the cushy chairs.

"How was she?" he asked, always wanting to know the blow-by-blow.

"Pretty teenager-like," I confided. "Haven't done it on a bunk bed since college. Why is sex always hotter when you're not in your own bed?"

"Because it usually means you're fucking someone for the first time."

"Or having a hot clandestine affair."

"That, too." He held up the bottle that was clutched in his left hand. "Want a glass?"

I shook my head no. "I had a little performance problem over at the dorm—too much of the grape, I guess. But I'm going to rectify that tonight after the salmon bake."

"Good man," Jack said.

"I've got to try to get some sleep." I glanced at my watch. It was 3:30 and the book signing started at 6:00. "I'm so wiped. And then I come back and Joy and my mother are going at it. Had to put that *fucking* fire out. I'm not sure this was such a good idea."

"We're almost there," Jack said. "It'll be a straight shot to Wisconsin. Two day gonzo. Head to the airport. Get tanked up. You'll be back at your desk in less than a week. Try not to stress about it, man."

"Yeah," I grumbled, wearily envisioning the road still ribboned out ahead of us, our final destination a distant chimera. I fumbled for my iPhone in my jeans pocket and set the alarm. I rose from the bed, lumbered over to the window and yanked the curtains closed.

Jack rose cumbrously from the chair. "See you in a few," he said, turning and heading out.

I closed my eyes. The weight of my world fell onto me like a knight's armor. Panic gripped me in its steel vise. I reached into my left pocket and shook out a Xanax and let it dissolve under my tongue for swift absorption into my beleaguered soul.

It seemed only seconds later the alarm went off, as if I had been administered an IV twilight anesthesia and had just come out of it. I glanced at the time on my iPhone. Two hours had gone by like a meteor streaking across the sky. It must have been a true REM sleep because I felt magically revivified. I showered and put on a nice button-up shirt, a fresh pair of jeans and some spiffy loafers.

Twenty minutes later the four of us were assembled in the Rampvan, Jack at the wheel and captaining us on bucolic roads back to the dominion of Persephone, a.k.a. the Linfield College campus. Joy, appearing mollified by my stern intervention, had groomed my mother for the event and dressed her in her nicest clothes. Jack looked aptly disheveled in his surgeon's scrub pants and pineapple-decorated Hawaiian shirt. Apparently unaware that white was not the wisest color choice for wine events, Joy was attired in a pair of cream-toned cotton slacks and a revealing black tank top. (Had she taken my earlier urging to heart?)

The lot was filling up when we arrived. We paraded over to the entrance of the college's Oak Garden where a long line was forming. I wended straight to the front of the line, where badges were being handed out, and found Julie running around like a chicken with its head cut off.

The partying had been going on a few days now and some in the crowd were growing obstreperously impatient.

"Miles! I was worried you weren't going to make it," Julie exclaimed.

"I'm here," I said. "Where's the signing booth?"

"I'll take you in," she said.

I gestured to my group. "I want to get my people in. I don't want them waiting in line," I demanded, pulling rank—and enjoying it for once!

"Of course," she said.

Julie found us all badges and we followed her into the Oak Garden. It was a vast area with large, spreading oaks ruling over the perimeter and providing shade from the still-searing sun. Round, red-clothed tables crammed the venue. Long tables, laden extravagantly with food and wine, and manned by local chefs and their respective staffs and sommeliers, festooned the borders on three sides. Orange-glowing Japanese lanterns were strung over the garden, lending it a preternatural aura. Julie led Jack, Joy and my mother to a center table where half the seats were reserved for us. The other IPNC participants sharing it—two couples with florid complexions and bottles from their cellars—greeted us affably.

As my dysfunctional family settled in, an impatient Julie pulled me by the elbow to the signing table. Pillared stacks of boxes of *Shameless* flanked the ends. On the lawn to the side I noticed additional boxes, still to be opened. Eager autograph hounds had already started forming a line and were raring to go. "This is where you'll be signing," Julie gestured.

"Okay," I said, distracted by what looked like a series of parallel fences on fire. Silhouetted figures moved in front of them, characters of a Javanese shadow-puppet show, in a kind of strange pyromancy.

"Come on, I'll show you, then you can start signing."

"Be right back, folks," I called out to the burgeoning line.

Julie ushered me over to where the eponymous salmon bake was underway. There were four long rows—maybe a hundred feet in length—of stacked oak logs that a small crew was in the process of igniting. To the side, *sous* chefs in white smocks wielding razor-sharp sword-sized knives were gutting gargantuan king salmon, expertly filleting them and then pegging them onto thick oak branches with a kind of crude, barbarian flair. "Once the fire gets really going," Julie was saying loudly over the shouting voices and the crackling flames, "they'll stick the salmon on those huge skewers in the ground and roast them just like the Kalapuya Indians did two hundred years ago. Flavor is unbelievable."

"This is quite an event you put on, Julie," I said, starting to feel as if I was coming on to a powerful hit of LSD.

"We spare no expense. These people are paying a lot of money. Come on."

She directed me around the perimeter. I stopped to grab a glass of Pinot from the Boedecker Cellars people, who, once Julie apprised them of who I was, were thrilled to oblige. Wine sloshing out of the too-small tasting glass, I walked briskly to catch up with the indefatigable Julie. She steered me to the far side of the Oak Garden.

"I wanted to show you where the charity event is going to take place."

"What's the charity event?"

She stopped in front of one of the college's brick buildings. On the lawn rested a fermentation vat the dimensions of a suburban tank pool, filled to the brim with red wine, and, in the heat, smelling badly oxidized. Constructed fifteen feet above it was makeshift scaffolding, with a 10x10 foot platform. A wooden stepladder leaned against the platform, on which I noticed–to my horror–was stationed a single chair.

"What's this, Julie?"

"The charity dunking apparatus."

"What?"

"You'll be up in that chair." She pointed. Then she swept her arm to the side of the contraption to indicate a prodigious bulls-eye–maybe three feet in diameter–mounted on a metal pole on which some artist had painted a cluster of red grapes five times scale. What looked like a primitive Rube Goldberg series of levers ran from the bulls-eye, feeding under the platform, where, to my increasing dismay, I could make out a trapdoor. Directly...beneath...the...hangman's...chair.

"Someone's going to get up there and..." I started to laugh nervously. She threw me a bewildered look. "That someone is you, Miles."

I telescoped my head into her face. "What? What're you talking about?"

"Didn't Marcie tell you?"

"No!"

"It's part of being the master of ceremonies," she said, smiling.

"You're fucking joking?" I glanced back up at the hangman's chair.

"I'm not going up there. I have acrophobia! As well as thanatophobia!"

"Miles, it's for charity. Portland's homeless shelter."

"Which I'm going to be in after I get up there and destroy my reputation."

"They're going to love you," she said, trying to be reassuring.

"Have you done this stunt before?"

"No. It's the first year. But we tried it out. It's fine."

"No, it's not fine, Julie. I wasn't told about this."

"We informed your publicist," she said testily. "It's in the contract."

I got out my iPhone. "This gives a whole new meaning to *double-booking*! Hold on a sec." I autodialed Marcie. She answered on the second ring.

"Hi, Miles," she said in that cheery, disingenuous voice of hers that I was coming to loathe.

"Marcie, I'm here on night two of the IPNC..."

"Did the books arrive in time?"

"Yes! That's not why I'm calling. You seemed to have conveniently forgotten to mention the WINE DUNKING CHARITY EVENT."

"That's part of the ten grand, Miles," she replied unflinchingly.

"Why didn't you run this by me?"

"I didn't think you'd care," she said, rapidly growing bellicose. "You've dumped spit buckets over your face, what's the difference?"

"You didn't tell me because you knew I would bail. This thing's fifty feet high," I hyperbolized. "A fucking gallows! And I'm paying you ten percent? Why don't you fly your fat ass up here and do a couple cannonballs into the wine, you Benedict Arnold!"

"It's unbeatable publicity," she said, ignoring the insults, to which, as a publicist, she was inured.

"Fuck the publicity. I'm already a rock star in the wine world, you cretin!"

No doubt thinking of her commission, Marcie tacked. "I was told it's all been checked out and approved by the proper regulators and it's completely safe. Ten grand, Miles, plus another guaranteed five on the books."

"Fuck. I'm calling PMK. You put the C back in woman, Marcie!" I hung up the phone and turned to Julie, who was shuffling nervously in place. I glanced up at the chair silhouetted against the night sky and sighed an emptying lungful of mounting anxiety. "That's a hell of a long drop," I muttered.

"It's not fifty feet, Miles," she said reprovingly.

"Fifty feet, fifteen. Some asshole hits the bulls-eye and I'm going into a vat of wine! You think Philip Roth would do this? Haruki Murakami? I'm an author! Not a circus act!"

"It's for charity," Julie pleaded.

"Looks like it was copied from the scaffold in *A Tale of Two Cities*," I chortled nervously.

"It may have been," Julie said with an arch glint in her eye, still ignoring, it appeared, my grave reservations about this ghoulish and mortifying exploitation of my ephemeral celebrity.

"My publicist failed to tell me about it," I said ineffectually, and calming slightly, a few more quaffs of the Boedecker inuring me to the humility that awaited. "But, fuck it! I'm sure it's safe, right?"

"Like I said we tested it this week and everyone had fun. No one got injured. Plus, it's a warm night. You won't have to wear the wetsuit."

"Oh, great! What about the mask and snorkel? Let's go full Hannibal Lecter, shall we?"

She laughed at my–ahem–gallows humor.

I dipped a finger in the vat of wine and tasted it. "What's in the vat? A mélange of all of the Willamette's great Pinots?"

She gave me a look of shock. "There's over a thousand gallons in there, Miles. That would be tens of thousands of dollars of our stuff. No, it's–don't kill me–Charles Shaw."

"Two Buck Upchuck!" I flung myself into her face. "You're kidding, right?"

"It'll be fun," she said, reaching for my elbow and leading me away and back to the signing table, adding sardonically, "besides, the IPNC took out a million-dollar life insurance policy for you."

"Oh, great. That's comforting. No wife, no kids. I drown, half'll go to my reprobate younger brother." I drained my glass as if it were Gatorade and I had just crossed the finish line in dead last, and handed it to her. "Get me another glass, Julie. ASAP. I'm going to have to get really shitfaced for this one!"

"Whatever you need, Miles."

"No promises on my behavior tonight! You'd better have paramedics on call!"

"Come on, you'll be fine."

At the signing table were some hundred wine aficionados, the line stretching all the way back to the blazing fences of oak, where lambent

flames tongued the twilight sky. I eased into a padded foldup chair next
to a young woman with a jaded emo countenance. A silver nose ring glittered from her prominent proboscis. A tattoo of a strawberry emblazoned her bare upper shoulder. Under the tattoo appeared the phrase: "Eat Me Wild." In front of her was a credit card machine, ready for the literary looting of well-heeled wallets.

"Hi, I'm Chelsea," she said in a high-pitched voice. "You must be Mr. Raymond."

"Miles." We shook. Her hand was lifeless and damp. "So, shall we get started?"

On cue, Chelsea stood, cupped her hands around her mouth and shouted, "All right, everybody, we're going to start the signing. Have your credit card or cash ready. It's fifteen dollars a book." She sat back down. "You're going to make a mint tonight, Miles."

"Yeah," I grumbled, "if I live through it."

She threw me a bemused look, then switched on her ingénue smile and started swiping credit cards and filling her little cash box with bills. The oenophiles descended on me once they had paid the tariff. Clutching their books, they all had a question or two for me—or more, if they were, and most were, bibulously inspired. Some wanted the book inscribed to someone special; others to people they disliked or considered philistines when it came to wine, and hoped my caustic personalizations would mirthlessly set on the path to higher-end appreciation. Business cards piled up on the table. Representatives for wineries as far away as France invited me to their *châteaux*. Wine dealers requested my presence at their shops, beseeched me to do a book signing or attend a tasting of rare Pinots. Women, still drunk from the day's bus tours and numerous seminars focused on *terroir* and biodynamics, planted their hands on the table and leaned over me with their breasts hanging out, blatantly flirting. A few room keys were pressed into my hand. Fuck, at one point I had a hallucination of what it must have been like to be Tom Jones in his heyday at The Sands. Where were the panty tossers?

Julie dutifully plied me with artisanal Pinots—Raptor Ridge, Anne Amie, the unfamiliar winery names became a blur—no doubt still afraid I would bail on the "charity" part of the festivities and hoping inebriation would inure me to any ludicrous vitiation of my public image. Now and then I would step away from the table for a breather and try to uncramp my signing hand. As I gazed out over the commons, the event was really starting to fill up. Everyone was drinking. Voices ricocheted. As night fell the flames from the jagged oak-flaming fences rose higher and burned brighter, furiously licking the sky. Their incandescent light poured through the gigantic Chinook salmon, primitively harpooned into the lawn, turning their flesh a translucent orange. The whole tableau of the festivities looked like the gateway to hell–a hell where the wines were big and bold, the women swarthy and writhing in sinful and libidinous naked-ness, the shirtless men goatish with erections–plunging its denizens into a Lethean realm of drugged oblivion. By night's end I fully expected to witness lascivious scenes of alfresco fucking.

I sat back down at the autograph table and continued inscribing books. A pair of middle-aged women, dressed for the sultry night in bra-less tank tops, leaned into me. "Whom should I make this out to?" I asked, trying to make myself sound as if they were the first to get their books signed that night.

"I want to lick every inch of your body," the redhead with the expensive breasts exploding out of a loose-fitting dress slurred, fastening her eyes on mine and not letting go.

Her brunette friend added, "And I want sloppy seconds," before som-ersaulting into a tittering laugh that had the hair on my arms standing up.

"Let's start with the inscriptions," I said. "Then maybe we'll see what transpires," I harmlessly–I thought!–flirted.

The red-haired one said, "Okay. Write: I want to *fuck you* Deborah–Love, Miles."

I did as she instructed, figuring she was entitled to anything her heart desired for her fifteen filthy-minded dollars.

Her friend said, "And I want to fuck you, too, Carol."

"I don't know if I have a sufficient supply of Viagra," I attempted to joke.

Deborah the Red whipped her tank top down and proudly showed me her prodigious breasts for a good few seconds, then closed up shop. Her friend splayed the fingers on one hand and raked her crotch while giving me a tongue wave. They sashayed off with their books into the teeming crowd, hula-hula-ing their prodigious bottoms while throwing me back-ward come-hither looks.

"Do you know them?" Chelsea asked.

"No. And that's why I don't believe in past lives."

She smiled a look of befuddlement, and resumed collecting the Pinot enthusiasts' money.

They kept pouring in, crowding in on me like whales beaching themselves involuntarily on the shore of my celebrity. Some arrived bearing bottles and glasses, demanding that I taste their artisanal Pinots. I was beginning to feel a little like Tod Hackett, Nathanael West's fictional set painter, at the premiere that spins out of control in *Day of the Locusts*.

More books, more Pinot enthusiasts. Then Natalie ethereally appeared out of apparent nowhere to semi-rescue me. She had in tow a modern-day Hemingway-esque Count Mippipopolous who was cradling a jeroboam of something French, no doubt Bourgogne *rouge*, any other grape variety constituting a desecration of the IPNC. "This is Miles Raymond," Natalie introduced me. "Miles, this is Harvey. Huge collector of Pinots. He's from the mosh pit."

"The mosh pit?"

"There's a group in the center—high-end collectors—and they've brought some really rare bottles and they're letting those who know someone taste them. Like me, for instance. It's called the Mosh Pit." She leaned forward and kissed me on the cheek. "You met the right woman, Miles." She turned to the corpulent man with the jeroboam, no doubt—judging by his excess avoirdupois—nursing a nasty case of gout. "Pour Miles a glass, Harvey." Natalie plunked a sommeliers' glass on the signing table. Cradling the jeroboam with both hands, Harvey, a little unsteady at the helm, emptied a healthy dollop into the Riedel. "'96 Gevrey-Chambertin *grand cru*. Clos de Bèze," he said, with full flawless, pretentious, French inflection.

"Ah," I remarked, pretending to have heard insider rustlings of the indubitably great wine. I gave it a swirl, put my nose into the cavernous opening of the Riedel and inhaled deeply. My olfactory senses were invigorated by the intense perfumed quintessence of a great hand-crafted Pinot. In the mouth, it caressed my palate like a candied ectoplasm that clung preternaturally until the last bit disappeared. "Nice," I said to Harvey. "What does one of those jeroboams go for?"

He spluttered into a loud guffaw, the laugh of a truly rich, truly obese man, a train without brakes, a steer being electrocuted to death. "At auction?" He furrowed his brow. "Ten thousand. *If* you can find it."

I took another three-hundred-dollar–by my inebriated math–sip. It *was* pretty magical. A beautiful balance of fruit and acidity, not one of those made-for-Parker 15.8% alcohol fruit bombs–often blasphemously bulked up with Syrah–which really traduces the variety. "I feel like I've been christened," I said, which elicited another earth-trembling guffaw. "Natalie, could you get me a plate of food, some of that oak-fired salmon, Indian style." I lowered my voice, "And later I'll do you Côte d'Or style."

A laugh shot out of her pretty, fellatio-friendly mouth. "Sure, Miles. Whatever you want."

She and the count threaded their way through the crowd, the festival-goers crowded closer and closer as the venue overflowed its peak occupancy. The Japanese lanterns strung overhead glowed brighter... and blurrier. The temperature was still humidly in the nineties, a sweltering heat wave, Natalie had informed me, that supposedly visits the Willamette Valley only once a year. Several young men, no doubt vintners from afar, having already crossed the vinous Rubicon, had stripped their shirts off and were now swilling Pinot bare-chested and pounding their chests like savages over a fresh kill and the discovery of fire.

A river of autograph seekers kept streaming toward the table, as though the line extended out of the Oak Garden and overflowed into the streets of McMinnville. I didn't know how many books I could sign before my hand would start looking like my mother's. The Clos de Bèze was still hitting me as if I had awakened in another world surrounded by sinuous nymphs.

Natalie reappeared with a heaping plate: the oak-roasted flesh of salmon, pasta primavera, farmers market mixed greens, and a truck farm of vegetables. She scissored open a foldup chair, plopped down next to me and splayed her legs. I continued signing while I picked at the food. Delicious, particularly the salmon, which I forked ravenously into my mouth to help my stomach keep pace with the unstoppable flow of wine.

Natalie asked with a wink, "Are the women behaving?"

"Are you kidding?" I slid over the pile of business cards and hotel room keys. "They're indefatigable. Unrepentant. Hornier than jackals in the spring."

"You're hot, Miles."

"Fuck, Natalie, I'm over forty, on the road to fifty."

"Last year I met this *vigneron* from the Côtes de Nuits. His teeth were stained brown from cigarettes and wine. His pores reeked of Pinot. He was one of those Frenchmen who only shower every other day. But when I tasted his wines, I fell in love." She pointed to the chest-high wall of hay bales demarcating the perimeter of the Oak Garden. "He fucked me on the other side of those bales last year. One of the best fucks of my life," she said, her eyes ablaze with the reflection of the fires, burning into mine with the intimation of an imminent reprise of that night.

"That's good to know, Natalie," I said, picturing her, as men are wont to do, naked and spread-eagled under some malodorous Frenchman ramming her with his pathetic little gherkin.

She rose loose-limbed from the chair. "I'll let you get back to your book signing. I'll be over at the Mosh Pit."

"And in a few moments I'll be up there." I pointed to the platform with the lonely chair high above the vinegarlike miasma of wine, meant to cushion my fall.

"You're kidding me?" she said.

I shook my head and threw my arms in the air in mock exasperation. "It's for charity. Plus, these people are so hammered I doubt any of them will be able to hit that bull's-eye. And if one lucks out, I could use a little swim in this heat."

Natalie kissed me on the mouth so fiercely I thought it might be a deliberate move to ward off all the other women. She turned and disappeared into the raucous crowd, which appeared, as the heat hung on unabated, to grow more and more native.

I kept signing. Chelsea kept slashing open more boxes and hauling out more books. More business cards, insistent, drunken offers to fly to this exotic place and stay at that incredible château or villa. It would all be a blur in the morning, the business cards and the hotel room keys the detritus of yet another wine-soaked bacchanal, discarded into the wastebasket in my suite. If that was where I woke!

Julie finally came to rescue me. "All right, it's time," she said. "Come on."

I gazed at the gallows in the distance. "I don't know about this, Julie."

She clutched my elbow and pulled me away. "It'll be fun. These people'll remember this one forever."

Glass in hand I followed her zigzag–as if I didn't know where she was leading me!–through the crowd. I stopped briefly at our table, where my mother, Jack and Joy were eating and drinking. My mother had made a friend in a jolly old man and they were trading anecdotes about life in the military.

"How're you doing, Mom?" I asked, placing an arm on her back.

"Marvelous," she said, holding up her glass.

"Are you getting enough wine?" I asked rhetorically, because half-empty bottles littered the table.

"Oh, yes," she said. She turned to the man who was sitting to her right. "This is my son, Miles."

The man half-stood, as if he still had shrapnel in his lower back, thrust out his hand and said, "The young fellow who wrote *Shameless*! It's a pleasure to meet you, Miles. Such a wonderful mother."

"Yeah, she can be at times."

"Oh, you be quiet," my mother said.

"Miles," Jack boomed. I turned. "When's the wine dunking?"

"How'd you know?"

"It's the talk of the festivities."

I glanced up at the platform over the vat of plonk. "Fuck, man."

"I'm going to put you down, dude."

"You can't afford the entry fee, Jackson."

He leaned back in his chair, so far I thought he was going to topple over, and laughed uproariously.

Joy looked like she might have been drinking a little, too, letting her hair down. Instead of that perennial scowl, her face had a healthy blush.

"How're *you* doing, Joy?"

"Fine," she chirped in the most animated voice I had heard since picking her up at Las Villas de Muerte. She *had* been drinking.

"Good. Glad everyone's happy. Duty calls."

I broke away from my anomalous, ad hoc family and continued my dead man's walk toward Julie, awaiting me at the foot of the stairway to the wine gallows.

"Are you ready?"

"No," I said, and power-chugged a grossly overfilled glass of the Clos de Bèze, a teenaged heathen hunkered down in a sewer main with a pint of Ripple, knowing the police are on their way.

"Let's go," she said, ignoring my renewed remonstrations. She began the ascent up the nearly vertical wooden ladder, employing her hands. I haltingly followed. We popped up out onto the platform and, fifteen feet above the lawn, I faced the unruly Pinot-soaked multitude, those who wanted nothing more than to see the guy who had championed Santa Ynez's overrated Pinots get his due–all in fun, of course.

Cued by some unseen sadist, a bright spotlight burst like a supernova over the heads of the crowd and illuminated the two of us. I squinted against the blinding glare and tented my eyes in what must have looked like a salute. The band ceased its mind-numbing Classic Rock so Julie could be heard over the PA system. I gazed in revulsion at my drunken persecutors. Julie took the microphone and attempted to get the revelers' attention. "Hello, everyone," she shouted. "I hope you're all having a good time."

Cheers erupted. Wine bottles were hoisted aloft. More men had dispensed with their shirts. So had a few women. Some of the males were now down to boxer shorts, even briefs, a smattering of women down to bras and panties. These semi-nudists danced unsteadily in place, a tribe initiating a sacred sacrifice in which a heart would be plucked from a still live, writhing goat and devoured while still twitching. The fires from the salmon bake silhouetted the celebrants in a fiery backdrop. I felt like I was at the throwing end of the Islamic Stoning of the Devil.

Julie, in a rising tone, soldiered on. "For a mere hundred dollars you get one throw at the bull's-eye..."–she gestured with her arm to indicate where the target was. The huge disk swung adjacent to the platform, parallel to my head–"to bring down this year's emcee... Miles Raymond!" Cheers and catcalls greeted her announcement. On that cue, another spotlight was switched on, illuminating the disk that, if struck, was going to trigger the Rube Goldberg contraption and send me plunging into the cesspool of plonk. "All the money goes to support the Daniel Jordan Shelter for the Homeless, here in Portland. A worthy cause. So, get out your credit cards and open up your pocketbooks. Here's your chance to send the famous author, Miles Raymond, the man who made Santa Ynez"–boos, catcalls, howls, yelps erupted from the assembled troglodytes–"synonymous with Pinot into a vat of his favorite grape: MERLOT!"

The ensuing cheers and laughter turned into a collective ritual chanting, a drunken chorus: "DUNK HIM! DUNK HIM! DUNK HIM!"

Julie extended her arm in my direction and melodramatically beckoned me to take the chair.

"Are you sure you don't want to put a black sackcloth over my head?" I shouted ruefully. Not waiting for an answer, I sat down and faced the cannibalistic throng. The chanting continued in a thunderous roar. An alacritous line formed behind a makeshift pitcher's mound. Next to it was a mesh bag filled with softballs. There must have been a hundred or more. Behind the bull's-eye was a net to catch the errant–I held out hope!–throws.

Each pitcher was announced by a young man at a microphone by the mound. "And now, from Ayers Winery, Bill Upchurch." A cheer went up from the crowd. Then the chanting. "Dunk him. Dunk him. Dunk him!" Upchurch threw wild and the crowd inundated him with mock execration. Each attempt was preceded by the same introduction. The line-up trying to take me down was predominantly male. I don't know if it was the height of the bull's-eye or the hurlers' advanced inebriation, but for a good $2,000, en route to Portland's most woeful, no one could get close. In my limited field of vision all I glimpsed was this silhouetted object tearing darkly through the spotlight. I braced myself each time for the gong, the spring of the trapdoor to open and the plunge of my limp, weightless body into the night. But it seemed, for a stretch, I was safe, as if I might escape ignominy at the hands of these high-end swilling, vengeance-maddened Willamette Valley drunkards. At one point I glanced down and saw Jack near the front, waving his iPhone to video each attempt at unseating me. I believed I heard him shout in frustration, "Fuck, man, give me the ball!"

As the futile throwing of softballs dragged on, Julie brought a bottle of some Willamette Pinot and set it down next to me. I filled my glass, growing more confident I might be spared a dousing in the despicable Merlot. Julie returned to the microphone. "Come on, people. Surely, someone can hit the bull's-eye," she exhorted the crowd. As more and more people threw wide of the mark, more and more contestants lined up, credit cards in waving hands. With all the errant hurls, reminiscent of Tim Robbins's wayward pitches in *Bull Durham*, it had suddenly turned into a competitive ego thing: who was going to be the one who could hit the mythical bull's-eye? After every missed throw, Julie would shout out: "And that's three-thousand six-hundred dollars for our homeless shelter." It was starting to seem like one of those games at the county fair that's deviously rigged so no one has a chance of winning.

I must have grown complacent because just as I was insouciantly refilling my glass a thunderous CLANG rang in my ears. Simultaneously, I was suspended in mid-air, bottle in one hand, wineglass in the other, and soon in full ignominious free-fall. The chair and I separated just as we hit the vat of wine with a resounding splash. I hadn't had time to prepare for the nosedive and collided with the wine in a fetal position, head forward. In the vat, a good deal deeper than I had imagined, I did a somersault and then, for a scary minute–or what seemed like a full minute–found myself in a state of aqueous vertigo, unsure which way was up or down.

Finally, frantically, I broke the surface like a feeding trout, wineglass and bottle held aloft, sputtering arguably the world's most insipid grape variety. The IPNC nut bags roared. They were absolutely psychotic with delight that someone had finally brought me down. Jack was dollying in on me for a close-up (he was directing again!), laughing his fool head off. Over his bearish head, I could make out my mother, at one of the front center tables, laughing uncontrollably, slapping her armrest like a single-flipper-ed seal. Natalie in the Mosh Pit was beside herself with glee. Where was Joy? I panned to where the line was. And there I found her, both arms raised ramrod upright in triumph. The organizers had given her, what appeared, a twenty-foot handicap, and she had nailed it on the first attempt. With my money!

Why write? I thought, as I was helped out of the vat by two strapping young men, *when I can just be a vinous Jerry Lewis character the rest of my pathetic life?*

Julie, over the microphone, through the roaring crowd: "Let's give a rousing round of applause to Joy Soriano. Joy Soriano, everyone!" Cheers and whistling and applause erupted.

The two burly IPNC aides hustled me back toward the ladder.

"Hey, wait a second," I said. "I'm not going back up there."

"Julie said to let you know there was enough time for another round. Plus, it's for charity."

Wearily, bedraggled and drenched in red wine, but having suffered too much humiliation already to risk breach of contract now, I mounted the stairs like the bleating sacrificial lamb I had unwittingly become.

Julie welcomed me back up with a broad smile and an outstretched arm. Into the microphone she hollered: "Miles Raymond, everyone! Give it up for Miles Raymond!"

Another roar of approbation for my "charitable" work, my good sportsmanship, and my willingness to look like a fucking idiot, erupted from the crowd.

"See," Julie said as the crowd's appreciation abated, "it wasn't so bad."

I stared at her cross-eyed and shook my head in disgust. While one of the muscular aides reset the trapdoor and the other repositioned the chair and toweled me off for another go-round, I turned to the primitives, whose upraised glasses and bottles might just as well have been cudgels and spears, and shot both arms into the night with clenched fists, as if I had triumphed over some ordeal of initiation vouchsafing me passage into their dystopian universe. The aide who had re-secured the chair gesticulated for me to retake my throne of mortification. Seeing the natives in such a state of ecstasy–had some thrill-seeking Portland hippie, homeless no doubt, spiked their wine with a powerful hallucinogen?–I gladly resumed my position and waited for the next detachment of hurlers.

Julie leaned once more into the microphone. "Our master of ceremonies has agreed to do one more sitting, ladies and gentlemen." Wild cheers and a cacophony of shouted words greeted her announcement. "So, get out your wallets. The winning throw will receive a free wine-tasting dinner with none other than Miles Raymond."

Fuck, I never agreed to that either, I grumbled to myself, slumped in the foldup chair over the re-rigged trapdoor. This woman was really overstepping the bounds. Was Marcie getting back at me for canceling all those engagements at the last moment because a wine tasting dinner had gone too long and left me the worse for wear?

The column re-formed, a Conga line of bloodthirsty neo-Dionysians, snaking rearward through the crowd. A contingent of Japanese–reputedly serious collectors of Bourgogne *rouges* and, it now occurred to me, serious baseball aficionados–their companions dressed in kimonos (in this heat?) moved to line up. The collective frenzy to bring me down a second time

had been kindled and the crowd was pressing in closer much like a rock
concert headlined by some hot new band.

The not-so-hot local band started up, heaping on more discordance into the stifling night. Once again, the hurlers were individually announced before their throws. There was the usual number of wild tosses from the drunken revelers; some of the charitable donors even fell on their asses in trying to take me down. A couple got close. One even grazed the bull's-eye, but didn't hit it flush enough to spring the trapdoor, though I heard the mechanism beneath me threatening to let go. Gazing through the glaring spotlight, I noticed a hooligan contingent of the crowd was converging on the vat, eager for an up-close look at my definitive fall from grace. As if the ultimate humiliation hadn't happened years ago!

I pounded the wine as names continued being called out, softballs hurled into the night, the crowd booing robustly with every wayward attempt. At one point I gazed up at the stars, scintillating in the galactic amplitude of the Oregon night sky. I thought about the trip and how in a few days it would be over. About my sudden, totally unexpected, ascent to fame, and wondered how in hell it had brought me to this demented wine festival, to this chair, just a spring-loaded trapdoor between me and public embarrassment. The women I had slept with and the lies I had whispered to them...

And again my mediations were interrupted: BLANG. A moment passed, and I was in a free-fall once more. This time I landed feet first. I came up spitting Merlot, only to find that some of the Pinot enthusiasts were now stripping off their clothes and jumping into the vat with me. In horror, I tried frantically to climb out, but they wouldn't let me. One psycho clamped two strong hands on my head and pushed me back down under the surface–and tried to hold me there! I shot up like a Polaris missile egesting wine from mouth and nose.

"What're you doing?" I raged in his face.

The crazed sociopath screamed back at me and, obviously drunk out of his mind, attempted to dunk me again. I swung a hard right and caught him on the chin. He brought a hand to his face, looking shocked, as if: Not at the IPNC. Surely not. But before he could register what had happened the redhead and her crotch-scratching girlfriend from the signing had elbowed him away and were bearing down on me, wading through the chest-deep wine with the others, a small rookery of deranged pinnipeds. Both of them had stripped their tops off and were propping up their–to them!–glorious breasts with cupped hands. Thus, instead of sagging into the wine these four bosoms were held aloft as if offerings to the gods.

"Come on, Miles," the redhead slurred, her maw a disorganized whorl of fat lips. "Lick me, you satyr, lick me!"

I turned away and once again tried to clamber out of the vat to freedom. The two evidently sex-starved women, and a few around them, got a hold of me and tried to pull me back in. Both hands clutching the rim of the vat in terror, I tried to hang on. I felt what I took, with a mixture of hope and dismay, to be a feminine hand slide into my pants. Rooting around for my cock, the hand managed to get a purchase on my scrotum and squeeze it like an exercise ball.

At last I screamed bloody murder. "Help! HELP!"

I surfaced after another terrifying dunking and found myself being mauled by the redhead's camel-like lips. A moment later, a loud splash sounded behind me. I turned. In the tenebrous light, there was Jack dog-paddling through the wine, coming to my rescue. With his ample girth he pulled the women away from me, slung an arm under my armpits and hauled me to the edge of the vat, all the while shouting: "Get the fuck away from my friend, fucking wine whores!" He brandished an angry finger at two fanatical Japanese men, apparent victims of inherited dwarfism, both cackling psychotically like hyenas. "And you, too, you fucking nimrods!" Even in *extremis*, I was grateful that he'd refrained from one of his many colorful ethnic epithets.

My trusty wing man hauled me over the edge and out. I crumpled onto the lawn in a heap, still coughing wine from my half-drowned lungs, and staggered to my feet, flailing my arms like windshield wipers stuck on high speed. The oenophiles who had leapt into the vat now disgorged from it like cockroaches from an NYC co-op cupboard opened at night. When Jack got hold of me and was dragging me away, the women and the guy who had tried to drown me had launched a half-hearted chase; now that I was safe, I took some pleasure in seeing them tangled up in their intoxicated and uncoordinated attempt to run, and toppling to the ground.

I sought asylum at the table where my mother and Joy were parked,
their eyes pinched shut with insuppressible hilarity. Everyone was laughing, but I was still terror-stricken. It was the highlight of the festival: Miles
Raymond, celebrated author, performing two cannonballs into a swimming pool of Merlot; Jake and Martin now drenched in wine from head
to toe. My mother and Joy were laughing so uncontrollably I worried they
were going to defecate in their pants, and in unison.

Natalie pried herself from the Mosh Pit and snaked through the crowd.
"That was great, Miles!" she shouted.

"Fuckers tried to drown me," I said, still shaking.

"Let's get you over to my dorm and take a shower."

I turned to Jack. "I'm going to..."

"I heard," he said.

"Did you see those fucking crazy chicks?" I asked him.

Jack touched his forehead to mine and held me by the shoulders. We must
have looked like two bighorn sheep head-butting over mating rights. "You are
living high, Homes, you are living high." He slipped a pill into my hand. "Now,
go fuck that Natalie chick's brains out. I'll get these girls back. You were awesome, man. You were awesome! Video's going to rock YouTube, dude!"

He released me, and Natalie took me by the hand and led me away to
another den of iniquity. I slipped the pill into my mouth and bit it in half.
By its distinct bitter taste I knew exactly what it was. Natalie ushered me
to the Mosh Pit, where she grabbed a magnum of some Pinot. A French
vigneron admonished, "Hey, hey, hey!"

"I'll bring it back, François," Natalie replied cavalierly, adding, "empty,"
as she pulled me away. Once we were free from the main crush of the
crowd we picked up our pace, and ran tangled-footed to the hay-bale
fence, tipsy Natalie no doubt flashing back to a year earlier and her vile-
smelling *vigneron*. Steadying each other, we clambered over the abrasive
straw and fell on the other side, laughing. Natalie brought the magnum
to her mouth, threw her head back and chugged it, her throat rippling in
glorious peristalsis. She handed the bottle to me and I aped her style.

"'04 Arnoux Romanée St. Vivant! That was the *vigneron*, Pascal
Lachaux," she exclaimed. "He's legendary. Beautiful, isn't it?"

"Not as beautiful as you, Natalie," I said, forearming spilled '04 Arnoux
Romanée St. Vivant from my face.

"I had to fuck him last year to get into the Mosh Pit to taste this," she confided loudly, delirious with drink. She took another healthy swig and passed the monster bottle back to me.

I exulted once again in the wine. Pinot at its most kaleidoscopic, exotic flavors ricocheting this way and that.

"It was worth it, though," Natalie said, her eyes wide and her face a little slack. She reached for my elbow and helped me up off the lawn. We half ran, half walked, tripping over uneven ground, back to the dormitory. Incoming freshman eager to lose our virginity, we giggled nervously as we stumbled up the stairs to her third-floor cubicle. We stripped off our clothes, knotted towels around our nakedness and crossed the hallway to a communal shower. Natalie killed the lights as I turned on the taps and got the temperature set to a luke-cool, the air was so hot. She slithered toward me in the crepuscular light. Her mouth found mine under the cascading water. With one hand full of dispenser soap, she found my cock and worked it into a stiff, skyward-yearning totem of concupiscence.

We lathered each other until we were a pair of seals in heat cavorting on a slippery, moss-covered rock. A tall woman, but manageably slender, she was soon hoisted up off the ground and harpooned with my pharmacologically enhanced erection. We kissed and fucked perfervidly–she was on the pill, we'd never had any STDs, we were teenage virgins anyway, so fuck it–and went at it as if time were standing still. In a drunken vertigo, we whirled around the shower room, a lovemaking top spinning out of control. Until that top lost its energy and toppled to the tiles in a tangle of wet, soapy limbs.

Back in her room we continued going at it, clawing at each other like feral animals unloosed in an amoral universe. She stopped me at one point, produced Pascal's magnum of '04 Arnoux and beseeched me to reenact the scene in *Shameless* in which I, uh, Martin, poured Richebourg on Maya's–uh, Renay's–pussy and performed cunnilingus on her. Naturally, I obliged, even if this pantomime was becoming a banal and embarrassing routine with women who were fans of the book. Careful what you wish for...

"Natalie Meunier," I said, as I tipped the magnum and splashed her pussy with one of Burgundy's finest. "Is that a *nom de plume*?" Without waiting for her reply, I buried my mouth in her wine-soaked nether region.

"It's my real name," she moaned.

"What a great name for a wine writer," I said, licking her until her hands found my head and boxed my ears and silently voiced: Don't you dare stop.

I peeked a glance without breaking my lingual stride. Her head was swinging back and forth, her neck muscles gone slack. She gazed unfocused at something in the fourth dimension.

When I sensed she was teetering dangerously on the precipice, I rose and entered her again, plunging deep into her forbidden wetness. Her eyes took on the fey expression of a clairvoyant's in presaging the end of humankind. I thrust wildly, having also glimpsed the Apocalypse.

We came together, our bodies tensing, finally slackening, our conflagrant lovemaking at last subsiding on sheets soaked with perspiration.

After a few minutes lying next to each other and catching our breath, Natalie rose from the twin bed and poured us more of the Arnoux. This woman, with her reedy figure, seemed to have no concept of satiety, at least when it came to wine or sex. But what wines! She was whisking me off to fabled Burgundy and, as a bonus, fucking me on the journey there! At last, I thought–risibly, I had to admit–my writing had paid dividends!

"I almost blacked out," she admitted.

"You did?" I said, sipping the Arnoux.

"I haven't been fucked like that in months."

"You're pretty hot, Natalie."

"You probably say that to all the women."

"True." I kissed her lightly on the lips. "But I never mean it." I kissed her again.

"Well, thank you, Mr. Pfizer."

I sat up abruptly, my eyes bulged with chagrin.

"I found the other half in the bathroom."

I fell back on the pillow and slapped a hand to my forehead in mortification. "Oh, Christ."

She propped herself up on an elbow and looked down at me. "Hey, don't worry about it." She grabbed my rudder and gave it a little pull. "You've had a lot of wine."

"Yes, I've had a lot of wine," embarrassment wrecking the magic of the moment.

"Ah, don't be sad, Miles," she cooed.

"I guess there's a pill for that, too, huh?"

chapter 14

Dawnlight poured in through the canvas-slatted blinds. I blinked awake, my head about as light as the Liberty Bell, complete with crack and tintinnabulation produced by the repeated impact of the clapper. On the twin bed, I found myself in a sweaty knot of naked body parts. I stroked Natalie awake. She reached, apparently instinctively, for my cock. The 50 mikes of Viag must still have been coursing through my bloodstream because my organ sprang to life from fallow, parched ground. We made love again, less intensely, more agreeably, ignoring each other's halitotic breath, sticky flesh and piquant bodily fluids.

When that session had come to another rousing conclusion, complete with fingernails clawing my back and intense eye-locking looks, I crawled over her and out of bed. I slipped into the change of clothes I had brought in the brown paper sack, kneeling before her as she lay on her side, her pretty head balanced on her hand. "You are something, Natalie. You are really something," I said, genuine feeling swelling in my heart. I took her free hand, held it in mine and stroked it. In my befogged vision I noticed a faded area at the base of her ring finger. The left ring finger.

"Are you married, Natalie?"

She smiled a somewhat distant smile, sighed through her nose. With the back of her wedding band-less hand she caressed one side of my unshaven face. "Yeah, I'm married. And... I have a kid."

"Oh." I felt like a sewer main deep within me had developed an air lock and the cloacal waste matter was backing suddenly up into my stomach. "Where is he?" I asked anxiously, half expecting an irate, hung over, oenophile–probably French!–to burst into the room wielding one of those machetes used on ceremonial occasions to open champagne.

"Back in New York."

"That's a relief."

"I'm sorry," she said.

"I think you and your husband should see a sex therapist," I half-joked, feeling around for a foothold on this friable precipice. I dared not look down lest I go mad.

She laughed, probably at my obvious mood shift rather than at the wit of my feeble remark. "Yeah, probably. We haven't done it like that in a long, long time." She took a momentary look inward. "In fact, we haven't done it in a long time, period."

"You must play a lot of Scrabble?"

She laughed in the affirmative.

"It's amazing how many women out there are in sexually unfulfilling relationships. Why get married? Why be with one man? All you're doing in the long run is consigning yourself to a life of sexual barrenness."

"Well," Natalie started as I found myself pouring from the Arnoux (at 7:00 a.m.!), "we don't all base our marriages on the illusion the sex is going to be great the rest of our lives."

A night of uncorking had softened the wine. The sulfites had blown off, the tannins had muted, and now it was all pure Pinot fruit.

"So, what then? You stay married and get royally fucked on the side when the opportunity presents itself?" That came out sharper than I meant it to, but I was feeling hurt.

"Something like that," she said. "Now that we live well into our eighties, I don't think it's humanly possible to fuck the same person for half a century or whatever."

"Probably right," I agreed. "But even if I started tomorrow, I'd have to live nearly to a hundred to test the theory. And I don't think Pfizer has a pharmacological solution to that."

She smiled. I smiled back, raked my hand through her long dark hair, mildly depressed, hung over, sleep-deprived, a touch of panic setting in at the thought of my roustabout freak troupe wondering on what shoals their captain had shipwrecked.

"If you'd known I was married before we slept together, would it have been any different?" she challenged.

"Probably not." I rose to my feet, trying not to wobble. "Can you run me back to where I'm staying?" I asked, blatantly impatient, and feeling a bit rooked.

"Are you angry?"

"Me?" I emitted a laugh that sounded bitter even to myself. "I was just starting to like you, that's all."

"Half our life is the tragedy of relationships." She looked up at me and smiled. "Paraphrasing Willa Cather."

"Well, with all due respect, fuck Willa. Fine prose stylist, but she always came across like a pretty frustrated dyke to me. How about that ride?"

"Don't be angry."

"I'm *not* angry. I've just returned to normal, happiness once again having narrowly eluded me."

The mordancy was not lost on her. She pulled herself together while I waited, refreshing my sommeliers' glass with another splash of the Arnoux.

We drove in a clock-ticking silence back to the Brookside Inn. It was another blistering hot day in the making. The digital thermometer on Natalie's generic rental reported mid eighties. The sky was a cloudless, immutable blue, the Sunday roads devoid of vehicles.

As before, I had Natalie stop at the turnoff. She slid the stick into Park and turned to me. "I'm going to be coming out to LA in Septembe–"

"Natalie," I chopped her off, "I have to be honest with you, too. I met this Spanish girl on the trip up. It was just one day and one night, but there was something special there. I'm thinking after I get my mother to Wisconsin I'm going to play it out, see what happens. My problem with seeing you on the sly is that every time I see you, when you leave it's just going to remind me how fucking lonely and empty I feel. Am. If you were available... you'd be my dream girl. I'd go all in. But, you're not. So, thanks, but no thanks."

"Okay."

"I don't want to get all entangled, then have to disentangle myself–it's just such an emotional rollercoaster," I said wearily, massaging my temple with the palm of my hand. "I had a great time, Natalie."

"I said 'okay,' Miles." She replied with a smile, at least. "I had fun, too."

I kissed her on the mouth, opened the door and stumbled out into the implacable early morning heat, already feeling lonely and empty... and stupid.

Fifty yards from The Carriage House I heard faint but unmistakable ululations from the ground-level floor. I quickened my pace. When I reached my mother's suite she was calling out frantically: "Joy! Joy! I have to go to the bathroom!"

I lumbered, a little buzzed from the Arnoux, into her room and found her, to my dismay, lying on her back on the bed, helpless. "Where's Joy?" I asked, sensing something calamitous.

My mother gaped at me, panic-stricken. "Oh, Miles, I'm so glad you're here. I don't know where she went. I've been calling and calling. I've got to go. Will you help me, please?"

Battling a hangover that felt like a sledgehammer pounding a submerged rock, I exhaled wearily and sprang into action. I rolled her wheelchair next to the bed, helped her sit up, and slid her over to the lip of the mattress. "Okay, Mom, give me your hand." She held out her right hand and I grasped it. I pulled her closer to the edge of the bed until I managed to get her feet to touch the carpet.

"I'm falling, I'm falling," she wailed in an exaggerated paroxysm of fear.

"No, you're not, Mom. Now, come on, stop being a baby."

With our right hands lashed together, I hoisted her to a tottering upright position, then eased her into the wheelchair. I rolled her into the bathroom, praying she wouldn't pee her pants, performed a mirror image of the previous transfer maneuver, exited the room while she urinated, apprehensive at the thought of Joy off with one of the randy Japanese Bourgogne *rouge* hoarders from the Mosh Pit at the Salmon Bake.

My mother called out that she was done and I returned to the bathroom, block-and-tackled her off the throne, and wheeled her back out into the main room.

"I'll go find Joy," I said.

"She's no good," my mother barked in a croaking voice.

"Mom, she's exceptionally good. More to the point, she's all we've got. So, just fucking cool it. It's your birthday today and we're going to go to this big champagne brunch. You like champagne, don't you?"

"Oh, yes," she said, her ill tempered expression instantly transmogrified by the mere mention of drink. "I love champagne."

"Okay. I'm sure Joy's just taking a walk somewhere."

"And smoking her goddamn Mary Jane!"

"All right, Mom, chill. Not everybody's perfect. Not even you." That extracted a chuckle from her. "I'm sure she'll be back soon to give you your bath." I walked out before she could start in on her litany of complaints, closing the door behind me so I didn't have to hear them trailing me like a pack of bloodthirsty coyotes.

I trudged upstairs. I noticed that the heavy door separating the upper floor rooms from those on the lower floor, usually left open, was closed. I opened to the unambiguous sounds of humans engaged in wanton copulation. Moaning. Grunting. Female. Male. More alarmingly, this noise was issuing from Jack's room. I crossed the hall as if the floor were booby-trapped and I were a snapper with a mine sweeper. The door was slightly ajar, so I ventured a peek.

The reality by which I was confronted was worse than I had feared when I thought Joy had gone AWOL. My eyes widened in horror at the spectacle that rudely greeted me: Jack lying on his back, Joy (!) doubled over him, sucking his fully—and I don't employ that term lightly—resurgent cock. Our demure little taciturn Filipina looked like a jackhammer run amok. The salacious tableau so suffused me with revulsion I just about vomited on the spot.

Instead, I drew a hand across my haggard face, hoped the image would be effaced—it wasn't—miraculously regrouped psychologically from the multiple consequences of this ghastly revelation, pushed the door open to about six inches, instantly summoning Jack's attention. Joy, oblivious of my presence, fed voraciously like a jackal on the carrion of his dick. He attempted to wave me off. In silent reply, I fashioned a face of outrage and pointed my index finger at Joy, stabbing it several times in her direction for emphasis. Then, as if pantomiming a desperate hitchhiker in a game of Charades, I jerked my thumb downward, making clear where Joy was *truly* needed.

Jack held up both hands, one of which was intemperately holding a sommeliers' glass half-filled with red, mouthing: Okay, okay, let her finish.

Disgusted, I crossed to my suite, ensconced myself within, and collapsed on the bed. I was still having difficulty processing the image of
Jack and Joy in unholy congress and the repercussions of *that* for the
rest of the trip. I had to keep my eyes open to ward off the appalling
picture of their incongruous coupling, but even then it wouldn't go
away, it stuck to my brain like an insect on flypaper–and agonized there,
still horribly alive.

Twenty minutes later, a sheepish-looking Jack shambled heavy-footed
into my suite and filled up one of the chairs with his bare-chested girth.
He sipped from the sommeliers' glass, apparently welded to his hand.
"She's with your mom now." I was gratified to hear a tinge of remorse.

I closed my eyes at last, exhausted. "I didn't think you'd do it, Jack. I really didn't think you would." I opened my eyes and bulged them out. "Joy?"

"The chick was all over me, man. You get a little wine in those Asians
and they go nuts."

I nodded in despair. "That's because they don't possess the gene that
helps them to metabolize alcohol." I looked over at him sharply and raised
my voice. "What the fuck were you thinking, man?! Huh?"

"We were just having a good time."

"What're you, going to fuck Joy all the way to Wisconsin while my
mother wails at the top of her lungs for her to help her relieve herself?
Which *I* just did, motherfucker!"

Jack furrowed his brow and waxed defensive. "Miles. Let me tell you
something. That chick's about to mutiny, your mom is such a fucking a-
hole. My fucking her is about the only thing that could save this trip."

"That is such fucking twisted logic, Jackson," I groused, pinching my
temple with my thumb and middle fingers to impede the blood now
throbbing into my hurting brain.

"Hey, I'm sorry, dude. It just happened. It was one wild fucking night."

"Fine. So, it's over now. I'm not going to dwell on it."

"Me either," Jack said.

A disconcerted silence fell over us. Birds chirruped out in the trees.
They didn't know anything about over-imbibition, hangovers, stroke-addled mothers, sex (me and Natalie, not just Joy and Jack) that never should
have happened. They just knew hunger and procreation, and maybe bliss-
ful avian contentment in flight.

I exhaled through my nose. "How'd your big guy hold up?" I inquired.

"Worked like a gem sans meds. No pain."

"I'm relieved to hear that."

"How was Natalie?"

"Fucking smoking. On paper, the *ne plus ultra*. But... she's married. Has a kid. Lives in New York, anyway. Though I'd risk hospitalization to get on a plane to see her, she's that hot."

"Just keep her in the coop, Miles. For when she comes out again."

"I'm over that. Too bad, though. We really bonded. There was never a forced moment, never a lag in the conversation. The sex was levitational. And she's *fucking* married!"

"What's with these married chicks today?" Jack said. "Fucking hornier than shit."

"You know what it's like. One, two years in, you're lucky to get licked. Five years, forget it. Maybe once a month when you're half asleep and don't know what you're doing. That's why there're so many women at this bacchanalia. They need to get away, get drunk on their ass, and get fucking pounded. They're not looking for commitment. In the winter they'll rendezvous in the Bahamas and fuck Jamaican kiteboarding instructors."

"Good for them," Jack said, toasting his glass to motiveless sex.

"Yeah," I said, "good for them."

"So, what's on tap for today?" Jack asked. "Another mystery tour?"

"No, it's my mother's birthday. We're going to take her to IPNC's champagne brunch, back at the campus in McMinnville."

"When's that?" Jack asked, rising to his feet.

"I don't know, starts at 11:00, goes to whenever. If we don't get too plastered, maybe we can check out of here and make a dent in the leg to Wisconsin."

Jack pushed himself up from the chair with some effort. "Okay, I'm going to try to get a little shut-eye."

"So," I said, "you'll just put the brakes on with Joy until we get my mom to her sister's?"

"No prob, dude. Besides, I think I ripped her up pretty good." He winked. "She might need till Wisconsin."

I smirked through my nose. Jack turned cumbrously. I heard the door close and Jack's heavy footfalls receding down the hallway. I closed my

eyes. All I could see was Natalie Meunier's naked, yoga-lithe body pressed
up against me, her widemouth smile looking at me joyfully as she humped
away with abandon. Oh, well.

In the middle of a sinister dream hurled down by an angry god, my
iPhone jangled.

Joy said, "Your mom wants to go to champagne brunch like you promised."

I glanced at the time. It was nearly 11:30. I'd slept four hours. Why
didn't I feel at all rested? "Okay, Joy, I'll be right down." I rang Jack's cell.

He answered grumpily. "What is it?"

"Champagne brunch. My mother's seventy-fifth. Remember?"

"Three-quarters of a century. Man. Do you think we'll ever make it to
the big seven-five?"

"The more probing question: Do we want to? Limp dicks and gray pubes."

"I hear you. Gimme fifteen."

A quarter of an hour later, on the nose, I was downstairs. Jack ran late
as usual. Joy—a little worse for wear—was trying to brush my recalcitrant
mother's hair and make her look pretty. "No, not like that," the patient
said peevishly.

"How do you like it?" Joy asked.

"Let me do it myself," my mother snapped, snatching the brush from
Joy's hand. "You're no good."

"Stop it, Mom. Stop it!"

She brushed her hair off her ruddy face with slashing strokes. She
needed a drink, but didn't have the courage to voice it.

Joy backed away. Jack sauntered in.

"How's the birthday girl?" he said in his booming voice, having obviously gotten a start already on the day's drinking. At my mother's non-
response, Jack grew silent, looked to me for elucidation.

"All right, everyone, let's go," I said, clapping my hands, hoping that
would disperse the mounting disquiet that everyone, for entirely discrete
reasons, was clearly feeling.

"I don't want to go," Joy said.

"Oh, come on," Jack tried to persuade her.

Joy's face hardened into a mask of silent contempt. Jack stepped
close as if to comfort her when I waved him off, shaking my head in a
tight no.

"What if I have to go to the bathroom?" my mother piped up, still locked in combat with her hair in front of the mirror.

"I'll take you," I said. "But, if we're lucky, you can hold it this once." I turned to Joy. "All right, Joy. Why don't you just relax, get some sleep? We'll take her off your hands for a few hours."

Joy swiveled her head to the side until her chin was touching her right shoulder and glowered at the flora.

The Oak Grove had been magically transformed. The dunking contraption remained, but the vat had been drained and disassembled. At the entrance where we signed in, a young woman informed us that a lot of people hadn't shown, unapologetically citing their crucifying hangovers, and invited us to take whatever table we favored.

With Jack in tow, I pushed my mother down a cement pathway and parked her at one of the many empty, umbrella-shaded tables. It was hot, that oh-so-rare heat wave still in lockdown over Oregon. Jack and I, both on little sleep, sat down listlessly. Within minutes, a wine steward appeared with a bottle. "Champagne for everyone?" he asked cheerfully, blithely unaware of the personal damage that the three of us bore.

"Oh, yes, please," my mother said on hearing the magic words.

He filled the three flutes on the table with a cold, zesty, pale-golden liquid, geysering with bubbles. He ground the bottle into a bucket of melting ice and departed with a chirpy, "Enjoy your brunch."

I raised my glass. "Here's to being seventy-five, Mom," I said.

"Happy birthday, Mrs. Raymond," Jack said.

We clinked all around. Smiles momentarily returned, though my inner telepath could make out thunderclouds on the horizon.

"I'm sorry I'm such an old cuss," she said.

"No, you're not, Mom. Liar."

She laughed. "You ought to just take me out back and shoot me."

Jack and I looked at each other and laughed. There were those moments her clouded mind cleared and she was downright perspicacious.

"Mom, you ever hear what Lily Bollinger said about champagne?"

"No," she said, enjoying another much-needed sip.

"'I only drink champagne when I'm happy, and when I'm sad. Sometimes I drink it when I'm alone. When I have company, I consider it

obligatory. I trifle with it if I am not hungry and drink it when I am.
Otherwise I never touch it–unless I'm thirsty.'"

My mother responded with a throaty chortle. "You know what Churchill said?"

"No."

"'In victory we deserve it, in defeat we need it.'"

"Well put, Mrs. Raymond!" Jack said, raising his glass.

My mother consumed her first glass with alarming alacrity. It rocketed straight through the foundered ramparts of her stomach lining and directly up to her half-necrotic brain. Her face all but instantly colored a refulgent red, her mood turned to golden sunshine and the world was once again a magical place where all her cares floated out to sea on a rudderless vessel of alcohol. Seeing this transformation and how elated the champagne made her, I unhesitatingly refreshed her empty glass before she could wheedle. She sipped it greedily as if she, like Jack and me, needed the libation to quell all her anxieties. Why not let us all enjoy our little oasis of peace? It would prove a mirage soon enough.

The mood turned buoyant. Champagne will do that. The IPNC was almost over. Two days to Wisconsin, dump my mother with her sister, and fly back to L.A. It had been a sometimes Pyrrhic struggle, but we were just about to enter the home stretch, Jack and I happy that we were on the declivity of the trip, as it were.

Halfway into her second glass, my mother raised her right index finger, shook it in place, and said, with bowed head and furrowed brow, "There's something I have to tell you."

"What's that, Mom?" A little facetiously–damn champagne!–I said, "Let me guess. The man you met last night fell in love and he wants you to stay in Portland?"

"Oh, no," my mother chuckled.

"What's the big confession? Spit it out."

She took another sip of champagne, and I saw, all at once, that it was a sip for fortification. A look of worry furrowed her brow. Her face pinched shut into an expression of darkening apprehension. Her head bobbed up and down.

Jack and I waited.

"I'm sorry," she said, tears hobbling her words.

I leaned forward and squeezed her forearm. "What, Mom? You can tell me."

She gathered herself, then dropped the bombshell: "I stole Joy's money and gave it to Bud."

I half sat up out of my chair. "What?!"

"I took it out of her purse when she was in the bathroom that morning, probably smoking her you-know-what. And gave it to him," she said through tears of shame. "All of it. Poor Bud. He needed it more than Joy."

My chin sagged on my chest. All that anguish and acrimony because my mother had decided to be charitable to her down-at-heel, ne'er-do-well brother.

"I'm sorry," she said, her eyes now flooded with tears.

"Why didn't you just ask me for money? Why did you steal it from Joy, then turn around and blame the poor girl? Mom. Jesus Christ! Have you lost your mind?"

"Don't swear."

"Jesus FUCKING Christ!"

"I knew you'd be angry with me, that's why I didn't tell you," she said, now crying uncontrollably.

"I mean, did you even think about the repercussions of such an act–let alone the morality–when you did it?"

"No," she peeped.

"Fuck!" In panic, I fished out my iPhone and hunted up the number for the Brookside Inn. Thank the good Lord I had stored it. Bruce's wife, whats-herface, answered. I asked her, calmly, if she wouldn't mind ringing the Rouge Suite. She tried to make small talk, but I cut her short and she cheerfully patched me through. The extension rang and rang. I hung up before Bruce's wife came back on to take a message. I scrolled through my call list, found Joy's cell and dialed that. Straight to voicemail.

"Who're you calling?" my mother asked, feigning innocence.

"Joy!" I exploded. "Who do you think, you fucking stroke-addled idiot? Do you think I'm doing this excursion for my health?" I slammed my phone on the table, rattling the cutlery. "I'm sure she'll be greatly relieved to hear Jack and I know she's not a lying, thieving OFW." I also, ironically, was relieved to learn this because I imagined, once Joy was apprised of the truth, that it would go a long way toward mollifying a rightly discontented, and possibly mutinous, if Jack wasn't bullshitting, traveling caretaker.

"She's probably smoking her Mary Jane," my mother said.

I brandished my champagne flute at her and locked my eyes on hers. "You're going to apologize–apologize profusely! abjectly!–when we get back. Is that clear?"

"Oh, don't talk to me like some child."

"Is that clear, Mom?" I insisted, way more worried at this point about Joy's welfare–not to mention my own–than my mother's.

"I promise," she said.

"And I'm going to be there when you do it. And we're going to offer to buy her all the cannabis she needs to get her to Wisconsin!"

My mother looked down, shamefaced. I glanced around. The brunch was a buffet. I wasn't hungry, and doubted Jack was either. Drinking copiously over a period of weeks without respite is an effective appetite suppressant.

"What would you like to eat, Mom?" I asked gruffly.

"Oh, a little of everything."

I rose and went over to the buffet line. Plate in hand, I piled on scrambled eggs, biscuits with gravy, maple pork sausages, and a ratatouille she probably wouldn't touch, brought it back to the table and set it down in front of her, hoping that she would have a myocardial infarction on the spot and spare me any more of this insanity!

"Oh, how gorgeous," she said, conveniently forgetting the enormity of her confession.

I noticed her champagne glass was full, which meant she was now on her third. When I looked over for the bottle, it was upturned in the ice, indicating that it was empty. I signaled the wine steward and he glided across the lawn. "We need another bottle." He pivoted in place and hurried off. My mother dug ravenously into her heaping mound of food. Every now and then she would stop to sing its praises. I had to remind her several times during her private repast to wipe her mouth with her drool-cloth where the food dribbled, which she always immediately did, not wanting to look like what she was: a stroke victim.

My anxiety mounting, I tried Joy's cell again, but the call still went straight to voicemail.

Since it was my mother's birthday I allowed her to have a fourth glass of champagne, trying to balance the celebratory nature of the occasion with Joy's need to be able to transfer her into bed.

When my mother had finished her mountain of food, the wine steward, in tow with some of his staff, appeared carrying a large slice of cake, a single candle stabbed into it and burning. They broke into an *a cappella* "Happy Birthday" and my mother glowed, tears forming in her eyes. It was quite possibly the highpoint of her life until... her face froze and went ghostly white. For a sickening moment I thought she was having another episode of congestive heart failure.

After the wine steward and his staff had drifted off, I said to my still dismayed-looking mother, "What's wrong, Mom?" She raised her one good hand shakily and cried. "What's wrong?"

Through her tears, with champagne flute in hand, she answered mortifyingly, "I made chocolate."

Jack looked at me for an explanation. I hung my head in despair, and he knew the interpretation wasn't good news. "i.e., shit her pants," I translated in an undertone.

"Oh, Christ," Jack muttered.

"I'm sorry," my mother blubbered. "I'm sorry."

"We've got to get her out of here and back to Joy," I said urgently to Jack.

Jack and I drained our glasses of champagne and straightened quickly from the table.

I leapt behind my mother, unlocked the brakes, and wheeled her hurriedly down the oak-shaded path and back to the Rampvan with Jack trailing.

The Rampvan now reeked of excrement. My mother's new white pants were stained brown on the insides of both thighs. She euphemistically apologized over and over through prodigious tears. "I'm sorry I made chocolate. I'm sorry...."

Jack tried to make light of the situation. "Mrs. Raymond, if that's chocolate, I'd sure hate to be the CEO of Hershey's."

My mother tried to laugh, but humor was beyond her as she sat in pants soaked with diarrhea.

We sped back to the Brookside, braked to a dusty halt, rolled my mother out and straight into her room.

"Joy?" I called out. There was no answer. "Joy?" My eyes raked the room. On the dresser I spied a folded sheet of inn stationery. I opened it. On it was handwritten: "I did not steal money. I did not hurt dog. Can't take care of your mom no more. I fly home–Joy." With the note was left

$2,000 in hundreds, her calculation of a pro-rated payment for services rendered-and now sundered!

It took a moment for the full force of this development to strike me. When it did, it T-boned me like a Ford Escort plowed into by a Lincoln Navigator running a red light.

Jack came up behind me while I held my head once again in my hands in despair. "What does it say?"

"She split."

Jack threw a backward look at my mother, his expression growing dismayed. I sucked in my breath. "Fuck. Fuck!"

"What're we going to do?" Jack said.

I looked up at him. "We have no choice," I said. "You've got to help me clean her up."

"What?" His oversized face disorganized into one of horror. "This was not in the job description, Miles."

"Jack. The woman has shit her pants. She has full left-side paralysis. She can't clean herself, okay? Joy has flown the coop. She's probably halfway to Manila by now. Do you think Bruce and Susan are going to help us? I don't. I need you to stand her up in the bathroom while I towel her off. We'll get her into clean pants. And then we'll figure it out from there."

Jack saw I was at the breaking point and, resigned to the grim duty at hand, grumbled, "Okay. Just tell me what to do."

We wheeled my excrementitious mother into the bathroom. Using all weapons at our disposal, Jack turned on the bath water, flung open the little window, and I opened the faucets on the sink. Positioning himself behind her, Jack hooked his meaty paws under my mother's armpits and stood her up from the wheelchair as one might a heavyset rag doll. I rolled the wheelchair out from under her and, the dirty work being my unannounced responsibility, peeled off her pants. Diarrhea was streaked all down the back and inside of both legs. The stench was overpowering. I shot a glance at Jack and noted that his nostrils were clenched and he was making every effort to breathe through his mouth.

With warm wet towels I painstakingly cleaned up the mess–my mother, that is to say–while Jack held her erect. She was blubbering how sorry she was, obviously humiliated to find herself in this opprobrious position on her 75th birthday. Jack never once looked down, uncomfortable, and understandably so, at seeing my mother disrobed.

It took a good twenty minutes—what seemed like an eternity—to get her washed up and into a fresh change of clothes. I sequestered the diarrhea-soiled ones, as if they had come off the back of a Chernobyl technician, in a plastic laundry bag and discarded the malodorous bundle in the trash outside. When we were done and had her back in her chair, Jack excused himself to go to his room.

I sat down with my mother and broke the news. "Joy left."

"It's my fault," she said, still a lachrymose mess.

"I don't know what I'm going to do," I said, a nauseating fear welling up in me now that the immediate crisis had been dealt with and the grim implications of Joy's departure opportunistically sunk in.

My mother wore a hangdog face, born of fatigue, humiliation, and her own farrago of fears. "You ought to take me out back and shoot me," she said again, this time sounding like she meant it.

"Don't say that, Mom. We'll get you to Wisconsin."

"*Me wan' to go home,*" she sang, mimicking Belafonte. But this time with significantly less conviction.

"I know." I rose from the chair. "I'll be right back."

"Where're you going?" She asked it in a rising tone of trepidation. With Joy gone, she had quickly shifted all her insecurities about who was going to care for her to me. And the realization of that burden was making me revert to my suicidal outlook, a standard when I couldn't sell a screenplay or a short story to save my ass.

"I need to talk to Jack. I'll be back in a few minutes. I'm not sneaking off anywhere, okay?"

"Oh, please," she cried. I heard the fear that her apprehensions were falling on deaf ears. That and her innate distrust of her dissolute son.

I plodded upstairs, my mother's voice calling out after me with a flurry of admonitions. I found Jack lying supine on his bed, fingers interlaced behind his head. The TV was on some sports channel, the volume was muted. A glass of wine stood on the nightstand next to him.

I slumped onto the bed and bent forward, elbows on my thighs, raking a hand through my hair. "Happy birthday, Mom," I attempted to joke.

"That was dark, dude," Jack said, with none of the usual bonhomie in his voice. "Dark."

I raised my head and looked up at him. He was staring into space, the gears in his gourd grinding. I'm sure he was cogitating on the 2,000 miles left to Wisconsin, absent the indispensable Joy. It was a dismal look that accompanied his thought process.

I decided to preempt the inevitable. "Look, Jack, there's nothing left for you to do on this trip."

He started nodding, as if to himself.

"With Joy gone it's not going to be much fun from here on out. The wine part's over, too. I'm going to have no choice now but to stay in the same room with her. You'll be all alone..."

"I don't want to bail on you, man," he said, though his tone suggested otherwise.

I shrugged. "It's a long drive to Sheboygan. Three gonzo days and she's home. A day or two of transition with her sister and then I can bid goodbye to the whole deplorable mess."

"Why don't you hang around here in Portland, see if you can find somebody?" he suggested, his mind already on a jetliner back to LA, two double Absoluts in the bar before takeoff, and an Ambien for good measure.

"By the time I find somebody, train them, I'll be stuck here at least a week. I'd rather just brutal it out."

"If I were you I'd take her back to that Las Villas place."

"No. This is something I promised her. She's going to be happier with her sister. I got into this, and I'm going to get out of it."

Jack kept nodding, as if his neck were mounted on a spring. "I feel bad, man. It's a rough gig."

"I'm used to it. I've done it before. I took care of her when her money ran out and I was trying to get her into assisted-living. I know the drill. You'd just end up in a hotel room all by yourself with nothing to do because"—I reached for his glass and took a healthy swig—"it's 24/7 with her from now until I deposit her into the arms of her sister."

Jack turned and looked at me, his still-unshaven face grizzled with gloom. "Are you sure, man?"

"It sounds like your buddy Rick's got an AD-ing gig lined up for you. You probably want to get back and lock that in. I can handle this. Besides, from Portland you can get a million flights back to LA. Once we get out into the hinterlands, your only choice would be Greyhound."

"I don't want you to think it's because of what happened this afternoon," he said, all but admitting that he had been thinking of leaving after the IPNC.

"We'll be laughing about that one for a while," I said, chuckling sardonically.

"Man, that mother of yours has got the bowels of a horse," Jack said, able to joke now that he'd been excused from his duties.

I laughed a laugh of evacuating relief. But it sputtered to an end as I envisioned the end of the trip without Joy or Jack... or Snapper.

Jack sidled close to me and hooked an arm around my neck. "If I were you, when you get Phyllis settled in, I'd go to Spain and just get out of this fucking place. Hollywood's killing you, man. You're not the same Miles Raymond."

"I know," I said. "When the movie hit, I vowed I wouldn't succumb to the cliché of fame and start dancing in the Conga line. Now, look what's happened to me? I'm a fucking mess." I pointed at Jack's wineglass. "Too much of that shit. No writing. Women I don't remember or who just fuck me because I'm Miles Raymond, author of one overrated novel made into a pretty good little movie that'll be forgotten in one year. I'm just playing into everybody's hand, drinking and whoring, and doing what they expect of me, all the while destroying myself, my gift, what vestiges of it remains." I looked at Jack. "Maybe I need a dose of reality to clear the jets."

"Well, you're about to get one now," he said, with a mordant chuckle.

"That I am," I said. "That I am."

The decision was cemented with a hug.

As Jack—his spirits lifted!—got on his cell to book a flight I hiked across the lawn, up to the Main House to check out. Bruce and Susan wondered why I was checking out early, not staying the night. I told them that I was eager to get on the road, not wanting to disclose the whole imbroglio, Joy leaving and all the rest.

With a palpable mutual sorrow, Jack and I packed up, got Mom secured in the back, and GPS-ed the Rampvan to Portland International. I double-parked at Alaska Airlines departures, switched the hazards on, then climbed out to help Jack with his luggage. We looked at each other for a

pregnant moment, then he wrapped his arms around me. He held on to
me for the longest moment. "Good luck, man," he whispered, his scratchy
beard pressed against my cheek.

"Yeah, I'll call you from the road, let you know how it's going."

"Do that," he said, reaching for his duffel bag. He smiled and nodded,
a sadness creasing his face. "See you back in LA." Then he turned and was
swallowed up by the teeming terminal.

I climbed back into the van, turned to my mother sitting in her wheelchair in the back. The vehicle looked, and felt, empty. Twin feelings, sadness and a sense of duty, possessed me. My stomach felt like a toilet with
no water in the bowl, vainly trying to flush. "We've got a long way to go,"
I said. I tried to do the voice of Barbara Stanwyck: "So, hold on to your
bladder, it's going to be a bumpy ride."

"Where'd Jack go?"

"Where you're headed, Mom. Home."

chapter 15

From Portland International, my mother and I, on our own now,
looped onto I-84 and headed in a northeasterly direction. In no time
we were climbing through a riparian gorge, paralleling the wide, rushing
Columbia River. Just before departure I had hit Google Maps on my laptop and computed that we could make the small town of Pasco by nightfall. I wanted desperately to get out of Oregon and away from all the
wine–I had abandoned dozens of bottles back at the Brookside Inn, and
that was after Jack's pillaging all he could cram into his suitcase–and put
as many miles behind us as possible.

At first, my mother seemed nervous with just the two of us aboard, her
nervousness manifesting in frequent requests to pull in at the various rest
stops. Every stop involved my wheeling her into the woman's bathroom, to
be met with glares–even with a handicapped person in tow! And too often
the handicapped toilet was occupied by some insensitive, perfectly able-bod-
ied woman. There was no way I could effect the transfer in the regular stalls,
so it was particularly galling to wait until some obese specimen waddled out
of the handicapped accommodation, after having taken her sweet time.

At the third pull-off where my mother exhorted me to stop, she
couldn't go. I scolded her for the false alarm. "We have a lot of driving
still to do to get you to Wisconsin, Mom. These transfers are not easy.
You can't be asking me to stop all the time. You've got to try to learn to
hold it, okay?"

"I'll try to be good," she said, sounding as if she now sensed the gravity of the new situation. "But, I'm afraid."

"What of?"

"You being able to take care of me."

"Well, I am, too. If that makes you feel any better. But, what's the worst than can happen? We die, right?"

"Oh, no," my mother said, chuckling at my cynical humor.

The landscape turned wooded, tall pines reaching for the fading light of the sky. Now and then our view was graced by a mountainside waterfall, spewing runoff from the snow-capped Cascades.

"Oh, it's beautiful," my mother would exclaim as we climbed toward the crest of the range. The weather had grown mercifully cooler with our ascent. AC no longer needed, I switched it off.

On the eastern side of the Cascades the landscape grew flatter and the forested terrain surrendered to sagebrush and wild grasses that the searing summer sun had parched a honey-colored brown. Here and there, harvested farmland dotted with bales of hay fled past as we continued east. The late afternoon sky turned a deeper and deeper blue as we rode on into twilight.

My mother and I didn't converse much on this first, short, leg of the journey to Wisconsin. When we did it was usually to negotiate her request to stop at a bathroom. I would ask if she could hold it and she would say she would try. Shortly thereafter, she would plead again that she needed to go. I don't know if it was the sleepless night, my legs sapped of strength from making love with Natalie into the raw hours of morning, or the fact that I desperately needed a drink to quell the jimjams jangling my nerves, but I was finding myself growing unappeasably querulous. It was only two hundred-some miles to Pasco, but the next three days were going to be brutal without Jack as my co-pilot and Joy as my mother's minder.

In the tiny interstate-bound town of Umatilla, we looped onto I-82. Though it was nearing eight o'clock, now that we were out of the mountains and in the flatlands, the air had turned hot and dry. The neon sign of a Wells Fargo branch flashed "92°," reminding us that it was still summer.

It was a short distance to our day's destination. Located on the inland side of the Cascades, Pasco, WA, is an arid, wind-swept town of fewer than 40,000, flanked to the west by the Columbia River, which hugged the I-82 almost all the way.

I rolled my mother out of the Rampvan and into the Best Western Inn, a relatively new, three-story motel with a high-ceilinged lobby. The receptionist raised her eyebrows at my request for a single handicapped room–which I'd neglected to mention in making the reservation–but at the sight of my forlorn-looking mother slumped in her wheelchair, she nodded thoughtfully and started punching keys–and more keys, making me aggravated.

"Could we kind of hurry it up? My mother's *really* got to go to the bathroom. And, unfortunately, I'm in charge of that detail," I added, my tone chafed with impatience. "Plus, I don't think you'd like it if she pissed in your lobby." (God, I was jonesing badly for a drink!)

The receptionist hurried up and got us checked in.

In the spacious, air-conditioned room I helped my mother go to the toilet. She must have been holding it, because she took one long rainstorm of a piss. When she was finished, I helped her up off the porcelain, pulled up her stretch pants and maneuvered her back into the wheelchair.

Back in the main room I wordlessly handed her the remote. She switched the TV on, found a local news channel and zoned out to that while I went down to the Rampvan to fetch a bottle of wine. Halfway back to the entrance I realized my mother would demand some, but all I had retrieved was a bottle of St. Innocent Pinot, so I returned to the van and found a bottle of rosé made by the same winery–and that had better do or I'm going to flip out, I raged in my head. After baking in the heat of the van all afternoon it was warm to the touch. I tracked down an ice machine, filled a bucket and plunged the bottle in. One could almost hear it going *ahh*.

"Where'd you go?" my mother implored as I came into the room.

I held up my bottle and her bucket. "Out to get you some wine. I figured you could use a glass."

"I thought you had abandoned me," she said.

"Oh, and get myself arrested for filial neglect. Just what I need, Mom," I said dismissively as I extracted the two corks. I grabbed the pair of plastic cups from the minibar, filled hers with ice and rosé and mine with the '08 St. Innocent Pinot White Rose Vineyard, a wine I'd never tried before, but which turned out to be astonishingly good.

"It's red," my mother said circumspectly.

"It's a rosé, Mom. Try it."

She took a sip. "Hmm," was all she said. Then she took another. And another.

Thanks to the wine, my mom's fears dissipated. I tried to hold back, but the strain of the drive and what still lay ahead hung over me like a gray June marine layer that refused to burn off.

Holding out her cup for a refill, my mother asked, "Where're we going for dinner?"

"If you're hungry, I'll order take-out. I'm too wiped for a restaurant." I obliged the refill request, but pointed a cautionary finger at her.

"How about pizza?" she suggested, downright perkily.

"Mom, your arteries probably look like the sewers of Paris already. Do you really need such unwholesome food?"

"I'm craving pizza," she said in a rising tone, her sugar levels dipping.

"All right. All right." I got on the trusty iPhone and pulled down the maps app. I was soon on the phone to a take-out place called Sahara Pizza. After some debate we decided on The Ultimate Sahara, my mother's choice and a grotesquely described monster of a pie.

As we waited for the pizza, I asked, "Are you looking forward to seeing Alice?"

She nodded introspectively, as if she had given the question less consideration than I had imagined. Sipping her wine, with the imminent reality of Wisconsin growing nearer, I couldn't tell whether she was having doubts now or there was something else on her mind. In her innocent and post-stroke way it was possible she had just fantasized about getting out of Las Villas de Muerte and hadn't weighed the repercussions of what it was going to be like to live at her sister's in Sheboygan–for the rest of her life.

Without looking at me, she asked, "Would you call to check up on Snapper?"

I closed my eyes and sighed. "They're probably closed, Mom."

"Could you please phone them?"

"All right!" I got up and went toward the door.

"Where're you going?" she bellowed.

"I don't want you to be privy to this call." I slammed the door between us, fatigue fraying my nerves.

Outside, the sun was dipping in the west. I scrolled through my recent call list, found the number for Lakeview Veterinary Hospital and tapped it. The receptionist answered. "Hi, this is Miles Raymond, the guy with the Yorkie who was HBC."

"You're learning the lingo," she said, remembering me.

"Is Dr. Ariel in?"

She put down the phone and went to check. Moments later, Dr. Ariel's voice came on, sounding guarded. "This'd better not involve anyone's tooth."

"No, no. That's totally healed. Thank you so much. No, I was calling about Snapper."

She cleared her throat and the line briefly went dead. "Well, he was getting better. We had him stabilized. But I'm afraid the damage from the original injury was too extensive. There's too much tissue death. It's compromised the circulation to his right hind leg." She paused.

"What does that mean?"

"The poor little guy's toxic from that leg. I was going to call you as soon as I got a chance. If we don't amputate soon," she said matter-of-factly, "he'll die."

I exhaled a sigh and couldn't respond right away, weighing a whole host of things—what to tell my mother? what decision to make? where the nearest gun store might be just in case....

"Mr. Raymond?"

"Wouldn't it be better just to put him down, Doctor? Amputation. Jesus."

"Dogs in general do really well on three legs," she said.

"Oh, yeah? Could he jump into my mother's lap?" I asked testily.

"Maybe," she fired back.

I went mute.

"It's your call, Mr. Raymond, but I'm not going to be the one who puts him down. As an alternative, if you want to sign him over to us, I'll perform the amputation on my own dime. And I know someone who'll take him. Someone he's grown very fond of."

"Yeah, who?"

"Me."

Oh, fuck, I almost spoke into the phone. "If I agree to let you amputate, I'll pay for it," I said.

"That's fine," she said, "but we're going to need your mother's consent."

In a rising tone, I said, "I'm not going to tell my mother that her dog is getting his leg amputated. She'll bawl the rest of the way to Wisconsin and I'll end up in a state mental hospital." Clearly, I had descended a long way from that balcony at the Academy Awards a mere four months before.

"She's the rightful owner."

"I have power of attorney," I said.

"Okay, that makes things easier."

"So, if he survives, you're willing to take him?"

"Yes," she said in a calm voice. "And if in the future your mother wants him back, she can have him."

"How am I supposed to get a three-legged Yorkie to Wisconsin?" I asked in exasperation.

"Your mother's dog is going to die if I don't take off the gangrenous limb," she hurried me along. "So, Mr. Raymond: Do I have your permission to remove Snapper's leg?"

I dragged a hand across my sticky, sweaty face. The pizza delivery car pulled into the lot. "All right, Doctor, you have my consent to do what's necessary to save the dog as long as you'll take him. I'm not going to tell my mother, though, he has to lose a leg. The image is too horrific."

"Just don't lie to her and say he died," she admonished.

"Why would I do that?"

"You wrote a book where all the characters based on you and your friend do is lie. I presume you know something *about* the subject."

A mordant laugh momentarily convulsed me. "You're right, Doctor. It's all about lying." I shook my head. I was getting flak from every side. "All right. Save the critter. I'll check back in a few days and see how he's doing."

"You made the right decision."

"No, you guilt-tripped me. Goodbye."

The delivery boy bounded up the steps, acned and monosyllabic. His meth-mouth smile at the $20 tip made me lose my appetite.

Inside, I caught my mother refilling her cup. "Mom, what're you doing?"

"Just a smidgen more," she said girlishly.

"Mom, I can't have you peeing like a racehorse all night. Who do you think I am? Florence Nightingale?" I set the pizza down on the nightstand. "Here's your Sahara with the works."

My mother had me bring a towel from the bathroom to use as a bib. I wrapped it around her neck, pizza not being the preferred food given her loose-jointed mouth. Halfway through her second slice–sausage, bell peppers and tomatoes plopping onto the towel–she asked, "What'd they say about my Snapper?"

"He's doing fine, Mom."

"Will he be coming home?"

"I don't think so."

"Why not?"

"I think it's unrealistic. And unfair to your sister Alice."

"Why?" she demanded.

I nearly exploded. "How am I going to get him out there, Mom?"

Her face hardened to granite streaked with red sauce. "I miss him."

I closed my eyes and held them shut, waiting for her mood to pass.

Out of the corner of my eye I saw my mother reaching for the rosé. I grabbed it just before her greedy paw could claim it.

"Mom, I'm the one who's going to have to get up in the middle of the night and help you to the bathroom."

"Just a smidgen more. For your poor mother who raised you," she pleaded.

"No. You've had enough."

Her expression turned sullen. "You're no good."

I sighed. Now I understood, first-hand, what Joy had suffered through. Not even a few more thousand could make her willing to stay. I rose from my chair. "Come on, Mom, let's put you down." I caught myself. Snapper. My mother? "I mean, let's get you to bed."

"First my medications," she said sharply, still indignant about my cutting her off. I knew the feeling.

Next to the "Dear Miles" note Joy had left me I'd found the book-sized zippered pouch that contained my mother's pills, with a separate note detailing the instructions on administering them. Coumadin, Lasix, Lanoxin, Cordarone, atenolol, aspirin, Ambien, ending with the application of a nitroglycerine patch over her heart. Modern medicine is amazing, I thought. It's regulating her heart, pumping her blood, thinning her blood, emptying her of excess water that's dangerous for a non-ambulatory person, and sedating her all at once. Polypharmacology and curmudgeonlinesss were keeping her alive.

"Now, my brace," she instructed, when we had finished with the meds. I dutifully removed the brace from her lower left leg and set it aside.

"Okay, now we'll put you to bed."

"I want to go to the bathroom first."

"Jesus, Mom, you're peeing like an incontinent dog."

"I've got to go!"

I wheeled her back into the bathroom and went through the transfer routine, waited in the doorway with my back turned while she relieved herself, and hauled her back into the chair and back to the bed.

"Now, undress me."

I closed my eyes and held my breath a moment. "Can't you sleep in your clothes?" I asked.

"No. Undress me."

With some difficulty, owing to the immobility of her paralyzed left arm, hanging like the trunk of a dead elephant, I pulled off her sweatshirt, trying all the while not to look at her naked body. But I couldn't keep it entirely out of view, and glimpsed her drooping, wrinkled breasts. Next, I peeled her pants off. That left her stark naked. With both arms I hauled her legs up onto the queen bed and maneuvered her stocky frame until it was correctly aligned. I covered her up as quickly as I could.

Helpless as a turtle on its back, she launched a barrage of admonitions. "You're not going anywhere, are you?"

"No."

"You're not going out to drink?"

"No."

"Good."

Finishing the explosive Raptor Ridge I found myself reaching for the half bottle of rosé. I stopped myself at the thought that I had six hundred miles to cover the following day, doing all the driving myself.

I climbed out of all my clothes, except my underwear, and slipped into the adjoining queen. When I heard my mother snoring I switched off the TV. I tried to fall asleep, but anxiety kept me pitched wide awake. Half a Xanax didn't do much to assuage the rising sense of dread, so I took the other half. I closed my eyes.... The mistakes I had made....

Sometime in the middle of the night I was rudely awakened by my mother crying out for Joy.

"Joy isn't here anymore, Mom," I said into the darkness. "It's me, Miles."

"Oh, I forgot," she said, sounding frightened and disoriented. "I have to go. I'm sorry."

Three times that first night I was roused from sleep to take her to the bathroom. I vowed then and there to cut the diuretics–damn the edema and the threat of congestive heart failure!–until we had made it to Wisconsin, fearing I would go mad and end up in lockdown.

chapter 16

The next morning dawned brilliantly blue, awash in sunshine... if you weren't in my head. I roused my mother early because I wanted to make Billings, Montana by nightfall, the first of two stops I had calculated in my insomniacal night on the MacBook. She asked me to bathe her, as Joy had done every morning, but I begged off, saying I would do it when we got to Billings.

She didn't like the break in routine and let me know it in a withering diatribe, which I let pass over me like a scudding thunderstorm. Dependent on me, what could she could do except whine until she wore me down? or I wore her down?

After a hurried breakfast at the motel, we got into the Rampvan and wended our way onto the I-90. Once on the interstate, I took stock of the fact that I hadn't slept much. My nerves were jittery, shot. As we passed through the mountain resort town of Coeur d'Alene, on a beautiful, placid, sapphire-blue lake, I checked the mileage gauge and saw we had gone only 165 miles! My brain was already fried; I needed Jack to take over so I could... have a glass or two of wine, it occurred to me with a sudden, sickening epiphany of self-loathing. With fear gripping me in a way any drinker would understand, I realized I was going to have to go cold turkey if I was ever going to deliver my invalid mother over to her sister in Wisconsin.

I tried to maintain my concentration on the road, but found myself dropping out, then suddenly swerving in panic when the tires jolted over the lane divider bumps. Coffee stimulated me awhile, but then dropped me back into that narcotized daze, the road undulating interminably out in front of me as if it had no terminus, or as if at some point, when I had fallen asleep at the wheel, it would hurtle me off the edge of the earth and debunk Columbus. Several times I considered stopping at a motel and just sleeping, even if that meant prolonging the trip, because it seemed almost an impossibility that I would be able to make the 600+ miles to Billings. And, more annoyingly, my mother's rest stop visits were starting to fray my nerves. It was all I could do to keep from exploding every time she blurted out in a rising tone, "I've got to go!"

We rode on through the beautiful topography of Idaho and western Montana, passing grassy valleys speckled with feckless livestock, grazing under an amplitude of celestially blue skies, punctuated here and there by mushrooming cumuli. The freeway was blissfully empty, but with every mile ticked off the odometer it felt like the minute hand on a condemned man's watch. There were moments when I was certain I was going to lose it. I debated more Xanax, but I feared falling asleep at the wheel. Under any other circumstances I could have enjoyed the freedom and exhilaration of a road trip, but I felt more like I had been kidnapped and someone in the back was holding a loaded gun to my head. My mother!

To maintain my sanity I called a few people and got back to others who'd left messages. I had a brief conversation with my book agent. She asked hopefully whether I had worked up a proposal for my next book. Giving my mother a backward glance, I told her I had something in the inchoate stage that I'd tidy up and ship off to her as soon as I got back to L.A. Though I was still angry at Marcie, I was emotionally weak and looking for any kind of solace, so I phoned her. I informed her what the new circumstances were and she commiserated with me for a bit until it felt like disingenuousness had crept into her words. I couldn't stand her shallowness anymore so I changed the subject to business. She ran some lecture and cruise ship proposals by me, but I told her I couldn't deal with any of them until I got back home—when I said *home* it sounded like some phantasmal place, an Edenic realm that I was moving ineluctably away from, not toward, as if I had taken the wrong road and was now circumnavigating the globe just to get across the street! I found my brain pullulating all kinds of foolish imaginings. Some made me laugh; some made me want to cry; some made me sure I was not long for this world.

I phoned Jack. It was barely noon and I could hear the familiar slurring in his voice.

"What's up, Miles?"

"Out here on the road. Seeing double. It's brutal, dude, it's brutal."

"I feel for you, man. Don't know what I would do." He burped some beer.

"What I'd love to do is pull over and go get hammered somewhere, but that isn't going to make my problem"–I glanced over at my mother whose head was lolled to the side–"go away."

"Hang in there. It's only a few more days."

"I don't know why I got myself into this mess."

Jack grew silent. This was not the partying, joke-a-minute Miles he had grown fond of. This was the dyspeptic Miles, the side of me that didn't appeal to him. I could tell he wanted out of the conversation when he said, "I've got to jump, Miles, this is Rick."

"All right. I'll check back with you later."

My mother needed constantly to urinate and was not shy about announcing the fact. On her fifth such request, I flew into a veritable rage: "Mom, to stay on schedule we have to make Billings. I can't keep stopping like this. I'm losing my momentum. Can't you hold it?"

"No. I have to go," she insisted.

"Maybe we should stop at a hospital and fit you out with a catheter and a bedpan?"

"Please. Stop."

I swept a hand across the desolate passing terrain out the window. "Where?"

"I don't care. I have to go, damn it! Next stop."

"You just went."

"I have to go! I'll pee in my pants!"

"Don't threaten me, Mom. I'm onto your wiles."

"You're just irritable because you want a drink."

"Fucking A I need a drink!"

I peeled off angrily at the next off-ramp. It led to a rural frontage road, fissured with cracks, weeds sprouting through them. I drove a long ways through barren nothingness, searching desperately for a rest stop or a gas station or anything. What the fuck was there an exit for? I fulminated in my sleep-deprived brain.

"I've got to go," my mother wailed.

In a moment of apoplexy, in the grip of white-line fever, I slammed on the brakes and threw the shift lever into Park. I scrambled out of the van, opened the side door with a slam, flipped the ramp down, jumped in and got behind my mother and pushed her out into the hot sunlight. I wheeled her across a stretch of dirt corrugated like a washboard by the summer heat and months without rain. She bounced in the chair as I roughly pushed her away, out of the view of passing motorists. I had no idea where I was taking her. Maybe to the edge of that fantasized cliff where I morbidly imagined hurtling her into the abyss!

Finally, out of eyesight of the freeway, I stopped, set the brakes on her wheelchair and crossly offered my hand. "Here. Give me your hand," I said, feeling the blood throbbing in my face.

"What?" she said, looking utterly bewildered.

"Come on, you're going to pee standing up."

"Don't make fun of me. I'm your mother!"

"You said you had to go. So, go!"

"I'm not going to pee standing up!"

I walked away from her and stormed back to the Rampvan, my rage unquestionably exacerbated by the fact I had had nothing to drink in close to twenty-four hours. I glanced back at the gutted case of wine in the back and debated opening a bottle to calm my nerves. But the consequences of a DUI, a mini-spree, with just me and my mother and the 1,000-plus-odd miles left to Sheboygan quickly chastened me, lashed me to the pillory of abstinence. In the moment of that realization I felt emotionally raw, naked to the world, on the precipice of a genuine nervous breakdown–the kind you see in movies where white-coated men converge on you with tranquilizer guns and straitjackets. I started to laugh at the absurdity of it all, the image of just me and my mother out in the middle of nowhere, she trying to piss and I attempting to hold to the crumbling ramparts of sanity.

My laugher stopped abruptly when, ever so faintly, as if out of the wilderness of my worst night, came my mother's cry, "Miles! Miles!"

The stress was too overwhelming. I broke down, clamped my hands over my eyes and wept. Her plaintive calling rang out louder, an echoic summons for help. I wanted to find a gun and put her out of her misery. Hell, both of us. How did I end up on this madcap adventure to Wisconsin? Why hadn't I seen the friction that was building between her and Joy and taken more drastic measures to mollify it? I hadn't been paying attention because I'd been having too good a time with Jack. With Laura, with Natalie... and my one unsinkable great love: Pinot Noir. I had at myself until there was nothing left but a bloody pulp of a conscience.

"Miles!" my mother caterwauled. "Miles!" It wasn't going to stop; it wasn't going to go away. She was the infant child I had encouraged–okay, pretty much forced–two women to abort... for just this *fucking* reason!

Maybe this was my fate. Maybe all the whoring and drinking post-movie success had landed me in this karmic enantiodromia where the world was now turned impertinently inside-out. Worse, there was no escaping it. An invalid mother, due to a series of cruel circumstances and poor planning, had yoked me to the earth. I was no longer Icarus soaring toward the searing sun. The wax holding my wings together had melted....

Spurred by an implacable sense of duty, I climbed back out of the Rampvan and trotted in to where I had abandoned my mother and her incontinent bladder. I was sick with worry wondering whether I–let alone she–could make it to Wisconsin. But as I ran toward her I grasped one thing: If I didn't surrender to every one of her needs, no matter how petty they might seem, this titanic struggle between the two of us would hurtle me off the deep end to wrack and ruin. In surrender–total surrender–as my revelation unfolded, there existed the possibility of sanity, of seeing this through.

There, on a small rise, alone, she sat in her wheelchair, her head thrashing around in a way that recalled a sick farm animal's, crying out my name over and over. I rushed toward her, tears blurring my eyes, and hugged her in the wheelchair. "I'm sorry, Mom, I'm really sorry." She convulsed in my arms, wracked with sobbing. "It's just been so damn hard. And now with everyone gone, out here in the middle of nowhere...."

It felt weird to hold her in my arms. I flashed back to when my father was officially declared dead and we had hugged. Her body felt so foreign to me then, as it did now. But I held on to her, because she seemed relieved that I was embracing her, reassured by the envelopment of my arms that it was all going to be okay, that I was strong enough to get us through it.

To her I had been the prodigal son, and to me she had always been the dutiful, but unfeeling, unaffectionate mother. Now, in this wretched moment of forlornness–her need to be cared for and my trepidation that I couldn't do it without Joy and Jack–we fused together in a palpably emotional exchange of mutual support.

"I know I'm a burden," she bawled into my ear.

"No, Mom. What happened to you couldn't have been prevented. But it doesn't matter. This is where we are now. This is where we are. Okay. You've got to have faith in me. You've got to believe I can pull this off. I know you think I'm a wanton drunk, and you're probably not too far off, but I went down a different path in my life that didn't prepare me for this moment."

"I know," she said.

"I'm going to get you to Wisconsin if it kills me. All right?" I said, forearming the tears from my eyes. "Now, let's go and find you a restroom."

I got behind the wheelchair, unlocked the brakes and pushed her off back down the slope. To passing motorists we must have looked like two souls in desperate need of salvation, lost along the road on our pilgrimage to Santiago de Compostela.

I rolled my still-shaken mother slowly across the dirt path to the Rampvan and got her resettled inside.

"Are you okay, Mom?"

"I was scared."

I hooked an arm around her shoulders. "I know. I'm sorry. I had a bit of a meltdown there. Maybe I need some of Joy's Mary Jane."

My mother smiled a laugh. "Oh, no, then you'll really flip out on me."

I laughed back and patted her on the shoulder. "All right, you ready to go?"

"Oh, yes."

I closed up the back door, circled around to the driver's side, climbed in, turned the key, and backtracked to the interstate. The mini-breakdown had served as a kind of anodyne; my resolve was not just restored, but stronger than it had been at any other moment since I'd made up my mind to undertake this journey. The decision to stop battling my mother engendered in me a massive sense of relief. I experienced a quieting of the mind, a suffusion of peace in every ravaged corpuscle of my emotionally raw soul. There's catharsis in surrender. Unfortunately, there's no catharsis in stopping drinking, only a cloacal upsurge of every thing wrong you have wrought.

At the next rest stop, felicitously a mere ten miles down the highway, I dutifully rolled my mother into the bathroom. As I waited for her to do her business, I spoke through the stall's door, "We'll stop at every rest area if you want to, so don't worry, okay?"

"Okay," she said meekly.

"I'm here for you until we get there, okay? I'm sorry I exploded."

"I'm such a burden," she said, starting once again to cry.

When she called out she was done, I helped her back into her sweat pants, draped an arm around her neck, and said, "It is what it is, Mom. I'm sure Hank, Doug and I weren't a lot of fun when we were toddlers."

"Oh, you were terrible. I could have brained you," she said, as I pushed her back out into the harsh sunlight, both of us laughing, albeit for different reasons.

We drove on. Through lush valleys framed by majestic mountains, creeks slashing blue tortuous swaths through them. Now and then I spotted fly fishermen whipping their rods back and forth to get just the right length on their casts before setting their flies on the rippling currents, envying them. I babbled to my mother and she babbled back at me–golf, men and women professionals, our low common denominator. Anything to keep awake, keep the white-line fever from engulfing me, and quash the panic that abstinence had beset me with.

On the open road, my mother, in a manifestly more relaxed mood, narrated a story from when she first met my father. A captain in the Air Force, he flew her in a light plane from her hometown of Sheboygan across vast Lake Michigan to Grand Rapids, where he resided. There were advisories due to thunderstorms, she told me, "... and he just flew right into them," she said, making a little whistling noise that mimed the sound of a projectile. "Oh, we could have been killed," she said. "I kept telling him to turn around, but he wouldn't listen to me. He was so reckless." I tried to picture my air force captain father with his Dennis Quaid *The Right Stuff* grin emblazoned on his face, oblivious of the meteorological perils, while others around him hangared their planes to ride out the storm in the nearest bar.

"But you made it, obviously?"

"Oh, that single-engine plane went up and down, up and down. I got soooo sick."

For some reason that made me laugh. There's catharsis in laughter, too. And I hadn't been finding much to laugh about the past couple days.

"You know, Rusty was stationed in Montana before you were born," my mother recalled.

"Oh, yeah?"

"We were in Helena. Oh, it was so hot in the summer. And we had *noooooo* air conditioning," she trilled, vividly recalling the time.

I marveled at the lucidity of her way-back memory compared to the spottiness of her day-to-day one. She often had trouble remembering if I had visited the previous day, but when you asked her about something that happened forty years in the past, it's as if time had embedded that memory into her consciousness and, though half the tissue in her brain was dead, she could journey back there and recall moments that one would have figured would have been out of her reach.

We reminisced in tandem with the countryside flying past, traveling back in time as we moved ineluctably forward in space. Somewhere out ahead, I was even letting myself hope, lay the prospect of a new beginning for my mother.

A hundred miles from Billings I noticed the tank was nearing empty. After we'd filled up and I'd toileted my mother and rolled her back into the van, I detoured into the convenience store and found two locally brewed handcrafted ales. Buying a bottle of each, I climbed back into the van and cracked the first. I tried to conceal this from my mother, but she hadn't lost her raptor's eye for the subtlest movements and changes in her surroundings, particularly when liquids were involved.

"Are you drinking beer?" she asked.

I showed her the bottle. "Just two," I said. "We're almost in Billings," I rationalized. "Because, I can't go cold turkey."

She nodded. I was only watching in the rear-view, but I'd have sworn that nod was accompanied by a look of understanding, even acceptance, as if, she, too, had once battled her demons and come a cropper. Of course, to question my drinking would have incurred the risk of my questioning hers. Whatever her motivation, she just said, "Oh." Then added, "Your dad liked beer."

The beer soothed my nerves as we rode past picturesque landscapes into Billings, Montana. Situated in the Yellowstone Valley, the city is engirded by gently sloping mountain ranges. The Crowne Plaza, where I had booked us, appeared in the flesh as on its Web site to be not only Billings's tallest building, but its nicest hotel to boot. It featured an on-premises restaurant, an essential after the day's punishing drive.

We checked into our handicapped-equipped room. On the tenth floor, it enjoyed a panoramic view of the verdant valley and snow-capped peaks.

After helping my mother go I lay down on the adjoining queen. My ears were ringing. I was exhausted, wanted desperately to sleep, but it was still light outside and I knew my mother was excited about hitting the penthouse restaurant and her requisite two glasses of wine. Me? I told myself those two beers were the last and that was it. It did not promise to be a fun night.

My mother held me to my promise to bathe her. Which I did, not without difficulty. Stripping off her clothes and transferring her from the wheelchair to the tub proved a complicated, taxing ordeal. For her as well, I conceded. Seeing my mother naked was going to take some getting used to, but when she asked me to help her wash her hair, I obliged.

After her bath, and in fresh change of clothes, she looked, even sounded—and smelled!—magically transformed, a different person. In her demure words, "a human being."

In my servicing her every need without protest, at least without vocal protest, as I still was annoyed by every rest stop pull-off, the tension abated considerably. Knowing I was there for her, she became concomitantly less demanding, as if a peace had suffused her back there on that godforsaken stretch of Interstate and banished a few of *her* irrational fears. I wondered, too, if the amelioration of tension made her less nervous because after my meltdown the intervals between pit-stops lengthened.

The Crowne Plaza's top-floor restaurant lives up to its name: Montana Sky. We were seated at a window—there is an advantage to being with a handicapped person when requesting the primo tables. The commanding views of the city—the most populous in Montana—and the neighboring mountains were spectacular. My mother, with her glass of over-oaked Chardonnay, was in heaven. With my own death-grip on a glass of tonic water I wasn't soaring where she was. But one glass would have become four, maybe more, and I couldn't risk it. Over mostly confabulatory conversation, I white-knuckled it through a pretty damn decent meal.

My mother haggled for a third glass of Chardonnay, but I enjoined the waiter—to the accompaniment of her vehement protestations—from complying with her request. She wasn't happy. Her harangue continued in the elevator, but lost its force as we turned our attention to the routine of administering her meds, removing her brace and transferring her into bed. Her bedtime routine finished, I climbed into my queen, dissolved a Xanax and an Ambien I filched from my mother under my tongue, and switched off the lights.

Soon, I was sweating heavily. I got up frequently to hydrate. The sheet turned sticky from my perspiration and I spread a towel between my body and the bed. As panic gripped me, I felt myself ever so slightly shaking. Maybe convulsing. Sleep eluded me as my mind, wired, ran wild to all things dark and bleak in my life. Again, I feared I was going to go insane, sure to wind up without knowing how I got there in a white-padded room screaming for Mother Mary, Jesus and Joseph. In my head everything was painted black with catastrophe. At one point I debated dialing 911 and having them whisk me off to the ER. As my mother snored away and I continued to suck the marrow of my own brain, pustulating macabre images and eschatological scenarios of every conceivable variety, I descended to the point of doubting I could handle life anymore.

My mother, awakened by my frequent trips to get water, asked meekly, "Are you feeling okay?"

"I'm detoxing, Mom."

"Oh," was all she said.

I wanted to talk but my mother wasn't the right person to bare my soul to. We had never had that kind of close relationship and it was going to feel awkward to open up, desperately as I wanted to. Because in this wretched moment, she was all I had.

"I crossed the neurochemical Rubicon, Mom," was all I said.

She didn't say anything. Maybe she was trying to unscramble *Rubicon*. Maybe she didn't want to talk about my drinking because it hit too close to home.

"The Rubicon is..."

"I know what the damn Rubicon is," she snapped, arresting me.

I fell silent.

"It's a river in Italy that Caesar crossed that meant an automatic declaration of war on the Senate. It was the point of no return."

I still wanted to explain what the *neurochemical* Rubicon is, but didn't dare. I lay there stunned. I never had gotten to know my mother.

"I'm not as dumb as you think."

There followed a silence, but in the silence my mind continued wreaking havoc. Sensing that my mother was still lying awake, I ventured, "Did you drink when you were pregnant with me, Mom?"

That must have taken her by surprise. She didn't answer. The question was decidedly too personal. And accusatory. And while we'd been accusatory for years, we had never been personal, and, as a result, my memories of growing up with her were scant.

"When I get you settled in Sheboygan it might be the last time I see you, Mom," I said, in the grip of fear, wanting to talk, wanting anything but the night and its implacable silence.

My repressed mother didn't like talking about herself, and my questions, I could tell, were upsetting her. She hoped silence would, well, silence me.

"It doesn't matter now, Mom, I just want to know." She remained stoically silent. I tacked. "What was your beverage of choice back then?" Again, my question was met with silence. "Wine? Beer? Scotch?"

After a long moment, she finally said in a low, croaking voice, "Beer. Pabst Blue Ribbon. Oh, your dad loved his Pabst's."

"So, you did drink when you were pregnant with me?" I asked, still quaking like a leaf in a stiff wind, my brow beaded with sweat, my body perspiring heavily through the towel.

The time lag was even longer. For a moment I thought she had dozed off. Then, out of seeming nowhere, her disembodied voice spoke, "I might have had a few beers," she admitted, her tone clearly indicating that she was not appreciating where I was headed.

"Every night?" I prodded.

"I don't know, Miles. I was depressed." She broke into tears, and then the floodgates opened, "I didn't want to have children. I had Hank, and then Rusty said he didn't want an only child because *he* was an only child and it had been hard on him. So, then we had you, and you two were such a handful. And then two years later we tried for a daughter and ended up with Doug. It was such a struggle when Rusty left the Air Force and started up his new businesses and I had the three of you all alone. And you'd run around and run around and you wouldn't obey," she said, crying her way through the recounting of the memory. "I wanted to travel, I wanted to see the world when I got out of the military. I wanted to go back to school and study journalism, or use my nursing degree and help the poor in Mexico. But with the three of you? It was impossible. I felt like my life was over." She broke down sobbing.

Suddenly I felt sorry for her. As if I had compelled her to dredge these laments at an age when all she wanted to do was blissfully forget. "You regret having kids?" I prodded gently.

"No, you've all been so good to me since my accident." My eyes had grown accustomed to the dark, and when I glanced over she was nodding her head to herself. "That's what kids are good for." Through more tears: "They'll take care of you."

There was a pregnant pause, then I dropped the bombshell. "So, why'd you leave the family, Mom?"

My mother fell silent, but this time it was a different kind of silent, the kind that told me I'd made her deeply uncomfortable. Which was not really my intent. The fragility engendered by my detoxing was not really her problem. But there was something I wanted from her. Something I had never gotten. "Huh, Mom? Where were you that year you were gone?" I waited. "With another man?"

Another long moment, this one unsettlingly interminable. "Yes," she said in a voice that sounded like it came from a completely other woman, one I had never heard before.

"Who was he?"

"His name was Paul. He didn't have children."

"What'd he do?"

"He was an internist. I worked for him as his nurse."

"You took a year off from the family and traveled the world?"

"Yes."

"Were you in love with him? with this Paul?"

The AC came on. Footsteps went by the door, rose and fell and then

another door opened and shut. "I don't know, Miles. It was a long time ago. I just know that you three were more than I could handle." Tears blurred her eyes. "At one point I wanted to give you all up for adoption, I was so miserable. I was having a nervous breakdown. And back then they didn't have the medicines they have today. They threw you in the loony bin. I was a nurse, I know."

I had been eight at the time, but remembered feeling a chasmic void I couldn't put voice or reason to. My brothers and I, gullible innocents, accepted our father's spurious explanation for our mother's abrupt absence, but every night we sensed, though we didn't articulate, the moroseness in his demeanor, the strain in his bearing. I remembered how, when she returned, an awkwardness had fallen over the household, a discomfiture that was hard to quantify. Something in our psyches had been permanently altered. Her hiatus was never talked about again. Swept under the rug, it was one of those lacunae in life that get plowed deep into the unconscious. And the whole Raymond family turned to the bottle.

"Why did you come back, Mom?" I wanted to know.

She sniffled. "For you kids."

"You felt guilty leaving us with Dad?"

"I hoped he would find someone else. I didn't want children. He did."

As the AC hummed, I tried to assimilate all this. "Do you regret your decision to come back?"

"I don't know," she said, growing miserable.

"Whatever happened to this Paul character?"

"He died recently."

I nodded in the dark, thinking.

"Is there anything else you want to know?" she whimpered.

"No."

"Do you blame me for your drinking?"

Now it was my turn to clam up. Her question left me nonplused. I didn't know how or when or why I had fallen prey to over-imbibition. But at that moment, I saw clearly why I had become a writer. "No, I don't blame you for anything, Mom." Given the debilitating effects of her stroke and helplessness she must have been experiencing recounting these painful memories, it wasn't fair of me to press her for more answers as to why I had become who I had become. In a lighter tone I said, "I absolve you of all guilt."

"Oh, that's such good news."

"No, I know who to blame. I'd love to blame you. Or the people who want to give me oceans of free wine. But I know better." I waited. "I appreciate your candor, Mom." I waited again. "We can't blame the past for who we are today."

She wanted desperately no doubt to switch the subject. So, out of the blue, she asked, "Why was Jack holding his, you know, thingamajig. I've been meaning to ask you."

I laughed at her euphemism for *cock*. "Well, he, uh, had an accident."

"What kind of accident?" my mother asked.

"Uh, well..." At Jack's expense, I spilled the whole story.

She laughed so hard, especially at my description of him in the OR. "I thought that's what Jack always wanted!" she said, riding the wave of humor with me.

"Yeah, but I think he wanted to be able to switch it on and off at will."

"Is that why he got divorced?" she asked. "Couldn't keep it in his pants?"

"Mom! Jesus."

"Well, you're grown up now. And I know you're no angel yourself."

I almost said, takes one to know one, but my poor mother deserved a bit of a break. "Yes, Mom, Jack cheated on his wife. More than once. Finally she couldn't take it anymore and threw him out, straight to the curbside."

"Is that what happened with Victoria?"

"Yes, I cheated on her. Near the end. I tried to make amends, but it didn't end up working. Now, she's with a new man and has a beautiful daughter and I'm a successful author, so it all worked out."

The room went quiet again. A few minutes later I heard my mother's light snoring. I felt a little better, but I couldn't stop trembling.

chapter 17

It was a long and insomniacal night. In my broken sleep I perspired through two towels and managed at best four or five pretty rough hours. Dark dreams assailed me like marauding armies. They were the same dreams I used to have before the success of *Shameless*: destitution, loneliness, the whole litany of my once-desperate existence. Had I come full circle? I wondered, as my mother, *her* Ambien evidently producing its desired effect, slumbered away.

In the morning, ragged and dreading the miles that lay ahead with no one left to share the duty at the wheel, I bathed my mother without voiced complaint. As I sponged her back, it dawned on me–our roles had reversed. Once *she* took care of *me*–made sure I was fed and washed and got to the doctor if I wasn't feeling well–and now I ministered to her, bearing sole responsibility for *her* needs. As I rinsed her off, a frightening realization struck me like a golf shot: Who would take care of me in my dotage? Jack? I laughed out loud at the thought.

In the grand lobby of the Crowne Plaza I parked my mother in front of a majestic stone fireplace, while I bought a coffee, two wedges of treacly coffee cake, and an orange juice at the in-hotel Starbucks.

It was still early when we got out to the Rampvan. I was so tired from the previous day, so drained by my first night of detox, I almost wanted to turn around and check back into the hotel and stay another night in

Billings—until I could rest up. But we had to move on, our mini-version of the Bataan Death March.

As I deployed the ramp, my mother said: "Could I sit up front with you, Miles?"

"Mom, that's going to be a difficult transfer. It's not like with the Prius."

"Oh, please," she pleaded. "You can do it. I want to see the country-side." She locked her eyes on mine, nodded a few times and wheedled, playing on my sympathies. "This might be my last trip."

Her words startled me for some inexplicable reason. "Okay, I'll try, Mom."

The Rampvan had a little step just below the bottom of the door. I would have to get her up on that step, then somehow lift her up into the seat. I considered summoning the valet for help, but it occurred to me that if I couldn't perform the transfer by myself, what would happen when we got out on the open road, and I had to get her out for a bathroom stop?

I wheeled the chair up next to the passenger side door and set the brakes. "Okay, Mom, we're going to have to do this in two stages. First, the little step-up, then into the seat. Okay?"

"Okay."

Bravely, determined to sit up front, she held out her right hand. I hoisted her out of the chair, as if I were some kind of human dockside crane. I managed to get her paralyzed left leg onto the step-up. Mustering all my strength, I grasped her torso beneath her armpits and practically heaved her up, into the van, and onto the passenger seat. Finally I swiveled her lower limbs until her feet rested on the floorboard. Pancaking the wheelchair, I disposed of it in the back, all the while worrying about the numerous transfers I would be required to negotiate between Billings and our next overnight stop, Sioux Falls, South Dakota.

In the driver's seat, I turned and looked at my mother, riding shotgun, Gilligan's Island hat and oversized sunglasses in place, looking ready for adventure. "Feel good to be up front, Mom?"

"Oh, yes," she said. She crooked her index finger and pointed it at nothing. "I feel like a human being."

I laughed and started the engine.

"It wasn't so hard to transfer me, was it?" she said.

"Well, I hope you can hold that obstreperous bladder of yours, Mom."

"I will. I'm not so nervous now."

I jerked my thumb toward the rear. "Otherwise? Back there for the duration."

"Okay."

"I stopped the diuretics. I don't think a couple days without them can hurt."

"That's good news." It was almost disorienting to hear my mother going out of her way to be agreeable. Maybe the simplest of things like making the effort to seat her up front were all it took to radically alter her mood. I was learning.

The GPS guided us back to I-90. It was a spectacular lazuline-sky Montana morning and the interstate was wide open. The kind of wide open where you can do 80 mph and think you aren't moving.

"Oh, it's beautiful," my mother exclaimed. There was something ineffable, but relaxed, in her mien. In her helplessness and absolute dependence on someone else for all her needs, Joy's untimely departure must have paralyzed her with even more anxiety. Now that I had demonstrated I could toilet her and bathe her and administer her meds, a measure of calm had descended. Not only was I capable of providing at least the essential care, I was no longer out all night, drinking and whoring and carousing. That, too, I now realized, had caused her no end of sleepless apprehension. I had finally morphed–evolved?–from the profligate son to the responsible one. She might have believed in my transformation more wholeheartedly than I did.

"How're you feeling this morning?" she inquired.

"A little shaky," I admitted.

"We'll be okay," she said confidently. "If you get tired, I can drive."

I turned and looked at her. She wore a closemouthed smile. "Pretty funny, Mom."

"We have to laugh. Otherwise, there's no reason to live."

"When did you become so sententious all of a sudden?"

"Oh, stop using your fancy words on me."

I laughed. "You knew Rubicon."

"Yes. I studied the classics. I read *The History of the Decline and Fall of the Roman Empire*. All three volumes," she added proudly.

"Really? I never read it."

"You should. You might learn something."

I punched her playfully on the shoulder. "Oh, getting feisty on me now, are we?"

"I'm no dummy."

As we drove on, through a kind of prosaic, postcard-perfect beauty, I discovered the miles went much faster when I kept up a patter with my mother. If I just stayed up in my head and white-knuckled the road the journey was going to seem like eternity.

"Do you have a girlfriend now?" my mother asked, as we dropped down into the high plains city of Gillette, Wyoming, a former boom town, thanks to oil, that had surrendered to one of the worst methamphetamine epidemics in the country.

"No, not really," I answered.

"What's with all this sex, sex, sex?" she asked.

"What?" I asked, taken aback.

"All these women," she drawled in her singsongy voice. "What does it mean? Does it bring you happiness?"

"Why are you asking me all these questions, Mom?"

She nodded inwardly, as if gathering her answer before spitting it out. "Well," she began, trailing off. "I don't really know you all that well, and you're my son"–tears hobbled her speech, but I was getting used to that, so I didn't admonish her to stop–"and when you drop me off at my sister's I'll probably never see you again."

"I'll come out and visit," I said automatically, but she could no doubt hear a certain disingenuousness in my tone.

"No, you won't," she said. "No one'll come to visit me in Sheboygan. Hank is afraid of flying, and Doug hates me, and you're too wrapped up in your high-falutin' Hollywood world." Her tears had subsided to sniffles. "And I won't be able to travel by myself." She paused. "You'll come visit when I die," she finished. For someone whose entire right hemisphere was nothing but dead cells, she was surprisingly knowing; along with a reptile's parietal eye, she'd developed a sixth sense. She could have been an oracle foretelling what was to come. Or not.

From Gillette we crossed into South Dakota on the western slopes of the Black Hills. The interstate gradually climbed in elevation and the landscape turned increasingly wooded. I lowered the AC and cracked open spectacularly unfold, almost growing monotonous in its pulchritude.

We'd been quiet awhile, dipping in and out of conversation, when I inquired, "How're you doing, Mom?"

"I'm fine."

"Do you have to go?"

"No."

"We'll stop for lunch, okay?"

"Okay," she said, in her new imperturbability.

We coasted down out of the Black Hills, bent off the interstate and pulled into the small town of Rapid City. I parked on a quaint downtown street whose sidewalk corners featured nearly life-sized bronze likenesses of past U.S. presidents.

We ate lunch at the ancient Hotel Alex Johnson–a single glass of Chardonnay for my mom, mineral water for me.

After lunch I wheeled my mother to the bathroom. It was becoming routine. She must have been really holding her bladder because it took seemingly forever to empty it.

With a little more difficulty, I managed to get her back into the passenger seat. I was bone tired and still a bit edgy when I climbed back behind the wheel for the second half of the leg to Sioux Falls.

Threading through downtown Rapid City and looping back onto I-90 I noticed an armada of billowy clouds had materialized out of the hot blue sky, bred by the rising humidity and bracing heat of the mid-afternoon.

Between Rapid City and Sioux Falls the passing terrain is monochromatically flat. Vast stretches of treeless prairie, broken up here and there by cornfields, flowed endlessly to the horizon lines, unpolluted sky as far as the eye could see. Once this area had been composed of a lot of small farms, but multinational agribusiness had long since wrested control of the land and the old farmhouses with their barns and silos were in a vivid state of dilapidation.

Beyond the small town of Chamberlain, an afternoon thunderstorm developed. The swift-moving clouds mushroomed and grew coal-shaded as they amassed. As in a partial eclipse, the landscape suddenly darkened. Far in the distance lightning flashed. A few seconds later thunder followed it out of the foreboding sky.

"It's getting closer," my mother said, growing excited. She motored down her window and half flung her head out. "Oh, I love the thunderstorms," she effused. "I missed them so much."

"Well, you'll get to see plenty to make up for that now," I consoled her.

"I know," she said. She turned to me. "Let's pull over, shall we?"

A thick rain had begun to pelt the windshield and the sky had grown so ominously black cars were switching their headlights on. "Mom, it's raining, there's lightning."

"I know," she said. "I want to be out in it."

"What?"

"Come on, don't be a stick-in-the-mud, pull over," she said, gesticulating to an approaching off-ramp with her one good arm.

I peeled off the interstate onto the off-ramp and pulled into a rest area. Motorists were huddled in their cars or scurrying back and forth to the bathrooms with articles of clothing and bits of car-trip flotsam held over their heads for protection from the cloudburst.

"Take me out into the rain," my mother said.

"What?"

She looked at me. "Take me out into the rain, Miles. Please."

"You're crazy, Mom."

"I know," she said, "I'm crazy!"

"You'll get soaked to the bone."

"I don't care. This might be my last thunderstorm."

"Okay, okay, I'll take you out, but just don't get all melodramatic about it, okay?"

We both laughed. I killed the engine, pushed open my door, and was soaked to the skin by the time I got to her side.

The transfer wasn't any harder owing to the pummeling rain, and soon I was pushing her out into it. The air was thick and humid and infused with a palpable electrostatic charge that goose-pimpled our arms. The lightning was closing in, marching both closer and lower, its jagged detonations burning afterimages on our retinas, the thunder trailing the flashes by shorter and shorter intervals. The boiling storm clouds unleashed a hammering downpour.

"Let's go back, Mom!" I shouted over the rain and lightning and thunder.

"No! Take me up to that hill!" She crooked a finger at a gentle rise off in the blurry distance.

"Take me up to that hill!" she insisted, undaunted by the crackling fulgurations.

Why did I want to argue? We had passed that point; now it seemed we were one. I pushed us to the top of a small, grass-covered overlook. The lightning grew closer, hurling itself to the ground in indiscriminate patterns. The storm seemed to swarm us all at once. The ear-splitting claps of thunder were deafening in sound and ferocity. The sky was brutish in all God's sublime fury.

"Mom, in that metal chair you're a lightning rod!"

"I don't give a damn!" she shouted. Her voice was carefree, giddy. As a lightning bolt rent the sky in two, she clenched her fist and raised it to the heavens. "Take me, God. Take me to Rusty."

Before I knew it, I was laughing. Her gesture, what she'd just shouted, was daft and at the same time weirdly profound. "He probably will, Mom."

"Oh, I love the rain," she cried out, tossing her head back and letting it drench her hair and face. "I love the rain." In her face I could see the teenager from pictures I had found when I had cleared out her condo.

And, like adolescent sex, the squallish storm was over almost as soon as it had begun. It swept away over the cornfields, its looming black epicenter casting a massive traveling shadow on the green flora.

We were both utterly bedraggled, but strangely exhilarated.

"You want to go back now, Mom?"

"No, not yet," she said. "We have to wait for the rainbow."

"How do you know there'll be one?" I asked, clutching my biceps, shivering.

"There always is," she said confidently. "Let's stay."

"Okay," I hooked an arm around her shoulders and gave her a tentative hug.

Within a minute the clouds were breaking apart, sunlight raying through and turning sections of the cornfield iridescent. The countryside, once the storm had spent itself, glistened. My mother's expression suggested that she was almost supernaturally one with the land's revivification.

Suddenly, she stretched out her good arm and pointed. "Oh, look," she exclaimed. "There it is."

I stared off in the direction she was motioning, looking for whatever she was trying to point out with that shaking finger. A great arcing rainbow had materialized in the clearing sky, framed by a backdrop of the retreating clouds, soaring majestically over us, at the very least making my mother a clairvoyant. I wondered for a moment whether the devastating stroke had vouchsafed her special access to the divine.

"There's our rainbow," my mother said, starting to cry, personalizing the atmospheric phenomenon as if it was of her own making, as if all the suffering she had endured the past few years had magically conjured this for her out of nature's elements.

I slung my arm around her wet shoulders and hugged her again, this time less awkwardly. "There's your rainbow," I echoed her.

"You see," she said, "He was listening."

Thunder reverberated in the distance, not nearly as loud as before, as the storm retreated over the prairie to wreak havoc on the next town in its path.

"He's calling," my mother said cryptically. "He's calling."

"Who's calling, Mom?"

She seemed confused by my question, as if I should be able to read her thoughts, as if we had grown so close during this journey that we were now inextricably of like mind. "Rusty," she said.

"Dad's calling?"

She nodded as if that were as certain as the sun setting. She raised her index finger and waggled it at the clearing heavens, as if to scold him. "Oh, yes," she said. "They're all up there."

I let it go unquestioned, let her have her private sacramental moment in some imagined place where the walls between the living and the dead are transparent. As the sky brightened, the rainbow's colors grew more vivid. I couldn't remember when I had last seen a rainbow. Certainly never one like this magnificent creature, the sky's own elaborately beautiful sand castle if ever there was one, soon to dissolve in the bluing and revived heat of the afternoon.

When the rainbow had begun to fade, dimming against a brightening sky, I wheeled my bedraggled mother down to the restroom.

Back in the van, I rummaged around for a towel I had cadged from one of the hotels and dried us both off. As if she were my infant child, I undressed her and got her into dry, clean clothes. I gave her a brush and she worked her sodden hair back off her glistening wet face. Finally, with some effort, I transferred her back up to the front passenger seat. While she waited I went into the restroom and changed myself.

Back on the road, we were both reflective. I could tell she was thinking about returning home, after so many years away, to Sheboygan. Our imminent arrival made it all too real and seemed to rekindle her fears about how it would work out rooming with her sister.

Near dusk, we got off the freeway and wended our way through Sioux Falls. The GPS guided us to the six-story Sheraton, the most expensive hotel in South Dakota's most populous city, just as the Midwest summer sky was purpling.

I pushed my mother into the lobby. The hotel was designed with the rooms arranged in a rectangular fashion, the lobby forming a huge atrium, rising all the way up, giving the place a spacious feel. It had been a long drive and we were both spent.

As soon as we were settled in another handicapped-friendly room I fell onto the bed. I just wanted to sleep, but my mother was hungry. Room service produced mac and cheese for her, along with the requisite glass of Chardonnay, and an overcooked burger for me. I kept to my regimen of abstinence, one more leg to Sheboygan weighing–a little less heavily now–on my mind.

"You should have a glass of wine," my mother suggested insidiously. "You earned one."

"That was a lot of driving," I chortled. "No, if I have one glass, I'll end up down in the bar and you'll never make it to Sheboygan."

"Would that be so bad?"

I was about to answer, but realized I had nothing to say.

After she had eaten, I dosed her with her meds, sans the diuretic, and prepared her for bed.

Once she was under the covers, her meek voice cooed against my back. "Could you give me a kiss good-night?"

I massaged her shoulder for a second. "You know we don't do that, Mom."

"I know. But there's still time to change."

I don't know why, but I couldn't overcome the awkwardness of something so commonplace, giving my mother a goodnight kiss on the cheek. I demurred, peeled off my clothes and slipped into bed. Employing the remote, I channel-surfed until I found a baseball game that held no interest. I dissolved a whole Xanax under my tongue and prayed for a restful night, one in which my mother wouldn't wake me to assist her in relieving herself, one in which I didn't shudder and sweat and squander the precious sleep I needed for the next day's drive.

chapter 18

My iPhone alarm woke me at 7:00 a.m. I felt a little woolly-headed from the Xanax, but otherwise amazingly restored. My mother lay supine on the bed next to mine, snoring peacefully. I had no recall of having toileted her during the night. Finding no towels between me and the sheet I assumed that the worst of my detox's St. Vitus's Dance was over. Something built up in me that, like the previous day's thunderstorm, had broken. I found myself on the other side, sober for the first time in months.

I was already dressed and ready to go when my mother's eyes fluttered open. "Miles?"

"Yes, Mom, I'm here."

"Oh. I had the most vivid dream," she said drawing out *vivid* in her singsong manner.

"What was that?"

"Oh. We were all in heaven and everyone was happy."

"Who all's *we*?" I said.

"The family." She stared off into space, into the abyss of her memory. "Now, I don't remember the rest of it."

"Do you mind if we skip your bath this morning, Mom? You had a pretty nice shower yesterday afternoon."

"Oh, yes. That was the best thunderstorm." She turned to me and said, "You don't have to bathe me. I'm fine. How'd you sleep?"

"Pretty well," I said. "Yesterday was rough. I wasn't sure I was going to make it. But today we've got less than 500 miles."

We took our breakfast in the room and checked out. I transferred her up into the front passenger seat so she could be next to me on the last leg into Sheboygan, the last leg of any trip she was likely to take, a tacit understanding that evoked a filial-maternal current between us.

The drive to Sheboygan featured flat farmland, much of it blackened where the ubiquitous cornfields had been harvested. The nitrogen-based fertilizers dumped on year after year, without crop rotation, having left the land looking scorched, it was as if we were traveling through a post-apocalyptic world imagined by Cormac McCarthy.

As we grew closer to Sheboygan, my mother grew more deeply introspective; her usual patter all but ceased. The fears and insecurities that had plagued her and given her the urge to go to the bathroom more than she really needed had abated. She seemed to drift in her thoughts to the huge body of water that was Lake Michigan, coming into view and disappearing off to our right, realizing she had come full circle to her childhood and, in completing that journey, glimpsed the arc of her life. Dusk gradually eclipsed the lake's expanse of cold blue and turned it into a black hole.

As we neared Sheboygan, I turned to my mother. "Would you rather get a hotel? Just this first night, I mean."

She shook her head.

"You seem sad, Mom."

"The trip's over," she lamented. "I didn't want it to ever end."

Her words struck an emotional chord and I felt sad for her–not me!–suddenly. "Well, we made it," I replied lamely.

"Oh, yes. We made it."

It had been a long day and she was tired. From the worry etched in her face, I felt queasy all of a sudden, at last grasping that the trip, and getting out of Las Villas, had been the real motivating fantasy, not the reality of moving in with her elderly sister.

Following the signs and the trusty GPS, I turned off at the I-43 for Sheboygan and drove a short distance to North 11th St. where her sister lived. It was near the point where the Sheboygan River, after snaking through the small city, found its way to the lake. In its heyday, Sheboygan had boasted a bustling port and shipyards. Later it became a bedroom community housing the hundreds working at the Kohler plumbing fixtures factory, a scant few miles to the east. Kohler was still there, but Sheboygan, once very working class, was thriving again, now as a tourist destination with its lakefront B&Bs and renowned golf courses. But harsh winters obligated the tiny city to shutter itself half the year, and the tourists to move to warmer climes.

My Aunt Alice lived in a small, rectangular wood-framed house outfitted with aluminum siding, on a block whose every house would by the light of day reveal itself to be nearly identical to the one next to it. I transferred my mother from the van into her wheelchair and pushed her up a narrow concrete path. Two steps leading up to the front door didn't concern me, now that I was adept at dollying my mother backward down longer flights, but it did concern me for her sister. The porch was so miniscule that I had to leave my mother on the concrete path while I rang the doorbell.

Alice answered the door. I hadn't seen her in years. She was tall, thin, with short-cropped gray hair and a countenance fissured by a half-century's tobacco abuse.

"Hi!" she said, "You made it." She gave me a brief hug. "You look so grown up, Miles."

"You haven't aged."

She smirked. "I've heard so much about you and your success."

I nodded, too tired to do the routine.

Alice stepped down the short flight of steps to greet the sister she hadn't seen in over twenty years. "Hi, Phyllis. How are you?"

"I'm fine." Tears welled in her eyes. She pointed her finger at me and said, "He took good care of me. He got me home."

Alice glanced back and forth between the two of us. "I bet he did." She didn't seem to know what to do next, no doubt taken aback by seeing her sister in this semi-infantile state. "Well, let's get inside," she said nervously. "It's chilly out here." Anxiety clouding her face, she stepped back up onto the porch and held the door open.

I leapt down and got behind the wheelchair. I swiveled it around and bumped my mother up the short flight of steps like a mover with a hand truck. There wasn't enough room on the porch to turn her around so I pulled her through the narrow front door backward. It was such a tight fit that the outer edges of her armrests grazed the molding, further disconcerting Alice. She smiled to mask her concern, shutting the door quickly against the night air.

We convened in the tiny living room. Its hardwood floor, half covered by a threadbare rug, was due for refinishing. The couch and matching chairs, coffee table and lone end table were '50s vintage and bore commensurate wear and tear. Alice's husband, whose name was escaping me, had worked at Kohler until a heart attack had felled him, about ten years earlier. They had two sons. One lived in Alaska working for a regional airline, and the other was in a federal penitentiary, serving time for tax fraud. While I'd been aware Alice lived on a fixed income, I'd not expected quite the reduced circumstances confronting us. The small house was surely her only asset; as I was to learn, her criminal son had gutted her savings with all his legal troubles and more or less bankrupted her. I took heart in the thought that the money I had agreed to provide Alice for care of her sister was a godsend.

My mother was enervated from the journey, but it was plain she was depressed about her new lodgings. After two decades in a cliffside, ocean-view condo in temperate Southern California, this down-at-the-heel house must have felt like a fall from grace. A step up, perhaps, from the necropolis that was Las Villas, but a plummet nonetheless. She had made it home, but this wasn't the home she had dreamed about singing "Daylight come and me wan' go home..." along with Belafonte.

Alice returned from the kitchen bearing the traditional Midwestern welcome for guests: a plate of cookies (purchased, not made from scratch) and a pot of coffee on a green fiberglass tray. We chitchatted a bit about the trip, but my mother and I were so enervated from the day's 500-plus miles–from the whole journey, with all its lunatic vicissitudes–that she started to grow irritable, grouchy, interrupting even more rudely than usual in the middle of an anecdote I was telling Alice. "I want to go to bed," she shrieked.

The way she said it, by her angry tone of voice, I came face to face with the fact that this arrangement might not work out. I was beat, a mere two days sober after a year-long bacchanal, and I didn't know if I had the stamina to oversee this transition, whatever its outcome.

I picked myself up off the couch and went outside and brought in her luggage. Alice was looking with an expression of deepening concern at my mother, whose head was slumped on her chest. My aunt had not grasped the severity of her sister's condition when she signed on, and worry corrugated the corners of her mouth. My mother had fixated on the fantasy of leaving Las Villas and Alice had concomitantly fixated on a fantasy of additional income. The reality of their cohabitation had never been thought out.

I dropped the two suitcases to the floor. The luggage alone seemed to crowd the little living room. "Okay, Alice, how about I take you through the routine?"

"Okay," she said gamely, rising to her feet. She had had many part-time jobs in her life of mounting debt, and she embarked on this one as on any other: learn the ropes. But now she was in her late sixties, and my mother's needs must have seemed daunting. She was likely thinking what many thought, that my mother should be in full convalescence. Except someone would have to drag her kicking and screaming. And that someone was me.

"Show me the bedroom," I said, reaching for that upbeat tone I was decidedly not feeling.

Alice led me to what had substituted for a guest room—or sewing room, or TV room, it was hard to tell. She had it made up nicely for my mother's arrival, thoughtfully adding the flourish of a vase of flowers on the night-stand. But the queen bed filled nearly all the postage stamp-sized floor space; there was no way the wheelchair would fit between the dresser and the bed for transfers. As Alice watched, I pushed the bed against the far wall, clearing enough space for my mother's bulky chair.

Before I wheeled her in I went to check the bathroom. To my utter dismay, I would be able to maneuver my mother in, barely, but the cramped space made it nearly impossible to reposition the chair and shift her side-saddle onto the toilet. *I* would be able to pull off the transfer, standing her up, pivoting her, and sitting her down, but Alice would have trouble, especially given the number of times she would probably be required to get up in the middle of the night before we could customize the bedroom with wall mounts and a portable toilet.

Naturally enough, my mother desperately needed to go. As Alice watched me execute the maneuver, her consternation visibly mounted. Fearing mutiny, I knew then and there that I would be staying much longer than I had planned.

Sitting on the edge of the bed, my mother holding a cup of water, I administered her meds. I explained each to Alice and told her I would write down how often it was to be taken. She listened carefully, but she kept compulsively dry-rubbing her hands as if she were about to leap out of her skin. Maybe my own anxiety disorder was genetic.

Finally medicated–the application of the nitro patch gave Alice another start!–and tucked in, she looked up at me and said with a chuckle, "Give me a kiss good-night."

I turned to Alice and said, "She always asks for a kiss good-night"–I returned my gaze to my mother–"but she knows we don't do that, do we, Mom?"

"No," she spoke with the voice of a child, "but I can ask."

I resorted to what had become my standard consolation move, grabbing her right hand in both of mine and giving it a squeeze. "You're home, Mom," I said. "You're home."

"I know. I wish Snapper was here." She lapsed into tears.

"Don't cry, Mom."

"I won't."

"You know what happens to big girls who cry, don't you?"

"They go back to Las Villas," she answered, per the badinage struck up in our journey.

"Or state convalescence. And you don't want to go there."

"Oh, no. I'll be a big girl, I promise."

"You don't have to worry, Mom, I'm going to stay the night. Okay?"

"Oh, that's such good news."

Alice, blinking back apprehension, met my eyes.

Back in the living room, I explained that we were going to have to do some customized adjustments to her house, but reassured her I would stay on as long as she needed.

"Okay," she said uneasily.

"And if it doesn't work," I said, "if you find it's too taxing, I'll find her a home."

"I'll try my best," she said, adopting a brave stance. "She's my Phyllis."

Alice made up the couch for me. She handed me the remote, but there really was no need to since she couldn't afford cable and only received low-band channels. This was going to be another problem for my mother, I realized; she loved her cable TV and its cornucopia of mind-corrupting channels.

After Alice had gone to bed I phoned Jack. The background noise made it evident he was in a bar.

"We made it," I said.

"What?"

"We made it. We're in Sheboygan."

"All right. I knew you had it in you, short horn." He sounded loud and boozy, dragging frequently on a cigarette. I didn't feel like narrating the ordeal of the last three days and imprinting it on his mind as I would normally be wont to do. Numbed by the alcohol, he wouldn't get it. He'd try to make jokes. And I was in no mood for humor.

"Anyway, I'll let you get back to your fun."

"How's the little critter Snapper?"

"They amputated his leg."

"Shit, man, why didn't you just put him down?"

"My mother."

"Thank God mine did a face-plant with a coronary."

"I'm tired, Jack. I just wanted to call and let you know that we made it safe."

"Excellent," he boomed.

"Yeah, excellent," I muttered.

It was another night of wrecked sleep, taking me in and out of dreams whose leitmotifs were loneliness, failure, desolation, madness and death. Twice my mother called out my name; both times I woke with a start and helped her toilet herself. The second time, Alice was roused and stood in the bathroom doorway in her nightgown, watching the routine with a frank mix of determination and despair.

"Once we get wall grips mounted and a portable toilet, you won't have to worry about this," I said.

The morning dawned a sparkling blue. Alice's weak Folger's did little to overcome my exhaustion. With Alice attempting to lend a hand, I got my mother up and out of bed, but bathing her in the small tub was a chore. We had to seat her on the edge of the tub and scrub her, then towel her down. Alice was going to have to improvise to make this work, and her disheartened look inspired little faith in her faculties of invention.

Worse, my mother had already taken to ordering her around as if she were
the help at Las Villas, not her sister and fellow elderly widow. If not for
the thousand a month plus expenses, she would have bailed. On the spot.

After a hearty breakfast of eggs, bacon and toast, I wheeled my mother
outside. Alice watched me reverse-dolly her down the steps, her face still
constricted in an expression of apprehension, a wrinkled hand tenting her
forehead against the slanting sun.

"It's a beautiful morning, isn't it, Mom?"

"Yes," she said, clearly unable to enjoy it with the tension budding in
her sister.

"Alice," I said, "how about you try to take her up these stairs?"

She nodded uneasily and came down, got behind my mother and
grabbed the steering handles of the wheelchair for the first time. Working
in tandem, we backed the wheels up to the first step. I took the reins again
for a moment and said, "It's not that hard. We angle the chair like this"–I
demonstrated–"and then we just come up"–I bounced my mother up the
first step–"one step at a time." I eased my mother back down to the pathway and looked at Alice, complete with a big, enthusiastic smile. "So you
give it a try."

Alice took hold of the handles again and backed my mother up to the
edge of the first step.

"Oh, no," my mother cried out, "I'm going to fall. She can't do it."

I fought to maintain the infinitely patient voice that I had worked hard
to manufacture, but it was at the breaking point. "Mom, she's going to
have to learn to do it until we can build a ramp, okay?"

"Oh, I'm scared," she said.

"Come on, Alice."

Doing as I had demonstrated, Alice angled the chair forty-five degrees.
As she pulled, I pushed and my mother easily went up the first step.

"See, it's not that hard."

Alice didn't look too convinced.

"Now, how about you try it alone? I'll be right here."

"I'm scared," my mother interjected, which only exacerbated her sister's
visible anxiety.

"Mom," I said, squatting to be at eye-level with her. "I'm here, okay.
I've got you."

"Okay," she said.

Alice again levered my mother to the forty-five degree angle. Not quite in possession of all my faculties, I failed to see, until a few seconds late, that once she rocked my mother up to the second step Alice would have to jump backward to the porch so there would be room for the chair. She managed to get the chair up to the second step, but she stumbled in the leap back and lost her grip on the handlebars. My mother hurtled toward me and I barely caught the armrests before what would have been a violent collision. It took only a moment to right her, but had I not been there she would have been pitched forward out of the chair and crash-landed on the cement pathway with God knows what injury, fractured hip being the worst imaginable for someone her age and in her condition. If this was going to work, we would need a Plan B.

I dollied my mother back into the safety of the small house. Alice sat down on the couch next to her, exhausted, out of breath. I remained standing.

"I'm going to get a ramp built, so you can bypass the steps," I said. "But first, I'm going to find a medical supply store and take care of this situation in the bedroom." I continued addressing her twin expressions of shock and dismay. "Alice, do you know someone who does handyman work, someone who could build a ramp from the walk to the porch?" I gestured to the front door, as if Alice had lost her focus. "And maybe take out that molding so the chair fits through?"

She nodded, all but catatonically. "Yes, I know a fellow who…"

"Could you call him and see if he can come over? Today?"

"Okay," she replied absently.

I was tempted to snap my fingers in her face to bring her back into the now, but stopped myself from treating Alice the way her big sister did. Instead, I directed my attention at my equally nonplused mother. "Mom, I'm going to go see to these errands."

At the mention of my leaving, she snapped out of her trance. "Oh, don't go," she said.

"I'm only going to be gone a couple hours, okay?"

"Oh, please don't go," she pleaded.

"I have to. We have to get this place outfitted for you, okay?"

"Okay," she said, surrendering to the inevitable.

I turned to Alice, "I'll be back shortly." I patted her on the shoulder. "This is going to work. Don't worry." She nodded. "There's a routine, and once you get it down, my mother's easy to get along with."

She wouldn't meet my eyes. The stoic Czech in her was trying to buck up, but the realist was foundering her resolve. Miles the glass half empty had suddenly become Miles the motivator. Not a role I had ever envisioned. I was playing it for my mother. This was her last stop.

In Sioux Falls I had used the Internet to locate lodging as close to Alice's house as I could find. The best prospect was the Sheboygan Hotel, which turned out to be a cheerless, four-story cinderblock structure offering all of the conveniences of a generic hotel, but little else.

I checked in and carried my bags up to my room. I lay on the bed, fatigued, and closed my eyes. I wanted to sleep. I wanted a drink. I wanted this whole nightmare to disappear. But every time I opened my eyes it was still there, staring me implacably in the face. Maybe it would be better just to resign myself to the fact that Alice, however well meaning, was never going to be able to take care of her invalid sister, and find another assisted-living facility. But the thought of researching homes in the area, taking my mother around, having her be interviewed and assayed, poked and prodded like a piece of meat, was even more dispiriting than the prospect of what it would take to make Alice and her tiny house work. If worst came to worst, I thought, a flare going off in my head, I'd find a full-time Joy to help out Alice and just bite the bullet on the bill. For a giddy moment I even thought about calling Joy, but when I imagined my mother and her together I decided it was my perfervid brain speaking.

Panic seized me. I had never been in this helpless position before. I wanted desperately to do the right thing for my mother, and I wanted to honor her wishes to stay out of a home, but I wondered: had we reached our own Rubicon? Had I let her manipulate me into keeping her away from nursing homes and hospitals? She was dragging me down into the quicksand of her infirmity. I was 2,000 miles away from my life. Agents were waiting on me, with patience that would not hold up long. I had no idea what my next book was going to be. Or if I could even turn on the computer and start writing! The blank page—never a problem in the past—was starting to haunt me. Was *Shameless* just a fluky success, my career a one-shot wonder?

I felt overwhelmed. My mother had turned into a great vortex of needs and I had fallen headlong into it.

I took a half a Xanax and pulled myself together. I thumbed through the phone book and found an agency that hired out nurses. They gave me several names with accompanying phone numbers. Next, I located a medical supply store and drove over and purchased a small portable toilet and some wall mounts. The proprietor directed me to a nearby hardware store where I bought a large screwdriver and a hammer.

I returned to Alice's where I found the two ladies sitting together in the living room. Alice was jabbering away when I came in, but my mother wasn't listening to her. I sat down on the sofa. The TV droned in the background. My mother looked depressed; she had lost her recently re-animated personality. She clearly wanted not to give expression to it, but it was evident to me that she was coming to the realization that Las Villas de Muerte wasn't so bad, that and the reality of living with her sister was a far cry from what she had daydreamed.

"Alice, did you get a hold of your handyman?"

"Yes," she said, with affected enthusiasm. "He's coming over this afternoon."

"Good. I've got the names of some in-home-care nurses. They'll come on a part-time basis to help you out. Until we can get the ramp built they'll be able to help you take your sister in and out, okay?"

"Okay."

"I'm going to figure out this bedroom situation." I turned to my mother. "Let's go, Mom."

I wheeled my mother into the bedroom, transferred her out of the chair and onto the bed. Then I angled her bed as they'd had it at Las Villas. I had her raise her limp arm to the level on the wall where the hand grip should go. I tapped for a stud and mounted the hand grip just within her reach. Next, I went outside and hauled in the portable toilet. I could see Alice's distraught gaze sweep the room as I hauled the box past her.

She watched from the bedroom door as my mother practiced getting up out of the bed and onto the toilet, using the wall grip.

"It's just like Las Villas, Mom," I said, hearing myself sound like a high school baseball coach.

"I'm scared," she said, reaching up tentatively. After several unsuccessful attempts she finally managed it. I had her practice it several times before I could be confident she could do it without supervision.

"You got it now, you think, Mom?"

"I think so," she said, a quaver in her voice betraying acute nervousness over the prospect of self-toileting, without me or the stout nurses at Las Villas, winding up on the floor, crying out in the night. "I'll try," she said, focusing intently on the wall mount, her voice already steadying. She threw me a sideways glance and a wry smile.

"You can do it, Mom. You can do it for me."

With great resolve, and the fear of another Las Villas in her eyes, she performed the maneuver unerringly and I found myself clapping.

"That's great, Mom."

She smiled like a kid who had just won the 4-H ribbon for her prized pig. Alice, looking on, wore a sour expression, as if she had just witnessed her retirement in miniature.

Undaunted, I transferred my mother back into her chair and wheeled her back to the living room. Alice was in the kitchen, preparing sandwiches. She brought out a plate for my mother: baloney, white bread, and potato chips. I declined the lunch, stopping instead at a burger joint on my way back to the motel, where I was hoping to buy some sleep before the handyman showed.

I lay once again on the bed, shut my eyes and tried to nap. The gossiping voices of the maids in the hall seeped into the room. Early afternoon traffic rumbled outside. If I didn't sleep, I was hellbound for a stress-induced breakdown. But my mother and Alice still needed me, so the breakdown would have to wait.

Abandoning hope of a nap, I phoned two of the numbers the agency had provided for in-home caretakers. The first shunted me to voicemail. The second was answered by a middle-aged woman with a husky voice. Greta, per the info I had scrawled on the hotel notepad. She agreed to swing by the Sheboygan Hotel for a chat. If that went even half well, I'd take her right to Alice's and introduce her to the Golden Girls.

Greta showed–thank you, wrecked economy!–right on time. A heavyset woman of Germanic looks that went with her name, she was dressed plainly in slacks and a blouse. She had grown up in Sheboygan, she told me, had worked for all the hospitals in the area and was semi-retired. She seemed qualified, and wasn't in a hurry to be anywhere, so we caravanned to Alice's.

When we pulled up in front of the house, Greta's Ford Escort swinging in right behind me, the handyman was applying a cloth tape measure to the steps. Alice was looking down from the doorway, these retrofits to her house not something she had bargained for in agreeing to take over the care of her sister.

The handyman, Dave–a beer-bellied guy with a graying pate–and I exchanged introductions. "It shouldn't be too severe an angle," I noted, "so Alice can push her up and down without any trouble."

"Won't be a problem," Dave said, lighting a cigarette.

"What do you estimate?"

He pulled out a pencil and a pocket spiral notebook, wrote down some numbers and did the arithmetic. "Maybe like five or six hundred."

"Deal," I said. "When can you get started?"

He thumbed through the grease- and paint-stained pages of his appointment book. "I could start next Monday," he said.

"Not sooner?"

"Afraid I'm booked up. Fall's coming," he explained.

I gestured to my mother. "Dave, we have a situation here. It's important that this happen now. I'm willing to make it worth your while. I mean, come on, how many hours will it take you to build a handicapped ramp?"

Dave cleared his throat. "Well, maybe I could move one of these roofing jobs..."

"Great," I said, chopping him off. "See you tomorrow?"

"All right," Dave said, a little bamboozled, but counting dollars in his head.

We shook hands and he walked back to his mud-spattered white van and clattered off.

I led Greta up into the living room and introduced her and my mother.

"Nice to meet you, Mrs. Raymond," Greta said, bending at the waist to my mother's level and extending her hand. My mother took Greta's hand, shook it briefly, and smiled. Circumspect with strangers, as had always been her way, she said nothing.

Alice reappeared from the kitchen with a pot of her coffee and a plate of cookies, looking more than a little relieved that reinforcements had been called in. We all sat and talked, but I was soon impatient to leave. My mother seemed to be reassured by Greta's credentials, but I saw Alice looking around at her tiny house, in which she had everything in order, and foresaw it being reluctantly transformed and claustrophobically

crowded by my mother's enormous needs and the infrastructure that
threatened to crop up willy-nilly around her.

"Could you start today, Greta?" I asked. "I'm going to make a stop at
the bank, and we might as well start your salary right now."

I don't know if she interpreted my over-eagerness as desperation, but
her expression made it clear she had things other than work on her mind.
However, she agreed to stay the afternoon and make sure my mother got
to bed okay.

I led her into the bedroom with my mother and showed her the ropes.
For Greta, stronger than Alice and a decade younger, the transfers were
relatively easy-once my mother got over her insecurities about having a
new person minister to her.

I left the three women to get acquainted and drove back to the motel.

Another half a Xanax knocked me out cold and bought me four or five
jagged hours of sleep. I might have gone all night but for the ringing of
my cell. It was, as I expected–not Laura, not Natalie, not Jack–my mother.

"Hi, Miles," she said.

"Hi, Mom."

"I just wanted to thank you for everything you're doing for me."

"How's Greta working out?"

"She's good, I think," she said, sounding upbeat.

"That's good."

"I just wanted to say good night."

"Good-night, Mom."

"I love you."

"Good-night, Mom."

chapter 19

The next morning dawned gray and breezy as if an early fall storm were approaching from across the lake. I braved breakfast at a dingy coffee shop and drove over to Alice's. Alice answered the door, and it was abundantly clear from her haggard appearance she hadn't slept much. She looked greatly relieved to see me.

In the living room my mother sat in her wheelchair looking sad and sluggish, as if she, too, had endured a particularly rough night. From the greasy, matted texture of her hair I inferred that Alice hadn't managed to bathe her.

"Phyllis fell last night when she tried to go to the bathroom," Alice said.

"Oh, no," I said. "Were you hurt, Mom?"

She shook her head, but her expression betrayed a tension that was brewing between her and her sister.

"It was difficult to get her back into bed," Alice said in an excitable tone, "but I managed."

I glanced at my watch and asked, more to myself, "Where's Greta?"

They both looked at each other and shrugged.

"It's ten o'clock. She should be here by now." I got out my iPhone, found Greta's number in my contacts and tapped it.

She answered on the fourth ring. In a speciously apologetic tone she said that she couldn't work for my mother, adding only, "She doesn't like me."

"You can't do a couple of days?" I pleaded, "Just until I can get someone full time."

"She should be in a home," Greta said sharply, and brusquely concluded the call, leaving me feeling shitty.

Both my mother and Alice took note of my heavy sigh, the load of our mutual problem compounded now.

"Can you take me for a drive?" my mother asked.

"Sure. Let's give Alice a break."

I dollied my mother down the steps, soon with a bit of luck to be a ramp, and steered her to the dirt-streaked Rampvan, which I had been hoping to unload, as it was costing me a fortune. "Where do you want to go, Mom?" I asked, after I had gotten her up into shotgun.

"I'll take you around to all my old haunts," she said sweetly.

"Okay, Mom. Let's do that." I felt acutely sorry for her that it wasn't working out like we had fantasized.

Her memory of Sheboygan was startling, almost crystalline in its recall. She directed me to the small downtown where she once hung out and smoked cigarettes and flirted with the boys, she told me, a vestige of the hometown coquette twinkling in her milky blue eyes. We drove slowly by a brown concrete department store called Prange's. "And I used to work there when I was in high school," she recalled.

"Oh, yeah. I want to see the tavern your parents owned."

"Okay. I'm not sure it's there anymore," she said wistfully.

She directed me away from downtown, drawing deeply from the recesses of her memory the directions. Next to a small business park we found a white, two-story clapboard A-frame with a faded green awning. Printed on the awning in elaborate script was "Grey Gables." Jutting out from the second floor was an old neon Schlitz sign. Above three canopied windows, in more neon lettering, the name of the tavern appeared again.

I parked out front and tried the door. The place was shuttered. The breeze had picked up and the tattered awning flapped like a pennant in a buffeting wind. I returned to the Rampvan and stood next to the open passenger window where my mother gazed out at the place her parents once owned.

"A lot of memories there, I'll bet, huh?"

"Oh, yes," my mother said, staring at it through watery eyes. "We had a big chicken dinner every Sunday that my mother would cook and every-one"–her voice soared rhapsodically to a singsong–"came from all over."

"Sounds like quite a time."

"And my dad would get horribly drunk. Then beat my mother." A scowl disorganized her face and she shook her head to ward off the memory.

"Good *and* bad memories, huh?"

"Oh, yes," she said. She pointed her index finger at the sky and shook it at some invisible ogre. "He was a mean man."

I circled round the front of the car and got back in. "Where would you like to go now, Mom?"

"Let's go to the quarry," she said.

"Do you know how to get there?"

She nodded confidently.

"What happened with Greta?" I said as I started up the Rampvan and followed her amazingly accurate directions to the quarry.

"She's no good," my mother said sharply. There was a pause, then she said, "No one takes care of me like you," she sniffled.

"I can't stay here, Mom. My life isn't here."

"I know," she said, resignation in her voice.

"You can't alienate these people like Joy. I don't know if Alice can take care of you all by herself or not."

"I'm such a burden."

We crossed the Sheboygan River and, following my mother's directions, as if she had a roadmap indelibly imprinted on her memory, mirac-ulously, I got us to the quarry.

I got her out of the passenger seat and pushed her close to the rim, looking out over the huge rectangular pit, as deep as it was wide. While I saw just stone and dirt my mother traveled back in time and witnessed a part of her childhood, perhaps some of her happiest times.

"This used to be filled with water," she said. "We would swim in there."

"Were you a good swimmer?"

"Oh, yes," she said.

We sat in silence, looking. The freshening wind rustled the brittle dead leaves still in the trees.

"I can feel fall," she said, shivering histrionically. "Brrr."

REX PICKETT

370

"It's coming early."

"Oh, yes," she said.

"Hey, Mom, I had a wild idea."

"What?"

"You want to go play nine holes of golf? I think I can get you into the cart. There's this great course just up the lake."

"Oh, that would be heaven," she enthused. "I want to get out of the car. I don't want to sit in some restaurant."

"Okay, let's do it."

We drove a few miles north of Sheboygan to Whistling Straits, an extraordinary tract that has hosted two PGA Championships. It's nestled along two miles of a bluff on the Lake Michigan shoreline. Not technically a links course, it has very much a linksland feel. It's got a rugged, almost ragged, windswept look, with nearly a thousand (!) bunkers and waste areas. There are almost no trees. Whistling Straits is composed of wild native grasses, mounds and knolls and radically sloping greens slippery as ice.

It was mid-week and off-season, so it wasn't difficult to get on. I didn't have my clubs so I had to rent a set. The course manager, when I explained the situation about my mother, was kind enough to assist me in transferring her into our cart. It wasn't easy. But once we got her in, her face lit up. She'd been quite the athlete in her youth and fiercely competitive. In college, she was the number one ranked player on the woman's golf team. She might even have been able to go pro. She gave it up to raise a family. When I was about nine my parents joined a modest country club. My father played, but it was my mother who took me to the course almost every day after school. I got involved in junior golf and enjoyed a bit of success. But at 14, called by the ocean and the lure of surfing, I gave it all up. I didn't touch a club for twenty years. It wasn't until Victoria and I divorced that I rediscovered the game. It was one of the only ways I had of dealing with my depression.

We rolled up to the first tee and I set the brake on the cart. The first hole was a stunning par-four. I corkscrewed out of the cart, pulled my rental driver, unsleeved a new ball and jammed a bunch of tees into my pocket.

"Are you going to play the back tees?" my mother called out.

"I don't know, Mom. This course is rated 76.7 from the tips. I've never played a course this hard."

"Play it from the tips," she urged. "What have you got to lose?"

I chuckled. When I was young she always pushed me to play from the back tees. In junior golf she would petition the organizers to move me up to the higher age divisions, so I'd face stiffer competition and become a better player. "Okay, Mom, I'm going to play it from the tips. Just for you. How're you doing over there? Are you cold?" The wind was freshening off the lake. It was mid-afternoon and the sun was arcing away.

"No! I'm fine. Let's go. I want to see you hit one."

I teed up a Titleist, took a few practice swings, as was my routine, and then addressed the ball. Shockingly, I flushed one about 260 yards down the left side of the fairway.

My mother clapped. "Nice shot, Miles."

"That'll probably be the last one you see from me today."

"Oh, no," she said. "You've still got a good swing."

We played on. With the rental clubs and the fact I hadn't played much in the last year, my game was rusty. The extreme difficulty of the course—especially from the pro tees—and the wind that was now buffeting off Lake Michigan didn't make things any easier. But that didn't diminish my enjoyment. Not only my enjoyment in playing a little golf, but in seeing how happy my mother was to be out there, on this gorgeous course, watching me play a game she loved.

As we rode in the cart we reminisced. "Remember that time you were twelve and you shot 75 and won the Stardust Invitational?" my mother said.

"Wow, your memory's amazing. Day to day, moment to moment, you're like some Alzheimer's person, but your faraway memory is incredible."

"That was a great day," she said. "I was so proud of you."

"It was probably the highlight of my life winning that 13-14 age division as a 12-year-old."

"Oh, no," she said. "You have more highlights."

"I don't know," I said, feeling drained, the trip having emptied me of so much.

"You could have gone pro," my mother blustered.

"I didn't have the patience for it," I said. "All the practice. You know...."

"You could have won the U.S. Open!"

"Oh, I seriously doubt that," I said.

"Why'd you quit?" she said. "You were so talented."

"The kids in the neighborhood thought I was gay." Our family was the only one in the neighborhood that belonged to a country club and playing golf was considered sissy.

"Oh, no," she said. "Those kids were so mean. I tried to get Rusty to move to La Jolla, but he was so cheap." She started to tear up. "Our lives would have been so different."

"Don't cry, Mom."

She crooked her finger at the sky. "I was born here," she said. "No one would have ever thought there'd be such a beautiful golf course like this some day." She nodded in reflection. "Oh, I wish I could play," she lamented. "I wish I could get up from that damn wheelchair and walk again!"

I slung my arm around her shoulder. "Are you cold, Mom? Do you want to go back in?" We had made it to the seventh hole, a staggeringly beautiful par-three, dubbed Shipwreck, that required a shot across a little inlet of the lake to a green that was perched right on the edge of the water. An errant shot, right or left, and you were poleaxed. Waves lashed the cliffs. The wind bent the pin sideways. There were no houses, no cookie-cutter condos, just pure, pristine golf.

"Oh, no," she said. "I don't want to go back. I'm having the best time of my life!"

"All right," I said, climbing out of the cart. I checked the yardage on my scorecard. 214 from the black tees. Christ! This was a full-on twenty-degree hybrid for me. I teed up one of the last of my dozen balls—as I had already lost plenty in the deep fescue—and took my customary practice swings.

I glanced over at my mother to make sure she was watching. She bent her right arm into an L-shape and punched her elbow into the side of her body. "Keep your right arm close to your body on the downswing. You've been coming over the top. That's why you've been slicing it all day." She chicken-winged her arm to demonstrate exactly what I was doing wrong.

"Okay, Mom," I said, chuckling. She had been my only swing coach; a damn fine one, too.

"And play for the wind," she continued advising. "Aim fifteen yards right of the hole."

"Mom, you're giving me paralysis by analysis," I joked.

She laughed at the old golfing adage she'd quoted to me countless times.

I took a few more practice swings, rehearsing what she had advised. Then I found my target just as she recommended: right of the hole so that the shot, if I pulled it off, could ride the wind toward the pin. "Okay, Mom, here we go. If I hit this green, I'm going to try to qualify for the Champions Tour," I blustered.

"You can do it," she encouraged. "I've seen you."

I took one more practice swing, set up over the ball, then hit the shot. When you really pure a shot you know it the moment the club strikes the ball. You can't even feel it on the clubface. It's like butter. It was. When I finally looked up, the ball had started out over Lake Michigan, but it was turning with just a slight draw, the way great pros like to shape it. As it arced, the wind caught it and started pushing it inexorably toward the pin. I must have pulled the perfect club because the ball landed on the green, took a few hops and rolled to within ten feet of the hole.

"Great shot, Miles," my mother exclaimed.

I stuck my club back in the bag, with triumphant force this time, and clambered back into the cart. "God, I hit that one good, Mom," I gloated, feeling strangely ecstatic.

"Oh, yes," she said. "See, you just have to listen to me."

"I haven't been listening to you for a long time, have I?" I said, waxing emotional.

"No," she said.

"But I've been listening lately. I got you to Wisconsin."

"I know," she said. "That must have been hard. Especially when Joy left us."

"It wasn't easy."

"And all your damn wine! I was worried."

"Well...."

"When're you going to get married again, Miles? You need a woman in your life."

"You're her, Mom."

"I won't be around much longer." She smiled, and raised her good hand to still my rising protest. "You know Rusty thought you might be homo when you started writing poetry."

"Oh, yeah? That's news. Well, I have nothing against gay folks. Half my agents have been gay. But I'm not. I love women."

"You don't have to tell me. What about that Spanish girl, Laura? She's pretty. Why don't you marry her?"

"Well, it might be wise to do a little dating first. Plus, she lives in Spain, and that's a long way to come visit you." I patted her on the thigh.

She gave me a withering look.

"And you know I have flying issues."

"Oh, for God's sake, Miles, stop being so neurotic," she blared. She wagged her finger admonishingly at me. "Get on a damn plane and go live your life!"

I turned and looked at her. I felt as if I'd run into a lamp post.

She bent her face toward mine. "Get on a damn plane and go buy that girl some flowers. They've got that street in Barcelona that's nothing but florists' little stalls."

"You've been to Barcelona?"

"Yes," she barked. "I've been all over the world." She gave me that withering look again. "Live your life. You're such a stick-in-the-mud with all your damn problems."

I looked into her sad, but defiant face. It occurred to me that she had been thinking this about me all along and now suddenly it all came exploding out of her. As if this were her last chance to be a real mother to her son. "You're right, Mom. I'm afflicted with too many neuroses."

"Live your life," she repeated. "It doesn't last forever."

Her words had a weirdly galvanizing effect on me I couldn't quite pinpoint. Or didn't want to.

We rolled off toward the green where I was hoping to make my first birdie of the day.

"Oh, this is such a beautiful place," she said, casting her gaze out over windswept Lake Michigan, which was now specked with whitecaps. "This is truly heaven."

We finished out the nine holes, my dozen balls now history in the dunes and grasses and water, but I didn't care. Playing golf, especially on tracts like this, always elevated me out of myself and made me oblivious of all the travails of my life. And to see my mother so happy for once, so exultant in the freedom that being out on a course like this evokes, lifted me out of my solemn mood.

It was growing cold as the sun dipped in the west and the lake colored gray. We carted back to the clubhouse. The course manager helped me transfer my mom back into her chair.

"Did you have a nice time, Mrs. Raymond?" he asked.

"Oh, yes," she said. "I wished I could have played. I once got second in the NCAA. I qualified for the U.S. Amateur three times."

"You did?" he asked, sounding surprised.

"Trust me. She had serious game," I explained. "She taught me everything I know about the game."

"Well, I'm glad you both got a chance to play Whistling Straits. Come back again and play all eighteen."

"We will," I promised as I rolled my mother to the lot where our car was parked.

Back in the car, I said, "Do you want to get something to eat? You must be starving."

"Oh, yes."

"Do you know a place?"

The hot dog stand my mother remembered on the shores of Lake Michigan was no longer extant, but we found a place called the Blue Lake Resort, a grand white manse built in the early '90s, now beautifully restored and operating as a resort for estivating Midwesterners. We were seated out on a patio with a panoramic view of the lake. The sky was sealed off by dark clouds and the water was a slate gray as far as the eye could see. The wind that appeared to herald an approaching storm while we were playing had kicked up the whitecaps with greater ferocity, transforming the lake into a churning sea of white.

We ordered seafood salads. I stayed with the mineral water while I allowed my mother one glass of Chardonnay. For a moment she was back in heaven, the wine affording her that ephemeral lift that, in her words, made her "fly with the angels."

"Once, Rusty flew me across the lake right into a storm. It was so dangerous."

"I remember," I said, flashing back to that image of my father as a young USAF pilot.

"We could have been killed." Tears leached from her eyes. "He was a good pilot, though. We made it."

"How're you feeling, Mom?"

"Pretty well."

"Did you have a good time today?"

"Oh, yes. It was the best day of my life."

"I'm glad. Do you think it's going to work out at your sister's?"

"I hope so." Her eyes squinted almost shut. "I don't want to go to the poor house."

"I'm going to try to get someone else to help out. We'll find someone. We'll make this work."

We rode back to Alice's in an introspective, clock-ticking silence. It looked to have been a splendid afternoon for my mother, revisiting a few of her old haunts, the flood of mostly fond memories revivifying her downcast spirit.

Alice, seeming to have sensed our worry, was busy preparing a pot roast with all the trimmings–food being her ameliorant for everything. I excused myself and went out and bought a bottle of over-oaked Chardonnay I knew my mother would like.

We ate in the living room. My mother and Alice reminisced about their past growing up in Sheboygan, traded stories about friends and relatives and boyfriends, both a little giddy on wine and the glow that came from sharing memories. Soon, my mother was sleepy.

As Alice looked on, still a bit timid, I administered the medications, then got my mother to bed. I eased onto the mattress and said, "You're not going to fall tonight, are you?"

"Oh, no. I was nervous last night," she said.

"Okay, good. Because I'm not going to stay here. You have to learn to live with Alice."

"I know."

Alice had drifted out. A moment later we heard running water issuing from the kitchen.

"But she's not as good as you are," my mother said confidentially.

"I have a life back in LA, Mom. People finally want to pay me to write screenplays and novels and TV shows. This is my time. I have to capitalize on it or *I'm* going to be in the poor house with you."

"Oh no," she laughed. Tears sprang suddenly to her eyes. "You've been so good to me."

"Don't cry."

"I won't."

"Give me a kiss good-night."

I rose from the bed. "Okay, Mom. Good-night."

"Oh, please."

"I'll see you tomorrow. Be a good girl, or we're going to have to take you out back and shoot you."

She chuckled uneasily. "Miles?"

"What now?"

"Could you call and check on Snapper? See how he's doing?"

"Okay. I promise. But, Mom, you're going to have to start accepting the fact that Snapper, if he pulls through, is not going to be with you anymore."

"I know," she said, resigned. "But, I'd like to know how he's doing."

"Okay."

On the way to the hotel I checked messages. The second in-home caretaker prospect had returned my call, saying she was interested in the job. My spirits were buoyed, at least briefly. I kept intoning in my head: this is going to be a process.

chapter **20**

It was another night of disquieting sleep. I called Alice first thing. She said that her sister had managed to toilet herself, but that bathing her was still difficult. I promised to come over and advise her on what she could to do to improve her performance.

I endured another dreadful breakfast at the same coffee shop because I was too mentally fried to figure out something new. Over runny eggs I called the Lakeview Veterinary Hospital. The receptionist directed my call to Dr. Ariel. She came on, sounding surprisingly chipper.

"So, what's the status on Snapper?" I asked.

"We took the leg off and... he's doing well."

"He's alive?" I said, hoping my surprise would mask my disappointment.

"He's very much alive. In fact, he answers to his name and acts like his old self." She paused. "Do you want him back?"

I sucked in my breath. "If you were going to get a three-legged dog to Wisconsin–and I'm not saying I'm going to–how would you go about it?"

"Get an animal transporter," she said. "Someone who'll accompany the dog on a flight."

"Do you know of such individuals?"

"I could find out."

"And Snapper's..."

"He's fine. He's hopping around like a little bunny rabbit. Unlike humans, he's not bummed out he's missing a leg. He's just thrilled to be alive."

"Great. Okay, let me get back to you, Doctor."

I dropped my hand with the phone to the bed. Maybe Snapper's return would perk up my mother's spirits, take her mind off the new, compromised, circumstances. Animal transporter! Christ. This was turning into one expensive hegira.

I autodialed Jack. He was asleep when he answered. "Jack?"

"That's me."

"Miles. I've got a job for you."

"More chocolate?"

I laughed. "No. Hey, you like to fly. Would you be willing to wing it up to the upper Central Valley, rent a car, pick up Snapper from the vet, then fly out here to Wisconsin?"

It took him a moment to wake up and process this seeming harebrained proposal. "What?"

"We amputated the leg. He's doing great. I think it would go a long way toward improving my mom's mood if we reunited the two."

"Have you lost your mind? I hate that little fucker. I'm not going to get on a plane with him."

"Jack. What'd I pay you for this trip? Ten grand, right? And I cut you loose halfway in. You owe me, big guy. Snapper'll be in one of those carriers. Grin and bear it."

"Fuck, man."

"I heard three-legged dogs are chick magnets."

"Really?"

"According to Dr. Ariel."

"Hmm. Interesting."

"Okay. That's settled. I'll make the arrangements and call back with your marching orders."

"Hey, wait a sec..."

"Jack, I'll see you tomorrow. With Snapper."

With a flurry of keystrokes I had Jack on an early morning flight to Sacramento, a rental to take him up to Clearlake, and on a flight to Milwaukee by noon, and another rental to Sheboygan. I put it all in an e-mail and exhorted him: "Don't disappoint me."

I called Dr. Ariel and told her to expect Jack. She seemed a little saddened by the news.

"I was getting attached to him," she said.

"Well, be a professional. Buck up."

She laughed. "I think it's a great thing what you're doing for your mother."

"Yeah, yeah."

After breakfast I drove over to Alice's to check on the two of them. The pall was undiminished, so I took my mother out for a drive. We went to the same restaurant on the water and she ordered the same entrée and the same glass of wine. Amidst meaningless chitchat, she admitted living with her sister was an adjustment, but she was trying, she would do it for me. I purposely didn't tell her about the arrangements to bring Snapper out, hoping the surprise–and the companionship–would further her resolve to make it work with her sister.

Dave the handyman made progress on the handicapped ramp. I don't know if my presence galvanized him or not, but he seemed to work with a fervor one didn't find in LA.

I traded calls with Jack all the next day, charting his progress. It proved to be a mad dash from Clearlake back to Sacramento, but he made the flight, Snapper cozy in his cage, albeit sans a leg.

I met with the second in-home caretaker prospect. She was an elderly woman, wheezing on mentholated cigarettes. I excused her, called the agency again and asked for another referral. Hell, I needed a referral for another agency, the way my luck was going.

Jack and Snapper met me in the lobby of the Sheboygan Hotel. Snapper, curled up in his cage, jumped up and began barking when he saw me. I reached a fist toward the lattice-door enclosure. "Hey there, little guy." I looked up at Jack. "How was he?"

"Fine. I felt a little weird, but, you were right, it's a chick magnet."

"Get some digits?"

"Got some digits." He puffed out his cheeks. "I'm tired, man. It's been a long day."

"I appreciate everything, Jack."

"I need a drink."

"Let's get Snapper to my mom first."

"All right," he groused.

We drove in his rental to Alice's. Outside his rental I released Snapper from the cage. His right hind stump was stapled closed and still healing, but he bounced around on his three good legs with surprising alacrity. I squatted down to be at eye level. "Hey, Snapper."

Snapper came toward me. I held out my hand. He gave it a playful nip, ran five feet in the opposite direction, turned and panted at me.

"Some things never change," Jack laughed.

I straightened to my feet. "Come on, Snapper. Let's go see Mom."

Alice answered the door wearing an apron. The piquant aromas of a meatloaf—my mother's favorite—wafted out from behind her. "Hi," she said.

"Hi, Alice. We've got a little surprise for your sister." I pointed at Snapper.

Alice's expression changed from one of seeming contentment to instant apprehension. "Oh."

"My mom's dog. The one who was in the accident. Trust me. I know he only has three legs, but he'll do a lot to occupy her."

Alice opened the door. My mother was stationed in her chair with a glass of wine, in front of the blaring TV.

"Mom," I said. "We brought you an old friend." I stepped aside to reveal Snapper. "Go get her, Snapper."

My mother almost fainted on the spot. "Snapper," she cooed. "Snapper!"

Instinctively, Snapper ran forward and tried to leap into her lap, but his attempt fell short and he toppled to the ground. He tried again, but he couldn't make it to her lap. I bent down and helped him up and placed him in her lap. My mother started crying. Snapper, clearly recognizing her, licked her face.

"Oh, this is the best surprise ever," my mother said. "This is the best."

Alice came out from the kitchen and forced a smile, hearing my mother exult over Snapper's appearance.

"They had to amputate, Mom. I didn't want to tell you, because I thought it would upset you."

"They amputated a lot of us back in the war," she said.

"The doctor said he should live a normal, healthy life."

"Oh, that's such good news," she said, letting him lick her. She turned back to Snapper. "Oh, Snapper, you're such a bad dog. But I love you so much."

I stood up. "Jack, this is my mom's sister, Alice."

"Hi Alice," Jack said.

"Hi, Jack."

"And, of course, my mother."

"Hi, Phyllis," Jack said.

"Jack's the one who brought him out, Mom."

"Oh, that's so nice of you," she said. "How much did Miles have to pay you?"

"Not enough," Jack said, and everybody laughed.

"Would you like to stay for dinner?" Alice offered.

Jack shot me a look of panic.

"No. Jack's a strict vegan. We'll find a place in town that has soy burgers." My mother smirked at me. "You're not going to get drunk, are you?"

"All right, Mom. Relax. You've both got my cell number. Any problems, call me, okay?"

Jack and I drove to downtown Sheboygan and stopped at a restaurant called the Rathskellar. It was musty inside, the walls cluttered with framed photos of local legends–legends if you knew who won the Wisconsin Polka Fest in '88.

We took stools at the bar. I half expected a guy in lederhosen with an accordion slung over his shoulder to appear and serenade us the place was so anachronistic. Jack ordered a pilsner and I ordered a tonic water. When I said "tonic water," Jack reared back and looked at me. "What's up with that?"

"I'm not drinking."

"What?"

"I sobered up out of Portland. Had to."

Our drinks came and Jack took a healthy quaff off his frosty one. "Is this till you get back, or..."

"I don't know, Jack. I feel better. I can deal with shit. And I've had a lot of shit to deal with since the IPNC."

The bartender placed some menus in front of us. Jack was fiddling with his iPhone, nodding to himself. "Wow, Martin West no longer drinking. I'm calling the trades."

"Bet they don't stop the presses," I said.

He had no response. Without libations as our low common denominator, it was strange how little we had to talk about.

"How's Byron?"

"Good."

"Ever talk to Carmen again?"

"Nah."

"The reality TV thing still happening?"

"Yeah. Goes in a couple months."

"That was one crazy trip, wasn't it?"

"One crazy trip," he echoed. I could tell he was uncomfortable with the fact I wasn't drinking. Maybe my not drinking was an inadvertent judging of his, I don't know.

The bartender returned. "You guys want to order something?"

Jack folded his menu and handed it to the beefy guy. "I'll pass."

"You sure?" I said.

"Yeah," he said. "I think I'm going to drive back to Milwaukee and take this red-eye"–he glanced at his iPhone to double-check the time–"back to LA."

"I got a room for you and everything, Jack," I said.

"I know. I just want to get back. You got your mom and the whole deal at your aunt's and shit..." He brought his mug to his mouth and drained the beer. He put a hand on my shoulder and said, "It's good you quit drinking, man."

We locked eyes briefly, then just nodded at each other. There was nothing left to say. It was as if, without alcohol, we no longer had anything in common. Stop drinking and you lose friends. We were on different wavelengths now. It was sad.

Jack ferried me back to the Sheboygan Hotel. We clasped hands in the peace shake, held them tightly for a moment, then let go.

"Call me when you get back," he said.

"All right. Sure you don't want to crash here?"

"No," he said definitively. "I really want to get back." What he really wanted was to get to the airport bar. Fair enough. He was drinking for two now.

"All right, man. Take it easy."

"You, too."

Watching him drive off I felt eerily like someone had just died.

chapter 21

I was yanked from a deep, disquieting sleep by the ringing of my iPhone. It was a frantic Alice calling, tears hobbling her words: "Your mother's been taken to the hospital. She fell unconscious."

I dragged a hand across my tired face. It was pitch black in the room. A digital clock read 5:11 a.m. "What hospital?"

St. Nicholas was located less than ten minutes from the hotel. Experienced at finding my way to the ICUs, I located my mother fast in one of the curtained bays, lying flat out with a ventilator strapped over her nose and mouth. She appeared to be breathing rhythmically, but of course once they get you into the ICU there is no mercy; their goal is to keep you alive no matter what cost, no matter what suffering, no matter how tragic and doomed the scenario.

I pulled up a fiberglass chair, sat down, finding my mother's hand on the mattress and giving it a squeeze. "Hi, Mom? It's me Miles."

She grew agitated, but her hand squeezed back. An anxious Alice hovered by the curtain, a fretful hand to her mouth.

I rose to speak to her. "What happened?"

"She was trying to go to the bathroom when she fell."

I nodded. "You've talked to the doctors?"

"They're pretty sure it was another stroke."

I looked down at my mother. The poor woman had endured so much—pulmonary embolism, stroke, heart attack, congestive heart failure, and now another stroke. Not to mention raising three obstreperous kids!

A nurse on the graveyard shift slipped into the bay and told us, in a consoling voice, there was no more we could do. She suggested we let my mother rest.

I spent the next two days wandering around Sheboygan with Snapper. And yes, half the women stopped to coo over him and chat me up. It was like walking with a newborn.

Several times I checked in on my mother. She was showing guarded improvement, but she looked bad. Alice fed me dinner both nights. She admitted that she didn't think she could take care of her sister, apologized if she had given me that impression. It was just too hard, she said. We let Dave go. I would have to find a home.

By the third day, after they had stabilized her, she was transferred out of the ICU and into a step-down unit she shared with another woman in traction, both arms and legs in multiple casts, held in place by various ropes and pulleys. My mother, hooked up to a feeding tube, was otherwise off life-support, sentient and aware of her surroundings. Her head listed more than before and the left side of her mouth sagged worse than I remembered. When she spoke it was monosyllabically, in a hoarse voice that seemed to be issuing from a bathysphere. The morphine compounded the already extreme difficulty she experienced in vocalizing her thoughts and moving her one good arm. Her expression was all but affectless.

"How are you, Mom?"

"O-kay," she barely managed.

"You had another minor stroke."

She nodded almost imperceptibly. "It hurts."

"Where?"

"Everywhere."

There was a silence. I held her hand in mine. She stared blankly into space. Her eyes had a kind of forlorn, faraway look, half in the corporeal world, half in the realm of the already dead.

"Do they want to keep me here?" she asked, enunciating painfully.

"For a while. Yes."

Her head lolled in my direction and she did her best to fix her watery eyes on mine. She spoke in a sepulchral voice. "You promised."

Her words nonplused me; no, staggered me. My heart raced wildly.
Despite the effort it clearly required she kept her eyes fiercely locked
on mine. "Miles," she croaked. "You–prom–ised."

"Where do you want to go, Mom?"

"Home." Belafonte's lyric sang in my head.

"Home where?"

Very weakly, she lifted her index finger and suspended it in the air.
"Where everyone is," she said, still disoriented, still with that voice that
suggested she was only half in the world.

"Everyone who?"

Her face grew disorganized as if she couldn't understand that I couldn't
understand. Or, worse, that I was resisting. Her expression suddenly
turned childlike, as if through the shifting clouds of misapprehension she
had spotted a patch of blue. "You know. The family." She nodded to herself with a close-mouthed, self-satisfied smile, content that we, mother
and son, were in unison.

I stared into her nirvanic gaze, focused on some spectral presence only
she could make out. As she stared absently into her private numinous
realm, I saw she had already gone, crossed her own Rubicon. Now, she
was asking me one last favor.

Her eyes floated off. At a shuffling of heels on the linoleum, I turned.
The attending physician, a young woman, sidled over, a clipboard pressed
to her chest. I got up from my chair and we drifted out of earshot of my
mother, who appeared to have been narcotized back asleep anyway.

"What's the extent of the damage, Doctor?"

"We won't know until we get her out of here and into rehab."

"But she's probably lost some more motor control? Her speech is more
aphasic. That much I can tell."

The doctor smiled, mildly impressed that the patient's scruffy-looking
son knew some of the stroke vernacular. "Probably," she said. "She's getting
old." She glanced at the medical history. "I can see she's been through a lot."

"Yes, she has." Tears formed in my eyes and I blinked them back. I
launched into the story. My mother living at home, then put into assisted-
living after a congestive heart failure, being miserable, and how I had
brought her back to live with her sister, and what an insane trip it was,
"And now this."

"I'm sorry," she said, glancing impatiently at her watch, more patients to see, more life-and-death situations to attend to, more grieving families to face with a stoic countenance. "At least she's alive."

"What kind of a life is this?" I said, fastening my eyes on hers. I was hoping she'd have an answer, but none was forthcoming. Certainly not the answer my mother had sought from her son.

"I've got to go," the doctor said, smiling. "Talk to her. That helps." She pivoted in place and walked off.

Between visits to the hospital, I wandered aimlessly around Sheboygan. I'd have taken Snapper, but didn't have the patience or focus for all the passersby who'd buttonhole us on the sidewalks. The storm that had been building had finally arrived to blanket the city with gray, impenetrable skies. Rain intermittently poured from the saturnine heavens. It was growing cold, the early fall portending another punishing winter. There wasn't much to do. Snapper was subdued, as if he sensed the gravity of the situation. Alice was in limbo. Grief and infirmity had arrived at her doorstep and she didn't know what to do. I couldn't leave. My mother's words haunted my every waking moment.

I stopped in from time to time at Alice's, but we had little to talk about except my mother, too gloomy a topic for extended conversation. Alice wondered aloud what would happen when she got out and I said that I didn't know, that I would probably have to put her in a home this time. "The dreaded end of so many lives," I muttered, more to myself than to Alice. It was unfair of me to bring this to her again. Why was I trying to get my mother's sister, no youngster herself, to look at the contemptible way, in this medically aggressive society of ours, we require people to die? I think she was relieved when I said her sister wouldn't be coming back to her place, that that was no longer a tenable option.

My handlers back in LA were understanding, and professed to be eagerly awaiting my return so they could send me on meetings and pimp me out for lush writing assignments. I felt divorced from the whole whirligig—entertainment business, wine world, clawing to get me to this pitch session or that tasting. The exaggerated Hollywood excitement to capitalize on the updraft of this evanescent fame barely registered.

I called Hank and brought him up to date. My older brother kept mostly silent, probably afraid that once our mother was discharged I was going to make a move to dump her on him. First our larcenous younger brother, now me, then him–Mom getting worse at each way station. After reassuring him I would put her in full convalescence if need be, I asked whether he had heard from Doug. In a fusillade of expletives, he said he didn't want to see or hear from "that fucking asshole." No one prepares us for this, I thought, as I let a bitter Hank go, reassuring him that I would take care of everything. My mother's dream of finding a reunited family in the afterlife seemed just that: a dream.

A week after my mother's stroke I found her in the step-down unit with a physical therapist on one of my many visits. They had taken her off the feeding tube and were, all over again, helping her to relearn how to eat. Yogurt dribbled from the left side of her mouth and the PT patiently wiped it up, encouraging her to try again. As my mother tentatively tried to spoon more yogurt into her mouth, I noticed that her coordination wasn't what it had been and she had trouble finding her mouth. More depressing, she appeared listless, torpid to the point of not wanting to soldier on with this wheelchair-bound, nursing home way of life. I couldn't tell whether it was the effects of the latest stroke, or just the fact she'd made clear, emphatically, that first visit: that she had given up on trying, on life.

The PT left us to spend some time together. Before he walked off, he said, "You're doing well, Phyllis. You're going to get back to your old self."

I smiled, but I wanted to smack him.

My mother ignored his encouragement, and stared sullenly into space. Her expression defied such optimism, no doubt an occupational necessity the PT had been trained to manufacture. What was he going to say? You're fucked up and you should be warehoused in a ward for people on the precipice?

My mother wouldn't look in my direction. Rain streaked the windows on the far side of the room. The bed between the window and my mother's was empty. "Where's your roommate, Mom?" I asked. Not that I cared greatly; it was just a way to break the silence.

The answer to my idle question came in a voice so dark and cold and angry it sent shivers up my spine. "She died."

In an effort to brighten the saturnine mood, I said, "They got you off the feeding tube."

My mother went on staring into space, as if any improvement, any exhortation to keep her in the fight, were an insult.

I let a silence ensue. All we could hear was the rain pecking at the window. "Snapper's doing well."

She nodded, as if she no longer cared. "Good."

"He's his old self, eating..."

"I don't care," she chopped me off. "They won't let him in the poor folks' home," she nearly shrieked.

This was a different woman. She had gone to the edge of death and been denied it too many times. We were locked in combat over one thing, and one thing only: her wishes, and my willingness to carry them out.

Still without looking at me, she said, "You promised, Miles." Her head lolled my way, and her voice gained in intensity. "You–prom–ised."

I stared into the dark tunnels of her eyes and swallowed hard. Death without dignity was everywhere in this hospital.

"I'm never going to get out of here," she said bitterly, her words garbled again. She turned back to me and demanded, "Get me out of here."

"Where do you want to go?"

She extended that crooked index finger, barely raising her hand. With an expression that might have seen through all the walls in the universe, she gargled, "Home."

"Home where? Back to Alice's?" I asked, whether in an effort to ground her, or ground myself, I can't say.

She looked confused. She became agitated, vexed by my inability or unwillingness to understand. "No," she said. "Home."

"Away from this misery?"

She nodded imperturbably and her face grew long, sad, the first sign of emotion I had seen in her since she her readmission. "Home." Then, chillingly: "Where my father and mother are. Where Rusty is." With supreme effort she raised her hand higher and pointed the index finger skyward. "You promised."

I made an appointment to see a doctor. My Xanax supply was depleted and, with my mother back in the hospital, I was chronically insomniacal. It was raining hard when I pulled up to the two-story cinderblock medical complex. In a small waiting room with a kindly receptionist manning a switchboard, I filled out my medical history. I had to chuckle to myself when I came to a series of questions regarding my psychological well-being–anxiety (yes); depression (yes); schizophrenia (probably). I lied on the form so as not to alarm the doctor.

A nurse opened a door and led me into a tiny examination room. She weighed me, took my blood pressure, and told me to wait. I asked her what my weight was and was mildly alarmed to find I had gained some fifteen pounds since my last office visit. I was too afraid to inquire about my blood pressure.

The doctor was a genial man in his mid-fifties, with thinning blond hair and a quiet demeanor. He glanced at my answers to the questionnaire, then at the nurse's various measurements and readings. "Your blood pressure's elevated," he said.

"What is it?"

"150 over 98," he said matter-of-factly. "Normally I would recommend putting you on high blood pressure medication."

I related in my most concise story-telling mode, as if I were pitching a movie idea to a bored and jaded studio executive, what I had been through with my mother, what had stranded me in Sheboygan, postulating that this could be the cause of my elevated blood pressure.

"So, what's the reason for your visit?" he asked.

I filled him in on my history of panic and anxiety, ending with, "I need a refill on my Xanax prescription. And," I added, "I'd like to get a sleeping aid." I looked him in the eye. "And none of this Ambien or Lunestra housewife crap. They don't work for me. I need something strong. Something that will knock me out. I haven't slept in days. I'm going to go mad if I don't get a decent night's rest."

He returned my stare. I hung my head, feigning–well, not really–fatigue.

And for some reason, the weight of everything unloaded: the emotional journey with my mother, the flukish success of the movie based on my book, my downward spiral into an ongoing, wanton bacchanal, going cold turkey and seeing the world in the raw light of sobriety. I broke down and cried. The doctor just stood there. I heard the scratch of pen on paper. Brushing back tears, I looked up.

The doctor handed me two small squares of paper off his prescription pad. "Don't go mixing these. The sedative is *very* strong."

"Sure, Doctor. Thank you."

"And no alcohol."

"I don't drink. Anymore."

That night, with the help of the Seconal the doctor had prescribed, I did sleep. Deeply, in an underworld of dreams that seemed to issue from somewhere in the wilderness of the collective unconscious. In one, especially vivid, I saw my mother and father, in their twenties, romance efflorescing, young and smiling and given to laughter. They were flying in a single-engine aircraft, my father piloting his girlfriend, the woman he was in love with, across Lake Michigan into a cloudless blue sky for a special dinner where he would propose to her. I snapped to consciousness with the incandescent realization that somewhere, deep in our dreams, or deep in unconsciousness, or deep in the afterlife, all conflicts and acrimonies are resolved. That it was consciousness that so unrelentingly afflicted us with suffering.

I parted the heavy gray drapery. The storm was clearing. The skies were lightening to a refulgent blue, dispersing swaths of clouds in the windy upper atmosphere. Sheboygan's streets glistened. I was groggy, but oddly refreshed. As I shaved I couldn't help but stare at myself in the mirror. Dark pouches underscored my eyes. I might be feeling stronger, but the trip had aged me.

Breakfast at Alice's was somber. I had taken to coming over in the mornings to keep her company, and then driving her over to see her sister. But I could tell the visits were wearing on her. Death is too slow in coming was what she would have said had she not been a Christian.

"I don't think I'm going to come today, is that okay?" she asked.

"Sure, Alice." It had to depress her profoundly to see her older sister and know it could just as easily be her. And who would be here for Alice when the time came?

I rose. "Come on, Snapper," I said. "Let's go see Mom."

Snapper jumped off the couch. As his owner was growing more frail, he was improving.

"You know I can't take him," Alice said.

"I'll find a home for him," I said. "Don't worry."

"Say hi to Phyllis."

I drove, Snapper riding shotgun, to St. Nicholas Hospital.

The hospital was sepulchral at this hour. I found my mother in her room, slumped over in her wheelchair. Her head listed onto one shoulder, the left side of her mouth sagged; overall, a grotesque visage. The early shift had bathed and dressed her. This was the first since her arrival here I had seen her in her street clothes.

"Mom?" I said gently, to rouse her. I couldn't tell whether she was sleeping or still in such a state of disorientation that she was less than half in the world. "Mom, it's me Miles."

She turned her head slowly and tried to meet my eyes. I had to squat because the heaviness of her head, coupled with the increased diminution of motor control, precluded her looking up at me the way she had even recently been able to do. "Hi, Miles," she said faintly, the words drawn out, her speech so aphasic, similar to that of an infant, decipherable only by the parents. Still, it was a lingua franca that we had developed over the years since her first, devastating, stroke.

I massaged her shoulder in hello. "How're you doing?"

"Not so well," she said, garbling her words.

A muscular young PT came bustling in. Though a different guy from the one I'd seen the day before, he said in the same cheery voice, "We got her up today."

"That's good," I said, unable to share his enthusiasm about my mother's ostensibly improved condition, but understanding that it was his job to put a positive spin on the most moribund of cases.

I found myself speaking without having thought through what I meant. "I was thinking of taking her for a drive," I said casually. "Maybe buoy her spirits."

The PT furrowed his brow. "Let me ask the doctor."

"Please."

Brimming with energy, he strode off.

I squatted down again. "Do you want to go for a drive, Mom?"

"Oh, yes," she said, "I want to get out of here."

"I've got Snapper here with me."

"Oh. You're a good son. My Snapper."

"Where would you like to go? It's a gorgeous day."

She considered for a moment, then nodded sedately. She lost her focus for a moment, then her eyes opened wide. A flicker of exultation, pushed by a remote corner of a receding emotional core, swept across her face. "Am I going home, Miles?"

"Yes, Mom," I said unhesitatingly. "You're going home."

She grew practically animated, a wan smile creasing her lanolin-shiny face. "Oh, that's such good news."

The PT returned with the doctor who, it occurred to me for some silly reason, had her whole glorious life ahead of her. She held out her hand. I took it and smiled at her.

"I'd like to take her on a little drive, if that's okay. Might be good to get a little sunshine."

"I'm not sure it's a good idea, Miles. Your mother's pretty weak."

"I think it would be good for her. Plus, I've got her dog in the car." I told her about the amputation to gain her sympathy.

She squatted in front of my mother. "Mrs. Raymond? It's me, Dr. Neiser. Do you remember me?"

Her patient stared blankly into her face and I feared for a moment that my mother wouldn't be able to get past even the most basic cursory examination to confirm she was still possessed of her faculties. But she rose to the occasion. "Oh, yes. How are you, Dr. Neiser?"

"I'm fine, Mrs. Raymond. Do you feel up for a drive with your son?"

That perked the old coot up. "Oh, yes," she exclaimed. She raised the index finger and added, "I need to get out. I want to see the sky."

"Okay, Mom," I said, chopping her off, fearful she was going to spin off into the dottily transcendental and reinforce the doctor's misgivings.

Dr. Neiser straightened to a standing position. "Her heart's very weak. We've had to double the nitro."

I could see she was torn, and not trending in my direction. "We won't be gone long." I lowered my voice. "I'm leaving tomorrow to go home. This may be the last time I see her alive."

Frowning, the doctor looked from my mother back to me, then, against all her professional instincts, she smiled and said, "Okay. Have a nice outing." She turned and walked briskly out of the room.

The PT, in the wings, said, "Do you want me to help you out with her?"

"No, we're fine. I've got a special handicap van."

He placed a hand on my mother's shoulder, squeezed it with his strong fingers and said, "Have a nice afternoon, Mrs. Raymond."

"I will. Thank you."

"All right, Mrs. Raymond. See you when you get back." He went off.

"Ready, Mom?"

"Yes. All my life."

For the umpteenth time I circled around behind her chair and took hold of the steering handles. We rolled through the door, down the length of a corridor, past rooms featuring demoralizing dioramas of every imaginable human debility, past the receptionist's desk and out through the automatic doors into the crisp air. The bright sunshine galvanized my mother to root around in her purse for her sunglasses, but she was having trouble. I slowed to a halt and helped her find them. I placed them on the bridge of her nose. I rooted out her favorite faded blue Gilligan's Island hat and slapped that on her head as well.

"Oh, it's such a beautiful day," she managed.

"It is, Mom, isn't it?" I replied, feeling one with her elation.

We pushed off again and, in the handicapped parking, eased her to a stop at the side of the Rampvan, and slid open the door. When Snapper saw her he started barking his fool, impish head off.

"Oh, Snapper, you be quiet," my mother scolded.

I rolled my mother into the back and set both the brakes. Snapper, with an adrenaline rush brought on by his recognition of his owner, leapt adroitly into her lap. My mother bent forward to let him lick her, talking to him all the while. It brought a smile to my cynical face.

I circled round the van, climbed into the driver's seat and turned over the engine.

St. Mary's Cemetery, where my mother's parents were buried and where she wanted to go, is a small-town Catholic burial ground set in a wooded area outside Sheboygan. It's a traditional cemetery that you don't see much of in California, populated with heavy granite steles, plinths and gravestones of all shapes and sizes.

It was blustery when I braked to a halt on the access road fronting the cemetery. I rolled my mother with Snapper in her lap down the ramp. The going was bumpy as we traversed the dirt path and threaded our way through the grave markers to where her parents' modest stones stood embedded in the ground.

"Are you chilly, Mom?"

"A little."

I went back to the van to retrieve the sweater that Alice had been thoughtful to give me when I told her I might take her sister out for a drive. I wrapped it around her shoulders. "Better?"

"Yes. Thank you." Snapper lay contentedly in her lap. She stroked his small head.

I stood next to her as she stared wordlessly at her parents' graves. No telling what images and emotions were ranging over the drought-stricken floodplain of her nearly destroyed brain. Was she journeying back in time? Or surrendering to the inevitable and the darkening of those bright blue skies?

After a long silence she said simply, without looking at me. "I don't want to go back to the hospital."

"I know."

"You promised."

I hooked my arm around her and gave her a hug. "You've been through a lot, Mom. You're a tough old bird."

She rasped a chuckle.

I hugged her tightly. Then, mustering all my courage, I said, having succumbed to her private idiom, "You're ready to go home?"

She stared at the grave markers for the longest time. Then, slowly, almost imperceptibly, she nodded.

I squeezed her shoulders and let go my hug. "I'll be back in a minute."

She wordlessly nodded, turned her eyes slightly my way, but said nothing.

From a brown paper bag stowed in the Rampvan, I removed a cup of yogurt and a plastic spoon. I dumped out half the yogurt and added the powder of fifteen Seconal capsules, stirring the mix until it was smooth. Trying to go on autopilot, following the steps I had rehearsed in my head, I walked back to where my mother sat still staring at the grave markers. She was mumbling something to Snapper but I couldn't make out what she was saying.

I fed her the half-cup of yogurt, spooning baby food to the child I'd never had—and never would. I stood behind her with my hands on her shoulders, both of us gazing out at the sea of gravestones.

As if one last thing had flared in her mind, she looked up, raised her heavy right arm and crooked the index finger, at some invisible god she invoked to help her understand this final moment. She grew momentarily agitated. "Miles?"

I squatted down. "Yes, Mom? I'm here. What is it?"

Her face bore the oddest, most innocent expression, as if she had come full circle back to infancy. "Where do you think we go when we die?"

I tried to take her question at face value. "I don't know for sure," I started, wanting to be profound, knowing I would come up short. "But I had a dream last night that seemed to say that we go to where all our conflicts, all the resentments, all the bad things that have happened to us, are somehow resolved. I don't know where. I don't know what it looks like, but it has to be a place where everything is made whole, where we are no longer angry or in pain or suffering, where we are somehow one with ourselves, one with our families, one with the universe."

My mother nodded, seeming to understand, as if my disjointed speculation were the oracle. "Oh, I hope so."

A wind blew through the cemetery and pushed some leaves over the grave markers.

"I'm sorry about everything that's happened," I started. "This whole trip and everything. It was probably a mistake."

She shook her head slowly and definitively back and forth. "Oh, no," she said, tears muddling her words. "We lived life!"

"That we did." And with her words I saw what this trip had meant. Not just to her. The point wasn't the transporting of an infirm woman to Wisconsin to die. It was the improbable journey itself. I looked back at her. Still petting Snapper, she was staring, again, at some fixed point in space and time. I looked away.

Leaves swirled and eddied as swirling gusts of wind kicked up abruptly and then died down just as suddenly as they had come up.

After what seemed like an eternity, I turned and looked again at my mother. Her head was slumped forward, her chin resting on her chest. Her eyes were shut. I levitated the back of my hand next to her mouth. I could feel her warm, but now weak, exhalations. I glanced around and there was no one in the cemetery except my mother, Snapper and me.

Then, the strangest thing happened. Snapper perked up his ears, leapt out of my mother's lap, raised his head to the sky and started yipping uncontrollably.

"Snapper," I admonished. "Snapper." But he wouldn't stop. I had never seen him in such a state. His yips were that of a coyote, yowling, echoing through the cemetery.

The Internet medicide advice said that "when using barbiturates it is important to stop the breathing manually." Unless I asphyxiated her she would take longer to die, and death might come horribly by her choking on her own vomit.

Following one of three recommendations provided on the site, I pinched my mother's nostrils shut and then clamped my other hand over her mouth. She struggled only a few seconds and went slack. I removed my fingers from her nose, but kept my other hand over her mouth until I could no longer feel breath.

After what might have been a minute, Snapper still yipping away, her breathing seemed to have ceased. Just as in her condo a few years before when she had had the congestive heart failure, a peace had settled over her and her face seemed haloed, in a permanent state of rest. I looked at her a long moment, could have sworn I felt her spirit or whatever ascending out of her, breaking free of the dilapidated body that yoked her to the earth, this pain she had borne with so much suffering. She didn't want to go back to the hospital, I kept rationalizing, and she didn't want to waste away the last months of her life in a nursing home. And: I had promised.

Suddenly, Snapper stopped his yipping just as quickly as he had started. It was followed by a plaintive whimpering, as if he, too, sensed what I had. He looked at me, and I looked at him. If we could have spoken to each other we would have said the same thing: she's gone.

I turned to my mother and placed my lips on her cold lifeless cheek. I put my arms around her. And took a look at my watch.

My mother quickly grew cold in my overdue embrace. I checked and double-checked for evidence of breathing, but there was none. I examined her cursorily in the fading light. Her chapped lips had gone motionless and her face had grayed. Feeling her wrist with my thumb, I couldn't discern a pulse. Just to be certain, I let another half-hour pass. In that half-hour I reflected on our trip. More than once I laughed through the tears.

I finally punched in 911 on my cell.

An EMS vehicle showed within ten minutes, its lights flashing. Two paramedics, a man and a woman, hustled over to where my mother was peacefully slumped in her wheelchair. After hearing how she had just lapsed into unconsciousness they checked her vital signs and went to work in a vain attempt to resuscitate her. Despite the fact they found no pulse they employed all-out heroic measures. Oxygen, cardio-push, adrenaline injections. After twenty futile minutes the female paramedic returned to where I was standing and said simply, "Your mother's gone."

I nodded at the inevitable, tears forming anew in my eyes. Had they miraculously brought her back from the dead this time I would have been out of my mind with rage. The fact that they used everything in their medical arsenal to resuscitate her I didn't blame on them per se; it was what the law required them to do.

Per the standard procedure, the male paramedic got on a cell phone to the Sheboygan Police. Another numbing twenty minutes passed before a squad car with flashing lights parked on the periphery of the cemetery. Two uniformed officers made their way over to the scene of my mother's death. After conferring with the paramedics, they approached me. Through tears, I told them that I had taken my mother out of the hospital so she could visit her parents' graves.

The cops nodded empathetically, signed some papers and handed them to the EMS crew so they could "move the body"–my mother!–into their truck and back to the hospital.

Dr. Neiser met me in the waiting room after performing a cursory post-mortem. We sat across from each other under bright fluorescent lights.

"Do you want an autopsy?" she asked.

I shook my head. "I think we know why she died."

"I always advise an autopsy," she asked. "There was evidence of petechiae."

"Pardon?"

She looked at me with cold, unblinking eyes. "Facial hemorrhaging."

"Which means?"

"Hypoxia."

I looked at her dumbly, waiting.

"It could be indication of asphyxiation," she elaborated. Our eyes met, but only briefly before we both looked away. "Of course, CPR was performed in the field. That could also cause hemorrhaging." She glanced away and wrote something down on the paper on her clipboard. She looked up at me. "I believe what happened was for the best."

I nodded.

Our eyes met in that same darting reluctance. She glanced down and wrote something more on the form. "I'm going to put cause of death as 'heart failure,'" she said.

I pressed my eyes shut to block another onrush of tears. "There was no failure of heart," I said enigmatically, before checking myself.

The doctor signed off on the death certificate and mortuary arrangements—more paperwork!—were made. Cremains to be shipped to a funeral outlet in San Diego where they would be held until I could pick them up and arrange for disposition at the Ft. Rosecrans Cemetery next to where my dad was interred.

chapter 22

Two days later I had a reservation from Milwaukee to Los Angeles. I'd turn in the Rampvan at the airport. With a couple hours to kill I drove along Lake Michigan, three-legged Snapper riding beside me, panting happily. The sky was blue and wind churned up little whitecaps. I rolled my mother's wheelchair–a kind of keepsake–down to the shoreline and sat in it. It felt weird, of course. For nearly five years she had spent her waking hours *only* in this chair. Sitting at the lake's edge, Snapper nestled in my lap, everyone else gone, I felt the same old loneliness start to claw at me. I got out the iPhone.

"*Soy yo*," I said, doing my best at the accent. "*LAU-ra.*"

"*Sí, es ella.*" That was followed by a moment's hesitation. "Miles?"

"Yeah." I hesitated. "Is that offer to come visit in Barcelona still good?"

I had a hard time with the rush of beautifully inflected Catalan that followed, but took the answer to be yes.

"I want to eat at the finest tapas bars in Barcelona and stare into the wells of your eyes. I want to take that boat to Ibiza that you were telling me about and run naked into the Mediterranean. I want to take a train down to Valencia and dine on the most exquisite paellas. I want to go to San Sebastián and eat at Arzak and that other amazing place I saw on Anthony Bourdain's *No Reservations* called Echeveria where the chef cooks everything over open coals, even caviar. I want to drink in your culture. Sound like a plan?"

"Okay. You sound, uh, *preocupado*."

"I suppose I am a little." I'd tell her later that my mother had just–that'd I'd just killed my mother. "I want to change my life. I want to see if what we had has traction, *tracción*." I laughed at that stupid unnecessary translation, stared anxiously out at the mottled surface of the lake. There were no boats, just a vast expanse of water. "*¿Laura?*"

"Yes, I'm here."

"I'm coming to Barcelona to fall in love with you."

I knew viscerally, in my distraught state, that I had stepped across the line, blurting something so ludicrous, so premature. We had only spent a day and a night together, for Christ's sake. Had I lost my mind? What was this newfound sobriety doing to me?

"*Tendremos un gran amor.* For as long as it lasts."

"That's how everything works. For as long as it lasts."

She said something else, affirmative sounding, in her native tongue. I caught about half of it.

"One other thing. I quit drinking."

"That's good, no?"

"I might have one glass if we go to Rioja."

"Okay."

"Or maybe two."

"Okay."

I told her I would call her when my plans were finalized and hung up. Next, I logged onto the Net and went to Amazon.com. I ordered Gibbon's *The History of the Decline and Fall of the Roman Empire.* All three volumes.

I thought I might learn something.

I looked down at Snapper. "What am I going to do with you, little guy?" Snapper looked up at me with dolorous eyes. *Fuck!*

The sound of the tiny waves lapping at the shore metronomically filled the void. I stared pensively into nothingness, the clouds now starting to bunch together. The last patch of sunlight on the water vacated, surrendering to gray.

Suddenly my thoughts were shattered by the roar of a light plane passing overhead, flying east out over Lake Michigan. I tented my hand to my forehead and looked out. Squinting, I imagined my father and my mother in the cockpit, in their prime, laughing. They were going to be engaged soon. Then married. Then have kids.

When the plane had passed I got up out of my mother's wheelchair, cradling Snapper in my arms, leaving it parked in the sand.

I cupped my hand over Snapper's head, brought it to mine and nuzzled his snout. I let him freely lick my cheek. "It's just you and me now, little guy." Tears welled in my eyes. "Let's go home."

THE END

Author's Note

Vertical, like *Sideways* before it, is a celebration of wine – all wine – and not any one particular winery or vintner. No winery or winemaker or anyone in the wine trade any capacity influenced the wines or wineries that appear in *Vertical.* As part of my research for *Vertical,* I held several large tastings with non-wine professionals and solicited their opinions. The wines that appear are a result of those and other efforts, and were picked as appropriate for the characters and the story. Please celebrate the hard work and achievements of all vignerons in the spirit of the *Vertical* journey. Finally, while many of the places described are real, *Vertical* is a work of fiction, and its characters are fictitious. Any resemblance to real persons, living or dead, is purely coincidental.

Rex Pickett
Santa Monica
November 2010